Love & Death

"I'm not after some lousy affair, Mattie." David held her in place though her fingers pried at his hand.

"You're hurting me."

"What do you think you're doing to me?" His lips were hard, drawn into straight lines barely permitting sounds. "I don't like being used."

"Used? By me? Haven't you got that backward?" She reached over for her dress. He shook her so she fell back toward him.

"What if I quit my job, Mattie? Devoted all my time to this gift of yours? Would you believe I loved you enough then?"

"It's not a question of love. It's more...more..."

"Power." The word formed ominously between them. "That's it, isn't it? Power. You're starting to feel it and you don't want to give it up."

POWER. The word seemed to echo in her brain. POWER. She shuddered, a sense of fear slowly creeping over her, a sense of horror.

Power. Over dead things!

"No!" she cried. "God, no!"

GIFT
OF
EVIL

Elizabeth Kane Buzzelli

BANTAM BOOKS
TORONTO · NEW YORK · LONDON · SYDNEY

GIFT OF EVIL
A Bantam Book / October 1983

ISBN 0-553-23740-3

Published simultaneously in the United States and Canada

Bantam Books are published by Bantam Books, Inc. Its trade-
mark, consisting of the words "Bantam Books" and the por-
trayal of a rooster, is Registered in U.S. Patent and Trademark
Office and in other countries. Marca Registrada. Bantam
Books, Inc., 666 Fifth Avenue, New York, New York 10103.

PRINTED IN THE UNITED STATES OF AMERICA

H   0 9 8 7 6 5 4 3 2 1

To Tony—
For so many reasons

Prologue

Rain dripped endlessly into the dead man's open eyes, giving him pools of tears he was no longer capable of crying.

Saturated cardboard and old newspapers from one of the fallen garbage cans draped over his legs while apples and oranges—browned, almost liquid—oozed through the fingers that had clutched at anything.

The little girl stood near the mouth of the alley where the man had fallen. Her eyes were huge as she turned first one way then another. Her bangs were pasted across her forehead; thin brown strands of hair clung over her delicately traced eyebrows and fell into her eyes.

Water from the rotted gutter overhead dripped onto her head and shoulders, but she made no move except for pushing her tiny hands to whiteness against the wall of the brick building behind her. Ridges in the brick pressed painfully into the plump mounds of her fingers but she wouldn't let go.

She whimpered. It was a small sound, traveling no farther than her own ears and lost beneath the noisy drumming of the rain against overturned garbage cans.

"Daddy," she called, choking off the word out of fear.

Rain ran down her cheeks, into her mouth and off her chin; it slid harmlessly over the surface of her new strawberry patterned, vinyl raincoat. The matching hat was lost, lying on the ground someplace, maybe near the umbrella one of the men had stepped on.

She opened her mouth to cry again.

"Me and the little one are going to the store," Daddy called back to the bedroom where Ma was. "Get you some Vernors and chips."

He winked at the little girl because they were sharing a secret, sharing the knowledge that the trip out into the rain was to test her new rain outfit. Three pieces—all matching.

She'd been begging him to take her out so she could wear it, promising him he could stay dry under her umbrella. He gave in. But then Daddy usually gave in.

"Just down the street. Just to the store."

"O.K. little one. But it's raining cats and dogs out there."

He helped her into the green sweater and then into the stiff new raincoat. He snapped the elastic of the hat under her chin.

Daddy carried the umbrella, refusing to open it until they were down the steps from their upper flat and out on the street.

"Bad luck to open an umbrella in the house," he warned, giving his umbrella lesson seriously.

She put her hand into his and they walked to the corner, Daddy stooping so the rain wouldn't get her. But it did anyway, and slid neatly over the surface of the new coat leaving her dry and snug inside.

Sometimes the edge of the umbrella would hit her on the head when he let it slip too far her way. Then the rain would get him and he would pull the umbrella back and they would both laugh as she rubbed the place where the umbrella had struck her.

"Just tryin' to get your attention," he joked, bending to put an arm around her shoulders and hug her. She could smell the wet wool of his work jacket and feel his whiskers on her face and she would grimace, pushing him away from her, fighting for freedom from this tall protector.

"Is that a way for Daddy's little girl to act?" he asked, hurt, when she pushed at him.

Not answering, she put a finger into her mouth, turning it this way and that, not sucking it but tasting the cottony taste of it. She took her time answering but finally nodded, yes, she was Daddy's little girl.

"And when she was bad she was horrid." He tugged at one of the pigtails sticking from under the brim of her hat and pulled the thumb from her mouth.

"Not horrid." She frowned up at him, hating to be teased. "Not horrid."

"Not horrid," he softened, agreeing. "A very, very good girl."

The men came from nowhere. There wasn't anyone on the street and then there were four of them. They were all around them at once.

"Shit. He's got the kid with him," said one of the men, huge and dark in a black coat with the collar pulled up so his face was half-hidden.

"Too bad," another said. Then sounds seemed to blend together. Words were said. Voices grew louder. One of the men, a man with red hair that stood up around his head like a clown's, pushed Daddy so that he yelled and stumbled backward. Startled, his hands went into the air. Another man pushed him harder, backing him down a narrow alley between the stores.

Two other men followed the two who were pushing Daddy. One knocked the little girl out of the way, dislodging the rain hat so it fell forward, across her face, and down. He stepped on the umbrella.

She started to cry and scream for Daddy. She pulled at one of the men but he pushed her so she fell, ripping her new white tights. Her school shoes were not only wet, they were scuffed in long lines across the toe and down the side. She bent and brushed at them, crying out, "Daddy."

The men seemed to be all over him. There were heavy sounds, noises like the ones her father made when lifting the couch for Ma, a job he hated and complained about the whole while he did it. Then there were hard sounds, painful sounds, like slaps and kicks. She couldn't see her father. It was getting dark and the rain obscured the group in the alley. All of them were huddled together, moving, making noises. And then there was one very loud sound, something like the sound of lightning striking close by, and the men were running back toward her.

She hugged the building. The men stopped, ringing around her. Eight eyes, like those of fighting animals, fell on her and she knew a nameless fear that had nothing to do with dark, or falling, or sleep. Words came out and hovered over her head.

"What do we do about the kid?"

"Can't kill her."

"Man—you crazy? She can identify us."

"Nah . . . too young."

"Leave her be."

A shrug. They drifted away, lost somewhere in the clouds of rain.

She stood very still for a time, waiting, listening. Then she dared pull away from the building to lean forward, staring down the alley.

"Daddy?" she called quietly, voice full of tears. "Daddy?"

No answer. They were gone, only he was back there. She dared to walk, slowly, toward where the men had pushed him, back in among the garbage cans.

He was lying down. His eyes were open but he didn't answer when she reached out and shook him. She shook harder, pulling at his wet jacket sleeve. She put her face right up to his as she did when she went into their room where he and Ma slept next to each other in the big bed, times when she wanted him to get up. She took his face in her two hands and moved his head, dislodging the rain collecting in his eyes.

"Daddy," she whispered to him in her secret-sharing voice.

His lips hung open, his head moved only slightly, but he said nothing.

She gave up trying to wake him; she sat beside him to wait.

It was cold on the wet alley floor. The rain ran a river down the middle; to get out of it she snuggled close to Daddy, but there was no warmth there any more. She pulled her legs up under the raincoat and hunched her shoulders so no more water would run down the neck of her coat and trickle slowly along her spine. She leaned her head against him, tears running, though she hardly thought about crying.

"Daddy," she whispered one last time before putting the forbidden thumb into her mouth. She savored the warmth of it, the familiarity of it. Her cheeks and lips made sucking movements. She let her whole body curl around that thumb as it became the center of the world. Soon her eyes began to close. The sucking stopped and then hurriedly started again as she flowed into and out of sleep. She moved only once, to put her other, cold hand into her father's pocket. Then she slept.

Part One

Part One

Chapter One

Golden haze, thick enough to swim in, surrounded her. She put a hand out only to lose it in the radiating glow that appeared to emanate from a point directly in front of her.

There the light was pure, a deep, blazing yellow with pulsing waves driving outward until, at the edges all around her, the light became a brilliant white.

Hypnotic—that golden center. Exerting force on body, a pulling force that brought her forward, toward that hot middle, though she fought to run from it.

Power over limbs was gone. Mind captured, pulled painfully as if to leave the body, dragged faster and faster toward the consuming center.

Brain must split the skull. No room. Light closed around. She felt it wash over her skin, growing hotter, hotter, only to cool. Only to have the golden center expand. A pinprick of color in the gold. And she went through it. Breathless. Pain lessening. Running along a strange road. Moving soundlessly across a yawning culvert, feet flying, elation buoying her.

A muddy stream coursed way below. A stream with something half in and half out of it, lying among weeds at the bank. Her head snapped. The scenery slowed...slowed ...halted.

She began to laugh.

It was the awful laugh which shook Martha Small into consciousness. She opened her eyes but even then the image of the dead girl faded only slowly as though engraved on the air around her. A shudder passed over her body. She put a hand to her lips, still not believing that laugh was her own.

The room was in early morning shadow; anemic November light angled beneath the yellowed, pin-holed shade at the window.

Voices from the kitchen at the other end of the upper flat filtered through the closed door. Ma. Bella Schwartz. Juliet Swiderski. The three neighbors and friends gathered daily to drink endless cups of coffee; to talk and moan over their widow's problems. Martha squeezed her eyes shut before remembering there was no escape inside herself either. Not with the vivid memory of that terrible dream and her unnatural response.

"Martha!"

Her mother's raised voice cut through the hollow morning like a siren.

"Martha! Time to get up. You'll be late."

She put her feet to the bare floor, gripping the edge of the sagging mattress for support and for strength. Another day. They got worse. Thirty-three years of a downward progression. Martha put her head in her hands, allowing herself a moment of despair before going through the usual propping up, before reminding herself of her many blessings. It was more difficult this morning to thank God for her job at the supermarket, and for her health, with the pall of that dream hanging on her like another skin.

Pushing her straight brown hair behind her ears with what, for Martha, was a defiant gesture, she got out of bed and found the slippers which had somehow been kicked far under the bed. From behind the flowered cloth covering her cubbyhole closet she pulled her corduroy robe and shrugged it on.

With her hand on the doorknob she stopped to take a deep fortifying breath before trudging the morning path to bathroom, to kitchen.

"Morning, Martha."

"Martha."

"Morning, dear."

They sat as usual, ringing the table, coffee mugs making circles on the faded oilcloth. Their aging bodies were hunched toad-like toward each other as if for strength. She felt all six eyes examine her, searching out some leftover of her younger life.

"Look peaked." Mother's face showed concern.

Martha poured coffee, kept her back turned, mumbled, "Bad night. Terrible dream."

She moved to the sink, leaned against it, sipped the black coffee while the eyes watched more closely.

"Just terrible," she repeated for them. Their eyes brightened, chins lifted, heads came up as they waited for details.

"I was in a field, or a marsh of some kind, being pulled along by waves of something I couldn't see. I couldn't stop. Those waves wrapped around me, pulled me on, right across a big culvert. I remember these tall weeds."

A nervous tic beat in her right cheek. She put a hand up to quiet it, the hand absent-mindedly caressing her skin as she relived the dream.

"Get on with it, Martha, or you'll be late to the store," her mother prompted, sighing and poking at the bunches of pink, plastic curlers on her head.

Martha watched the three friends exchange the look that meant they hoped she would be done and gone soon. They did look forward so to mornings when grievances were still fresh after sleepless nights of thought about the lives that brought them here to Mt. Eliot Street on Detroit's east side.

"The weeds were all brown, from frost I guess. The water next to'em was about half frozen. Dirty looking. The place was...so...lonely."

She wrapped her arms across her chest, shivering under the worn robe. She tried to flick her lank, colorless bangs out of her eyes but the hair settled back into place.

Got to get ahold of myself, she thought. Shouldn't let a dream do this. Thirty-three, for God's sake. Too old to be spooked by a bad dream. Acting as if it were real.

So afraid. Always so afraid. Everything in life bigger, uglier . . .

She felt weighted down as if life kept her pinned in place. Never married. Never loved. Unloved. Unlovely. Still at home with Ma.

Plump Bella Schwartz shifted impatiently in her chair, tugged at the black babushka covering her freshly permed head, and rolled her eyes.

"Well," Martha attempted to marshal her thoughts against that part of her mind always on watch for Harriet's impatience, for laughter turned against her. "I was dragged over that culvert against my will and forced to go round the side, down to the bottom of an embankment. I went as close as I could to the water and there was a . . ."

She drew in a breath as the picture flashed back before her.

"I tell you, Martha, you're gonna be late to the store and Mr. Koch'll be mad and maybe fire you and then what, I'd like to know?" Harriet's nasal voice was raised to pierce Martha's self-absorption. To her friends she added, "Just that chit of a pension from the union. How're we supposed to live do you think? It's just awful what things cost. If my Donald knew how little I'd have to get by on he would've been a lot more careful with that car. Thank God Martha don't drive. Can't stand to ride in the things myself. Not since the accident. Martha either. Doesn't want to own one. Wouldn't let her anyway. So what if she's old enough? I tell her I'm too scared. Can't stand the thought. Nothing to argue about. Can't afford one. I always say first the bills, then the frills. Isn't that right, Martha? Isn't that what I always say?"

The lady friends nodded earnestly through all of this. Martha nodded too then raised her voice, going on with her story. "There was a girl's dead body inside that pipe." She shuddered, closing her eyes at the horror of it. "Jesus, it was awful."

"Shouldn't take the name of the Lord in vain, dear," Juliet Swiderski mildly reproved her. "Father Pawlowski says even when you say 'Oh God' like that, not thinking or anything, it's a sin. I asked him..."

"That sure was one hell of a dream," Bella interrupted Juliet as she always did. Juliet shot her a menacing look and tightened her lips to silence the words she would like to throw back at Bella.

"But let me tell you," Bella went on. "I've had some worse than that. One I remember—just terrible. This big guy was chasing me and I ran and ran..." Bella paused, switching directions abruptly. "Girl wasn't raped was she?"

Martha's throat tightened.

"Just a dead body," she mumbled, rinsing her cup and wiping the coffee stains from the sink. "No way to know what happened to her. But she had on these jeans, frayed at the bottom, and a dark blue jacket, and she had this yarn—yellow yarn—holding back her hair. Red hair. And there was a green ski hat beside her. It was so real."

"Well, if she had on the jeans, couldn't have been rape," Bella concluded and lost interest.

"Speaking of dreams," Juliet said, intent as usual on hearing only the thoughts within her own head. "I read in the *National Enquirer* where dreams only show what your secret wishes are."

"And my secret wish is to find a dead body?" Anger bubbled inside but it was useless to indulge herself. From long exposure Martha knew she had no weapons to counteract theirs. They could nurse grudges for days, use guilt as a force more potent than physical threat. Their silence and tight-lipped remarks wore away the edges of even the most indomitable rebellion.

"You know I don't mean that at all," Juliet pouted, turning to Harriet for sympathy. "Really, your daughter does twist a body's words, doesn't she?"

A shrug and a wave of both hands that as much as said "I give up" sufficed to placate Juliet.

"If you wanna know what I think," Bella said, puffing up her chest, resting her spare chins on it, and fixing Martha with a look, "I think this goes right back to your Daddy's accident. Now, now," she quieted a small disturbance from Harriet. "I know you both don't like to think about it, but it should be brought up every once in a while so you two don't get to brooding on it. You're both the same about that, you know. Both the same. Only mention it in passing. Scared to really talk about it. But it don't do no good. Not at all. Just look at your daughter's dream, Harriet. An accident and a person dead. Now don't you think that's Donald she's dreaming about?"

Harriet came forward in her chair. With quicker movement than Martha had seen her make in years, she slammed her hands on the table, attempting to quiet Bella. Her usually bland, expressionless face drew in on itself in indignation. She sputtered and tried to warn Bella to silence with a glare.

"Now. Now. Now." Bella threw both hands up to stop her friend's anger. "No use trying to bury the whole thing. Poor Donald died in an accident. Martha here was too little to know what was happening, but sure she's heard about it over the years from different ones. Probably just buried it away. Now she dreams of a dead person. Some awful accident. Stands to reason, don't it?"

"No need dragging poor Donald out of his grave to explain away some silly dream. You know how Martha loves to carry on about things."

"Got a headache," Martha mumbled beneath the quarreling voices and went to the cupboard for aspirin: a huge bottle in among Harriet's liver pills, pain pills, and laxatives. She shook three from the bottle, ran a glass of water, and downed the aspirin. Closing her eyes a moment, she stood very still as if expecting instant relief from the pain. There was none, and the darkness behind her lids frightened her, as though she could be dragged back there again.

The dream had been so real. She could still see the dead girl clearly. All so terribly clear. Colors: yellows, blues, greens, browns; and, as she saw it in her mind, the body seemed magnified, the colors even more intense.

Nothing to do with the death of a father she couldn't even remember. Nothing.

She rubbed at her temples, attempting to ease the pain there. Nothing helped. The pain seemed to have a power of its own that could swell and burst.

Never had she experienced anything just like this. Why couldn't she get her concern across to the trio behind her? They never listened. Not really. Most people didn't. Too trapped in their own thoughts.

"What I was trying to say, Martha," Juliet pressed on doggedly, "is if that girl in your dream was raped—God forbid!—it could show that's what you've got on your mind and it's botherin' you. I read in the *Enquirer* where this one psychiatrist says all dreams are really about sex."

"Ha," Bella laughed, poking Juliet on the arm. "I wondered how long it would take you to get around to sex. Now, shame on you, get your mind out of the gutter."

Juliet's small face puckered, her wrinkled and freckled skin knotting with disapproval. "It's not in the gutter. And you're a fine one to talk."

"I didn't say it was rape...." Martha wearily tried to put in, but they were off into one of their daily, circular arguments which never were resolved but died instead from inertia by nightfall.

Martha moved passed them as they squared away for battle, escaping to her room to dress.

Hers was the farther of the two bedrooms in their upper flat. It was also the smaller, with a narrow overhead peak against which, even after all these years, she still banged her head.

She closed the door softly behind her, got her clothes from the closet, dressed, then stood at the window, allowing herself a few more minutes of the privacy she craved but seldom was allowed except, perhaps, brief moments at night when the news was finished and Ma didn't complain of being left alone, or a little while on Saturday afternoon when she cleaned the room and changed her bed, taking time to sit at the narrow window where the maple beyond filled the sky with bare, silver branches and made her think of European forests where wolves stalked lonely riders on horseback; mountainsides with skiers threading difficult courses through tall trees; places where life was filled with challenge and people lived as she only read about in her secretly stashed magazines.

"Eight-twenty." Mother's voice ripped through her quiet.

She got the black umbrella out because the sky threatened rain and took a second to glance at her reflection in the large, mahogany dresser that had been part of her parent's wedding suite. Running a hair brush once more over her impossibly straight and thin hair, she sighed as it did nothing to improve her appearance.

She pulled the string to shut off the overhead light and walked quietly back down the hall, hoping they wouldn't notice her.

It was a game, leaving before the women whipped out shopping lists for her to fill after work. That always made her late coming home.

"Death." Juliet was sighing mightily and wiping her eyes with one of a bundle of tissues she kept in her sweater pocket for these frequent bouts of hers. "Everywhere you look, nothing but death. You see in this morning's paper where another girl's been kidnapped from out in St. Clair Shores?"

They didn't give Martha a glance as she made her way past them. Too much into their topic of the day, probably carry on until night with breaks in between only for the necessities of life. It was as though they still argued with dead husbands, using each other as surrogates for the missing men who had up and died before they could get in the final word.

At least their attention was off her. Martha shut the door behind her and hurried down the steep stairs to the street.

Chapter Two

Black gutter water swirled with rainbow plumes of oil slick washed down from a body shop mid-block. The usual double beat of pistons hummed beneath morning horns and squealing brakes as the small factories shaping plastic parts for the auto industry swung, uninterrupted, from night to day shift and sleepy men rushed to beat ticking time clocks.

All the sights, sounds, and smells of her street corner greeted Martha as she waited at the bus stop across from their building.

The rain began again, forcing her to open the umbrella quickly and fumble with a plastic rain scarf which could not be coaxed from its electromagnetized pouch, no matter how she tugged.

She was alone. As usual. Except for school children across the street going toward Pierce Elementary over a few blocks. No one ever went in her direction—north. Nothing out there for these people. The men went south, toward Chevrolet's Hamtramck Gear and Axle plant. The women went nowhere.

Koch's Market was out beyond the Seven Mile Road. It serviced clusters of small white houses, which there outnumbered the tool and die shops. Young mothers with babies lived there and gathered in the market to pass the time of day with other young women, their babies straddling blue-jeaned hips and sucking unhappily at rubber pacifiers.

Wind whipped the umbrella. She held on, praying it wouldn't turn inside out and leave her standing there looking like a fool, holding a broken umbrella. Happened once. Long time ago now.

She noticed the child because she walked alone. Groups of children pushed and shoved for position on the sidewalk across from Martha but this little girl walked by herself, between two bunches of the others.

It had been the same yesterday morning, the first time Martha had ever seen this little girl.

Her head was bowed into the wind. The long raincoat she wore was too big. Looked as if it was handed down from an older child. It caught between her knees, tripping her as she crossed Nevada with the light, her small feet stumbling up the curb, an arm circling the corner telephone pole for support.

The child stood still, other children passed as if she didn't exist. No greetings. No offer of help. Nothing.

As Martha watched, the little girl lifted her head,

almost lost beneath a flapping rainhat. Their eyes met, held, filled with curiosity—one about the other—then the child turned back in the direction of the school and walked off.

No sign of recognition, though the same thing had happened the morning before. Not even a smile passed between them. Martha understood. That wasn't a child to smile easily or warm to strangers. That was a girl who feared many things. Martha didn't know the child, but how well she knew the way that girl felt, and lived, and suffered. No friends. Every gust of wind an enemy. Every passing schoolmate a potential threat.

Martha shook her head, pulling her eyes from the tiny figure bent into the wind who was pushing her way to school. It was self-pity she felt. She knew that. Pity for the child she'd been, who never fitted in, never had a friend to buffer taunts and cruelty.

You wanna sit by me?

She'd been in the fourth grade. Even now the thought of how she had hoped and believed that Sally Florek really wanted to be friendly hurt her.

You wanna sit by me? I've got a secret. Me and Jane and Delia. You wanna know what it is?
She stopped talking to cover her mouth with one hand and giggle, making Martha giggle too then squirm with delight that she could giggle like the other girls.
The secret is M.S. Don't tell.
She called two other girls over, told them she'd told Martha the secret was M.S. They all laughed. One ran over to where Steve Craig was bouncing a ball against the side of the school. She told him and he laughed too. Martha laughed with each of them over the M.S. secret all that day, whispering M.S., as they did, to break them up. What M.S. was didn't matter. Only belonging mattered. Being part of THEM.

Martha watched as the child reached the next corner and stood off to one side, waiting to cross Mt. Eliot with the safety boy. The boy ignored her. Pretended he didn't see her standing there. She crossed with the next group of kids, careful to draw back as they reached the far curb. Careful to keep the group ahead where she could watch them.

M.S. had meant "Martha's Shoes." Because Ma couldn't afford new shoes, all fall Martha had worn oxfords with big cracks where the upper shoe had pulled away from the sole. Somehow she'd convinced herself it didn't matter, that no one would notice. Until Steve Craig came up to her on the way home from school that day.

Stupid. Don't you know M.S. stands for "Martha's Shoes"? You been laughin' at yourself all day. You're really dumb.

When Sally Florek got hit by a car Martha wouldn't sign the get-well card Miss Spencer passed around the class. She couldn't bring herself to forgive Sally even then.

Wind tugged at the umbrella again. Water splashed from behind a passing car and soaked Martha's legs and shoes, chilling her. She knew there would be no warming up today. Koch's was so cold now. Those new electric-eye doors stayed open longer than a human being with sense would hold them. And her cash register right in front of the doors. Her friend Patsy's register behind her. Patsy was always shivering.

Patsy suffered even worse than Martha from the cold. Her nose was raw and ran all winter long. Her hands became more and more chapped as temperatures dropped, until her fingers cracked open in places and blood smeared the keys as she punched her register. Once she tried working with gloves on but punched the wrong keys, overcharging Mrs. Kozak for kielbasa, which she still heard about.

And this was only November....

Chapter Three

"Just look at these goddam hands." Patsy held her hands out for inspection as Martha came through the electric-eye doors. "Old bastard's too cheap to up the thermostat. Next I'll be punching this thing with bleeding stumps." She smacked her register then changed the frown on her narrow face with prominent chin and outsized jaw to a smile. Here was Mrs. Taorimina shuffling up to her counter, mumbling over her string bag as she came. Patsy gave a shrug and threw a smile Martha's way then turned her attention to the hunched woman.

"AND HOW ARE YOU TODAY DEARIE?" Patsy leaned forward toward the woman. "Got your Ex-lax? Good. Good. Don't wanna have to call a plumber now, do ya?"

She laughed and the old woman put a hand coyly over her mouth to hide her shy merriment.

"You're a one, Patsy. No tellin' what you'll say," the woman chided mildly.

"If you can't have a little fun, what'sa use of living? Am I right?" She was bending earnestly from the waist toward the woman, one hand resting on her hip, the other draped across the dog food cans lined down the counter. Her stiff, bleached hair never moved as she wagged her head.

"You're right there, Patsy. You're right there." The small woman beamed and gratefully joined in Patsy's head shaking.

Martha moved passed them, back to the office where she asked Mr. Koch for her cash drawer.

The store wasn't busy yet. Too early. Patsy could handle the few lined up at the register. They were regulars. Dailies. Coming as much to exchange a few quips with

Patsy as they did for the one or two items they bought. Widows mostly. Women whose only social life consisted of shopping trips to Koch's Market, where they gathered in knots of conversation next to the Wonder Bread, in little self-pitying cliques in front of the meat they couldn't afford to buy, in nervous lines at the registers where gossip titillated their piqued curiosity.

Martha often marveled at Patsy's way with the old women. Though her manner was always deliberately patronizing toward them, for some reason Martha never could fathom, they loved it, even choosing Patsy's register over hers.

To be second choice sometimes hurt. Especially when the person was someone she liked, like old Mrs. Taorimina, who often brought both women little gifts of homemade cookies.

The one time Martha had tried to be like Patsy, calling Mrs. Krupa "dearie," the woman had snapped off an angry retort about "minding your manners" and Martha never again had the nerve to try. She figured some people just had a natural way about them. But not her.

As the morning advanced the store got busier, with few breaks in the lines until almost eleven o'clock. Patsy packed the groceries in Mrs. Fender's rolling cart and waved good-bye. A free moment. Rubbing her hands tenderly, she ambled over to lean against Martha's counter.

"So what were you sayin' before about a dream? I was busy. Couldn't really listen. Must've been a bad one. You looked pretty awful when you came in this morning."

Martha described it again, as she'd tried to do earlier. Patsy listened, better than the others had, but her only comment about the dead girl with the green ski hat was "Jesus, that gives me the creeps. Why the hell you dream about dead bodies? Dream about men. I guarantee you'll be smiling, not looking sick."

She laughed, leaning back to eye a young woman who walked in. Patsy whispered, "Get her. Look at those tight pants. What's she cruisin' for, I wonder? See those high-heeled boots she's got on? K-Mart's had the same thing for sixteen-ninety-five last week. One of those blue light specials. Should've got me a pair. I like 'em, don't you?"

Mr. Koch, arms crossed, was standing just behind

them. He cleared his throat for attention and frowned. Flustered, Martha straightened her brown bags and feather-dusted her register while Patsy went to look out the front window between soup displays, coming back when he was gone.

"What if your dream was true? You ever think of that? What if that's something in the future? Wouldn't that be terrible?"

Martha shuddered at the thought. "I didn't know this girl. She wasn't somebody I'd ever seen before."

"But still there's people who can see the future in their dreams. Once I went to a fortuneteller and she looked into this crystal ball and saw all kinds of things about my future. And almost all of them came true too. I remember she said I was going to take a long trip that summer and that's the year I went with my friend Sylvia out to California—to Disneyland. And she said I was going to change jobs, and I did too because Krieger's wouldn't give me three weeks off to go out there so I quit and got the job here." She paused to eye another young customer, fluffing out her white-blond hair and running a fingertip around her wide mouth to clean up the bright lipstick. "So you see, maybe your dream really means something."

"I hope not. I'd hate to think that girl was alive right now and I could warn her." Martha shivered and bundled tighter in her heavy cardigan.

Patsy shrugged. "If you could see into the future for real, you could make a fortune. Look at that guy who bends keys with his mind. I seen him on Mike Douglas and Johnny Carson and Dinah Shore and even on Gil Tabok's talk show. Imagine the money he's makin'." She shook her head at the inequity that must exist when a man makes money from so little and she couldn't get more than three-sixty an hour.

"Crummy day." Another break in the stream of customers found Patsy blowing her nose and wiping viciously at it. "That damn cold rain seems to blow right in here, don't it? Maybe we should just walk out. If we both threatened to quit, he'd have to do something. Naw, now don't get upset. I know you can't quit. Just thinking."

She settled into a miserable huddle against her register,

coughing, wiping her nose, and thumping her feet to keep them warm. "I'm never going to get warm today. Remember last year? My feet didn't thaw till June."

Martha was doing no better than Patsy. She kept her cold hands in the pockets of her sweater when she wasn't pushing keys. Her soggy shoes never dried so that now her feet were lumps of ice, void of any feeling beyond discomfort.

The day was passing slowly. Martha thought ahead to what was on TV that night. Since that promised little beyond "Laverne and Shirley," she thought about buying a magazine from the rack over in the produce aisle but decided against it. Mother needed Bengay. There was no toilet paper in the house, and Mr. Koch had some over-ripe bananas for her—a whole bag for a quarter. She only had three dollars left till payday. No money for a magazine. But she would buy herself a Hershey's with almonds, she promised. And save it to eat later in her own room, where she wouldn't have to break it into four pieces to share with Mother and her friends, who always took everything.

The rain stopped just before five. Early night turned puddles to reflecting pools where street lights burned. Patsy and Martha both hesitated over the newspaper box at the corner, debating whether the news looked interesting enough to warrant the expense.

"Look, headline says they found that girl who was kidnapped out in St. Clair Shores. Guess I'll get one," Patsy relented and deposited her coins. Martha thought of the evening ahead and decided she could spare the money too.

"You want to go shopping to K-Mart's with me Sunday?" Patsy asked as they parted at the corner, bus stops in opposite directions. "I think I'm going to get those boots after all. Let me know tomorrow, O.K.?" She waved and ran for her bus.

Liver in tomato juice.

Martha knew as soon as she opened the door and the smell swept down the dark stairway to mingle with the street damp and scorched heat escaping from the ceramic shop on the lower floor. She patted the Hershey bar in her sweater pocket for strength to get through dinner and beyond, to the evening, when she dared escape to her room.

"Stop raining yet?" Harriet looked up from the stove as Martha deposited the bananas and toilet paper on the table and held the Bengay up to prove she hadn't forgotten.

"Uh huh. Just damp and cold now."

She shook out her sweater and hung it in the hall closet, then set the umbrella in the bathtub to dry, stopping as her eyes caught her reflection in the medicine chest mirror.

Dark circles ringed her eyes, making them seem even larger, standing out from her face as if in fright.

Period due any day. Probably why she felt so tired and irritable. That, and, of course, with dreaming as she did, her night's sleep wasn't restful. Tired.

Hair even more bedraggled than usual, if that was possible. A permanent would do some good. "Body perms" they called them at Susie's Shoppe, where her mother went. But there wasn't enough money for that kind of thing.

Should she go shopping with Patsy this Sunday, she wondered? Be kind of nice to be with some woman who wasn't fifty-five or older, but how much would the trip cost? Bus fare. Lunch, probably. Even if she didn't buy anything, she would have to spend a few dollars....

"You know what Bella was tellin' us today?" Harriet chewed the liver and dished more mashed potatoes onto her plate as she spoke. "This disc jockey is taking a whole bus load up to Toronto for the superbowl of bingos. Just the kind of thing we've always dreamed of going to. You know the bingos at church are nice. I look forward to Wednesday nights, that's certain. What a thrill this would be." She stopped to chew and sigh. "But it takes money, like everything else."

Martha carved the liver to small, stringy bits then pushed them around in the pallid sauce, hoping she could leave most of it without her mother knowing.

"Wouldn't that be something, though? I mean actually going there? The prizes will be big, really big."

The bits of liver she had finally put in her mouth formed a lump which didn't diminish no matter how she chewed it. Impossible to swallow the mass.

"Of course Juliet claims she doesn't have the money. It's only a hundred-fifty apiece." Harriet glanced guardedly at Martha to see if she was getting through. "But I'd bet she'd get it if the rest of us was going. Coffee?"

Martha shook her head, hanging stolidly on to her silence in hopes it would persuade Harriet to stop talking. She bent farther over her plate.

"You know..." Harriet looked up and laughed lightly, jostling her sausage curls. "I was thinking that maybe you'd rather go on this trip than to Sea World next summer."

Martha shook her head, stopping her mother before she could go further. "Can't," she said while pushing the lump to one side with her tongue. "No vacations till summer."

"Hmmp, I'll bet if you asked Mr. Koch'll be glad to have you take off now." Harriet eyed her daughter as she mumbled over the food in her mouth.

"No vacations until June he says," Martha said and choked on the wad of meat, hurrying from the table to the bathroom, where she stooped over the toilet, ridding herself of the unchewable mass.. She tried to calm her heaving stomach before going back to face what she knew was only the first salvo in an escalating war.

"You'll only need Friday and Saturday. Not a week," the voice followed.

When she went back to the table and took her seat, Harriet was sulking. She cut, chewed, swallowed her meat with deliberate precision as if to prove that hers was always the perfect example. Martha felt her throat tighten even more.

"Liver's good for you. And it's cheap too. You know you don't make much money. And Lord knows I try..."

Martha sat in silence, stiff in her chair, eyes on the wax fruit centerpiece whose bright colors looked muddy under a gray pall of dust.

"You won't even see about getting those days off, will you?" Mother pouted, pushing her plate vigorously away as if she were foregoing food forever.

"I can't, Ma."

Martha had finished the dishes and was hanging up her dish towel when Juliet knocked timidly and came in, as she did every evening, in time to watch "Bowling for Dollars." Bella was the usual fifteen minutes behind.

Harriet's complaining voice was raised to reach Martha, who sat at the kitchen table with the newspaper she had bought and tried not to listen to her mother tell about her uncompromising daughter. Then the phone rang.

Martha had it before Harriet could hurry out from the living room. It was Patsy. Martha made a gesture to show it was for her, but Harriet only mouthed "Who is it?" and remained standing in the archway, hands on hips, listening.

"Did you read the paper yet?" Patsy's voice crackled over the wire.

"Just about to," she answered. "What..."

"Get it. Get it," Patsy ordered. "Weirdest thing I ever heard of in my life. You're not going to believe it. I've got the shivers. Just wait till you read it. Got it there?"

"Yes... uh, just a second." Martha set the phone down and got the paper from the table. "OK. What is it?"

"Look at page one, about that girl that was kidnapped and murdered. Got it?"

Martha found it and began reading.

"Get to it yet?" Patsy's voice demanded.

"Get to what?"

"Read! Read! You'll see."

Martha began reading the story aloud:

"The body, located by a fisherman who asked not to be identified, was lodged in a culvert which carried water from the Shiawasee Drain into the Clinton River. 'I knew right away it was the missing girl,' the fisherman told reporters, 'because I'd heard that description this morning on the radio.' The witness went on to describe the navy blue jacket, yellow ribbon in the victim's red hair, and a green ski hat found beside the body...."

Harriet, listening, gasped and brought a hand up to cover her mouth. Martha stopped reading and looked from the paper in her hands to her mother, her body turning very cold.

"See?" Patsy was demanding from the phone. "See what I mean? Remember that dream you told me about today? You didn't hear that description on the news last night did you?"

"No. I'm sure I didn't. I don't remember anything at all on last night's news about a missing girl. But..." Martha stopped to think as Harriet rushed back into the living room to tell the other two women. She felt the bands of pain tightening around her head again. Her brain filled with a fog that blocked thoughts. A sense of panic grew but beneath it was something more. Something inappropriate. Something she had to hold in. Laughter. She wanted to laugh. Everyone would think she was crazy. She must be crazy.

"Ain't that the weirdest thing?" Patsy went on. "I remembered right away, about your dream. It was like you was there or something. Jesus, how could that happen?"

"I don't know. I just don't know." Martha's voice was quiet as the three women gathered to stare, open-mouthed, at her.

When she hung up all three women demanded details and took turns reading the article and shivering.

"Why, you must have what they call second sight," Juliet marveled and clucked in disbelief.

Martha shook her head nervously. "Must of heard it somewhere. Had to."

"But that fisherman didn't find the body till today," Bella pointed out. "How'd you dream where the body was before it was found, huh? Explain that one."

"If you ask me," Harriet offered, "it's unnatural and best forgotten."

They were all looking at her strangely. Martha glanced from one face to the other, frightened by what she saw in them.

"You're right, Ma. Best forgotten. Some crazy coincidence." She pushed through them, explaining that her head ached, and hurried to her room. She shut the door and turned on the little bedside lamp whose soft, yellowed light didn't hurt her eyes. The Hershey bar was still in the pocket of her sweater, out in the hall closet. Though her stomach complained of hunger, she couldn't confront

their accusing faces again. They'd looked at her as if she
were crazy. As if something were wrong with her. Something terribly wrong.

Chapter Four

"Esther, hey, Esther!"

The young woman with intricately corn-rowed hair,
strands ending in golden beads, turned from the little
bar she was about to enter when she heard her name
called from across the street.

"Gary! Hey man." She raised a hand in greeting then
smiled, stopped short, and frowned as the succession of
her thoughts showed across her dark face.

She turned back on her high-heeled black shoes as if
to hurry inside the small bar, its marquee proclaiming
disco in bare lightbulbs.

"Hey, Esther," the man in the car called again and
beckoned her to him.

She made a motion of reluctance with her hand. For a
minute she hesitated, one hand on the door, not happy at
the interruption in the evening ahead of her.

Freddy just gone into Twinkie's Place. He'd be pissed
if she didn't follow—fast. Not a dude to play games, still,
Gary Jones was her husband's best friend. He didn't like it
when he caught her out like this, with other men. But not
a mean guy. He'd tell her off some. Take her home. Never
try to cause her trouble. Never.

"Come on, Esther," Gary was motioning from the car.

With an eloquent sigh she gave another shrug of her
shoulders, rolled her eyes heavenward, then smiled and
ambled slowly, seductively, her tight jeans moving like skin,
over to the car to lean in the window.

"What you doin' here, girl?" Gary cocked an eyebrow
at her.

"Jist havin' some fun." Petulance worked best in this spot, Esther knew, and she played it with a pout.

"Who you with this time?"

"Freddy."

"Come on. I'm takin' you home."

Not in the mood to be hurrying home on a cold Friday night, Esther leaned against the car and looked back toward the bar with longing. "Hey Gary, whyn't you get off my case?"

He firmed his jaw line, stuck it out, tapped his fingers along the edge of the steering wheel, and waited.

"Freddy's gonna be mad," she said.

"Too bad. You married, girl."

"Aw, he's working. Always working. I gotta have fun sometime." Her voice shifted from sexy to a keening whine.

"You wait and go out with your husband. Now come on. I'm takin' you home."

With a last try at rebellion, Esther stood back away from the car and peered in at Gary.

"You sound funny. What's with everybody tonight? Everybody's bein' mean. You sound mean, Gary. And just look at your eyes. You look different. Somethin' wrong? You ain't mad, are you? You never been mad before about this."

"Come on, Esther. I'll take you home." There was a knife-edge to his voice. He heard it too and put it down to being tired, being sick and tired of picking his buddy's wife up in bars around town and carting her home. Like he was some damn watchdog.

He felt a strange anger rising and pulled himself out of it.

None of his business. She wasn't bad, just too young to be tied down.

When she was in the car, scowling and angry with him, he reached over and locked the door she'd slammed behind her.

"How come you actin' so strange tonight?" Esther stuck her chin out and demanded of him.

"Not."

"Are too. Even your eyes. Never seen you like this before. Somethin' happened at work, don't take it out on me. You just get me home, O.K.?

His jaw hardened as though his teeth were clenched. His eyes gleamed; there could be fire behind them.

"What's with you, Gary?" Something about him frightened her, some vague sense that was intensifying as they drove. Fun-loving, easy-going Gary. Not like him at all.

"Can't you answer me?" she sat forward, trying to look directly at him.

His eyes turned toward her briefly and ran over her like a butcher looking over a cow. She felt the hair along her neck rise and her heart stop, then begin to beat double time.

"Gary?"

Again he didn't answer. They drove with her huddling away from him. He wasn't taking her home. No way. Heading out Woodward Avenue now. Passed Six Mile Road toward Palmer Park.

"You better take me home." Her voice weakened. Strangled. Stopped.

He pulled into the park. The roads were dark. With a single fluid move he turned the car into an opening between trees and stopped out of sight of the road.

"Now listen here, Gary..." She tried to muster outrage but stopped dead as he turned toward her, eyes brimming with hatred, lips pulled back as if in anguish. His hands came up and the expression on his face changed to one of overwhelming need.

She gave a weak laugh and hit at the hands moving toward her.

"Now, Gary. Hey man. You don't wanna scare me...."

The last thing she heard was a growl coming from deep inside him. To her frightened ears it was a sound a mad dog would make, or an animal about to make a kill.

Chapter Five

Horizontal stripes of filtered light coming through the venetian blinds cut across her bed and up the sloping walls. She had forgotten to close the blinds last night to shield her from the prying eyes of neighbor men entering and leaving the old clapboard Nevada Inn across the street. Ma got upset when she didn't close the drapes. Warned her about those men. Leering. Drunk. Lusting after women.

For three nights there had been no dreams, at least none with the incisive clarity of the dead girl dream, none she remembered except this morning's dream of Daddy, standing in the downstairs doorway, tall, dour, dressed as he always did for work: blue shirt, dark blue drooping pants, black lunch box under his arm.

He lifted a hand, waving good-bye to Martha, on his face an expression of intense worry. Bending to accommodate the bulky lunch pail, he fit his stiff-billed cap over his head, adjusting it so that it sat correctly, his longish brown hair creating a fluff around the edge—and he was gone.

Not much, as dreams go, but a familiar one. Except that Daddy's face was growing less and less clear and when she woke Martha was no longer sure he even looked like that.

Sunday. The one day in the week she didn't have to go to Koch's.

Sunday. She lay in bed thinking of her father. There was no pain in his absence any longer. There used to be. It had grown worse for years, instead of better, as she clouded over the father who really was and replaced him with a blue collar composite of Robert Young and Ozzie Nelson. From as far back as she could remember she had cut pictures out of the paper, anything that had to do with

25

the union he had belonged to: pictures of men on strike, photos of union leaders boarding planes and attending conventions, union picnics—men with wives and children, anything. It was a link with her father, these men with perpetually serious faces, angry men carrying grievance signs, men warming at fires lit in old metal barrels, men eyeing the cameras suspiciously. She knew their lives had been his life and it helped somehow to pile up the scrapbooks, to go over them, pore over the pictures, and feel she carried on for him.

So different from the man Ma spoke of. According to Ma, he worked, he ate, he slept, he went fishing with the boys, sat at the Nevada Inn nights with the boys, and finally was killed in his car on the way home from a fishing trip to Harsen's Island with the boys—the only one to be injured, impaled on the steering wheel, his chest and lungs crushed. That was the man Harriet talked about, not the man Martha knew from her dreams. Two different men.

She stretched and turned within the burrow of warmth her quilt created, allowing herself a few minutes more of privacy, time without Mother poking in her thoughts, picking apart her life as if something salvageable might have landed in the rubbish.

There was a light tap on the door. Harriet stuck her head, resplendent with pink plastic, around the edge of the door and inquired in a cracking morning voice, "You going to ten o'clock mass? It's almost nine now. You'll have to hurry."

Martha nodded and got up. Mustn't give her an excuse to sulk. She hadn't been too happy about the shopping trip with Patsy. She wasn't pleased at the thought of a girl like Patsy—a man chaser, Mother thought—having influence over Martha, but they'd been friends for almost three years now. If Patsy had been going to turn her into a barfly, as Harriet feared, it would have happened by now. Bella'd always maintained you can't make a floozie out of a silk purse, which evidently—since the worst hadn't happened—was true.

Martha smiled and drew on the black wool skirt she wore yesterday. Good enough for church.

* * *

"Uncle John and your Aunt Jenny are coming over later. Make sure you're home before they leave or I'll never hear the end of it from Jenny." Martha was back from mass, still dressed in her Sunday coat, a tweed she'd gotten a few years back when Penny's Ladies Shoppe, down the street, had closed. She also had on her good black gloves.

"What time are they coming?" Martha mumbled as she dug in the bottom of her purse, searching for coins she may have dropped to add to the three dollars for bus fare and lunch she had managed to wheedle out of Harriet.

"About three." Harriet, peeling apples for one of her apple cakes, glanced meaningfully at her daughter. A glance that carried the years of putting up with her husband's sister and her prying and moaning. Martha always liked Aunt Jenny because she was tiny and dark like Daddy, and when Martha was little never forgot to bring her candy or a comic book. But Martha didn't dare let Mother know, so now she returned the long-suffering look with an understanding smile.

"I'll be home no later than four," she said.

The store was filled.

"Let's get those boots first." Patsy was dressed in high, backless platform shoes, a corduroy jacket, and full make-up, from deep plum lipstick to deep brown eye-shadow.

Over lunch at one of the orange formica tables in the plastic cafeteria, Patsy was full of her Saturday date with the current "Bill." But she soon overchewed the meager details, which included an old movie and a drink at a topless bar where "Bill" had sat speechless, leering at the bare-breasted dancer with inverted nipples up on the small stage.

"By the way," she interrupted her description of the luckless dancer as an idea came back. "You read the paper today? Or listen to the news last night?"

Martha shook her head no. "We only get a paper on the days I buy one at the store, and I fell asleep last night before the news came on. Why?"

"Well. There's another girl missing over on the east

side. They gave her description. I figured maybe you'd dream about this one. You didn't did you? Well, maybe that other was a fluke. Or maybe this one's a runaway or something. But anyway, try not to hear the description and let's see if you can dream about her, O.K.?"

Martha was shaking her head. She choked on her tuna salad and put out a hand to ward off further discussion.

"No. Don't talk like that, please. I don't want to dream those dreams. Please no." Tears flooded her intense eyes. Patsy patted her hand and looked around to see if anyone was watching as she tried to quiet her.

"Shhh. Jesus, I didn't mean to upset you. I just thought you'd be as curious as I am to see if it really works."

"I'm not. I don't want it again. It's...it's like I'm crazy. Like something's wrong with me." She pulled a handkerchief from her coat pocket, wiped at her eyes and blew her nose, well aware people were looking at her now. "Even my mother acts like something's wrong with me. And Bella. Juliet. It's getting me so upset.... I could just kill 'em. You don't know.... Sometimes I just hate all of them...." Her face flushed a deep red. Her hands clenched into fists, knuckles whitened. "I can't stand it. The way they look at me. Can't stand it."

"O.K. O.K. Calm down. Sorry I mentioned it." Patsy waited while Martha fumbled with her damp hankie then gave up finding a dry spot and used K-Mart's paper napkin to blow her nose. "But you will tell me if it happens, won't you?" Patsy pursued. "You wouldn't try to keep it to yourself or anything, would you?"

Martha gave her a long look, moist eyes glaring. Finally she nodded yes, agreeing that she would tell. Anything to change the subject. To get on with this shopping trip, her big escape from home.

Getting off the bus at her corner later, Martha noticed Uncle John's car parked at the curb outside the door. She cringed, nerves knotting, knowing what was ahead: the appraisal, the interrogation...

Movement across Nevada caught her eye, distracted her. That little girl again. Leaning against the building, watching.

The same lone girl, brushing the toe of one shoe in the gravel of the narrow parking lot. At first she looked shyly away, then turned back to stare at Martha.

All she must own, Martha thought, noticing she wore the same oversized raincoat though the day was dry. On impulse Martha waved.

As if struck, the child snapped upright, foot ceasing its careless scuffing. Solemn face and eyes became alarmed. Plain face clearly shocked. She made no move to return the salute, only stood very still, waiting, as if preparing to run.

Knowing only too well what fear can do, Martha quickly opened the door to the upper flat and closed it behind her, leaving the child to the safety of the empty street.

Dear God, how she remembered that fear—fear of any friendly gesture from strangers, fear they might hurt her as Ma and Bella warned. Fear they might laugh. Wanting, always wanting, to take a hand offered but too unsure to chance it.

She shivered slightly though the stairway was oppressively hot. Memories were best left dead. That girl stirred too many. Martha hoped she'd never have to see the child again.

The three were seated at the kitchen table. Aunt Jenny was aging, Martha noticed as she kissed the papery cheek. Her dark hair was overcast with white. Her pale blue eyes were colorless now, almost gray. And when she smiled she looked worn, as people sometimes do who wrap themselves in a perpetual shroud of imagined tragedies and discontents.

To Aunt Jenny's sorrow, her tragedies were always those of other people, never hers. Except, perhaps, her brother's death, twenty-eight years ago, which widowed Harriet and left Martha fatherless. And her parents' deaths within two years of each other. But they were old and no one gave her much sympathy through her ten years of mourning—least of all her husband John, who was only too quick to point to their three married children, all strong and doing well, with healthy, well-adjusted children of their own, not even a divorce to wrinkle the benign surface of Jenny's life.

"As well as can be expected," Jenny sighed and gave her usual noncommittal answer to Martha's inquiry about her health. She patted Martha's cheek and shrewdly took in every new fine line in Martha's forehead, every hint of gray in her hair which might have appeared since the last inspection.

"Any prospects, Martha?" Jenny launched into her ceremonial litany of questions.

"How's the job?"

"Do you ever go to the beauty shop? You should *take* the money. You need a body perm."

"You being good to your mother?" This was from Uncle John, who only had the one question, delivered with a scowl as if his disapprobation was enough to prove his concern over his brother-in-law's widow and child and absolve him of any further responsibility which might threaten his bank account.

Martha answered the questions appropriately but didn't let the words touch her. They didn't mean to criticize. It was just expected of people, a way to show they cared.

When they left Martha's her eyes were heavy. Her body tired, aching. She wanted to wait for the news. To get the description of that missing girl so if she should dream about her—and it was likely because Patsy had firmly planted the idea in her mind—at least she would be able to explain away the dream.

But she was exhausted. The stress of constantly buffering between Aunt Jenny and Mother had been too much. She went to bed at ten-fifteen.

This time she was on a city street, but there was no life anywhere around her. The sidewalk, on both sides, was lined with huge brick warehouses, all boarded and abandoned. Their shadows covered the walks and darkened the street so that Martha felt as if she were groping her way along even though the sky overhead, between buildings, was blue.

Her feet were being made to rush over the broken concrete. She tried to hold back, to avoid her destination, but it was as if she were trapped in fast-forward motion that threatened to topple her if she resisted.

The number on one of the warehouses was in large

yellow letters. Martha noticed as she hurried past: 113. And just beyond number 113 was a break in the line of brick walls and a small, abandoned house set back from the sidewalk in a weed-blackened yard.

She didn't want to go up that walk or place a foot on the porch where missing boards and loose planks threatened unsafe footing. But she had no choice. It was go on, straight ahead, through a living room with peeling wallpaper and a broken couch that hung to one side. It was gag on the odor of urine and of smoke laying thick on the air. And choke on the smell of decay. And something else.

It was open that filthy basement door, pushing beer cans and cartons from in front of it as she pulled, to look down into darkness where a single circle of light fell on the sprawled figure of a girl lying face down with her head and arms on the bottom two steps.

The girl was black, with her hair corn-rowed. She had on a short red jacket, jeans, a black high-heeled shoe on one foot; and a black patent leather purse lay on top of her body, as if it had been thrown down after her.

The spotlight on the body faded. Martha closed the basement door and left the house.

She awoke to the awareness that there was no sense of fear this time. In fact, she felt more at peace than anything else. At peace and...well...satisfied. As her conscious mind took over she shuddered at the memory, imposing more conventional emotion on the experience. Still the satisfaction remained. Even though it had been a dream of another dead thing.

Chapter Six

She didn't want to tell anyone. No one. She lay listening to the morning voices coming from the kitchen. It was best to keep some things to herself. Maybe they wouldn't notice the change in her. She got out of bed and went to the bathroom to delay.

"What I mean to say is," Juliet went on after many interruptions, "that Martha's probably still a virgin, don't you think, Harriet? I mean, cause she's never dated boys, not really."

"I pray to God she's still a virgin," Harriet frowned in Juliet's direction. "What else should an unmarried girl be? Even though...there was that one boy in high school."

"The one who got sick and threw up all over her?" Bella broke into choking laughter again. Juliet reached over and pounded her back, showing her distaste for such display.

"Well, but you see what I mean?" she went on once Bella had quieted down. "Thirty-three years old and never been kissed, so to speak. That can't be good for the girl. Maybe that's why these strange things are happening."

Harriet bristled at Juliet who grew smaller and quieter, pushing her plump body up farther against the hard back of the kitchen chair. Harriet saw her advantage and pressed on. "All the good sisters stay as they always were, don't they? And the saints? And what about priests? They can't marry and they're all right."

"Ha," Bella dropped the syllable and smacked the table, making their cups leap into the air. She shook her head to show how wrong they were. "That's a laugh. I know stories about priests that you wouldn't believe. Why..."

Martha looked into her own eyes in the bathroom mirror. There was something new there, different. Something was happening which she did not understand and it frightened her. If she could just hang on. If others didn't know. It might go away....

"Well here she is now. Morning, Martha," Bella smiled as she shushed the other two.

"My, but you don't look well, Martha. Peaked." Juliet blinked and assumed a worried expression.

"Not another one of those dreams, was it?" Harriet knew her daughter enough to see that those huge blue eyes were unnaturally bright. Something was definitely wrong with Martha.

"Was it? Another dream?" Bella demanded, clucking her tongue. "Like the last one?"

Martha poured coffee and attempted an evasive answer.

"What was it this time?" Juliet asked, turning to the others to say, "Girl disappeared a few days ago, remember? You see a black girl in your dream?"

Not wanting to commit herself, Martha tried to escape to her room but was stopped by Harriet.

"You hear, Martha?" she insisted. "Was it a black girl in your dream? 'Cause a black girl disappeared down on the east side."

She nodded, hoping now to escape. But the three exploded with wonder, demanding she describe the dream and then quizzing her about every detail, forcing her to relive it until she finally ran from them, slamming the bathroom door behind her. Even here she could still hear their voices, shrill and angry with their excitement.

"I've got a paper at home that gives the girl's description," Bella said, moving her chair back, large body bumping the table as she got up. "Course I didn't pay no attention at the time. But let me run home. Get it. We'll see if Martha's description matches, like that other time. Wait for me, Martha," she raised her voice. "I'll be right back."

The other two hurried her, eager, though uncertain why, to have Martha proved—well—different.

Martha prayed she could get off to work before Bella, not much of a housekeeper since Herb's death, found that newspaper and returned. There was no doubt in Martha's mind the descriptions would match. Something was happening she didn't like or understand. And, short of never sleeping again, she was powerless to stop it.

The bus appeared as Bella came rushing out of the gate of her cyclone fence, waving a newspaper over her head at Martha and yelling. Martha pretended not to see her as she boarded her bus. She took a back seat and focused her burning eyes straight ahead.

Chapter Seven

"Whew! You look like a pile of warm manure!" Patsy greeted Martha as she walked into the store.

Martha gave a wry half-grin and thought how nice it would be to lie. To say no, nothing wrong, and end it. But she didn't lie easily, not even to herself, not even to protect herself from curiosity.

Strangely, though, even as she shied away from Patsy's attention, there was something in her that sought it. Something that preened and stretched when Patsy's eyes were trained on her. She had never known this limelight before. It felt good, somehow, as if it were her due. As if she were a spoiled child parading for applause.

"Bad night." She shrugged but gave Patsy a look that invited closer attention.

"Another dream?" Patsy's voice was properly hushed, her look attentive.

Martha shrugged again, as if to pass the subject off. She had seen Harriet use this trick to elevate interest in some little piece of gossip, some tidbit of news. It was too bad she hadn't learned more, paid closer attention. She wouldn't feel so adrift in a world where everyone seemed to know his niche and how to protect it from intrusion. If she'd been more attentive she would be an expert by now at dishonest secret sharing which shared little. Was it Harriet's fault? Probably not, she thought. Just another of her own faults.

"Well, if you won't tell me what it was about, your dream, forget it." Patsy had been at her all morning. Now, between customers, she was leaning against her register, huddled in a huge cable-stitched sweater, hands jammed into her pockets. She sniffed and looked away from Martha. "Here I thought we was friends."

34

"We...we are," Martha stammered. "I just don't...don't like to think about it."

"Hmmp." Patsy kept her eyes averted, rubbing her icy hands together as if she had more to consider than just Martha.

Breathing deeply as she gave in, Martha said, "O.K., Patsy, I'll tell you, but don't tell anybody else. Promise?"

"Who would I tell, for Christ's sake?"

While they snatched a few minutes between customers, Martha described the dream.

"Like that other time." The penciled circles around Patsy's green eyes made her resemble a giant panda. "Only this girl was black, eh? Hey, so's the one who disappeared."

Martha nodded. "I know."

"I cut out the description yesterday and tucked it in my purse." Patsy bent beneath her register to rummage in her bag. "Here. Now you tell me what you saw again and I'll check it out."

"Well, she had on a red fake fur jacket. Jeans. And black high heels. A black pa-"

"-tent leather purse." Patsy read from the clipping she held. They both stopped, breath barely coming.

"You realize that it's this girl the police are hunting for? They haven't found her body yet. And you know where it is?" Patsy's voice escalated with her enthusiasm.

"No. No, I don't," Martha shook her head violently. Denying. "It was just a dream. A dream."

"Well, just look who's here!" Patsy turned to greet a group entering the market. "Look Martha, it's your mother. And her friends. Let's just see what in hell they think about all this."

"Afternoon Patsy." Harriet Small managed a smile for Martha's friend. "Afternoon Martha."

"What brings all of you here?" Patsy listed slightly to one side, standing as she was with arms folded. She cocked a penciled eyebrow at them.

Ignoring Patsy, Harriet held a newspaper out toward Martha, indicating with a jab of her finger the article Patsy had in her purse.

"I showed her already," Patsy said.

Harriet's surprise was evident. "You know about this one too?"

Patsy nodded. "I've been telling Martha that if what she's got is an ability to see the future, she could make herself a lot of money. People do it all the time. And I ain't so sure most of those are genuine."

Bella and Juliet, behind Harriet, began clucking and talking to themselves.

"Well, personally," Harriet stiffened and showed her distaste for money, "I think she has a responsibility."

"Sure, so do I," Patsy answered quickly. "I'm only saying what others do with their gifts."

"She's right, you know, Harriet." Bella stepped forward, adjusting her heavy dark wool coat over her large bosom and removing her black scarf as she heated up with the discussion. "She really has a point there. If this is handled right, why, Martha stands to get famous."

"But the gift is from God," Juliet sputtered, scowling deeply as she considered what they were saying. "She shouldn't make money from it."

Mr. Koch, standing silently with arms folded, watched his employees and the old women going at it, until finally he stepped forward, demanding "What's going on here?"

Seeing that Martha was at a loss to explain, Harriet spoke up. "You might as well know. Everyone will soon. Martha's been having dreams where she can see the future."

"Mother!"

"Well, not the future maybe, but she located bodies of people who've been murdered. Before the police find 'em."

Mr. Koch drew his dark brows together heavily and thought for a moment before shrugging. "She should see a psychiatrist."

Juliet jumped to Martha's defense. "There's nothing wrong with her. This is a gift from the Lord."

He shrugged again and walked away waving a hand in dismissal. "You're all nuts. Trouble is none of you women have enough work to do. Martha, didn't I ask you to do cigarettes when you got the time?"

Male skepticism dampened their enthusiasm and Martha gratefully excused herself to go put up the cigarettes, avoiding the meaningful looks that the women were directing at her.

Soon a few others joined them, stood listening intently and staring open-mouthed at Bella who had the floor.

They all turned toward Martha who ducked her head to escape stares.

Stately Mrs. Kozak zeroed in first. "Is it true, what Bella Schwartz has been telling us? You see the future?"

Martha shook her head. This afternoon promised to be a long one, with her mother and her two friends still hovering over her at the store, and now more women gathering around her.

"She's just shy." Juliet took a little step forward and smiled at the women as she reached out to pat Martha's hand.

"But I don't...I..."

"I, personally, think it's frightening too." Bella maneuvered just a bit in front of Juliet. "I don't think I'd like to see dead bodies either."

"But it isn't something to be ashamed of," Harriet put in. "A gift from God..."

"You're damn right it isn't anything to be ashamed of," Patsy added, giving a little shake of her stiff white hair for emphasis. "If it's a ticket out of this shit hole, I'd take dead bodies any day." She nudged Bella and laughed. The woman didn't respond.

"I'm not ashamed. It's just that..." Martha stammered as she tried to defend herself, knowing it was impossible against this phalanx of women intent on a new, exciting development in their lives. They were already jockeying for conversation rights on the subject, with Harriet, due to relationship, definitely in the lead.

"Well, I think she should report this to the police," one of the women said.

"You know, you're right," Bella seconded.

"I'd say so," tiny Mrs. Taorimina piped up in a high, grating voice. "That's every citizen's responsibility."

Bella, quickest into action, was looking about, asking, "Who's got some paper? I'll need details. Who's got paper and pencil?"

Harriet frowned, unhappy over the loss of control here. Bella certainly could be pushy.

"I've got paper and pencil in my purse." She nudged Bella slightly aside, dislodging her from the center of the group. "I'll write it all down and you call the police. Go find the number while I write. Better be downtown, where they got homicide. And make sure you talk to a detective. No officer who just answers phones or nothing like that."

They crowded close, listening as Bella gave the man on the line the description of the dream. There was much whispering among them.

Bella turned from the phone a minute. "He wants to talk to you, Martha." She held the phone out to her, but Martha declined, shrinking back from it and waving it away.

"She's too shy about this whole thing," Bella said into the phone while glaring first at Martha and then Harriet, as if she should do something with her daughter.

"He wants to know if you can remember anything more specific about the street. Did you see a name or anything?" Bella demanded of Martha who had retreated to the edge of the group. She shook her head no.

"No, that's all, she says. Well, I know it's not much to go on, but she can't lie to you, can she. That's all she saw. Seems to me..."

Bella stopped, listened a while longer, her face reddening and drawing up in indignation. "Well...yes ...Martha Small. My name is Bella Schwartz, Mrs. Schwartz, but I'm calling for Martha. Yes, she works here at Koch's Market on Mt. Eliot. That's what I said, Koch's Market. Well...we thought it was our duty to...yes...good-bye."

She turned to the others and gave a short, embarrassed shrug while replacing the receiver. "He thinks I'm a nut."

Chapter Eight

The little guy bounced his basketball along the broken sidewalk to the corner and back, not stepping on cracks so he wouldn't break his mother's back. That's what the girls always said: Step on a crack, break your mother's back.

He didn't believe stuff like that anyway. Not now that he was eight. Knew better.

But still—best to be safe.

He measured his steps carefully along the pavement. Stay off a those cracks.

Don't know what's the matter with James Robertson. They were playin' nice, havin' fun with the new ball, when James just socked him and ran on home.

Play by myself then.

He grabbed the orange ball and tucked it under his arm, hunching up his shoulders so his jacket collar would keep that cold wind off his neck.

Nobody else around to play with. Not supposed to go over to the playground by the school. Saturday. Nobody be around. Too cold. Still—maybe. And he'd like to get somebody else to play with. Have 'em see his new ball....

He didn't usually disobey but today felt different, like it was all wrong anyway. He put a foot off the curb into the street then followed it with the other.

Going through the opening in the chain link fence he could see there wasn't anybody else there.

So what? Try to get it through the hoop.

He bounced the ball a few times in the dirt as he'd seen the big boys do. It got away from him. Trying to catch it, he kicked it instead, sending it over behind the school where the portables were set up for extra classes. One of 'em would be his homeroom next year, when he went into fourth grade.

He found the ball behind the narrow aluminum building. Clumsily he bent to pick it up then noticed the boy standing there, leaning against the wall, watching him.

"Hi Leroy," the little fellow greeted, happy to see someone he knew.

The young man lifted his head in greeting and lackadaisically shifted feet, pulling upright.

The small boy had seen this kid hanging around the school grounds before. Mostly the teachers ran him off, but he always came back, tried to get in ball games with the younger kids. Some of the kids called him names.

"You wanna play?" Unafraid, the little boy marched up to him then stopped.

Something wrong with Leroy today. Eyes looked like he was really mad at somebody. The little boy took a step back, then another.

Leroy pushed himself away from the building, springing into a crouch.

"Leroy. You scarin' me." The little boy's eyes were huge, big brown orbs in a light brown face.

The older boy grinned but it didn't change his face. His lips peeled back, showing his teeth.

"Come here," he said, the word an angry deep noise in his throat. "Come here."

"Uh-uh." The little boy dropped his ball and turned to run. He heard the scrambling on the gravel behind him, heard a rush of breath, then a hand hit him across the back of the head, sending him painfully rolling over and over, gravel biting, scratching, tearing at his face and hands.

When he sat up he was crying.

"Why'd you..."

When he looked up it was into a face like none he had ever seen in his short life. There was hatred there—eyes blazing, body taut, shaking.

"Leroy." This time it was a soft pleading sound. "Leroy."

But Leroy kept right on crawling toward him.

Chapter Nine

Martha sensed that the thin man with dark, tousled hair was looking for her, though she couldn't have said why she thought so. It had never happened before, and she had no idea who he was or what he could want with her. She just knew, with a sense of fatality that something was about to happen. Another one of those uncontrollable, life determining events she dreaded getting ahold of her, shaking things up.

His dark eyes went back and forth over Patsy and her and then did a fast survey of the store as he scraped his feet self-consciously on the dark matting just inside the door. His narrow face, kept averted, was neatly divided into geometric planes by fine high cheekbones and a strong chin colored slightly by the shadow of a beard. He coughed, patted the pockets of his no-color overcoat, and advanced on Patsy.

"I'm looking for Martha Small," he said, deep voice catching halfway through. Obviously ill at ease, it was just as obvious that he was usually in control.

With an instinctive fear of authority, Patsy frowned and didn't answer. He turned to Martha, inquiring, "Miss Small? I'm Detective Sergeant Bernabei."

She nodded, fear welling inside. No one who came unexpectedly like this brought good news. Could only be trouble of one kind or another. Something—like her father's accident—that would destroy.

With clumsy movements that snatched and missed at a pocket, he finally pulled out a wallet which he flipped open importantly to expose ID and a badge.

"It's not my mother, is it?" Her voice fell, stifled by the hand she put up to her mouth. "Nothing's wrong, is it?"

He shook his head quickly, betraying concern that she not get frightened. A hand automatically went out to comfort but fell back to his side.

"Nothing wrong. No trouble," he assured. "I just wanted to talk to you. Just a couple of things I'd like to clear up." He took a small black notebook out and flipped through it absentmindedly, seeming to need an excuse to avert his eyes from her stricken face.

She didn't protest, this thin, colorless woman, or carry on. Only stood waiting with a stoicism that could be heart-breaking if a man allowed himself to feel pity for timid souls caught up in legal machinations they didn't understand. But Sergeant Bernabei hadn't asked that Mrs. Schwartz call. He wouldn't have sought this frightened woman out if she hadn't started the wheel going herself.

"A Bella Schwartz called me yesterday." He referred to his notes, flipping pages, though he had no need to, having spent hours of his evening going over everything on this murder, including his report of this phone call, still puzzling him because it was so distinctly out of the ordinary. An odd piece which didn't fit anywhere. "Said she had information on the murder of Esther Shell. . . ."

"Not about the murder," Patsy, standing protectively beside Martha, put in quickly. "It was just about her dream of finding the body. It happened once before—that girl down in the Shores. She dreamed about that girl too and when they found the body, the description of the place exactly fit Martha's dream. That's why this friend called you—it seemed like a duty to report it, and you can see Martha's kind of shy."

He nodded, looking from Patsy's face, with its dark slashes of penciled eyebrows where her own had been shaved, to the sallow faced woman whose brown bangs hung almost into her huge, round eyes. What a study in contrasts, he thought, watching the one eye him coldly as if she expected a battle at any moment while the other half-cowered against her friend and looked guilty of whatever he might choose to charge her with. The blonde's hostility would set the tone, he knew from experience, and he would get nowhere. He had been drawn here as much out of curiosity as from his responsibility to official business.

Obviously this cowering woman who lived miles from that abandoned house where they found the body knew nothing about the murder. And anyway he was almost certain it was a friend of the girl's husband who strangled her in some misguided burst of loyalty to the buddy he thought was getting a raw deal. There were only minor details to clear up on that and they would have a warrant for the guy's arrest.

This visit was on his own time. Because the coincidences, the similarities bothered him. As he had been talking to Bella Schwartz yesterday, Tim Randolph, another detective, had been taking a call from a party store owner reporting a dead body one of his resident winos had told him about. A dead body at 115 Sizemore.

The first thing to strike him at the scene had been the yellow numbers—113—on the warehouse next door to the abandoned house. If it had been longer ago than fifteen minutes, he might have missed the connection between the phoned report and the actual place. But it wasn't. And on seeing the numbers, he took out the notebook and checked the other details—all matching to an astonishing degree. Matching, as if this Martha Small had been at the scene, or been told about it by someone who was. Seemed important enough to check out.

The last thing he was willing to believe in was psychic experience.

Until now—here—looking at the frightened woman. Even the psychic explanation made more sense than her being involved in this in any other way.

He pulled back a bit from the encroaching blonde and changed his tactics. This Small woman would be more accessible without her hovering angel. Maybe he could put her at ease, get her to trust him so he could learn the truth about how she knew where the body was. Then he could forget the psychic business.

"Maybe this is a bad time. Because you're working." He smiled directly at Martha, excluding Patsy purposely. It was a quick, shy smile. "I'm off duty right now. Will you be through work soon?"

Martha nodded, ducking her head to turn quickly to Patsy for help.

"Why don't I wait outside in my car and drive you

home? Or maybe there's a place close by we could go for coffee. Someplace where we could talk?" He smiled again, feeling an odd compulsion to touch the woman's trembling hands, assure her he was all right, wouldn't hurt her.

"Just a minute," Patsy reared back and fixed him with a knowing stare. "You better whip out that ID again. I don't like the sound of this."

He complied, holding the wallet open as she squinted over his picture. "Just a second." She turned to her register for a piece of paper and a pen and proceeded to copy down his name and badge number.

"You can call downtown if you'd like to confirm it," he offered to expedite her investigation.

"No," the quiet woman pulled away from her friend. "I'm sure you are who you say you are, Sergeant. I'm through at six if you don't mind waiting."

"No ma'am." He touched his forehead as he once had when he wore a patrolman's cap. "It's the light blue Chevette right here in front." He left.

She phoned and told Ma she had to work a little later than usual.

"Not short in your register, are you?" was the swift reply. "Don't let him cheat you. If he wants to take it out of your paycheck again tell him that the girls at the A&P don't have to make up shortages, not since the union came in. Tell him that. You mention union and he'll shut up right away." Harriet paused briefly for breath. "But don't make Mr. Koch mad. I don't mean that. God knows where you'd get another job. And be more careful with your change. You know you sometimes get absent-minded and you could give change for a twenty when they only gave you a five. But if..."

"I've got to go." Martha hung up, not even giving a time when she might get home.

It was with a mixed sense of trepidation and importance that Martha walked up to the blue car and waved good-bye to Patsy, who moved reluctantly toward the bus stop, turning frequently to keep Martha in sight.

He was out of the car when he saw her, inviting her to get in and shutting the door after her.

The interior of the car was warm. He'd kept the motor running for heat as he waited, and Martha welcomed the thick, snuggling feel after another day of damp cold at her register.

The little car smelled of leather upholstery and books— no tobacco smell, nothing unpleasant. It was show-room clean inside. A tape deck played the intricate horn of Chuck Mangione in low tones that pleasantly soothed her, as did the detective sergeant's shy smile when he asked where they might go for coffee.

"Or maybe we could have dinner somewhere? I've got to eat too. And I am taking up your time." With timid self-preoccupation she missed the keening note of loneliness beneath his words.

David heard himself asking this stranger out to dinner and caught the pleading tone in his own voice, caught it and was embarrassed, dismayed that his need was this close to the surface. It had been a long time since he wanted to sit and talk with a woman. On this job, opportunities to meet women were not scarce, but the kind he met, especially since being promoted to homicide, were not the kind a guy took home to mother. The women he dealt with all day were either crying or cursing.

Sitting there, waiting for this Miss Small, he had not really been thinking about her at all. Nor about being lonely—since he never thought about that anymore, the state being a perpetual one which had created its own niche inside him, as familiar to him as the place where he retained memories of his dead father. It was her stricken face that touched him, brought out a protective sense he thought he'd mastered but evidently had not. His vulnerability to pathos made him smile. He muttered under his breath, "Ma, you'd be proud of me. Still a good boy." Paying homage to the mother who, with basic Italian upbringing, raised her boy to "have respect."

Now he heard the plaintiveness in his voice and switched to gruff nonchalance. "But then, I am a stranger to you." He shrugged as she was making small protests of "I couldn't. No thank you."

"And you've probably already got plans for this evening."

She shook her head, face deadly serious. "No, nothing except I have to wash my hair. It's just that I know you're busy and I don't mind waiting for dinner."

"Well..." He felt she wanted him to press but couldn't. "If you're sure...then I guess I'll just ask my questions. At least I can drive you home. If that's O.K."

"Yes. I'd appreciate that. If you don't mind."

"Now—" he reached around for his notebook and pen again, fumbled with them comically, retrieving them with her help as the pen was about to roll down into the seat. He muttered, "Thanks." She suddenly grinned at him, a sense of impish fun bursting through that thick overlay of fear.

"You'll have to write fast," she teased. "It's almost dark."

He smiled back. Their eyes met and held, something passing between them that neither could describe but both knew felt good, felt like acceptance. He put the notebook away.

"Was that the truth? About your dream?" He got down to business, but softly, a sense of friendliness behind the words.

"Yes," she said.

"You know," he wouldn't look her way now, "the police don't believe much in lucky dreams."

He paused.

"What do you mean?"

"We found the dead girl."

She felt her breathing stop, held suspended. Something leaped inside her, something agitated, excited, pounding as if to be let out. "Dead girl, dead girl, dead girl"—words knocked against her skull. "Dead girl, dead girl, dead girl—number two."

She felt her lips move involuntarily. Curve up into a smile.

Don't let him see. God, don't let him know something's wrong with me.

He was looking away, she could only see the outline of his face, the dash light and the glow of the street light on the corner creating a silouhette against the glass. Her breath came again, in one long expelled sigh.

"And it was just as Bella told you? Just as it was in my dream. Right?" She whispered the words, listening to them. Was the tone right? As it should be?

"That's about it. And I have to tell you it struck my partner and me very funny. You know. Odd. We figured there were only three possible explanations for a coincidence like that." Here he stopped to swallow nervously. "One is that you somehow stumbled on the body in that house; and two is that someone you know did, told you about it, and maybe you felt you couldn't keep quiet and made up this dream to cover it."

She was very still, sitting primly. A straight-backed shadow. When he stopped, she asked, "And the third possibility?"

"That you had something to do with the murder."

He heard her catch her breath. She said nothing. He waited, feeling cruel and stupid.

Her voice was throbbing with tears when she finally spoke. "I don't know how to clear myself of any of those charges. Except I swear it was a dream. And remember how Patsy told you about the dream I had before this one? About that girl out in the Shores?"

He nodded, but realized she could not see him and cursed the darkness that was isolating them into their own forms of misery.

"Yes, I recall that now." He pushed in the cigarette lighter, just to have something to do.

"You can't think I had anything to do with two murders, can you? I don't even have a car."

"A friend could have a car. Maybe a boyfriend."

"I don't have a boyfriend. I don't even know anyone with a car, except my uncle. Oh—NO—don't suspect him now!"

"Look—" he was nervously twisting the wheel. "I'm starved. Couldn't we get something to eat?"

Her voice was small. "I'm not really hungry. I'd ask you over to our house, but mother wouldn't have cooked enough, and anyway, tonight it's creamed dried beef on toast."

There was silence between them.

"If you're through, I'd like to go home," she said. "I...I don't feel too well."

"Sure," he started the engine. "Which way?"

She directed, then asked, "Am I really under suspicion?"

"Not really. It's just so strange." He sounded put out.

"I didn't want Bella to call." Her voice was wistful.

"But she did. And here I am."

There was silence between them again.

"I see what you mean," she said as she pointed to the curb next to her building. "It sounds terribly suspicious. But it really was a dream." Her voice caught, held, and waited dismissal.

"Guess you'd better run on in." He was oddly disappointed. He had expected something more. Either the pleasure of exposing a charlatan or the joy of believing. He had neither.

She didn't escape as he expected her to, but sat for a time with her hand on the door handle.

"Am I still under suspicion?" she asked, turning toward him, the streak of light from the upper flat shining on her eyes and then on her tongue as she licked at her lips.

"No. I just don't understand this at all."

"I'm not a liar," she said softly. "It was a dream. Both times."

"That's so hard to believe." He was shaking his head. She sat a while longer.

"I'm sorry."

Instinctively his hand went out and found hers braced on the seat. He squeezed it briefly, let go as the hand fluttered excitedly away. But she brought it back. Touched him. Ran her fingers along the back of his hand as a child might, exploring the dark hair growing there, feeling his roughened skin. "I am sorry." The voice was a whisper. "But it's the truth. Only dreams."

"You know something," he said. "I believe you. I only hope my partner does." He'd had to clear his throat to answer. He was aroused by her but knew if he made a move she would run.

She was out the door, leaning half in from the sidewalk. "Does that mean you might come back?"

In his confusion, his guard slipped. The words came out all wrong.

"If you'll let me."

Christ, he thought, I sound like a kid, a damned kid begging for favors.

She shut the door without answering. He watched as she glanced up at the windows and hurried through a door set in the side of the old, wooden building.

"Damn it," he smashed a fist against the wheel. "Damn it."

Chapter Ten

"Who was that drove you home?" Harriet demanded as Martha took off her coat, tangling herself in the torn lining. Juliet, setting the table for Harriet, smiled a hello.

"Someone who came to the store to see me." She hoped to avoid the word "police." The women panicked at the idea of turning the eye of the law toward themselves, their only experience with policemen being the men in uniform who stopped speeders out on Mt. Eliot or broke up fights in one of the small factories on the street.

"Not a boyfriend?" Juliet smirked.

"I'm afraid he was from the police." She paused to let it sink in. No matter how much she claimed she didn't want to upset them, breaking the news and listening to the shock waves it produced was a gratifying sensation. It had always been this way. She told herself the right thing to do but did the opposite, especially with the three women. Something in her enjoyed exciting them, tormenting them. But then they were so easy to torment. They could be upset so quickly. It was as if all of them, including Martha, needed drama, excitement, anything to shake up the plodding days.

"Wha...! What do the police want with you?" Harriet was standing at the refrigerator, reaching for the bowl of creamed dried beef to heat for Martha. She broke one of her own rules as she stood with the door open.

"It was that phone call Bella made. They found the body. Just the way I dreamed it. Now they think I either know the murderer, or killed that girl myself."

"Ooh, no." Juliet was rocking on her chair, hands at her mouth. "I told Bella. I told her. Nothing but trouble. You know how she always thinks she's right. Can't tell that woman a thing. And now—*this*."

Harriet made an attempt to wave Juliet's whining voice away as she shut the refrigerator and moved over to a chair. "But they can't really suspect you, can they?"

Martha shrugged and took a small enameled pan from the cupboard to heat some of the beef for herself.

"But you say it was just like in your dream?"

She nodded.

"Then . . . then this is the second one like that. I don't understand. What's happening, Martha? What is it?"

She turned to face her mother, accepting the honest confusion, but meeting it only with her own. "I don't know, Ma," she said. "I wish I did know so I could stop it."

"Are the police coming back? I mean, will they come here?" Juliet wanted to know.

"He said he wanted to talk to Bella."

"Ooh, just wait till she hears," Juliet thrilled. "Whyn't you call her Harriet? See if she's on her way."

Harriet shook her head. "I don't go looking for tornadoes."

Juliet snickered and rolled her eyes as Bella walked in soon afterward.

"What's going on here?" She was in a good mood, a hearty smile on her face. "Something's burning." She pointed toward the pot on the stove which Martha was happy to attend to as Harriet told Bella about the police.

"Told you not to do it." Juliet folded her arms and affected an air of injured innocence.

"Phooey," Bella exploded. "You all stood around telling me it was our duty to call." Her face lost its red jauntiness as it sank into two double chins and a scowl. "What the hell they want with me anyway?"

"Don't know," Martha mumbled over a mouthful of charcoal tainted creamed dried beef. "He thinks we murdered the girl."

"What!" Now Bella was screaming and swearing at the top of her lungs. "What the hell's the matter with you people, gettin' me into something like this? I never had no trouble with the police in my whole life until now."

Martha rather enjoyed the woman's hysteria. The growing excitement in the room felt good, so different from the usual exchange of meaningless sentences. It was as though, now that the police had taken notice of them, they were of more value. Good or bad wasn't really at stake here. Their immortal souls weren't in danger. But outside attention was focused on them. And especially on Martha.

Especially on Martha. At home. At work. People were looking at her. Seeing her. Whether or not it was in fear, as Juliet now betrayed in her stares, or anger, as in Bella's narrow eyes, or bewilderment, as in Harriet's regard, or even a mixture of awe and puzzlement, as Patsy, Mr. Koch, and some of the customers had shown—they were still looking at *her* and not using her as a mirror to hold up to admire their own reflections.

She rinsed her dishes at the sink and tried not to listen to Harriet soothing Bella while Juliet maliciously blew small blasts into the whirlwind. When she finished the dishes, she turned, only to have them stop talking and look toward her expectantly.

"I'm tired tonight," she said, elevating her chin and leaning casually against the sink. "I think I'll spend the evening in my room."

"What about me?" Bella wailed, making Martha turn back to them.

"Why should you worry? You know we didn't murder anyone."

"Yes...but..."

"Goodnight."

When the phone rang later, Martha sensed it would be for her and resented having to leave the shelter of her room.

But she was summoned. Harriet held the receiver toward her, covering the mouthpiece with her hand and mouthing the words: "A man."

"Miss Small? This is David Bernabei. Remember, I saw you earlier? About this Esther Shell case?"

"Yes."

"Well, I've been thinking this thing over ever since I left you and I just can't seem to get this dream of yours out of my head."

"Really?"

"What? Oh...yes..." A pause. "What I'm trying to say is that I believe you, about these dreams. I really believe you. From meeting you I could tell you weren't the kind of person to be mixed up in a murder. You get to know people pretty well in this job."

"I can imagine."

"Well, what I was thinking was maybe you could take a look at some of these other missing person cases, where we suspect homicide. I've got three right now. And see if you can find 'em."

She hesitated. "Is this some kind of a test?"

A pause from his end of the line. "I guess you could say that," he said.

"I'd really rather not. I've gotten into all the trouble I intend to for a while."

"It could really help.... I mean if you saw something—anything—we could go on."

"Please Sergeant. I'd rather not do that or encourage this...eh...this..."

"Talent?"

"No...please," her voice slipped. She was afraid she was going to cry.

"Well...then...could I just come talk to you?"

"What for?"

"I thought we could talk. I...you interest me."

"I'd rather not." All three women were waiting as she spoke, nodding and hushing each other lest a word be missed.

"I don't mean as a policeman, Miss Small. I just...felt comfortable with you. I thought maybe you felt the same." His voice held disappointment.

This time she caught that other quality in his voice. It led her to qualify her dismissal of him. "Well...if you want to come by after work."

"Tomorrow?"

"That will be all right."

"Six, right? This time we'll have dinner. O.K.?"

"All right."

"Good. I'll pick the place." He hung up.

The three women seated in the living room pretending they had not been listening were on her as soon as she hung up.

"Was that the detective?" Harriet asked, turning from the green rocker.

When Martha nodded that it was, Bella got up to turn the sound on the TV down more. Juliet didn't even fuss, though the program was one she always watched.

"Well?" Bella demanded.

Martha shrugged. "He seems to believe me, about the dreams. Even wants me to help him with some cases where the bodies haven't been found yet."

"Oh, my!" Juliet's eyes widened.

"I don't think you should do that." Harriet looked worried.

"She should too. You're going to, aren't you?" Bella demanded.

"I told him no."

"What? You've got a chance to clear my name and you refused him?"

"I'm sorry. I just don't want to tempt fate by trying to bring these dreams on. Haven't we had enough trouble already?"

Bella turned on Harriet. "Talk to her for heaven's sake. Tell her to help him and he'll leave us alone."

All of this was too much for Harriet. She certainly didn't want to be in the middle. "She's thirty-three years old," she quickly told her friend. "Old enough to make up her own mind."

Bella sputtered. Martha turned to go back to her room.

"How did you leave it with him?" Harriet asked. "I mean, did he take no for an answer?"

Martha shook her head. "Not exactly. He's meeting me after work again tomorrow."

"What for, if you said you wouldn't help him?"

"I don't know. He said he would like to see me. We're having dinner."

"Hmmm..." Harriet frowned. "I don't know as I like this. He's a man. You be careful, Martha."

"Oh ha!" Bella exploded with relief. "So that's what this is all about. The man wants a date and has to go through all of this rigamarole. God, men have changed since my day. They didn't pussy-foot around then. They liked you, that was that."

"So he's a beau?" Juliet was fighting to keep up in this unfamiliar maze of excitement.

Martha shook her head violently and blushed.

Harriet frowning, was deep in thought, lines cutting around her mouth and between her eyes. "I'd rather you didn't have anything to do with him, Martha. We don't want trouble. There's been enough..."

"Go on to your bed," Bella laughed and waved at her. "I'll bet you whatever you want that you won't be dreaming of no dead bodies tonight." She winked at Juliet in relief and ignored Harriet as she got up to raise the sound on the TV.

Chapter Eleven

The blue Chevette was there at quarter to six, parked at the curb in the first measurable snow of the season. Martha could see the car through gaps in the Campbell soup displays, but she couldn't see him though she craned her neck and attempted to get a glimpse of the interior of the car.

Patsy caught her and laughed, shaking a finger. "You don't look all that shook up to me," she teased. "What's with this guy? Last night you were like a ghost when you went out of here. Now look at you, blushing and jumping around like a sixteen year old."

All Martha could do was smile self-consciously in answer and try to keep her eyes off the car until time to check out.

He must have been sleeping. Slouching in one corner,

his head back against the window, he snapped upright when he heard her tap at the glass.

"Hi," he smiled, slipping the car into gear. "Mind if I pick the place?"

"Not at all." She sat back against the seat, surprised at not feeling nervous. She was relaxed, almost happy to see him, stretching her arms out unself-consciously to relieve the tension from hours of register and stock work.

"Tired?" His voice was soft and warm, his eyes on her.

"A little." She blushed, heat creeping up her face.

"Hope you like this place we're going to. It's one of my favorites. You like Italian food, don't you?" There was no trace of the professional policeman in him tonight. Eager to please, he was almost shy. In the dim light of the dash, she could see his smile come and go quickly. She was shocked by how strongly she desired to reach over and touch him. Made her feel silly as she used to feel at high school gym dances, where she would smile as boys paused to size her up and then ask the next girl to dance. She told herself to be careful.

"I've only had canned spaghetti," she said. "I don't get to restaurants much. We don't have a car. Oh—I told you that before..."

"Believe me, canned spaghetti isn't Italian food. You should taste my mother's cooking. She's great."

"You live with you mother?" The question was innocent.

"If you mean am I married, the answer is no. Don't worry."

"I...I didn't mean anything." It embarrassed her to realize she should have inquired last night, when he first asked to take her out, but the thought—of his not being exactly as presented—hadn't occurred to her. As naive as always, she thought, and laughed at herself.

"And yes, I live with my mother."

There was a time of silence between them in which he turned on the radio and flicked the dial back and forth before shutting it off again.

"You want to hear music?" he asked, taking off slowly from a red light. Snow was accumulating in the streets now.

"No. No, thank you." She searched her mind for a safe subject. She knew all about small talk, and how a woman was supposed to be bright and witty and keep the conversation going, but every sentence she formed sounded stilted when she ran it through her head. They settled for an amiable silence.

The restaurant was on a downtown side street, unprepossessing, almost a store-front exterior with a small sign in the window reading Romolo's. An old place with carved moldings and wooden pillars and rows of tables with red-checked cloths.

"Would you like wine?" he leaned forward to ask as they scanned the menu.

"I . . . I don't really drink."

"You don't—or you haven't before?"

She smiled at the distinction and admitted she hadn't before.

Over wine, a trace of the cop crept back into his smile. She stiffened, suspecting his next move, and listened carefully.

"I wanted to talk to you tonight because my head's been going around and around ever since I met you. I told my partner I believe in your dreams, and he thinks I'm crazy." They both laughed. "But the trouble is I do believe you. Or at least I want to believe, which is the same thing." He settled back, avoided her questioning eyes by playing with the squat wine glass.

"I could use your help." His voice dropped so that a couple at the next table could no longer listen in. "If you're for real, that is."

Unexpectedly, she felt anger at this challenge to prove herself. "I don't know if I'm 'for real,'" she said. "I only know what's happened to me. I didn't ask for it. Believe me, Sergeant. I haven't been happy . . . happy since this whole thing began. I . . ."

"I'll tell you the truth," he interrupted. "I really want to believe you. I do. You know, it's strange that I've come this far with you. Believing, I mean. In my job you learn not to. Too easy to believe the worst. This whole business is kind of new to me. And to be honest with you, Martha—I can call you Martha, can't I—good—well, it feels good."

"But how can I help? What are you talking about? I have no control over it."

One of his hands fell on hers, as if for support. It

seemed to Martha every eye in the place must be on them, every ear trained their way.

"I've got a picture of a little boy here." He started to reach into his suit pocket, but stopped. "Maybe you read about him. Just disappeared. His parents—a really nice couple—they call all the time, just to see if any of us found out anything. At first they called because they were sure he was alive someplace. Now they call because they want to be able to bury him. It won't end for them until we find the body."

"But I told you, I have no control over this. I can't perform like a...a trained seal." She shut up quickly as the waitress brought large bowls of minestrone and performed a sleight of hand with the grated cheese.

"I've got this friend—well, really just a man I met when I worked vice. He's a hypnotist. Used to have an act at the Blue Dove. I called him about you and he says he could train you in self-hypnosis. Maybe help you bring on a trance. Maybe get the same information your brain is feeding you through dreams."

"I don't want to start tampering with it. I'd like to just leave it alone. Maybe it'll stop the way it started—suddenly."

"And if it doesn't? What then? He says you'll probably sleep better if you can release this force through self-induced trances. And he says it's a snap to learn how."

She was shaken, yet the prospect of untroubled sleep was attractive despite her fear.

"But...Sergeant..."

"David, please."

"David. I'm afraid of whatever it is that's got ahold of me," her voice dropped, she choked slightly. *"I'm really desperately afraid. There's more...more you don't know. I can't go on...not on purpose. You don't know...."*

"But why? Why does it scare you? I should think..."

"Because it's unnatural," she whispered the words at him, leaning across the table. "Maybe it's even...evil."

His face showed amusement, then a little doubt. "You mean like some devil's got ahold of you?"

She nodded vigorously, shaking even her unflappable bangs. "Don't laugh. Please. I'm afraid of it."

He considered for a moment then said finally, "I don't think so, Martha. I don't think it's evil. Too much a positive force." His voice fell. "No, I believe you are blessed. I don't mean like a saint or anything. I just mean you've been given a different capacity than most of us have. Somehow you sense a troubled spirit and locate the source of its trouble. No one would want to be left dead in an old culvert, or in a heap of trash in a basement. You help them be found."

She sat very still, considering what he had said.

"I help them be found. . . ." she repeated his words, a touch of awe in her voice as the meaning shook her. "I help them be found. Contact the spirit world, you mean. Never thought about . . . about being dead."

She smiled slightly now, smiled at the sudden awareness of something alien, but interesting, moving into her life. Maybe she needn't fear it after all. Not if this man was so certain. A feeling of joy and sharing such as she couldn't remember experiencing in a very long time swept her, until she wanted to throw back her head and laugh.

David reached across the table, between plates, to take one of her hands in his. The hand he held was chapped. She might have been ashamed at another time. But not now. She left her hand in his, her touch light and fragile, expressing her desire to welcome him before her mind took over with its burden of fear and shame and distrust. Slowly she drew away.

"Will you help me?" he whispered.

"When do you want me to meet your friend?"

"Tomorrow night. He'll come to my house."

"Oh, no. . . ." she was already retreating.

"My mother'll be there. Bring your friend, Patsy, too, if you want to."

"I don't know." Her face was lowered over her plate, head shaking. "I wish I could just go back to being me, the way I was." She pushed at her salad.

"Do you?" His question caught her unawares. She glanced at his face and read things there about herself she didn't think he knew. There was truth there, about a time before the possibility of him, truth about a time when she was noticed just about as much as the prepackaged hamburger by customers, Mr. Koch, even Mother. At least now she'd been granted a bit of individuality. So what if it was the same sort of interest that a freak show might create?

She was just beginning to realize that attention and limelight felt good.

No. She did not really want to go back to the way she
was. Not really.

"Will you pick us up?" she asked hesitantly. "I don't
have a car, as I..."

"About seven, all right?"

"That's fine. At my home. I only work until twelve on
Saturdays."

"Great. And," he fumbled at his shirt pocket, "let me
give you my card. It's got my home number and my
extension downtown. Just in case you have to get ahold of
me."

"And I'll look at the picture of that child," she smiled.
"But later, when you take me home."

He nodded and attacked the lasagna verde with a
wide smile.

"He looks so little." She examined the picture of a
smiling black boy, about eight or nine. He could have been
any of a million children, but this one was missing. Gone
from his home for no reason. Martha could feel the panic
a mother would feel knowing this boy was alone somewhere—out there in the cold and dark.

He wore a striped T-shirt and blue jeans rolled at the
bottom but falling squarely over the tops of his old sneakers.

Tears stood in her eyes as David took the picture from
her and shut off the overhead light in the car.

"Now you see why I want help."

After a time she said, "Do you always feel this personally responsible?"

"Only with the kids. They're the ones that hurt."

She knew she should get out, go in. Mother probably
up there watching. But she couldn't. Not just yet. Not at
this moment. She felt encapsulated with this man, isolated
in a white world which forgave the ugliness of Mt. Eliot
Street. Perhaps if she opened the car door the blanketing
silence and stark beauty would metamorphose back to
dirty street, ramshackle buildings, and throbs of manufac-
turing shops. With unaccustomed selfishness, Martha wanted
to have it all for just a while longer.

David leaned his head back against the seat, sighing.

"You know," he said. "I thought I knew it all. Had seen everything, and knew everything. Then you come along and shoot it all to hell." He paused briefly. "There was this one child. Just a baby. When we found her there wasn't a bone in her body that wasn't broken. Her eyes were closed. There was blood coming out of every opening." He stopped, voice breaking. "Her mother and her boyfriend had taken turns beating her because she'd wet her pants. They were toilet training her. Only she didn't live through it. That one hurt. Really hurt...I wanted to kill those two bastards, beat them until blood came out everywhere on them. But I couldn't. I had to watch them put their heads together and talk about lawyers while the kid died. You know, something hardens inside you when you see things like that. Especially the kids. Yeah, the kids always get me."

He paused again. She said nothing.

"And then you come along, like a sign saying 'See Bernabei, maybe you're not so smart after all. Maybe there really is something beyond this.'" He turned toward her and put out a hand, reaching across the seat to where hers rested on the cold leather. She felt his fingers entwine with hers, felt his grip tighten until he was drawing her toward him and kissing her softly, his lips undemanding.

After she got out of the car, lips burning from the brush of his whiskered face across them, she stood in the doorway of her building waving good-bye to him, suffused with a kind of warmth she'd never known before, a welling, overfull feeling of desire and contentment.

A movement in the snow, something at the street corner caught her eye. A furtive movement. Not a night for walkers. In the light from upstairs Martha could just make out the outline of a child—that little girl—the same one, huddled beside the telephone pole.

Martha made an exclamation of surprise and took a step toward her. It was late, too late for her to be out. And so cold, snowing.

The thin, peaked face turned attentively to Martha, who stopped herself from rushing to the child. Their eyes met briefly and held.

Timidly, slowly, the little girl, face shadowed, eyes indistinct, raised a hand to wave.

A shudder went through Martha's body. This wasn't right...only a child. She took another step toward the girl, slipped, caught herself on the building. When she looked up again, the child was gone, the corner empty except for gusts of snow-laden wind whipping around the front of the shop.

Martha shivered as the wind bit through her coat.

Why was the child following her? Why did she hang around like this? Something was terribly wrong.

Martha welcomed the blast of heat inside the door, and even welcomed the barrage of questions from the waiting women, forgetting everything but pleasure at the attention being heaped on her and thinking no more about the little girl still out in the night.

Chapter Twelve

During the night the snow turned to rain and washed the white world into city sewers. Also, during the night Harriet awoke and listened to sounds of Martha's restless sleep and worried because her daughter was changing. This thing with the dreams was affecting her. She was quieter. Stood straighter. Wanted to be alone so much. And now there was this policeman. They shouldn't be involved with the police. Only mean trouble. But Martha said they'd gone to dinner, that it wasn't any trouble that brought him back.

Harriet lay in bed listening to the sounds through the wall.

Not that she didn't want to see Martha happy. That wasn't it at all, she told herself, and stopped to listen again as the bed in the next room creaked. Moaning sounds came through the wall. Chilling in the dark.

"I saw the little boy," Martha whispered into the phone then raised her voice when David complained he

couldn't hear her. "I found the little boy. From the picture
you showed me last night. I had a dream and—oh, David—
he *is* dead."

He said nothing. Silence. Finally, in a resigned voice,
he asked, "You're through at noon today, isn't that right?"

"Yes." She listened while eyeing the archway into the
kitchen, where the three sat huddled over coffee cups. She
didn't want them to hear.

"I'm through at noon. That's right. Yes, I saw the
place. It looks like an old garage, or an alley where the
garages are all of wood, and they lean and seem to be
mostly unpainted. And there's a big American flag somewhere in it. I'm not sure about it, but I remember,
and—yes—I'll be waiting and I'll tell you all of it then.
What? Oh—yes, tonight is fine. For dinner? Patsy too?
Well, I guess so. You're sure your mother won't mind?
Well—then—yes."

Patsy flicked at her counter with lackadaisical swoops
of the dirty feather duster. Beneath, stored as if for a time
of shortage, were gray piles of used Kleenex and half-
eaten bags of peppermints.

Cold played around her ankles. She'd noticed they
were getting redder, with tiny blue veins standing out. Just
like her mother—God forbid—varicose veins. Patsy could
envision years of hugely swollen legs. Nights of pain. One
morning she had wakened to the sound of her mother
crying, trying to pull her red and blue legs—immense, like
two bloated sausages—over the kitchen floor to the
bathroom.

Shuddering, she ran a painted fingernail down the
course of one of the still tiny blue tributaries. This damn
job! She shouldn't be on her feet. Should be at a desk job,
secretary, receptionist, not standing on this cement floor
for long hours like this.

Martha should be in any minute now. Patsy kept one
eye out for the hurrying, stooped figure. She wanted to
know how the date had gone, worrying she had not
warned Martha what could happen. So goddam naive,
that one. Thirty-three, but might as well be eight or nine
for all she knew. Not even those things a woman knew
from birth. No guile. No wariness.

After all, this guy was a cop. Decent of him to take Martha out to dinner. Poor kid never had a real date. Least he could do. But still, Patsy thought, I better warn her gently that he might be using her.

"Goddam men," she muttered, putting the lipstick away and grabbing up a hairbrush, running it over her hair before Koch saw.

When Martha finally came to work, Patsy could sense she was excited, happy. She wasn't smiling but her cheeks glowed red from the cold; the color brightened the blue of her eyes; those limp bangs were parted and drawn back on each side in two sweeps of hair. She looked younger, almost pretty. It seemed a shame to deflate her, to bring her down with warnings like those old ladies would, but it had to be said. For Martha's own sake and Patsy's peace of mind.

"Hi." Martha was breathless.

Patsy watched her prepare her register drawer, turning to smile quickly. "How'd it go last night?" she asked.

"Nice. Very nice." The smile was bright, fleeting. "He took me to an Italian place downtown. The food was really good."

A customer interrupted but Patsy, unable to control her curiosity, was back at Martha as soon as the woman's groceries were packed. "Anything else happen besides just going to the restaurant?"

Martha colored, lowered her voice. "We sat outside talking for a while. And...he kissed me."

"That all he did?" Patsy walked over close to Martha, keeping her voice low so no one would hear.

Martha nodded.

"Well, just you watch out," Patsy warned. "Maybe this guy's O.K. and just maybe he wants more than dreams out of you."

Martha looked back at Patsy.

"I'm thirty-three," she said, a wistful lilt to her voice. "Maybe *I* want more than dreams too."

Patsy understood and felt her insides wrench at the knowledge that someone else knew how she felt. Knew that same frightening loneliness. She hugged Martha with a swift squeeze. "I know," her voice broke. "All those years

ahead seem just too much to stand all alone, don't they?
Years of this store, or some place just like it, 'cause I don't
know nothin' else. And goin' home to an empty house.
Even those marriages where they fight and scream all the
time seem better than just...nothing." She controlled her
face and pasted a big smile back on as old Mrs. Taorimina
tottered up to her counter.

"But still you be careful of him," she whispered to
Martha over her shoulder. "I don't want to see you get
hurt."

Chapter Thirteen

There was embarrassment between them. Probably because of the kiss, she thought. But still she wanted to
touch him, could feel a hungering, almost undeniable
need to reach across and put her hand on his arm and feel
him beneath the gray overcoat. Make him aware that she
would take care of him and keep that sadness away if it
were in her power to do so.

Could this be the love everyone was always looking
for? Could love be connected with the electric spasms she
felt in her groin at the sight of his man's beard over his
narrow cheeks and throat? With what she felt watching his
hands—long-fingered, deft to carelessness—manipulate the
steering wheel with a caressing, sliding motion that made
her skin ache with the need to be touched?

She instantly suppressed her desire and wondered
momentarily if this abnormal longing wasn't another manifestation of her difference. She *was* different. Her dreams
proved that. Proved something was wrong.

Her head was hurting again. She had taken aspirin
but the pain was worse than ever now.

"I thought we'd go over to his neighborhood—the
kid's. Start there," he said, turning toward her as she

rubbed at her temples. He frowned, hesitated, pulled to the curb. "You O.K.?"

She nodded yes. "Just a headache."

"How about some lunch? Be O.K. if we just grab a hamburger at McDonald's so we don't lose time?"

"I've never had one. Are they good?"

"Sure they're good. Especially if you're rushed. Jesus, I didn't think there was an American alive who hadn't had a Big Mac."

"There isn't too much I have had."

He turned a sympathetic look on her. "I'd like to change that," he said, reaching for one of her hands. "You've got your skin all red. Really bad head, eh?" He put his fingers there and gently caressed her, moving in soft circles, very slowly. Soft circles that soothed the pain.

She lay her head back against the seat, letting those delicate fingers ease the pain. Her eyes closed.

He slid closer, not missing a single gentle arc. His fingers moved down to trace her cheekbone, caress her cheek, run along her jaw, push her hair gently, thrillingly away from her ear.

She wanted the hand to go on, to move over her whole body and heal her of all pain, but he stopped, pulling away, leaving empty space between them that seemed filled only with her desire.

"You're really something," he breathed. She was sitting up again, eyes open, feeling cheated, even angry. "You're sure not what I thought. This is... I mean... there's a lot more to you than I thought at first. You really took me by surprise." He was shaking his head, starting the car. "I don't want to take advantage of you, Martha. You're vulnerable, I can see that. And I don't want to hurt you. Please don't let me."

After a stop for lunch they began canvassing the area again, hunting but uncertain of what they hunted. The houses were small, mostly wood, white, neat. There were street after street of them, all with detached garages at the back, also of wood. White. Neat.

They rode in silence, awkward with each other now.

"Where I was everything was more dilapidated," she said frowning after a while. How were they ever going to find that one alley out of so many when it was already fading in her memory? She only remembered the United States flag—but who flew a flag in an alley?

"We'll work our way south now." He turned on to a main street. "This neighborhood kind of decays the farther south you go. Buildings get older."

Still there was nothing. Two and a half hours of nothing.

"I'm sorry I don't recognize anything," Martha said.

"We just haven't found it yet." His tone was resolute, no slight edge of doubt.

Here the houses were rundown. Only three streets over from where the boy lived, but in a westerly direction David had not tried before.

"This looks possible." She noted some boarded houses and alleys lined with brown-sided garages, some with windows out, leaning as the garages had in her dream. But they'd been unpainted. And what of that flag?

She was exhausted. Tired from work, unsettled sleep, and now, the certainty that she was going to fail.

They were well passed the place before her brain triggered any response. The realization struck them at almost the same time.

He backed the car to where the alley bisected the block. Dirty. Garbage littered. Blowing. A rusted tin can meandered through puddles. And the garages leaned. They were white—but unpainted.

The garage door facing the street, on the corner lot, was closed. It was crudely painted with wide stripes of red, white, and blue.

"Your flag?" They were both almost afraid to breathe.

She murmured, "Yes," and pointed to a garage three down from the corner. White but just barely so. The windows were broken and stuffed with cardboard. A sense of familiarity washed over her so vividly that there could be no doubt in her mind what would be found in that third garage.

He got out and walked down the alley, turning in beside the building she had pointed to. He moved out of sight. She waited. Not long. He was walking back toward her, head down, face hidden.

Getting in, he had only to nod. Tears were running

down his face. He pounded his fist against the wheel, then pounded again and again. Swearing as he pounded.

He needed someone to touch him, to quiet his hands in their painful charivari. Why couldn't she bring herself to comfort him? Why couldn't she just touch him?

She sat straight. Face expressionless. She had already seen the small body, hidden beneath filthy burlap sacks; seen the features of the face; seen that one hand partially eaten by scavengers. She knew the horror of it, but didn't know how to ease the shock for him.

"I should be used to this by now." His teeth were clenched. "But I can't accept it. So damned unfair. So damned unfair."

She turned away so he couldn't see her face. It was daylight, middle of the afternoon, no dark to hide in this time. She felt the laughter deep inside her, felt it swell and rise, choke her, until it had to be covered by a cough and a hand over her mouth, a hand that hid the awful smile she wore.

Chapter Fourteen

The hypnotist's breath smelled slightly of the garlic that had spiced their dinner. It wasn't unpleasant, just more intimate than Martha was used to, as close as he was, straddling a stool in front of her.

His nose was prominent, with a gypsy hook to it. His smile a tight arc that displayed small, even teeth. Martha liked him well enough. There was something soothing and personal in his deep voice. Something familiar there as he took her hands in his before placing them in her lap, instructing her to keep them limp and to concentrate on his voice.

His name was Tolly Pritchard. He was going to teach her to reach a stage of relaxation and concentration he called self-hypnosis. But first he would hypnotize her, teach her the mechanics; then, in a few weeks' time, they could move to self-hypnosis so she could control her visions, order them to a constant usefulness not possible now, dependent as she was on the dream state.

"It'll take practice," he warned. "But you'll learn. Should be no problem. First you have to trust me, then we'll explore your capacity to be hypnotized. You do trust me, don't you?"

He leaned forward, smiling in a teasing way that cut through her defenses. His eyes looked directly into hers. She began to relax, to concentrate on his voice, attempting to shut the others out. It worked only for a moment. Concentration was elusive, broken by the upheavals of the day.

Neither of them had really felt like going through the motions of this evening. But it was planned. His mother cooking from early morning. To brood, they agreed, wouldn't bring back the child or change the sorrow of the parents.

She had met them. After David called downtown and put the wheels of investigation in motion, he had gone the three blocks to one of those neat white houses to break the news.

The tall black man in blue work clothes of an auto plant worker knew as soon as he opened the door. His wife held him close and comforted him. There was resignation and relief on her face.

David explained Martha's dream to them, the two understanding the words but looking at her in disbelief.

"You saw our Billy in a dream?" the man asked, staring wide-eyed at this unlikely psychic.

"Then his spirit must have contacted you," the boy's mother grasped the implication and looked almost jubilant. "He wanted us not to worry anymore, didn't he? He's all right now. No matter what he went through, he's all right now. Thank you," she whispered and put her arms around Martha, kissing her cheek lightly. "Thank you so much."

Thank you so much.
Torment. Happiness. Horror. Pleasure. Pain. All at once. Warring. All equally frightening.

Thank you so much.

She didn't want to be thanked. It made her angry.

Too difficult to concentrate on this man. Others were there, watching, making her self-conscious. Especially Mrs. Bernabei sitting across the room, black-oxford feet planted firmly and squarely in front of her. Plainly showing her distrust of all such goings-on. Just as plainly showing her dislike of Martha. Something in the way she had surveyed Martha's dark flowered dress and shoes that needed new heels warned Martha that this woman wasn't looking for a friend. It was obvious by the questions she asked that she suspected Martha's intentions toward David.

She was a big sailing ship of a woman, Mrs. Bernabei was. Her rich dark hair shot through with pure white streaks. She had pulled it into a fat bun at the back of her head. She must have been beautiful once, fine white skin, high cheekbones, large dark eyes. But now her bearing was more military than womanly.

"I take good care of David," she said, pointedly looking toward Martha. "Clean his house. Cook his meals. Entertain his friends. What more does he need, eh?"

Martha could only smile a little and shake her head nervously to show there was nothing more she could think of. Patsy made a move as if to answer but Martha silenced her quickly with a frightened look.

"Relax now," Tolly Pritchard instructed her once again and made a shushing sound toward Mrs. Bernabei, who had mumbled something about the evil eye behind his back.

"Do you see the light?" His voice was soft, low, insidious. "You see the light. Fine. Just watch it now, think about it, move toward it and breathe. That's right. Deeply. Slowly. Very deeply now. You are relaxing your body. Your legs. Your arms. Your neck. Your head. Now follow the light. We'll be here with you. Don't be afraid. Let your mind spin away, after the light. Let it be free to roam. Let it go."

His voice stopped. She tried to concentrate, but the light kept going out, or it became Bella Schwartz's face, laughing at her. The attempt was useless. How could she possibly concentrate when she knew they were all staring at her? All she could think of was whether her dress was straight. Were all the buttons buttoned? Why hadn't she washed her hair this afternoon? Did it look greasy in this light? What if her nose ran and she didn't know it?

"Is it working?" she heard David whisper. A twinge of pain started at the very back of her head.

"Too much goin' on here, Dave," Tolly answered. "Better some place quiet, maybe just the two of us. We'll try another time."

Later, as they had cake and coffee, Patsy tried diligently to engage Tolly Pritchard in conversation, but he deftly feinted and ducked and kept his questions going across the table to Martha and David. She gave up using charm and sat sulking over her cup of tart black coffee. She wanted to smoke but didn't dare. Not in this house. His mother'd probably stand next to her with a can of Lysol.

She had hoped for better things from this date. She'd never met a man in show business before. At the places she hung out a gal didn't get to meet many men who weren't married. And all of them worked for the Big Three in one plant or another, and really, after a while, they became almost interchangeable—one worrying about what kind of car to get next; another wanting a new dirt bike to take up to northern Michigan; another fretting about his bowling game. And each preferring to be in the bar with his buddies rather than with her, only dating because the other guys suspected him if he didn't.

The disco dates she bragged about to Martha were mainly illusory. There had been two. And once in a while one or another of them did take her to a nice restaurant, but the way they talked it up when they were back in the bar made Patsy wonder who the date had been designed to impress.

Thirty-five and still having to preen and simper. Still having to pretend awe at masculine strength. Still having to enter into their childish jokes on each other—sneezing powder, for Christ's sake! Still having to laugh when she goddamned well didn't feel like it. And still having to pretend transports of joy over their fumbling, jack-off love-making that from the first time—at fifteen, in the back of a Ford—hadn't come anywhere close to her idea of what love-making should be.

Shit, but she wanted a real man. Just once. She wanted tenderness. A caress that touched her hair, her lips, and didn't telegraph demands. She could almost be jealous of Martha. Of all people! But David was nice, if kind of quiet and intense. You could see he liked Martha, even seemed a little awed by her. But—oh, ho—that mother was a different kettle of fish. Martha'd better be careful or she'll be ground up and made into meatballs!

Tolly turned and smiled.

Maybe, she thought. Maybe...

Neither Martha nor David said much during the drive home. Tolly'd asked Patsy to stop and have a drink with him. He wanted David and Martha to join them but Martha's head was hurting again. This had been a hard, draining day. She wanted to go home. She wanted quiet. And, most of all, she wanted David to stop pressuring her to go on helping him.

"I know you don't want to think about it, but you can't just deny the power you've got." David's voice was rigid, deep with impatience.

"Yes I can." She hugged her arms tightly across her chest as if to compress something growing inside. "Yes I certainly can. I'll deny it and keep denying it. If it ever happens again I won't let anybody know. Then maybe it'll go away."

"You wouldn't do that." He softened his tone, reached across the seat to take her hand. She let hers lay limp and unresponsive in his.

When she could, she drew her hand away. After a time of staring out at block after block of darkened buildings Martha cleared her throat. "I can't go on with it, David. Can't you see that? I can't go on. Something terrible will happen to all of us."

His "goodnight" was curt. After the emotional strain of this day she wanted nothing more than to shut her door and cry until she was washed free of fears and hopes and responsibility for others.

When she opened the door to the upper flat Aunt Jenny and Uncle John greeted her. They were seated at the kitchen table. Their faces were grave. Something was wrong. They only came across town on Sunday afternoon so Uncle John could avoid traffic and night driving. This was Saturday. It was late, very dark. Only one of those dreaded family disasters: death or scandal would bring them out.

Uncle John frowned, looked embarrassed. Aunt Jenny looked smug.

"Where's Ma?" Martha asked, fearing the answer.

"In her room lying down." Aunt Jenny's words were clipped short. She wasn't going to volunteer information. Big moments like these were hard to pry away from her. She savored news-breaking and collected facial expressions, voice tones, emotional outbursts for future ruminating over with friends who liked detail.

"Tell her." Uncle John rolled his eyes and turned away in disgust. It was clear he would rather be home in bed watching the late show, than here, facing a long dark drive.

"What's wrong, I asked you?" Martha's face was burning. She took a step toward Aunt Jenny that was part threat.

"She says her whole world is falling apart. Tonight it's newpaper reporters. Seems you found a dead body today? Or something like that. Now just what is going on here, young lady?" Aunt Jenny stood with her arms protectively crossed on her chest, very much into her role of Harriet's avenging angel.

"Reporters? I don't understand. Yes, I did help a policeman locate the body of a missing child, but I don't understand about the reporters." Martha felt as though her head would whirl off her shoulders. She no longer wanted any of it, not the uproar, not the constant feeling of guilt they all placed on her, not this spotlight of inspection trained her way. And now—more. Reporters.

"How can you help locate a body? You find it or something?" Uncle John demanded swift, rational answers so it could be ended and they could leave.

"In a way, yes." Martha removed her coat and pushed past Aunt Jenny to the hall closet. "But I won't discuss it tonight. I'm tired and I'm going to bed. If Ma called you, you better see if she wants you to stay on or go home. I can't take anymore."

With her back turned, Martha walked to her room, went in, and shut the door, knowing she left two astonished people behind her.

Chapter Fifteen

Monday morning.

Patsy was in transports over Tolly Pritchard. They'd stopped on the way home Saturday night. "Just for a drink, but a nice place," she told Martha. "And he's supposed to call this week. He's really nice. Don't you think he's nice?"

Martha agreed.

"How're you and David getting along?" She eyed Martha shrewdly. "Anything happen?"

"We fought about those damn dreams. I told him I didn't want to have them anymore. And he talked about how important it was, and how it's my life's work and went on until I just couldn't stand it."

"Gee, that's bad. Really bad. Did he call yesterday?" She shook her head no.

"Hmmm." Patsy's mood fell. "I'd sure hate to see you go back to the way things were before. I mean, at least the dreams brought something into your life. At least, there's David. And you're goin' out, havin' fun, not just sittin' around with your mother and her friends. Those dreams kind of made things happen in your life, don't you think? And mine too. Look, now I met Tolly."

"I know," Martha said. "But it's so awful that my life gets better on the dead bodies of other people. I don't like that somehow. Something's wrong, Patsy. Something I can't explain." She hesitated to go on, revealing herself at what cost? But she had to tell someone. "It's as though there are two of me." Her voice lowered, hushed with the implications of what she was about to say. "Two of me and I can't control them. I have these feelings, strange feelings that aren't right.... I..."

Patsy smirked. "Do you mean about David? Is that it? You mean you got the hots for 'im? So what? It's about time. I don't know how you stand it, all the time without sex. Jeez—that's not even normal."

Martha shook her head, embarrassed and also unhappy at being stopped just when she was finally going to tell someone the things going on inside, things which were driving her crazy.

"No. It's not that," she tried again.

"Look," Patsy put an arm across her shoulders and hugged her. "I'm not your Ma or her friends. I know what's what. No need to be embarrassed with me. I know what it's like to want a man. To want to be more than a daughter all your life. And if I was you I'd grab him and get him into bed as fast as I could. That's where marriages are made, don't kid yourself. Get him into bed and if he's a decent guy next thing he'll want to marry you. Make an honest woman of you," she laughed and squeezed. "Of course, if I was you I also wouldn't listen to me. What in hell can I know when I'm thirty-five, unmarried, and the furthest thing from a virgin you ever seen."

They both laughed, comfortable with each other, but the moment was past when Martha could tell her those terrifying things about herself. Could tell her about that part of Martha that was enjoying these deaths.

They were soon busy. The regulars gathered early to pick up a few things and tell tales of weekend events—so many fights, so many grudges after family gatherings that had to be unloaded someplace. And when a woman gets old, with no one left to help carry the load of indifference—cruelty of daughters-in-law, sons-in-law, children—well, any stranger will do.

After that first rush there was a lull during which a young woman, camera slung around her neck, walked in, looking about with a professional eye.

"Oops," Patsy exploded. "I forgot to tell you, Martha. Mr. Koch thought this stuff about you helping the police would make good publicity for the store. He called the

Grocer's Spotlight first thing. I'll bet that's the reporter now."

Martha had only a minute to give Patsy a pained look before they were lined up, Mr. Koch on one side of Martha, Patsy on the other, and told to smile. Then there was a shot of Martha alone at her register. And then a shot of Mr. Koch in front of the meat counter, holding up links of his German sausage.

"You mention I make it myself," Mr. Koch urged, following the young woman through the store after she had asked Martha questions and received reluctant answers.

When the woman left, Martha returned to her register, dazed at the attention. Customers stopped her to find out what was going on. So much happening so fast. Too fast to be assimilated.

"Martha! It's for you. Your mother," Patsy called from the front, holding the phone out to her. "Hurry."

"Come on home, Martha." Mother's voice was high and excited. "Tell Mr. Koch it's urgent. WDIV just called. Guess who's coming over here to interview you? You know that Tilly Hines who does the five-thirty news? She's the one called me. She's coming herself to talk to you about finding that body. They're going to bring cameras and all so's they can tape you. I told her I'd get you home."

"Oh, Ma. I can't leave."

"Just tell 'im you'll mention the store. Then he'll let you go. Now, I told her yes. There's no stopping it. So you just come on home. And leave enough time to change and fix your hair. You don't want to look bad. Oh...oh, and another thing, the *Detroit News* called, man left his number for you to call back. He wants a story too. Oh...and there's a special delivery letter waiting here. You want me to open it?"

"I don't...wait...I..."

"Might as well, don't you think?" There was the sound of paper tearing and other voices in the background. Juliet—helping. And then Mother was back on the phone. "You're not going to believe this, Martha. I can't hardly believe it myself. Well, what do you know...."

"Ma please. I've got to go. What is it?"

"For goodness sakes! You're never going to believe this, Martha."

"MA!"

"It's from the parents of that child you found. There's a check here for five hundred dollars. Five hundred dollars!"

Again there was excited conversation on the other end of the line.

"What for?" Martha's voice was strangled. "Isn't there a letter?"

"Yes. Yes. Just a minute now. Here we are. It says, let me see here.... 'Dear Miss Small. We can't thank you enough for what you've done for us. You've given us peace of mind at last. It is as though God worked through you to help us. We want to help with your work. May you always use your dreams as the instrument of God that they are. Maybe our little donation will help you help someone else in need. Bless you and thank you. Pray for us....' And then they signed it. Well, what about that. You know, Martha, maybe I've been wrong about these dreams being nothing but trouble. Maybe they really are a blessing. I think I'll go see Father Pawlowski about it. Make sure it's not the devil's work or anything."

"Yes, Ma," she answered wearily. "You go see the priest."

"And you know what else just hit me, Martha?"

"No, Ma. What?"

"Five hundred dollars is enough to pay for at least three of us to go to Toronto. It's like it was meant to be, don't you see?"

"But that money was meant for other things. I don't..."

"What better than to make us all happy? After all, that's why God gives these strange gifts to people like you. And I'm sure Bella can pay her own way."

"I can't go. Remember."

"Oh—that's right. The vacation time. I forgot." Her voice filled with self-pity. "Just forget it then. We'll just forget it."

"No, Ma. Listen. That's all right. You three go. I guess you deserve at least that much."

"Well...no...I couldn't do that," Harriet's voice trilled and hesitated, attempting martyrdom but not succeeding. "Well...we can talk later. You come on home, O.K.?"

"Yes, Ma." Too weary to fight. "I'll come right home."

*   *   *

The news crew was gone, leaving Bella and Juliet in a tizzy of excitement. So grateful to Martha. They were dressed in their best, the dresses usually reserved for weddings, kept covered in plastic cleaner bags at the back of the closet. Juliet's was blue chiffon with rhinestones at the throat. Bella's was flowered silk with a jacket to match. Harriet had settled for a simpler dress. Martha wore a plaid skirt, white blouse, and green cardigan.

Martha couldn't help but preen just a bit under all the attention turned her way.

They were having ham sandwiches on TV trays in the living room. Harriet sat in the old morris chair under the darkly framed Bleeding Heart of Jesus. Juliet and Bella, prim in their good clothes, shared the green slip covered sofa. Martha had the best chair, with footstool. The five-thirty news was just coming on.

"There she is." Juliet beamed at all of them as there appeared on the screen the woman who, just that afternoon, had been with them in that very house.

And then there was David. The woman interviewed him outside the police department. He described what happened and how it was through the dream of one Martha Small that the body was found.

"That's you." Bella leaned over, tapping Martha's arm. "See how he's giving you credit?"

"Here we are. Here we are," Juliet crowed, pointing at the TV showing the same room they sat in, same faces frozen as the camera panned over them.

"Ooh, remember when he did that?" Juliet couldn't contain her excitement.

"Shhh," Harriet hushed them all.

Martha was reading the letter: "...sending you this check to help with your work..."

"Then they sent you money so that others might be helped?" the blond woman was asking. "Evidently you intend to help others with your gift then."

Martha watched herself bow her head, noted her hair looked dirty again, watched herself furtively race her eyes back and forth as if for help, watched herself gulp and smile fleetingly, and recalled how nervous she had been and how concerned she was over making a fool of herself.

She didn't want anyone laughing at her. And—maybe—David was watching. She prayed the phone would ring.

"I hope to," she was saying, haltingly at first, then more confidently. "I hope to. I feel I'm just the instrument through which God works. If I can help some poor unfortunate be found and buried, or maybe even some day help catch a murderer, then I want to help. How could I stop? If the dreams continue, then so must my work."

She listened to her voice, which didn't sound like her own, and heard the unfamiliar words. She watched herself sit straighter, flick her hair back from her face, part her bangs with both hands, and push the hair away from her face. She watched as her shade smiled willingly and frankly at the woman.

Within her spinning mind, her own echoing words drilled expanding tunnels of awareness....

"...it's my duty to follow this gift I've been given...."

"Yes," she breathed from behind the three entranced women, staring at themselves on television, smiling inanely as one does when not certain whether to be proud or embarrassed.

She felt the "yes" in her shrunken soul that once had hoped for so very little.

She heard it echo in her brain as it turned her away from banality and red knuckles, aching feet and dark nights in a lonely bed with only magazine men for lovers.

Yes!
Yes!
Yes!

Before the show had finished, David called.

Chapter Sixteen

Shadows of nude males and females stretched up the wall and on to the ceiling, cast by a row of black, human-shaped candles—effigies—lining one shelf of the shop. One was burning, head and torso were gone, soft black wax was cascading down the legs. The sight fascinated Martha. She found it difficult to tear her eyes away, watching as the flame devoured the figure with the inexorability of disease.

A strange place—Lilith's Occult Book Shop. Strange and disquieting, Martha thought as she stood just ahead of David inside the door a few days after the TV interview, her eyes warily roaming the floor to ceiling shelves, most of which contained books, cans, and bottles. Every inch of space was in use.

On the walls not covered by shelves were tapestries with strange angular people in jocular positions. They seemed indecent, though they were not. It was the playfulness implied, playfulness set directly next to open books displaying grotesque depictions of the devil, of strange symbols.

"To rid yourself of an enemy." A voice sing-songed the words in a high, Jamaican accent. From the back of the shop a golden brown woman stepped forward, one of her hands gracefully pointing toward the row of candles. "Take one, anoint it with oils, burn it. No one will trouble you.... Hello." She came forward, hand out to take one of Martha's. "I am Lilith. And you are Martha Small."

"But how..."

Lilith shrugged, hands going up to indicate there was no cause for surprise.

"I don't mean to frighten you, my dear. Sometimes I forget how intimidating I and my shop are to the uninitiated."

She put a calming hand on Martha's arm and laughed, turning toward David. He stood with his hand on the door handle and closed it carefully behind him.

"Ah, yes." Lilith threw her hands in the air as punctuation. "And you are the detective, David Bernabei, was it? Yes, yes, a friend of Tolly Pritchard. And he sent you to me to have me reassure Miss Small about her newly aroused psychic power." She turned back to Martha, taking her hands and drawing her forward into the shop. "Isn't that right, my dear? You are afraid of the power you find stirring in you. An' you wan' me to explain it to you. To help you understand. Nothing is easier. I envy you. Just comin' to it now. All the joy of discovery, the exploration of your power.... Come sit down with me now." Lilith folded her flowing robe neatly over her body and sank in one effortless movement to a sitting position on the floor. She patted the space beside her. "Sit."

"I'll stand," David mumbled and busied himself examining the books.

"You find bodies. That man told me this." She cocked an eyebrow toward David. "Dream. Dream of dead bodies. Locate people who have been murdered." She stopped.

"It frightens me."

"But why? All my life I have strange things happen." She shrugged. "With some people that is a gift. A talent. I don't question such things. Neither should you."

Lilith drew in a deep breath, settled her straight back and shoulders, and fixed the hem of the robe to lay perfectly around her.

"There is a name for your gift. Divination. You are a diviner. The word sings, does it not? Sings of God—the divine—a diviner. You are able to divine that which is hidden. You are able to uncover bodies so that souls in torment may be freed. Don't be afraid, my dear. Be thankful you are so blessed." She put a hand up as Martha started to speak. "But there is more I have to tell you. The means of your divination, the way you dream of these dead bodies—this is not really a dream, you know. You are there. Your spirit flies. You go places where these lost souls are hidden."

"But how..."

"It is a part of your self, a part connected to the

unconscious, called the etheric self. It is able to leave your earthbound body and travel wherever it must. I have written on these studies. Articles."

"But . . . leave my body? You mean my mind? My mind wanders?"

"No, no." Lilith frowned, impatient. "Let us call it your soul. It is that part of you which is spirit. A higher self, one freed by sleep or trance to travel, to move about. Why yours feels compelled to locate dead bodies, I cannot tell you. But a reason is there, buried somewhere inside you."

"Can I make it stop?" Martha leaned toward the woman as if to get within her protection.

"Maybe. But it would take a great effort of will. And that might be very bad for you. This is happening for a reason. To force it to end could turn that need in another direction. Even against yourself."

"But these experiences are terrible."

Lilith shrugged. "I know that. And yet for some reason your etheric self becomes locked on spirits in trouble. I don' know why. But I know that such an ability as you have exists. Know it because my own mother had this gift. Back in Jamaica. She told me once how her brother—she had a great love for him—went to Kingston one day. They lived out, away from the city. Well, she worry so much about him that night she dream of him, dream she walk down a dark street and see him standing with two men. She walked up to him and tell him to come home right now, that he be in danger. The next day he come home very early, frightened because he was almost robbed, grateful to my mother for saving him. It seems two men were about to rob him on a back street in Kingston when my mother—looking like a ghost—came up, warned him, and disappeared. That scared the men so they run."

She paused, letting her story fill the space between them. "You see? It is possible to project your astral body. It is a gift given to only a few. You are fortunate. But, as you see, not abnormal. You're not insane."

Martha breathed deeply. Felt relief coming over her, easing the tensions of the past weeks.

"Thank you," she whispered, reaching out to touch

one of Lilith's hands lying placidly in her lap. "It's a tremendous relief to know I'm not crazy or anything."

Lilith threw back her head, eyes on the ceiling, and laughed. Then she hugged Martha.

"You wait. I will read the tarot for you. Cards say if this gift will bring happiness. Be better you know."

She placed a carved wooden box between them on the floor. David joined them, settling to the floor with creaks from many unused joints.

Inside the wooden box was a rectangular package wrapped in rose silk.

"The tarot cards," Lilith indicated. "They must be properly cared for: their own box, silk wrappings. Now, first an indicator card. A card which is you. Brown hair...hmmm...I will choose the Queen of Swords. Yes. She will be your indicator."

Lilith went through the pack of garrishly illustrated cards and selected one, putting it on the floor between them. "That is you." She patted the card showing a regal woman, sword in hand. "Now you must shuffle three times, and cut the cards three times with your left hand, moving toward the left, and then I will lay the cards to tell your past, your near future, and the distant future."

When the shuffling and cutting was done Lilith laid the cards out in the form of a cross with a staff of four cards beside them.

"This first card," she indicated one lying directly on the indicator card, "is the High Priestess. I must first concentrate." She rested her head in one of her hands, eyes closed. The three sat in silence. The black candle began to sputter weakly.

"Your cards are dominated by the major arcana of the tarot," Lilith lifted her eyes and said to Martha. "This means that other people dominate your life. Your future and your past have been and will be run by others. To avoid this you will have to fight, I don't know if you have the strength. We will see. I will go on now. The High Priestess: she is the card of hidden influences. There is some force which is ruling you. It may be an inner force. It may be an outside force. I cannot tell as yet. Not clear to me. The cards are not exact, you see, but must be read in relation to the cards around them. And even then the message is not...not certain."

She reached out and touched a card lying across the first.

"The Devil," she said, indicating the horned, pentacled satyr. "But not to worry. Not to worry. He is not always a bad fellow. Here, hmmm, let me see. He is in the position of forces which will work against you. He is black magic. I don't like that. Not at all. Black magic. Bad use of a force. This is not good. Not good. No, no, don't let it upset you. The cards only tell what might be. Everyone can change their destiny. You need not be ruled by fate. This man, this devil, he also shows that material things will rule you."

Martha gave a half-hearted chuckle. "Not much chance of that."

"This next card I would expect to find in this position. We are now in your past and the Moon card tells of psychic power unfolding, becoming a part of your life. But it also tells of deception, of someone who has been treacherous, done you harm, a harm you cannot forgive."

"I don't know of anyone." Martha's large eyes turned to David for help then back to Lilith, who was staring at her intently.

"It is there. Deception. Secret enemies. There is hatred here. It is very strong. And you don't know about it? I don't understand." She shook her head again. "This is part of your past. You should be aware...."

"But I'm not," Martha insisted. "There's been nothing in my life like that. I would know."

"Hmmm. The cards always tell me the truth. But this is like reading for two different people. It's never happened before. Let me go on. See if they change somehow."

She straightened the cards, touched them lovingly, closed her eyes a moment before continuing.

"Six of Cups reversed. The past is very strong in you. It has a great hold. In fact, the rules by which you live your life are those of a time passed. It is as though others have pulled strings, dictating your life for you. But that will change. You see this next card: the Nine of Cups? That is the wish card. You are going to get your wish. Great material wealth is coming to you in the near future.

More than you have ever dreamed of. And you will break
the bonds of your past. Wealth will buy you independence,
what you long for most, though you hardly dare say such a
thing aloud. And here, ahhh." The woman caressed a card
labeled the Lovers. "Here is a choice between two men.
Two lovers. It could be a happy choice for you, but this
next card, Strength reversed, says that you will abuse the
power given you by your new-found wealth and love. This
might get in the way of the lover you should choose. It is
not clear to me. What is becoming clear is that there is
something within you, something you fear."

Lilith licked at her lips. Her eyes went to David's face
but darted away as he returned the look.

"And this next: Queen of Pentacles reversed. Those
around you are fearful too. They mistrust the person you
will slowly become, but the Magician is ahead of you. He
tells me you will win out, that you will draw on your
higher power to achieve all you want to achieve. Your
power is great. You will dominate. But the final outcome is
indicated by the Tower. Your last card. The card which
tells what will happen ultimately. It tells me there will be a
great change in your life. It will not always be for the best,
but it will occur anyway. This hidden thing in you, this
thing that comes from your past, will rule. I don't know
what it is. I can tell you no more than I have. But you
must be wary. It can change you for the better, or it can
destroy you."

She gathered up her cards quickly, wrapped them,
and slipped them back into the wooden box. "I'm sorry I
cannot be more specific, but the cards, they don' seem
clear. Or maybe it's me. Maybe today was not a good day
to read your cards. So many influences around us."

"Oh, yes, well, thank you." Martha made a move to get
up as Lilith was doing. Lilith put out a hand to stop her a
moment. "I've never seen a fall of cards like these before.
You seem to be torn in two—two separate people. One
wants to go forward. One wants to go back. I can't tell you
what to do. That's for you to choose. You must shape your
future by your choices. I wish you good luck."

"Thank you. And thank you too for reassuring me
about this talent I've been given. I feel better. Not so
afraid," Martha said.

"Yes. Yes, the gift." Lilith was frowning at her. "It is natural, as I said. But you must also be careful of it. It mustn't rule your life. You must stay in control."

"I will," Martha promised and smiled to assure Lilith she understood. "I will take good care of it."

Chapter Seventeen

In the days following the phone rang again and again.

Aunt Jenny: "Just thrilled!" by it all, but scared to death for Martha. "Such an unpleasant thing to do, find dead bodies."

Reporters.

A mother, sobbing out a story of a runaway child. "Can you help? Please? I'll pay whatever you want, only help me. I can't sleep. Can't work. I'm sick all the time just thinking about Rose Ellen and what could have happened to her."

A mother: "Oh my God, I'm going crazy. Jamie wouldn't run away. But that's what the police say and they won't look anymore. Please..."

A mother: "Please..."

Martha took the phone numbers. Promised to call back. She hung up after the last call and dialed David's number.

"How do I begin?" she agonized.

"Then you've decided to go on?" His deep voice poured salve on her jangling nerves. She felt the tightened muscles throughout her body begin to relax, her heart beat slowed.

"Yes. Lilith convinced me that what's happening isn't abnormal. I want to help. Maybe I don't even have a choice anymore. But I can't do it alone."

There was a pause, then, "I'll help you, Martha. We'll set up a system to deal with the calls, letters too. We'll work out something together. Don't worry."

It wasn't the words that excited her. It was the husky promise underlining the word, the sensual music playing across her brain and causing her breath to catch. She ached to touch him, her fingers tricking her with the solid feel of his arm in their tips. She wanted him to hold her, feel him hard against her. All the words from the panting love stories she'd hidden in her room filled her brain. She urgently wanted to live what those fictional women lived and feel what they felt. Passion. Only a word until now, but she could imagine it, could imagine herself nude in bed with David, hands on his warm body—but there it stopped. All she knew of love-making was clinical, a voyeur's view, much of it ridiculous when she pictured the scene. Had to be more than the mechanics of the act. Had to be emotion, desires like those she was feeling. Had to be aching need. Otherwise why all the books, all the songs, the endless words written in praise of love? Had to be more than magazines could tell. And she wanted it all.

"Take the phone off the hook now Martha," the low voice whispered in her ear. "I'll see you tomorrow, after work. We'll work things out together. And, Martha, practice the self-hypnosis that Tolly taught you."

"I've been afraid," she admitted, hesitated, felt guilty in her admission.

"It's time."

"Yes." She was still reluctant. "I guess you're right. It's time to face up to it, isn't it?"

There was a pause. She heard him draw a deep breath.

"I hope money isn't what changed your mind," he said, waited.

She thought a moment, searching her mind for the most honest answer. "But I'll have to be paid if I do this full-time."

"Yes. You'll have to quit your job. And you'll need enough for expenses. That's all. Not a lot. Don't turn yourself into a sideshow freak."

"I'm not like that." She was hurt and slightly angry at the implication, and at the breaking of her lovely, erotic mood.

"Don't forget where your gift comes from," his voice warned.

"I'm not likely to, David," she answered. "But, still, it's a way out for me. Just think, maybe I won't ever have to punch a register again." Her amazement at the miracle of deliverance showed plainly in her voice. "If only I can figure some way for Patsy to make it out of there too."

"I wouldn't move too fast if I were you," he warned again. "Not yet. What if your visions stopped?"

"Another supermarket, I guess. But don't stop me, David. Not now. Don't have doubts, please. I've overcome them. I'd rather be dead tomorrow morning than work another day in that store. Don't you see, David? Maybe this is the beginning for me. I've prayed long enough...."

"I'll figure something for you too." She was crying along with Patsy, who stood behind her register, hunched and miserably cold as well as miserably unhappy. "If I make enough money maybe you can be my secretary or something."

"You don't mean it. You'll forget you ever knew me," Patsy sniveled, blowing loudly into a tissue and wiping at her eyes. "But you know I'd do anything to help out. I'd be grateful to get out of this place. Especially now. You hear? He's not hiring another girl to replace you. Mrs. Koch's coming in to cashier. For Christ's sake! His wife! Who the hell will I complain to?"

"She'll never stand for the cold. Might be a good thing." There was a strange, alienated something in Martha's voice, the slightest hint of displeasure. Patsy's ears keenly distinguished the tone. She knew what was happening. It was the underlying sound in married friends' voices when they told her not to be unhappy about her single state since at least she got out of the house nights. And the sound in male voices when she complained about her job and they told her she should be happy to have one at all. It was impatience. It signaled an ending.

Martha heard the sound in her voice too. And recognized that she was so eager to see the last of this place she didn't want any consideration, any guilt, to hold her back. She knew Patsy didn't blame her. How could she? She would be as eager.

Martha escaped, promising to find a way out for

Patsy, leaving her to watch as she ran out to David's car. Leaving her to the Mrs. Taoriminas and Mrs. Kozaks. Leaving her to Ex-Lax jokes and the old "sweeties" and "dearies."

Martha shut the car door, sank into the seat, and startled David by laughing aloud. Laughing until tears ran down her face, and he, reaching over, shook her, evidently fearing she was hysterical.

David grabbed the frail arms and shook slightly. There were thin bones beneath soft flesh. He shook again to stop the laughter. It made him uneasy, the sound, out of proportion, somehow not fitting. And the flesh, not roundly woman-like, but puffy, more like holding on to a child.... he shuddered and pulled away. He didn't understand himself but supposed it had to do with this strange situation. He hadn't come to terms with her psychic power yet. Hadn't yet been able to accept it without fear.

"Sorry, Martha," he mumbled.

Her eyes swiveled toward him, meeting his, startling him even more. They burned with anger, were turned on him with what seemed to be menace. A chill ran across his skin, causing the hair along his neck to rise. She said nothing, only stared.

"Martha?"

The fire in the eyes died and she looked away. After a few minutes he noticed tears sliding down her cheeks. He reached out to take one of her hands. In his concern for her he didn't even notice how different her flesh felt now. How warm and firm her hand felt in his.

He didn't notice that it was as if a different inhabitant had moved into the body.

Chapter Eighteen

A gushing Juliet was bad enough but a gushing Bella Schwartz was obscene. Martha would have paid as much again to be rid of the unholy trio for their weekend in Toronto.

Ready to go. Juliet's hair had been frizzled and hennaed by Susie at Susie's Shoppe de Beaute in honor of the trip. Bella treated herself to a blue wool coat with a magnificent collar of raccoon that began below her statuesque bosom and muffled all of her neck and most of her head in brown fur.

Harriet had her hair cut, truncating the well-trained sausage curls at half roll, so that now her head was a sea of breaking waves frozen at full crest and doomed to tremble in mid-air. She wasn't happy with the look but accepted it as she once had the rows of sausage curls, as inevitable and at least new.

After weeks of talk, they left. And Martha, exhausted from demands made on her by David, by the women, by petitioners, gratefully embraced the first extended quiet of her lifetime. Two nights. Three days. She stood at the kitchen window looking after the cab driving the women away. The first relief she'd had after weeks of having them underfoot night and day.

The cab disappeared. She sighed, was about to turn from the window when a movement just below caught her eye. The swiftest of impressions. A head ducking out of sight. Small. Brown hair. Of course, that child again. That lonely child. She had seen her often recently, but always just for a moment. As if the child were afraid. Curious but afraid.

She turned back to a sink full of breakfast dishes and

89

a bucket left sitting on the linoleum, a reminder from Harriet that the floor needed scrubbing. It could wait. All of that could wait.

She walked into the hall, was going to call Patsy. Had every intention of calling Patsy because, until now, she hadn't found the time. She put her hand on the phone then decided not to.

She couldn't bring herself to break the silence, especially since Patsy would probably head right over to keep her company—the thing she wanted least.

David would be coming soon. They had work to do. Business to discuss. Patsy would be in the way. It was bad enough having the three women always there, butting in. Bringing Patsy here to disrupt their one quiet weekend was too much to ask. Too much.

Selfish, she told herself, taking her hand from the phone and going into the bathroom to run hot water into the old-fashioned, claw-footed tub. A hot bath, a magazine, the luxury of an hour to herself. She went into her room to rummage through the dresser, hunting for a free sample of bath oil she'd hid.

Selfish, she told herself again as she slipped into the steaming water. Then she carefully rested her head against the cold enamel and laughed aloud.

Things were better now. With David's help she was interviewing callers, deciding on those she might help, and had actually helped three children be found—all dead.

And she was beginning to master the trance state. Tolly Pritchard was helping on Wednesdays, the women's bingo night at church. He had successfully hypnotized her several times now, a post-hypnotic suggestion that assisted her into a semi-trance on her own. She had even begun to see shapes and people before spontaneously coming out of it. It wouldn't be long, she knew. And once that was mastered, perhaps she would see the murderers, be able to identify them. Imagine the headlines then!

She smiled at her ambitions but felt no guilt about them.

She stretched, slipping further beneath the water, letting the oily surface lap up around her neck, lick at her chin. The heat penetrated everywhere, infusing her with the delicious sensation of being overpowered. She gave in to it eagerly.

Things were not merely going better they were going beautifully.

The dreams continued, sought after now so she could match pictured faces and descriptions to visions of hidden, buried, lost bodies. Each time it worked David's respect for her multiplied along with his reverence for her "gift." She was a diviner, he reminded her of Lilith's words, one who sees the future, or the past, or remote present through some process of divination: throwing bones, reading clouds, tea leaves, dreams. A long tradition, reaching into antiquity, preceded her. Diviners were blessed and cursed, worshiped and abhorred, angel and devil. They were as mundane as willow-twig water witchers, or as divine as Jesus. She was in strange company.

She and David were together almost every day now. In his spare time he helped her help frantic parents. Even his working hours were spent solving cases with Martha as his sole source of information.

He kissed her good-bye at night and hello in the morning, never moving beyond limits he delineated for himself. There seemed now, in their relationship, a kind of reverence that she began to find cumbersome, as it proscribed the violent emotions she was feeling for him.

She ran a hand over her wet and slippery body and knew she had to have him. Must break through that wall of awe to the man beneath, the man she wanted. She wished, now, she had experience at exciting a man. She wished she knew the things Patsy knew. Even knew what Harriet and the others knew. As it was, her self-confidence and ego were suffering even as pride in her accomplishments and celebrity grew.

She got out of the tub and dried herself using two towels. Unbelievable luxury. She dressed.

The flat so quiet. Old building arthritic in its joints.

Friday night. She rolled the TV into her room and shut the door, ignoring even the ringing phone. David was on a case, he'd said. Couldn't see her that evening.

Saturday. Routine reasserted itself and she cleaned

the flat and went grocery shopping at Spinski's store down Mt. Eliot, a trip she dreaded and put off until necessity forced it.

David called about six. Still embroiled in a case, he said. Couldn't be there until tomorrow.

Sunday. He came to dinner. A dinner of the only dish she knew how to make.

"Spanish rice," she announced, serving him a huge portion which came from the bowl in one mighty glob and descended to his plate with the weight of a boulder.

More of the Pinot Noir he brought was poured, enough to flood a field of rice, and soon he was able to push the plate away with a satisfied pat to his stomach.

"Good," he praised, smiling across the table at her.

Picking up their glasses, they moved, arm in arm, into the twilight of the living room. Martha was only too aware of the contrast between this circle of dark, overstuffed furniture and threadbare carpet with his own pristine home—still in plastic wrappers. She felt shamed by the Bleeding Heart of Jesus hung on dirty gold cords above the sofa and by the ancient floorlamp with chain pulls.

He noticed her change of mood.

"Not angry because I didn't eat more of your Spanish rice are you?" He looked up as he settled himself on the sofa. He was half teasing, unsure of himself. "My mother made me eat before I left. Afraid I'd starve on the way over, I guess."

"More likely she knows what kind of a cook I am."

"I thought it was good," he protested.

She went back to the kitchen for the wine, placing it on the glass of the coffee table. She sat on the sofa, one cushion's width away from him, kicked off her shoes, pulled her legs under her, and let her skirt ride up a bit over her knees. She left it there.

Noticing his glass was empty, she leaned forward and poured him more wine. He was beginning to relax, to ease down against the cushions and loosen up, even pushing his loafers off.

Carelessly, she dropped her hand flat on the cushion between them as he talked about an aunt of his who was expected to his house later that evening. Would she like to go back with him? The aunt would really like to meet Martha.

She stalled, not saying yes, not saying no, and turned a reluctant smile on him to show she didn't want to go but didn't want him to either.

They sat without talking for a while. His eyes finally dropped to the hand resting invitingly between them and he pushed his fingers to where they just touched hers.

She pretended to pull way. Then, smiling, giving in, came back to where they touched. He moved his hand on top of hers, tracing the outlines of each finger before entwining their fingers tightly together.

Their hands were hot and moist against each other. It was an oddly sexy union that had all her senses on alert. Waiting.

Still he made no further move. Martha grew increasingly angry as she stifled a desire to throw herself at him and be done with it. She withdrew her hand violently, surprising him.

"What's wrong?" He sat up, leaning toward her, hair loose and falling across his forehead.

She pouted, turning her face away, pretending interest in the ancient movie on TV. "Nothing," she said.

"Come on. There is too. I can tell."

"Nothing. Really."

He moved closer, attempting to recapture her hand. His thin, powerful hand covered hers roughly. He held on to her.

"What is it?" his voice dropped as his head bent close to her, breath playing through her hair, touching her skin.

"I . . . I don't know," she said, a tear falling. "Maybe you better go."

"Not like this." His arm slipped across her bent shoulders. "Come on, tell me. I won't go until you do. Don't you know that what affects you affects me?"

"Why?" She turned wet eyes on him.

"Because I care how you feel. That's why."

"Care about me? How would I know that? I don't really know how you feel. You treat me like a sister. Then sometimes I think you really care about me . . . and then I . . . I don't know . . . it's all mixed up."

"But you know I care. Look how well we work together. How..."

"Work! Is that all we have is work?" Her large eyes, outlined and mascaraed now to add to their size, accused him.

"No." He moved away slightly, narrow face undergoing a series of conflicting expressions as he attempted to understand their quarrel. "Of course not. We've become very...well...close friends."

Her eyes roamed over his face, taking in his eyes, his lips soft with drink and conciliation, his strong chin where his dark beard already shadowed the lines of his face, and she turned away as if at some secret sorrow.

"I care, Martha," With his hand he turned her face to his and kissed her lightly. "I care very much."

She let her head droop against him so that his lips rested on her forehead where he kissed her again, many times. She turned completely toward him, putting her arms around him, and looked upward, wetting her parted lips with the tip of her tongue so that he would see and know she wanted him.

David kissed her, then pulled away.

"Whew, we'd better watch that kind of thing," he joked and moved even farther down the sofa. "Aren't your mother and her friends coming home tonight?"

Martha, with nervous movement, clasped and unclasped her hands in her lap. She turned her head away from him, anger keeping words locked in her throat.

Leaning toward her, as if she might not have caught the question, he said again, "Your mother's coming home tonight, isn't she?"

The look she shot him was quick and devastating. The words were cold. "Not until later."

They sat in an awkward silence until David made a tentative move toward her. He reached up and lightly placed his hand on her shoulder, causing her to turn to him. She noted the look on his face, the uncertainty in his eyes, and knew she had won.

He pulled her close, kissing her, his lips hotly parting, his tongue meeting hers with force as he pushed passed, thrusting between her lips and into her mouth, probing, alive with curiosity.

Slowly he moved again, bringing her up to meet him.

The second kiss was more agonizing than the first. When his hand covered her breast she almost screamed— the touch was like nothing she had ever imagined. She helped him with the buttons, helped him as he hesitated at the hooks of her bra, and sighed deeply as he closed his hand on her bare breast. It all felt so good and so natural. Her body was crying to crawl inside him somehow. She arched toward him, crying aloud as emotion moved her.

"Touch me," he whispered into her hair, caught in the bristles of beard and trailing into his mouth.

"I don't know how," she whispered back as her mouth traced a line down his chin and throat.

He felt for her hand and pushed it down until she felt the urgent hardness in his pants, moving against her hand, straining upward.

He moaned and moved his own hand desperately, reaching under her skirt and pushing up fast and hard against her. At the touch a convulsive explosion hit her. She came, but her passion was in no way diminished.

She helped him with his clothes and hers, marveling at the size of him.

He laid her down on the sofa, beneath the Bleeding Heart of Jesus, and made love to her until they both cried.

Later they picked up their clothes, showered together, and went naked to her bedroom where they lay down on her bed and slept in each other's arms.

Harriet's voice calling "Martha, oh, Martha. We're back" woke them. The excited twittering of the other two was background noise.

Martha poked David frantically, then shushed him with a finger on his lips.

"My mother's home," she whispered, struggling against an urge to laugh.

He was instantly awake and scrambling for his clothes.

They heard Harriet say, "She must be sleeping. I'll go wake her up."

Martha giggled as David tried to get both legs in one leg of his pants. She called out, "I'm here, Mother. I'll be right out."

She reached for her robe, draped on the bureau and whispered cruelly, "Come out and meet them when you're dressed."

"I can't." He panicked, looking around for another means of escape.

"Then jump out the window." Coolly she tied the flowered robe around her and opened the door.

"Here she is," Bella called, spotting Martha in the hall. "Come see what we brought."

"What a trip! What a trip! How can I ever thank you, dear?" Juliet fumbled for a tissue to wipe the gathering tears.

"I'm just happy you enjoyed yourself," Martha smiled at them, feeling she was looking down from a towering height, her smile and eyes measuring the distance between herself and the women.

"There you are." Harriet came in from the bathroom. "You left a mess in the tub."

"I'll clean it tomorrow," she answered laconically. "Anyway—hello. You could say hello before nagging, you know."

Surprised, Harriet was thrown off center by Martha's criticism. "Well, yes, you're right. Hello, dear. Were you too lonely?"

"No. I was busy." She smiled brightly at the three weary women. "David came to dinner today. He kept me company."

"Such a nice man," Juliet began, only to pause dramatically at a noise from down the hall. "What was that? I heard something."

They all looked toward the archway leading to the hall, stopping to listen, holding their breath, eyes huge.

Martha broke the tension with a light laugh. "That's just David," she said, pulling her robe closed where it gaped at the neckline.

The eyes turned toward her. Not a word was spoken as they took in the state of her hair, the robe with no sign of a nightgown beneath.

After a time of racing thought, Harriet dropped her eyes, saying, "So he's still here, huh?"

Martha smiled broadly and nodded, disconcerting the

three women who had no defined responses to so bizarre
a situation.

Harriet turned, hiding her confusion with motions
over the coffee pot and cups. The other two took seats at
the table, staring at the archway with enough trepidation
to warrant the arrival of the devil.

He looked so magnificently tall in the low archway. As
fresh and flushed and satisfied as any man had ever
looked. Martha beamed at him, noting with amusement
his formal nod to each woman and their set smiles and
nods in return.

Martha could hardly believe that she was enjoying the
situation. The worst predicament of her life, and she
could only think how funny it all was. So unlike herself. As
if another Martha had always lived in her, just waiting her
chance. A Martha who loved to look pretty, to wear nice
clothes, to be independent. Free.

It was bewildering, her metamorphosis, to her as well
as those around her, she supposed. But she planned
more. As if catching up on years of being crushed by
poverty, her mind was running wild. She could be anyone
she liked. Anyone. And no one could stop her because her
freedom wasn't based on pleasing a boss, or a husband's
largesse. It was centered on her. She was the center of her
universe for the first time in her life.

It felt so good.

They would have to get used to it. There would be
other changes. Beginning with this upper flat. She wanted
out. Never to be embarrassed by seediness again. Never to
be cold. Never to be hurt because an old lady chose
another register. Never to be unloved.

When David was leaving Martha reached up and
kissed him, though the women watched. Bella and Juliet
left soon afterward, still without comment, although Martha
knew they would have plenty to say when they hit the
sidewalk.

Martha waited for Harriet's explosion.

"I'm glad you weren't lonely," was Harriet's only com-
ment as she cleared away the dirty cups, head kept down.
"I think I'll leave these tonight. I'll do 'em in the morning.
Just so tired. Did I tell you I won fifty dollars? I did.
Might get some new drapes for the living room."

"I've got a better idea," Martha said drily. "Let's get a decent apartment."

Harriet looked into her daughter's face for the first time that evening. "What ever for? What's wrong with this place?"

"Everything. And the money's coming in now. Why shouldn't we live decently? Someplace where those two can't camp everyday."

"Bella and Juliet? They're my friends. I couldn't leave them." She shook her head. "We're fine right here. I never expected better. Don't plan on gettin' it now."

"Mother, I'm serious," Martha challenged. "Those two always here, whispering behind my back. Why do you have to have them here? What is it you owe them?"

"Owe them?" Harriet's eyebrows escalated, her face a mass of guilt and confusion. "Owe them? Nothing. Nothing."

"Then it won't matter if you never see them again. We have to get a decent place to live. A decent place where decent people live."

"This place was always decent before. You do what you have to, Martha." She left the kitchen as if bent under a great weight.

"Won't I ever though," Martha raised her voice after her. "You just watch me. All of you—just watch me."

Part Two

Chapter One

Something was wrong. Very, very wrong. Something that could not be—was. And Martha didn't know what to do, was immobilized, standing on the sidewalk in front of the tall, downtown Detroit building where she now lived high up in a beautiful apartment. She stared down the walk of large cement squares toward the corner beyond her building and clutched her bag of groceries as if it were rooted in place and could support her.

The child stood on the corner, watching her. That same little girl. The one she felt so sorry for.

No, it was another child that looked like the one she'd seen before, she told herself, not daring to believe her eyes. All kids look a lot alike, don't they? Working too hard. Could be her eyes. But...brown, stringy hair sticking out of a floppy rainhat, oversized raincoat, a small foot lazily brushing the sidewalk.

The girl leaned back against the corner street sign and continued to watch Martha.

Couldn't be. Martha started forward. Couldn't be. That little girl was miles from here, back somewhere on

Mt. Eliot Street. No way she could get down here by herself. No way in the world. Even if she knew where Martha moved, she would have no means of finding the place.

Martha stood very still, watching the little girl who looked directly at her. Their eyes met and held. Her serious look mirrored Martha's, as if she too was shocked by the encounter.

Both held still until the child slowly raised her arm in a familiar salute.

"This is too much," Martha mumbled to herself. "I'm going to see what's happening here." She moved forward, shifting the grocery bag from left to right arm. Her direction and step were purposeful.

The child snapped upright, large coat swinging around her thin legs. She regarded Martha a moment then took a step backward into the street.

Martha slowed, afraid to frighten her into the path of a car. That small face, with fear written on it, tugged at her memory and made Martha cautious. "Wait a minute. I want to talk to you," she called after her, signaling the child to stop; but the little girl took another step, then another, turning to hurry across the street where she ducked between parked cars and was gone.

"Impossible." Martha was standing at the corner scanning the opposite side of the street in both directions. "Can't be the same one." But she knew she was wrong. And somehow that certainty beneath her denial frightened her, made her almost faint with fear. She reached out and clutched the street sign that the child had leaned on. She was tempted to run her hand down the metal, to feel if it was warm, to prove that the child really existed and wasn't some new phantom sprung from this psychic world she had tapped. But she wouldn't allow herself the luxury of proof.

She clutched the groceries tighter and turned back toward her building. Company coming. Be there soon. Mother et al. First time she had let them all descend on her. Needed composure to get through the afternoon.

Still...she looked over her shoulder one last time before entering her building. The corner was empty.

*   *   *

He perched on the edge of the nubby, white sofa like an uncomfortable Humpty Dumpty, knees spread to accomodate his paunch, expression apprehensive as he eyed the glass cubes of tables in front of him, pale Chinese lamps nearby, other breakables within his reach.

"Relax, Uncle John," Martha laughed and offered him coffee in a heavy stoneware mug, giving him something tangible to hang on to. He juggled this too, giving her cause to worry about her white carpeting.

"Nice place, Martha." Aunt Jenny smiled, nodded, and twittered like a little bird on an uncomfortable perch as she accepted a tea biscuit then looked about for a place to put it and, finding none, popped it into her mouth.

"Mattie. I'm called Mattie now. Snappier, don't you think?" Martha/Mattie smiled brightly.

Bella was seated squarely upright in the middle of a gold and white tapestried sidechair, knees spread, skirt hoisted so the tops of her nylons showed where the dark rim of material cut into her fleshy thighs.

Juliet primly touched a napkin to her lips and sipped her coffee with overly delicate mannerisms, clearly awed by her surroundings.

Harriet helped Mattie serve then went out to the kitchen with the coffee pot, still frowning over the girl's insistence on entertaining in that white living room and not in the kitchen where people belonged when they drank coffee and ate cookies.

At least Martha...er Mattie—she was having trouble with that new name. At least she'd finally had them over to visit. Months already here in her own apartment and she hadn't asked before. Like she didn't want to see them. Not that she'd asked this time, but at least she'd agreed to have 'em.

Snide remarks from Jenny about "the girl's manners."

Hurt comments from Juliet.

To say nothing of Patsy—calling every week to get news of Martha, not daring to call Mattie herself: "Don't wanna bother her. I know she's busy." Promised that girl a job, that's what Mattie did. Now don't seem inclined to live up to that promise. Not even calling to say hello.

Well, Patsy wasn't invited but Harriet couldn't worry about her too. Enough to keep Jenny and Juliet and Bella quiet.

"Mother." Mattie was standing behind her.

"OOH!" Harriet jumped. "You scared me." She patted at a place where she supposed her heart was located.

"I wanted to ask you, do you remember seeing a little girl—five or six—hanging around the building where you live?"

Harriet's face moved from thoughtful to curious. "A little girl? Which little girl? Lots of 'em go by on their way to school. Which one you talkin' about?" Harriet watched the carefully made-up face of this new daughter of hers as she made a move to answer quickly then became guarded, hesitated before speaking.

"Oh—just a little girl. Always wears a raincoat and a rainhat. Looks poor. Lonely kid. She used to hang around our corner. We'd wave at each other now and then."

Mattie was leaning forward, more eager than she was letting on. Harriet watched sweat break out on Mattie's forehead. That always happened when she was nervous, ever since she was little. Harriet frowned at this new and surprising Mattie.

"Too many kids go by. Don't know one from the other."

"Oh." Mattie was disappointed. "Just thought you might know her. Know her family. Always in a raincoat. That's unusual...."

"What kind of raincoat?" The question was out before Harriet could think to stop it. She didn't really want an answer. Something told her she didn't want to know. Desperately didn't want to know. Her breath caught inside her as if hung up on a spike. A hand moved to her heart.

"Oh—I don't know." Mattie's pretty face became thoughtful. "Kind of faded. Clear background. Red splotches on it. Red flowers, figures—maybe big strawberries."

Harriet's breath strangled in her throat, held until her face turned red, eyes bulged, and she put a hand out to Mattie for help.

"Ma! What is it? Here, sit down. Sit down. Water? You want water? What's wrong. Ma? What's the matter?"

Harriet sank into a chair and closed her eyes, leaning

her head on one hand while the other beat at her chest until breath came again.

Release from pain. Good. Unless she thought again of Mattie's words. No. Coincidence. Coincidence, that's all. Nothing to get upset about.

Mattie was kneeling before her, face all concern, a glass of water in her hand.

"Drink some, Ma," she offered. "You feelin' better? O.K. now? Good. For heaven's sake, what was it? What happened to you?"

Harriet took the glass and sipped delicately at the water. She turned to look straight into Mattie's large blue eyes. No, no knowledge there. Nothing mean, hateful. She hadn't done it on purpose. Just coincidence.

"Just a spell." Harriet gave her a weak smile. "Old age does that to a body. Gives 'em a weakness. I'll be O.K. You go on in with the others before your Aunt Jenny gets the idea you're ignoring her."

She had been talked into this by Harriet. Into having all of them over. Harriet had called earlier in the day, told Mattie she was bringing them that afternoon. This time she had given in.

"If you have to, Ma. I know I should've asked Uncle John and Aunt Jenny over before now. But those other two, well, you know how I feel about them. Yes, I know they're your friends. All right. If we have to have the mob scene let's get it over with. But no more than an hour. Understand? I'm really busy...yes...but...O.K."

She had sighed in the quiet of her apartment, wishing suddenly she could divorce herself from all of them, except Harriet of course. They didn't fit into her new life. Could be an embarrassment. She still cringed when she thought of that first TV interview, last November, with the three women overdressed and smirking at the camera.

Thinking of them had made her remember Patsy, another irritant. She should have called her. She should have kept in touch, shouldn't have cut her out of her life so drastically. Should, should, should...Jesus, how tired she was of hearing *Should*.

She had walked across the silence of her living room over to the huge windows and looked down at the view from her twentieth floor apartment. She had watched a freighter slowly make its way down the Detroit River.

Windsor lay over the river. A ragged waterfront quickly petering out to flat fingers of marshland stretching into Lake St. Clair.

She could see the lake from her apartment high over Detroit. Could see where the Detroit River emptied and opened into the wider expanse of water.

Her windows shone. High above bare trees. High above the dirty city. Up in a second layer of high city with birds and air for neighbors and the Renaissance Center nearby.

Fitting, she had thought on first looking out this window. Her and the city, both experiencing a renaissance.

And the apartment. A cloud floating above the death and violence below. White plush carpeting. White walls. Walls of windows. Light—great rectangles of light. And all so clean. The air here squeaked in her mouth. Had a cutting edge to it, never laden with imprisoned dust. Nothing was old. Nothing showed threads beneath pattern. Nothing was covered. No throw rugs, no doilies, no slipcovers. Only light, space, air.

Free—for the first time in her life. And she had hope. The tremendous weight of old women's anxieties was lifted, a burden she didn't even know she carried until it was gone. She had dreams.

To hire Patsy would have meant chipping away at all of that. It would have meant being burdened with the past again.

She had watched a car crawl the Windsor shoreline and admitted she wanted no more reminders of the "good old days." She could afford Patsy. That wasn't the problem. There was money, coming in regularly now. Many people calling for help, willing to pay the thousand dollar fee to locate a missing person. Still, this new life was costing plenty. And old habits of thrift wouldn't let her spend money on help, at least not yet. She had told herself it was good business to have this new apartment, to dress well. People put little faith in a woman who looked no better than a storefront gypsy. She had told herself all of these things then told herself she simply didn't want Patsy.

* * *

"How much rent you pay, Martha?" Uncle John looked around, assessing.

"It's Mattie now. I'm called Mattie, not Martha," she quietly corrected again.

"That's right, Mattie. Your mother said you'd changed your name." He smiled. Aunt Jenny smiled.

"How much you pay?"

"Plenty."

Aunt Jenny gave her an indignant look: "plenty" wasn't the answer she wanted to hear.

"Your cousin John pays three-hundred-fifty a month. Includes everything. Electric. Gas. Water. Everything but the phone. You pay that much?"

"A little bit more," she answered, getting up to pour coffee for Juliet who sat toying with her empty cup.

"More!" Uncle John whistled and looked around again as if to see what he'd missed in the first appraisal.

"Furniture's all hers too," Juliet added from her store of "Mattie" facts gleaned from Harriet. "This isn't a furnished place, is it, Mattie?"

"Seems like you could have got a better deal than that," Uncle John said.

"Possibly. But I wouldn't have the place I want, would I?"

"I . . . suppose not. As long as you've got the money. People generous with you, eh?"

She nodded.

"And you generous with your mother?"

She frowned at him, not knowing how to frame the words she wanted to say. But he wasn't waiting for her answer. Something else was on his mind. He cleared his throat, leaned toward Mattie, his hands clasped between his knees, blunt-toed workshoes splayed out and set like doorstops into the deep pile of the white carpet.

"About your mother, Mattie." He waved a hand at a sound of disapproval from Harriet. "Jenny and me have talked about this, about you having your own apartment. And while it is nice and all, we still think your place is at home, with her. It just don't seem right that she should be left alone like this, after all the years you been to home with her." A scowl crossed his face as he warmed to his subject.

Aunt Jenny sat purposefully forward also, nodding. "That's right, Mattie. You should be to home with your mother."

Old guilts stirred in Mattie. Inured responses to adult criticism made her cringe.

As if apologizing, she said, "But I asked her to live with me."

"And she said no. Now what the hell did you expect?" Uncle John's voice patronized her; he gave an amused smile. "You know your mother's gettin' on in years. Now, now, Harriet, this has to be said," he quieted Harriet's weak protest with a raised hand.

"Harriet's gettin' on in years and you can't change old ways that easy. You're the one should change your ways if you ask me. You're the one should make the sacrifice. You're still young—won't hurt you to pull up stakes here and move back home."

At first she only stared at him, too angry to answer. She felt something inside stir and catch itself and stir again, growing in size until it was too large to contain. She knew she was supposed to be quiet, to bow her head and accept what was heaped on her, to follow the lead of the other women and be respectfully quiet while this fool made his pronouncements. SHE WOULD BE DAMNED FIRST!

"The hell it wouldn't hurt me." Her voice came slowly from a place inside her where she felt something burst open. All heads snapped up in shock. Martha swearing! At Uncle John! No one spoke to him like that. No woman, that's for sure.

"Now you listen..."

"Shit." She formed the word precisely, her lips curving around each letter's sound. She formed it so he would hear distinctly and understand. "I will never go back to that place. Do you understand? Never. I've put in my time. And I think I've been hurt enough already without giving up my whole life...."

"Hurt? Hurt? What do you mean, hurt?" Bella, who had been unusually quiet, burst out now, pulling her plump body forward in the chair that trapped her.

"Shhh...shhh." Harriet waved weakly at her friend and put a hand on Juliet's fluttering fingers. She turned frightened eyes on Mattie.

"Now, now, now, Martha. Your Uncle John only means to say what's best for us all." She tried to calm all the ruffled feathers.

"Not what's best for me," Mattie countered. "And it's Mattie, Ma. Mattie. Can you remember that? Mattie?"

"Yes, dear. Well...Mattie. Your Uncle John here just cares about all of us, that's why he said that."

"Hmmp." Aunt Jenny had crossed her arms on her chest and was glaring at Mattie.

"That's it exactly. And shame on you, girl, for..." Uncle John tried to get the floor back from the women but lost out as Juliet, unable to sit quietly another minute, began to sputter in a naughty-naughty voice:

"I'm surprised at you, Martha..."

"Mattie," Mattie sighed and corrected.

"Well...yes...if you want...Mattie. I'm surprised you'd say we hurt you."

"I didn't say all of you deliberately tried..."

"Personally I don't remember ever being unkind to you. Nor Harriet either," Bella interrupted and received an indignant look from Juliet. "It seems mighty ungrateful to me for a daughter to slap her mother in the face like this."

"How've you been hurt, Martha?" Harriet asked, tears in her eyes. "What are you thinking about? What is it?"

"Now, Harriet." John stopped her. "That's enough. The girl isn't thinking of anything at all. Just being ungrateful."

"That's how they all pay us back eventually, don't you know." Jenny pouted and took a tissue out to wipe her eyes, which filled with self-pitying tears.

"But I'd like to know how she feels she's been hurt, John." Harriet turned in her seat, facing him, protesting.

"No use digging up the past. What's done is done. Martha's just gettin' used to a new life, shakin' off the old. Guess we'll have to excuse her, give her some time." His voice changed, there was conciliation in it now.

"But these dreams and visions. There's more to 'em, John. More you don't know." Harriet hurried on, talking to John alone, shutting Mattie out completely as they were used to doing. "Could they be caused by..."

"THAT'S ENOUGH, HARRIET," John's voice rose, threatened. He raised himself slightly from his chair. Bella scowled. Juliet gasped. Jenny smirked.

Mattie wanted them to leave. Her head was hurting again. She didn't know why she had been so rude to Uncle John. She knew better, knew it would all come back on her. Why had she done it?

Quickly she offered more coffee, more biscuits, then ushered them gratefully out, balling her fists and beating on the doorframe after shutting the door behind them.

Damn. Damn, she muttered. Damn, damn, damn them for bringing the squalor and violence of their lives into this place. Damn them.

She went into her pale cream and white bedroom to choose a different outfit. David would be there soon. And she wanted to shower first, to scrub off their fears and petty tyrannies. To be rid of them all.

When she emerged from the shower her mind was clear, off the past and on to the future and her gift. That was what was important, this blessed gift which was going to save her from them, the tool she would use to escape, to...

What was she thinking about? Suddenly it seemed as if it weren't really her thinking at all. As if she was losing control of her thoughts. Yes, she looked forward to whatever might be ahead, but why had she felt compelled to swear at Uncle John? Why treat them all with such contempt? That wasn't how she really was. God, she thought, biting at her lip, I'm changing and I don't have the power to control how I change. She shook her head to clear it again. Won't think. Won't allow it. Wonderful things in store for her. She just knew it. That's what she would concentrate on, not on things that frightened her.

Thirty cases successfully solved. Runaways, murder victims. One man lost in the northern woods while snowmobiling but found alive because she directed the search. He sent her five thousand dollars out of gratitude. There was even a woman who had disappeared and was thought dead. Martha saw her, very much alive, enjoying herself at a disco in New York with a man who looked suspiciously like a friend of the husband. Each case was a new challenge. But with each came the fear that the power might leave. That was one fear she couldn't control. It was too pervasive, too central to her entire existence. It wasn't even the horror of finding dead bodies that frightened her now, or the horror of that undeniable joy which came afterward; it was losing the power that scared her, made her lie awake nights torturing herself with thoughts of going back to the old life.

There was no going back. Death would be preferable. No more upper flats. No more drafty supermarkets. And no old, drab Martha.

Mattie. Mattie now. The clipped name provided psychological distance from Martha. A distance she needed, especially when she thought of the cringing woman who could be waiting around the corner, waiting for Mattie to fail.

She hung her silk robe in the closet, choosing a pale gray suit and lavender blouse. At the mirrored dressing table she ran a brush through her lightly streaked hair, arranging the permed curls into a casual, uncared-for-looking perfection. She applied her make-up as taught her in one of Bonwit Teller's make-over sessions at Somerset Mall, blending the blush into the base, the three shades of shadow from lashes to brow, highlighting her huge eyes with mascara, and downplaying her narrow lips with pale lipstick in two shades, to add fullness.

She leaned back, examining the work of art she had created. She gave a quick laugh of pleasure. Gone, gone—the old, dowdy Martha. Mattie was one of her own magazine ladies now. Sophisticated. Worldly.

She added gold chains and a watch. Not a Cartier, but there were still dreams. She still made promises to herself. Knew this was only the beginning.

There were more worlds to conquer. She could only be stopped by a very few things. One loomed ahead. David. Not sure what to do about him. He had changed so. Even more than she. Held back, stifled enthusiasm, warned her to go slow, expressed doubts about the gift. And *that* she could no longer tolerate. Her own fears were enough to deal with. Something had to be done. She didn't know what. She loved him, more than she had ever guessed she could love. But he couldn't be allowed to stop her, to limit her. Something had to be done. She didn't know what.

When he came in, opening the door with his own key, she could tell he hadn't slept well. Dusky smudges surrounded his dark eyes, making them appear sunken into his head. His jacket collar was up. His hair was wind-blown.

Tolly Pritchard was with him.

He handed her a fistful of letters picked up at their box in the main post office and gave her a quick hug. Mattie took David's jacket and the gun which he always had to wear. She kissed him on the cheek.

"See, if you lived here you wouldn't have all this running back and forth," she whispered to him, smiling.

"If you would marry me we wouldn't ever have to be apart," he countered swiftly with his old refrain.

"Just you, me, and your mother?" She raised a penciled eyebrow and turned to greet Tolly.

"Look at this." Mattie handed David a letter she had just opened, sliding it across the kitchen table where they sat going over the daily requests for help. "It's from a Bobby Sanderson, a public relations representative. Says he would like to represent me. Says he could manage my career as well as get me publicity."

"Just what you need, more publicity. You get plenty of that now." David scowled and returned to the letter he was reading. It contained a snapshot of a young blond girl.

"But he says he could make me known nationally. Even internationally. Says he could arrange a speaking tour." She read the letter again. "He even says he could get me booked in England and Australia."

David looked up, frowning, a deep cleft developing between his eyes, which appeared to squint at her. "What for? We can't keep up with the requests coming in now."

"Oh yes we can." She brushed away the objection. "What we need is some real help, though."

"A secretary?" Tolly looked up from the letter he was

recording in a ledger of possibles. "What about your friend, Patsy? Seems I remember you promised her a job."

Mattie said nothing, sitting very still with her head bent over the letter she was reading. Finally she asked, "You still see Patsy, Tolly?"

"Well, no, not really." He colored slightly, looking uncomfortable.

"Why?"

"Oh, I don't know. Not much in common, I guess. She's not really my type." He gave a laugh.

Mattie lifted an eyebrow, considering his remark. "Hmmm. And how do you think she would fit in here?" She indicated her bright apartment. "Or on my speaking engagements?"

David looked up but said nothing. She watched as Tolly thought about it.

"Not at all, to tell ya the truth. But," he shrugged, "you sure changed."

"Yes. But that's different. I . . . I . . ."

"You're sharper than Patsy?" David's question had an ironic tone to it. "Or just richer?"

"David! For Christ's sake, don't start on me again. I've already been given a double dose of guilt today. Please, I don't need you adding to it. Anyway, I only meant that as a secretary I need someone very professional. A secretary, not a supermarket cashier. But if you think that's too hardhearted an attitude we'll just forget it and keep on struggling as we are."

"Then you won't need a public relations man either." David pushed the letter away. "To tell the truth, Mattie, I think you should cut down on these appearances, not plan on more of 'em. You should be using this talent of yours the way it was meant to be used. It's been bothering me, Martha . . . eh . . . Mattie, that we're abusing it. This whole thing's been bothering me. We're still investigating the deaths of the little boy and the girl out in the Shores—that other one is solved—but something doesn't sit right. Something I can't put my finger on."

"You've been spouting doom and gloom for the past two months." She gave a chilly smile, causing Tolly to look uncomfortably from one of them to the other. "Are you expecting a bolt of lightning to strike us? The earth to open and swallow us? What? For God's sake, David, what's going to happen?"

He shrugged and looked away from her set face, dropping the subject.

They worked without speaking. David's silence began to get on her nerves, guilt stirred. She probably had been bitchy. And this Patsy business...well...

"Why don't I call Patsy tonight," she said after a time, surprising both men and herself. "Sure. I'll call Patsy." The load of guilt lessened.

Tolly smiled a cynical arc. After a brief laugh he said, "Hey, why not? And since this is give to the needy night, why don't we all go out to dinner together. I'll call her. Be just like old times. Right, Dave boy?" He reached over and slapped David's back. David scowled as Mattie and Tolly had a good laugh.

Chapter Two

"I'd never thought I'd ever see the inside of this place." Patsy looked around Aldo's Restaurant and blinked her heavily mascaraed eyes. "And you!" She looked back to Mattie. "I wouldn't hardly of known it was you, Martha."

"Mattie."

"Yeah—Mattie. You really look great, you know?"

"Thanks Patsy. You're looking well too."

"Oh," she shrugged at the suggestion and patted at the back of her colorless hair. "You know me. Beauty shop every week."

Tolly and David consulted the menu and called over Aldo, the barrel-chested owner, to have him suggest the wine. Patsy stared, leaning toward Mattie to ask, "Is he the *real* Aldo?"

Mattie nodded and spoke quickly to drown out Patsy's

excitement. "How are Mr. and Mrs. Koch? And all the ladies at the store?"

"Just fine," Patsy beamed. "Always asking about you, but of course I didn't have much to tell them except what I read in the newspapers. Not hearing from you at all. Did your mother tell you I called every week, just to see how you were doin'? Well, I did. You didn't have your phone in at first. Then I figured I wouldn't bother you. I could tell from stories in the papers how busy you were."

"You should've called."

"I couldn't do that, Martha."

"Mattie."

"I couldn't do that, Mattie. After you didn't call and I didn't hear from Tolly again, I thought it would be too much like begging. Hell, I've got my pride." She patted Mattie's hand on the table. "I was so thrilled when Tolly called today. He tell you he asked me to a club where he was performing? We had a great time, but then I didn't hear from him again until this afternoon. I guess he's not too reliable," she had lowered her voice. "I don't mind telling you, Mattie, I'd begun to lose hope—of ever hearing from either of you."

"I have been busy. Very busy."

The men ordered for Patsy, who threw up her hands at the length of the menu. Mattie ordered a salad and a light veal dish.

"We still have work on a case to do tonight," she explained. "I don't like to be too full when I have to go into a trance."

"You learn to do what Tolly taught you?"

"She's great at it," Tolly put in. "Soon she won't need any help from me."

"Gee, that's terrific. You really just see all these people then? I mean, no more dreams or anything."

"I still dream, but I have more control over the process now."

"Still seeing just dead people?"

"She's been finding dead ones, live ones, lost ones, and want-to-be-lost-ones," David put in. "Only thing she can't do yet is see 'em ahead of time, or see who the murderer is."

"And that's disappointing," Mattie added, a finger

twirling one of her gold chains as she looked around and waved to a Junior League acquaintance at a corner table.

Patsy noticed. Mattie knew she noticed.

"Why would you want to see murderers?" she asked. "Wouldn't that be dangerous?"

"Just think of the murders I could stop from happening if the murderers knew they would be caught."

Patsy thought awhile, then shrugged, digging into her plate of fettucini Alfredo.

"If you don't need me later, I'll just take Patsy home." Tolly offered as they sipped at tiny glasses of strega.

"Maybe you should be with me, Tolly," Mattie stopped him. "This case is difficult. I seem to have trouble getting focused on the girl. I'd like to try again and then, if nothing happens, I'll have to talk to her parents. Visit her home."

"Is this one dead or alive?" Patsy asked.

"I don't know. That's what we're trying to find out." Mattie was annoyed at the interruption. "So, maybe you'd better plan on being with me, Tolly.

"Maybe Patsy would like to come along and watch you work," David put in.

Mattie looked doubtful. "I don't usually do well with strangers there."

"Strangers?" Patsy's face was reddening as they talked about but around her.

"Well, maybe it would work. What do you think, Tolly?" Mattie asked.

He considered. "You're in pretty good control. I don't see how it could hurt."

"Well, we'd better get going then," Mattie said somewhat impatiently. "I'm tired and I don't want to be at it all night." She pushed back her chair, preparing to leave.

"Just a minute, Mattie." David put a hand on her arm and looked meaningfully at Patsy. "Patsy hasn't finished her spumoni yet."

"Look how fast she goes into the trance state," Tolly was stage whispering to Patsy and David. "She hardly needs me anymore."

Mattie was seated in a wingchair before the large window overlooking the river. at first she sat in a relaxed

position, breathing normally, eyes closed. As the three concentrated with her Mattie's facial muscles slackened, her
color faded, and her breathing slowed and deepened.

On her lap, she cradled the graduation picture of a
young girl with long blond hair and a "cheese" smile.

Mattie's manicured fingers rested casually on the picture,
acting as antenna of her mind.

Patsy, fascinated, still felt strangely uncomfortable with
them. The apartment subdued her. The odd lack of color.
The cold lines of mahogany antique chests and modern
cube tables stunned her. There certainly was a lot to know
about having money. This wasn't what she'd ever thought
to do with it—not those oriental rugs, for sure. The
wall-to-wall—yes, as deep as possible. That's what she
would have. But everybody's different, she knew. That's
what makes the world go round, she decided.

Mattie was mumbling, her head falling forward on to
her chest.

Christ, but didn't she look good. Really classy. It was
hard to believe it was the same person. Such a mouse
before. Wouldn't listen to anything about doing something
with her hair, wearing make-up. No interest. Now, all of
a sudden! Look at this! She was touched by God all
right.

Mattie's breath was coming faster again. Patsy could
hear nothing else in the high-ceilinged room but her
breathing and the low moans she gave.

Mattie's eyes opened and took some time to focus,
reminding Patsy of a lidless store mannequin, posed as if
arrested in midair.

Finally she smiled at David and then at Patsy and
Tolly.

"Not too successful," she admitted, reaching to the
side table for a drink she had waiting there. "Something
kept getting in the way. You'd better call the girl's folks
and arrange a meeting so I can go over her room and the
neighborhood. Familiarize myself with her life. I don't
know what's the matter. It's as if I'm being blocked somehow."

"Do you want me to do that for you?" Patsy leaned
forward, offering.

Mattie smiled, but shook her head. "David knows the
people, Patsy. He'll take care of it."

Tolly, frowning, asked, "What's the problem here? Can't reach a deep enough trance?"

Martha shook her head again, setting the loose curls around her face to bobbing prettily. "I don't think that's it. There's something about this case that I just can't grasp."

"What's it all about, Dave?" Patsy swiveled around to face David, beside her on the white sofa.

"Eighteen year old girl. Carol Frejan. Never came home from work one night. Worked at a small office down on Jefferson. Happy kid. Going to marry a boy in law school at Wayne State. Nothing to run away from. No sign of violence. But she's gone. Car and all." He turned toward Mattie. "Did you see anything? I mean, you know how sometimes what you see is only a symbol for the place. Anything at all?"

Shrugging her shoulders, Mattie frowned deeply and rubbed at her eyes. "It seemed I was in a room. Maybe a church, because there were candles in holders along the walls. It was dark. Maybe there was a person in the room. I don't know. I couldn't see enough before it was gone."

David and Tolly shook their heads, David finally saying, "Not enough to go on."

"Look." David rose, tugging at his pants and buttoning his jacket over his holster. "You get some sleep and we'll try tomorrow. Maybe a dream will solve it. Or maybe this is just one we can't solve. We'll take Patsy home. I'll be back in the morning."

The look she gave him made Patsy turn away and fumble with her coat and purse.

"You're not coming back?" Mattie's eyebrows were raised, her voice hurt, childlike.

"Not tonight." He bent to kiss her. She turned a cheek to him. "I'm tired. Honestly."

"Mother complaining?"

"What? Oh, yes, she has said I'm never home anymore. But I am tired tonight. And some things have come up I want to think about. I'll see you in the morning."

When they had gone the apartment was quiet. Mattie went to the desk where she had laid the letter from Bobby Sanderson, the public relations man. Her eyes ran over it again: tours, TV shows, maybe even a book.

She turned off all the lamps in the apartment and went to stand at the window that looked down on the shimmering water, lights in all directions, right across an international boundary. Over there—Canada. Another country. And she could look across all of it. Why not even more? she asked herself.

Why not even more?

Chapter Three

The call had come into the department. David had been impatient at first. Murder cases brought the nuts out of the woodwork. Always someone either wanting to confess, someone ready to tell him how to solve the case because they saw Columbo solve one just like it, or someone who knew his Uncle Frank just had to be the murderer.

But a cop couldn't afford to brush any of them aside. You just never knew when the real guy would break and confess, or when a real witness would call.

"Bernabei? I gotta talk to you," the voice said. Unusual that he knew his name, David thought. Most of them just took a shot at anyone who answered. This was an older man, black, by the sound of him, his words thickened. Not a Southern voice. Not heavy into Black English. But experience told him this was an elderly, black man. And frightened.

"What can I do for you, sir?" David automatically went into his chin-in, professional voice.

"I say I gotta talk to you. It's about this girlfriend of yours and these here visions. I think there's more to it all than you know. I kept quiet this long. Didn't want no trouble. But I can't get it outta my mind. No matter how I try, I keep thinking about it. Somethin's funny here, I tell you. Somethin' I can't explain, but then I ain't no cop either. That's your job. That's why I got to talk to you."

"Could you come down here? I could see you this afternoon...."

"Me in a police station?" There was a chortle from that end and then a cough. "No I don't think so. Listen, can you meet me somewheres? How about the Chez Pussy Cat on Forest?"

"Maybe you better tell me more before I agree to meet you anywhere. I'd need information."

"I tell you, it's about that girl and her visions. They're not right. That ain't no power from God...."

David felt his body go cold. Not from surprise. He felt none. It was as if the words had been said before, maybe in his own brain. Maybe they articulated a deeply buried fear he had been harboring for some time now.

His mind tried to turn aside from fear, to grasp onto more ordinary circumstances, to retreat from facing anything that could touch Mattie, could hurt her.

Still, he told himself, this guy could just be another religious fanatic.

"If you're going to go into some tirade about God and the devil you'll have to excuse me, sir, but I've got a lot of work..."

"Now just hold on a minute there. I've got real information for you and..."

"Could I have your name?" Impatience leaked through his usual politeness.

"I'll give you that in a minute. Now just hold it a second here. I can tell you don't believe I know a damn thing about this business. But I'm here to tell you I do. I tell you I'm tied up in it as close as your girlfriend is, this Martha Small. And I know things you oughtta know."

"Then go on, tell me."

"No, I want to meet you face to face. I want you to know I'm not lying to you. How about this evening, say eight o'clock at the Pussy Cat like I said?"

"Sir, do you know how many calls we get from people who think they know something? If we tried to meet all..."

The voice interrupted, "You know that little chile you found in that there garage? That little boy was my grandson." The voice broke, hesitated. "Now you believe I need to talk to you?"

* * *

The bar was dark. A layer of smoke hung in the air like autumn mist. David felt he was going into a cave. It was like a private club, a sleazy private club for the down and out.

The faces turned his way were all black. He was an intruder here and he knew there wasn't one soul in that bar who hadn't already spotted him for a cop.

A man suddenly appeared under his nose. A stooped man, thin, dressed in a baggy brown jacket and dark suitpants. "Hee hee, knew I'd recognize you right off," the man laughed, words sneaking out from behind yellowed, craggy teeth. "Come on in the back. Lester says it's all right." He nodded toward the bar where a fat man stared at them as he drew a beer.

He led to a table between a darkened jukebox and the door to the men's toilet. The man pulled out a chair for David then sat down himself, wiping at the table with the sleeve of his brown jacket. "Place ain't the best, but good enough for what I gotta do."

"And what is that?" David felt stiff. He sounded impatient. A means of intimidation he had learned early as a patrolman and fell into unconsciously with suspects and witnesses.

"Tell you some things. And tell you that there are some things I cain't tell you." The man nodded as he spoke, as if agreeing with himself, bolstering some resolve he had made.

"You want to give me your name first."

"I don't mind tellin' you now. Alfred Williams. It was my grandson what was murdered and found by you and your girlfriend." There was accusation in the man's voice. He sounded as if he bore some grudge. David knew he would be better off to let it go and just let the man talk, have his say.

"And I been thinkin' ever since then about this here coincidence that happened. But let me tell it all to you." He took a deep breath. "You know that girl what was kidnapped out in St. Clair Shores and your friend was supposed to of seen? Least wise that's what the paper said. Well, that girl was the granddaughter of this guy I used to know when we was union organizers together, back some years ago now. Ain't that strange, two of us, old friends, both lose a grandchild like that? And that ain't all. You know the other one she found? The Shell girl. That girl was the daughter of another man I knew in the union. Still in the union. Pretty high up now. You see what I'm gettin' at? You see now why I wanted to talk to you? And I'll bet you your friend's father was a union man too."

"So? What's that got to do with anything?" David was getting more and more impatient. He hated having his time wasted, especially when he had so much to do.

"Well, now lookit here. All involved with the union some way. Don't that seem strange to you?"

"Look here, Mr. Williams. I'll bet that if you take any three people in this town, two of 'em will have some connection to a union."

"Yeah, but I bet you those two won't have relatives murdered around the same time."

David stopped and thought a while.

"You want a beer?" Williams asked, licking at his pale and shriveled lips. David only shook his head, put off by the smell of the place.

"Are you trying to tell me that because of this union connection you think Martha Small had something to do with the murders? 'Cause if that's it, I have to tell you you're way off base. I've checked her out and there's no way she could have murdered those people. No way possible."

"Then maybe you got to look at ways that ain't so possible," the man nodded to emphasize his words. "'Cause I tell you I know that girl's got more to do with 'em than she's tellin'."

David gave a short laugh and got up, leaning over his hands on the table. He was tired and didn't want to have to hear any more. "Sorry, that's impossible."

"You ain't gonna listen then?"

"Sorry. You're not telling me anything."

"Could be more die."

David shrugged. "She finds 'em all the time. That's 'cause she's psychic."

"No. I mean more die who've got ties to the union."

David turned to walk away, his mind already on his car parked outside. "Like I said, that's two out of three or better in this town. To predict that is like predicting it'll snow next winter."

"How 'bout if I give you some names of people I think will be hit next. Only one or two more. Maybe three."

"You goin' into the psychic business too?"

"No. I just know."

"Well, you just wait and see. And you let me know if you turn out to be right. Deal?"

The elderly man just looked at David, not answering. David turned and left the bar, sorry now that he had wasted his evening.

Chapter Four

Before stepping from the lobby to the street Mattie found herself hesitating, eyes going left then right, searching.

It was almost a ritual, this fear before leaving the building. And more and more often she had reason to fear. The child was there. Just standing. Waiting.

There was no hesitation in the wave now. As soon as she spotted Martha the hand went up and a wide smile crossed her plain, narrow face, moving up to her eyes, lighting them with a pathetic relief.

The situation was becoming intolerable. Mattie ignored her, refused to wave back. Once she even spoke to the doorman about calling the police or some agency about the girl. But when she had turned to point her out she was gone and the man said he didn't recall ever seeing a child waiting on the corner.

Today Mattie opened the door and hesitated. She was there. She waved. She hopped on one foot, overjoyed at the sight of Mattie.

Repulsed and angered, Mattie took a step forward,

meaning to run after her if she had to, to catch her, get her parent's name and number, and see that she got home. Stayed there. But as Mattie took steps forward the child took as many away. Mattie, embarrassed and frustrated, stopped in the middle of the sidewalk, raised a fist, and shouted, "Get away from here and stay away or I'll call the police."

The child, running now, turned around, floppy hat falling down her back and dangling on its elastic. She raised a hand and waved again. The sound of childish laughter floated back to where Mattie stood, fear and anger immobilizing her.

"I can't figure it out," she was earnestly telling David over lunch. "This child just hangs around my building until I come out. She's getting to be a real nuisance, David. I mean, after all, she's out there at all hours."

He was sipping at the Scotch he'd ordered, head down, half-listening.

Exasperated by his lack of interest and fearing to show how bothered she was, Mattie turned to study the menu, growing as quiet as David.

The London Chop House was hushed, the well-to-do luncheon crowd too mannerly for more than polite conversation.

"Afternoon, Miss Small. Nice to see you." Max Pincus, the gray-haired owner walked up to their table and bowed.

Mattie nodded grandly and smiled, noting peripherally that others were now taking notice of her.

David, studying the menu before ordering, gulped at the prices as he always did. It was going to cost forty dollars or more just for lunch. He couldn't see it himself, but she said it was really a business expense and that they had to eat, didn't they? Had to be seen.

"I talked to my mother last night." He cleared his throat and folded and unfolded the heavy gold napkin on the patterned plate in front of him.

"About what?" Her brows shot up though her eyes lighted on him only briefly. She was still annoyed with his lack of interest in her problem with the little girl.

"About us getting married."

"I bet that went over with a big bang," she laughed.

David shrugged and said nothing.

"Well?" Mattie demanded. "What did she say?"

His smile was weak. He played nervously with his knife. She softened toward him. His mother wasn't one of her favorite topics.

"She was happy for me."

"And?"

"Wished me luck."

"I'll bet."

"And said you'd fit right into the house, wouldn't have to worry about cooking or housework getting in the way of your work."

"My. How very nice." The sarcasm was thick.

"Come on, Mattie. She's old and scared."

"I know. I know." She relaxed her look of scorn, then turned expectantly toward the entrance of the dining room as a man walked in.

"I told her we'd probably have our own place and that she could keep the house. I'd still pay all the utilities and . . ."

The man was tall, with hair the color of wet beach sand. He had a trimmed beard to match. With a lifted finger he summoned one of the waiters, bending slightly to talk to him.

He had on a beige suit, jacket open to show a vest with gold chains.

The waiter pointed and the man looked toward Mattie, caught her eyes on him, and raised a hand in salute.

"Seems all the obstacles are out of the way," David was saying. "All that's left is for you to name the day."

She didn't answer, looking instead toward the tall man approaching their table. They smiled at each other. It was a conspiratorial smile, as if they already shared secrets.

"Miss Small?" The man stopped beside them, making a mocking half-bow.

"Yes. And you must be Bobby Sanderson," she greeted, putting a hand out for him to grasp firmly.

He agreed he was Bobby Sanderson. She introduced him to David, who stood, frowned, and shook hands.

"The name's familiar, but I don't recall . . ."

"Please sit down, Mr. Sanderson." She indicated the third chair, then turned back to David. "Remember the letter from a public relations specialist? That was Mr. Sanderson. I called and asked him to meet us here today."

"Bobby, please." The man sat down, rearranging his silverware and napkin and removing the single rose which decorated the table, setting it on the table behind him. He frowned slightly, eyes sweeping the area. He appeared to accept what he saw and relaxed.

"Why didn't you tell me?" David's face paled. "We should have discussed this."

"And you call me Mattie." She was smiling at the man, ignoring David. "I'm afraid my friend is upset with me. He usually handles all my business, but this I took care of myself and forgot to tell him. Forgive me, David. I am sorry." She turned to him theatrically, her voice emphasizing "forgive me" but her eyes empty of feeling.

"Well, I can't say I am." Bobby Sanderson rubbed his hands together and summoned the waiter with a nod, requesting a Chivas Regal and soda. "And—if I may call you David? Fine. I think I can show you how my help can be beneficial to you both."

"You don't *need* a press agent, for God's sake," David growled at her, feeling his face begin to burn. "It's bad enough now."

Equal to the occasion, Bobby Sanderson laughed politely. "Not a press agent, David. A public relations man. And that's one helluva lot more than a press agent."

"Your letter mentioned things you could do to spread word of my work world-wide." Mattie leaned forward, her large blue eyes pinned on him.

David snorted and turned away.

"Right." Bobby looked quizzically at the side of David's head then turned an understanding smile on her. "But why don't we have a drink, calm down, talk later."

Later, over coffee, Bobby dared open the subject again. Mattie was receptive, even eager to hear his plans.

"Well, to give you a short version of my services," he cleared his throat and concentrated on her, just slightly working around so his back was to David, "What I've done for others is to get their names known nationwide, with stories in all the major newspapers, through story ideas I offer to magazine free-lancers or directly to editors. Then

I arrange a tour, take you coast to coast when the time is right. On the tour there are interviews with local newspapers, radio shows, TV shows, even major talk shows. That's if I do my work right. By then you'll be a well-known name." He paused, watching Mattie's face. "How's it sound so far?"

"Impossible, but great."

"Again, if I do my job right, the tour will not only pay for itself, but will put you on the road to sky-high profits. Once you're a big-name psychic you can demand the very highest fees." He paused. "Let me ask you—what do you charge now?"

"To locate a body?" she stopped to think. "Well, I don't always charge, because some can't afford to pay. And I don't charge when I can't find one. But if I do, I like to get a thousand dollars—so I can carry on my work, you understand."

"A thou? Chicken feed!" He laughed out loud. "You don't know what a good thing you've got going here. Psychics are hot, really hot. And able to do what you can do? No end to the profits. No end."

"This talent of hers is supposed to be used to help people." David smacked his demitasse cup on the table, causing others to stare. "Not to fleece them."

"David..."

"No wait." Bobby put up a hand to stop her angry remark. "Certainly she should help people. That goes without saying. But what's the matter with making money at the same time? A lot of very rich people get into trouble too, you know. Why shouldn't they subsidize the ones she does for nothing?" He eyed David coldly, calculating how far he should go. He then continued, "You don't make up the difference to Mattie when she takes on charity cases, do you? I didn't think so. So you're not out a dime. Hey, haven't you ever heard of women's lib, man? Women don't want to be exploited anymore."

"I've never exploited Mattie." David looked toward her, but she had turned away from him, looking instead across the room.

"Then you shouldn't object to her making as much as the other psychics. Some of 'em make thousands each year just from lecturing at colleges and these town-hall series."

"When is she supposed to do her work?"

"Plenty of time. I won't interfere with that." He smiled at Mattie, whose face softened slightly.

"She's got something special here," David said doggedly. "Why should she be making a fortune off it? And what if it goes away? I mean, leaves like it came? What then?"

He shrugged. "Then it's over." Bobby paused, turned to Mattie again. "Well...how's it sound?"

"Sounds fine to me," she said. "The more my name is known, the more my work will spread."

"And the more money you'll make," David muttered.

"Then I'll get busy." Bobby ignored him. Spoke directly to her. It was half question, half statement.

She nodded, putting out her hand. "Come see me tomorrow."

"Shouldn't we discuss this a little more?" David asked, surprised by her quick decision.

"Why?" Her eyes flew, startled, to his face. It was obvious David would never understand. She would have to make the necessary moves without his approval. She wanted what Bobby Sanderson offered. Wanted it badly. Would do whatever she had to do to get it. Even if that meant David got hurt. Nothing would stop her. Not now.

Chapter Five

"Don't see how you could just go ahead and hire that guy." It was late afternoon but David was still angry, shaking his head at her. His face was flushed, features working themselves in and out of tight, disturbed expressions as he glared at Mattie and then out the large windows of her living room.

"What have I done that's so bad?" Her ingenuousness put him off stride. He turned, paced back and forth, then stopped to glower.

"You don't know, huh? You really don't know?"

She moved close to him, ran her arms up and around his neck, pulling his tense face down to hers. She turned her enormous eyes on him with a teasing look that, childlike, begged to be forgiven. For a few minutes he stood erect, pulling back from her. She moved in a little closer, cuddling against him. Soon he relented and put his arms around her.

"Still don't like it," he murmured, softer now, bending to bury his face in her hair.

David noted the feel of silk against his hands; he inhaled the expensive perfume. So different. Could he hold her back?

He looked down and bent to kiss her.

"Let's make up," her husky voice suggested against his chest as her arms snaked up over his shirt and began slowly, seductively to unbutton the top buttons. With three unbuttoned she pulled his shirt open and kissed his chest, face burrowing into the dark ringlets, teeth catching at the hair, pulling until he yelled and tried to push her away.

"You little..." He pulled her hair, forcing her head back so her eyes would look into his. Her lips were open, breath coming faster, deeper. He brought his mouth down to hers, kissed her until his lips felt bruised, his tongue felt lacerated by the force of hers darting at him, pushing, probing, demanding something of him.

He felt her hands at his shirt again, frantically working at the buttons. Felt her tugging at his belt.

"Come on." He exhaled the words in a shudder, pushing her backward toward the bedroom.

"No." The word was forceful. "Here. Let's stay here. By the window. Now."

"So much glass. Someone will see...." He pushed at her hands, stopping them, holding them.

"Who? A bird? Who the hell cares anyway?" The words were impatient. She drew back, hair disheveled, mouth reddened, lips swollen. A smile crossed her face. It teased him. Dared him. She was mocking him.

Letting himself relax, letting go completely, David threw his head back and laughed. "If you're game then so am I."

He slipped her dress from her shoulders and let her

push it down over her hips to the floor as he cupped her bare breasts and kissed each in turn. Still standing before the huge, open windows, he put his arms around her and lifted slightly, signaling her to hold on, to wrap her legs around him and let him enter her standing as they were with the city and river as backdrop.

"Gorgeous," she breathed into his ear. "Wonderful."

He pulled her hard against him again and again until he held her very still for a moment, until the world around them diminished and they were rocked with their own passion.

Afterward, they slid down into the white carpeting to lie in each other's arms, fingers still exploring flesh, words still gushing, until they began to tickle, to giggle, roll about on the floor, and exhaust each other in play.

Finally quiet, they lay in each other's arms in the fading light. He rolled toward her, tracing "I love you" on the mound her hip made.

He asked again, "What about getting married? At the restaurant I asked you to set the day for our wedding but you didn't answer me."

She was still a long while, face turned from him. She frowned. "I don't know if this is the time, David. With this whole divining thing mushrooming like it is, and—well—now I'll be away on tour for a while. That's no way to start a marriage."

He said nothing, moving to place an arm up and across his eyes, imperceptibly leaning his body back away from hers.

Neither spoke for a time. She waited, moved up to lean on one elbow and look down at him. His body was covered with a fine mist of sweat. The dark curls on his chest glistened, some were matted against his skin. His body was long, lean. Skinny really. Knees bony. She traced a pulsing blue vein down the arm shielding his eyes. On impulse she leaned her head to his chest, listening to the hollow sound of his heart beating.

He remained motionless, keeping her locked away from him.

"I love you," she whispered toward him. "But I can't give all this up now. Not now, David."

She stopped, awaited some response from him, but he lay still, mouth firm, breath measured.

"Do you know what I mean, David? Do you understand?" She touched his arm, saw the flesh ripple under her finger, felt him pull away. "I love you. Can you love me enough to know why I can't think in terms of limits yet?"

His arm came down between them. Slowly he opened his eyes and fixed her with a hurt glare. "And marriage to me would set limits. Be like caging you."

She shook her head, waining to get this over with now, end it, so she could talk of plans, the future, without having invisible borders placed around her life. Feeling impatient with him, she made a move to get up, but he reached out and grabbed her arm, painfully squeezing it.

"I'm not after some lousy affair, Mattie." He moved up even with her, holding her in place though her fingers pried at his hand.

"You're hurting me."

"What do you think you're doing to me?" His voice snarled the words at her. His lips were hard, drawn into straight lines barely permitting sounds. "I don't like being used."

"Used? By me? Haven't you got that backward?" She reached over for her dress, pulling it toward her, ignoring the hand digging deeply into her upper arm. He shook her so she fell back toward him.

"What if I quit my job? Devoted all my time to this thing of yours? Would you believe I loved you enough then?" he demanded.

"It's not a question of...of love." She halted, trying to think. "It's more...more..."

"Power." The word formed ominously between them. "That's it isn't it, Mattie? Power. You're starting to feel it and you don't want to give it up."

POWER. The word seemed to echo in capital letters through her brain. POWER. She shuddered, not understanding why this sense of fear was slowly creeping over her, this sense of horror.

Power. Over dead things! Like ... like some maggot feasting and swelling on dead flesh.

"No!" she cried and put her hands to her ears to stop him from eating her alive with hideous words. "No! No! It's not power. God! Dear God! No..."

He held her then and shushed her, letting her cry against his bare chest. They were both on their knees, facing, arms about each other like two drowning people. After a time, when she was quieter, he pulled back and tilted her face, wet and streaked with tears, up to him.

"No, you're right. You have a talent. A special talent, Mattie," his voice soothed. "And you're right about getting married. We'll wait awhile. Until you get used to all this. Until..."

"I love you, David." She clung to him, fingers denting the skin of his back.

Gently he pulled her away, turned her in his arms, and settled back to the floor, cradling her against him.

She tried to speak. Her voice cracked. She tried again.

"You don't think I can lose it, do you? I mean this psychic power. I don't think I could stand it." Her tongue licked out at her dry lips. "I couldn't bear that. Not now. How cruel it would be. What kind of God would give a miracle then snatch it back?"

Her body grew rigid beside him. David quietly hushed her with soothing strokes of his large hands over her mussed hair, down her temples where a frantic pulse beat, down her cheeks, her arms, her back. She trembled slightly then relaxed.

"It won't happen," he assured her.

"At first all I wanted was for it to go, to leave me in peace. It was so awful—those dead people—seeing them, knowing I knew what was impossible to know. But now—I feel so different. Everything seems so strange. Like I'm seeing the world with new eyes. Or I'm seeing it for the first time. David, I've got to tell you something. Something that's frightened me since this all began. Please listen." She reached up and quieted him with a gesture. And don't think I'm crazy or anything, but..." She paused, gathering courage. "From the beginning, whenever I found one of those people, I felt...almost happy. I'd get upset, you know that. I was horrified, sickened, all the things I would expect to feel. But there was this other thing—this happiness too. It...it scares me."

He hugged her to him and gave a short laugh. "Nerves. That's all. They do funny things. I should know. I've seen people in all kinds of tragic situations. Sometimes nerves play tricks. Make you react differently than you feel you should. Sort of like wanting to laugh out loud in church. That ever happen to you? Well, like that. Responses get mixed up. I wouldn't worry about it."

"But this is so calculated. That's all I can call it. Calculated. Not a nervous laugh but more as if some part of me I can't control enjoyed the deaths."

"Nerves," he answered her again and checked his watch. "Look, I gotta go. Let's leave the marriage talk on a back burner for now. But don't think I won't bring it up again."

"Just give me time." She got up, noticing it was dark out now and she was standing, naked, before the open window. With a laugh she tossed her head and walked with a deliberate, sexy swing into the bedroom, leaving an embarrassed David to gather his clothes and, in a crouch, make his way to the bathroom.

He made drinks and brought them out to the living room when they were both dressed. She was sifting through the mail. He set her drink down beside her, bent to kiss her neck. She didn't look up, her pale, curly head remaining bowed away from him. He cleared his throat.

"A man called the other day, called the department. Turned out he's the grandfather of that little boy you found in the garage." He paused. Her eyebrows went up. He had her attention. She waited for him to go on. "Didn't want to say anything before but...well...he thinks you had something to do with the murders."

She sighed. "We've been all through that. You know I couldn't possibly be involved in any of them. How many have there been now? You think I killed them all?"

"He questioned only those first three. Said all three were close relatives of men who were union organizers years ago. All in the same local with him." David stopped, watching as she listened closer.

"Union?" Surprised, she sat back to look at him. "My father was in the union. In fact, until recently, I collected anything in the paper about Father's union, Local 16. Just a way of keeping in touch with him. That is kind of strange, don't you think? Not that it could mean anything."

He could see he was worrying her and didn't want to, not even out of revenge over this Sanderson guy.

"I told him two out of three people in this town have union connections..."

"But he said they all worked together." She was frowning now, thinking.

"Doesn't mean anything. Shouldn't've even told you. Just forget it. Now about this Sanderson guy," he changed the subject. "You really think he's going to do you any good?" He straightened, stretched. He wanted to touch her but somehow no longer felt free to do so. She stared at nothing, her eyes fixed on the far wall. Something was between them again, as it had been before they made love. Something he didn't understand but found impossible to bridge. It was as if a crevasse had opened at their feet and they stood on opposite sides. If only he could reach across...

She sighed, lifted the drink he had fixed for her, and leaned back to look up, mind reluctantly following what he said. "Hmmm? Oh, Sanderson...I hope so. Be great to have news of my work spread, wouldn't it?"

He shrugged, bewildered by yet another change in her. Euphoric now. Back to saving the world.

"You want the truth? I think this is getting away from you. I mean with this PR man and all. Tours, talk shows—sounds more like a carnival to me."

She stood and walked stiffly away from him, turning when she was in front of the windows. The lights of an airplane, blinking like a syncopated star, beamed behind her in the night sky.

"What are you really afraid of, David? My losing control of things or your losing control of me?"

He hesitated, growing angry again. "I won't even answer that one," he finally said. "It's your business if you want to turn yourself into a road-show freak. But I can't help but feel you're perverting what's been given to you."

"Perverting?" she exploded, hands on hips, large blue eyes snapping with anger. "Perverting according to whom? All you want is for me to stay under your thumb, solve your goddamned cases for you, make you look good, and get you promotions. I've gotten you one already, haven't

I? And now you figure you'll cement that convenient relationship by marrying me. Then you, and your mother, can both keep me neatly in my place. Right? Am I right?"

Her face blazed. She walked toward him, slowing her pace to match the rhythm of her words.

"I've had enough of being under people's thumbs. You understand? I'm going to be free of everybody. Choose my own direction. And if that doesn't suit you, then you better get out of my life right now 'cause I'm not looking back for anyone."

"Free of me? Is that what you want?" he was yelling back. "If it weren't for me you'd still be back in that supermarket. But you're damn right I'll get out of your life. I'll never give you that chance to say I stood in your way. What the hell you need me for now? Right? You got your PR man. Get him into your bed and you've got me replaced completely. Bitch."

He grabbed his jacket from the back of the sofa and headed for the door. Mattie stood in the middle of the room, arms hugged about herself, head bowed under his barrage.

Before he could get to the door she gave a strangled cry and ran after him, tears running down her face.

"David, please." She wrapped her arms around him. "David, I'm sorry. I didn't mean any of those stupid things I said. It's just that I'm so afraid. So afraid of going backward, back into that old life, I feel as if I have to keep fighting against it. But I don't want to fight you. I don't. I love you."

She lay her head against him and cried until he put his arms around her and rested his head down near hers, whispering into her hair that he loved her too, would always love her, hoped they could stop tearing at each other.

The anger exhausted them. That and the futility of what they desperately wanted to feel—but somehow could no longer.

When the door closed behind David, Mattie got her purse from the hall closet. She took out a handkerchief to dab at her eyes without spoiling her mascara and then the business card Bobby Sanderson had given her. She dialed the number embossed on the card.

Chapter Six

The girl was alive.

Through a haze, glowing iridescently like a streetlamp burning in a storm, she lay in a cameo of light on an old flowered sofa, huge green blossoms twining around and over each other in grotesque pattern, her prone figure covered with a ragged quilt. Her blond hair was in tangles. Her eyes were open, staring despondently. One of her arms limply encircled her head.

Golden halos of candle flame burned on the wall, high above the couch. One candle guttered out. The room was slightly less bright. Her chest heaved, held, and sank in a huge sigh accompanying a turn to her side. Her hands cradled each other beneath her cheek, the posture of a sleeping child. She closed her eyes.

The light slowly faded until a single candle flame burned hugely. Then darkness.

Angered, feeling cheated, Mattie came out of the dream to the empty darkness of her room.

It was the girl all right. Still alive. But where? Where?

She turned over, punched the pillow into shape, and went back to sleep.

When the ringing started she incorporated it into the new dream she was having. Within her mind she answered the doorbell, opened the door—but still the bell rang again, waking her this time.

Ooh...head was aching...

So the girl was alive. But no solid clues as to where she was being held.

The doorbell again. Three jabs. One after the other.

What time was it? She came to and rolled over to check her clock. Eight? Who would be at her door at eight in the morning? No one expected. David knew better. She slid out of bed, grabbed up a silk robe she had thrown over the chaise the night before, and pushed her feet into slippers.

Angry at being disturbed so early, Mattie had prepared her face to show displeasure when she opened the door, carefully leaving the chain on.

There was no one there. Thinking they—whoever it was—had given up trying to wake her and headed back toward the elevator, Mattie closed the door quickly, slid the chain loose, and opened it wide, stepping halfway into the hall, ready to call out to whomever stood at the elevator bank waiting to go back down.

Again, no one. The hall was empty.

Then—a sound. From the other direction. A muffled giggle.

Her head snapped around. No one. Empty!

But...

The giggle again. A high, childish titter, seeming to come from just around the bend of the corridor.

Pranks? Someone playing a childish prank on her? Of all the...

She took a few steps toward the corner where the sound came from then stopped, body tensing, going icy cold. Something caught her eye. A garment showing slightly, as if someone hid just out of sight, the hem of a red-splotched raincoat alone giving them away.

The child! My God! The child! Here?

How could she have gotten into the building? Wouldn't the doorman have stopped her? Mattie's mind searched for an explanation.

No, no, not necessarily. Many times she had come and found him nowhere in sight, off on some errand or other, or sneaking an extra coffee break.

But to find her apartment from so many? Was the child even old enough to read? She wouldn't have thought her that old. But she could have asked. Who wouldn't help?

The sound of a stifled giggle cut through the astringent silence of the corridor. Louder. Wanting to be noticed. The triangle of raincoat moved, disappeared, pulled back from sight.

There was a sense of expectation in the air. Mattie felt it. Her skin was prickling, ears alert. Something was waiting...

She looked down the hall again, taking first a tentative step toward where the child hid and then shivering as if struck by cold breath. She pulled back.

The child was there. Could possibly be caught. This whole thing explained. But now the idea made her head swim with fear, made her reach out to steady herself against the wall. It was too late for sensible explanations. Whatever that little girl was about it was evil, something best left unexplained. Left unknown.

But could it stay that way? Mattie's mind, panic-stricken, floundered from rational to irrational thoughts. She'd come all the way to the twentieth floor now. Was getting closer. How soon before...before...

What? What, for God's sake? Before what? her mind screamed at her.

She backed slowly toward the doorway, taking one step at a time, feeling her way along the wall.

Just get back and lock the door, she told herself, eyes riveted on that corner. Just get back.

She felt the doorjamb with nervous fingers and breathed easier knowing she would be in the safety of the apartment in seconds. Would make it...

The triangle of material showed, moved again, widened, grew, and a head tilted out, hat and thin hair hanging as if from a rag-doll. The face showed surprise, then disappointment, then anger; the child quickly jumped into the hall, raising a hand and running toward Mattie!

Mattie leaped through and slammed the door after her, testing the locks and snapping the chain into place. She leaned against it, washed by a greater terror than she had ever known, and aware, with sudden conviction, that the terror was in response to a very real, even mortal, danger.

There was a noise from the other side of the door, a scuffing, as if someone stood there—waiting. And then a tremendous thud, and another. Powerful kicks against the wood.

Mattie took her hands from the door, fearing she could be touched through the panels. She backed into the dim morning light of the living room, backed into a chair, and sat without blinking, her eyes watching the door.

Her mind was torturing her. This morning had changed things—drastically. The child was inside now, had real access to her. And it was she, not the child, who ran.

The doorbell rang again at nine. Mattie was still in her robe. She sat up, immediately alert. Afraid.

"Mattie?" a voice called. A voice she knew. With relief she answered, letting in Bobby Sanderson, briefcase in hand, large smile greeting her. She felt her body shaking and held herself tightly together, not wanting him to see, to suspect...

Her eyes swept what she could see of the hall. Empty.

"Nice place. Real nice place." His eyes went over the apartment. "Got a lot lined up to show you." He smiled jovially, striding across the room, lifting his nose to sniff the air. "No coffee?"

"Thought you might be David," she said to the back of him, disappointment evident.

He stopped dead, theatrically turning toward her with exaggerated gestures. "Don't tell me you two are fighting?" He shot his brows up. "Hope it wasn't on my account."

She shook her head, motioning him to the sofa as she crossed to the kitchen door, promising coffee. "No fight."

"Doesn't he live here?" he called after her, bringing only a laugh in response through the half-open door.

He shrugged, removed his jacket, and settled himself, his expression one of pleased surprise as he made a mental note of this additional fact for his file.

"You know something?" he was asking when she came back with coffee for them both. At his question she raised her eyebrows. "I just can't see you two together. Worlds apart, you two." He stopped, shook his head. "I could tell David was a cop from a mile off. He just doesn't have the class you have."

Mattie sipped her coffee, noting that her hands had stopped quivering. She remained quiet for a moment, not certain how to answer him. He meant it as a compliment, but he was still out of bounds, and she wasn't experienced in handling employees.

"I think..." she began, hesitated, and began again, "I think my friends and relationships have nothing to do with my life as a psychic. The business angle is the reason you're here. Maybe we should stick to just that. All right?"

With a gesture resembling a tip of a nonexistent hat, Bobby settled back, sipped at his coffee, and cleared his throat.

"Just one more thing."

She nodded.

"When I represent a client I have to know everything there is to know about that person. You get what I'm saying? I don't like nasty surprises. And I don't like cleaning up after the garbage's been dumped. Follow? That means if I'm going to do the best possible job, I have to know every corner of your life. I'm not peddling you as Miss Purity of 1982 if you sleep with ten different guys every week. So while you think this whole thing is none of my business, I want you to know that it is. And from here on in everything that happens will be my business." He paused, set his cup down on the glass table next to him, and leaned forward, earnestly clasping his hands together. "If that isn't straight at the outset, we better forget this whole business. That's the way I operate."

She sat through the verbal scolding without a word, watching as his expression hardened. Something in his attitude didn't sit right with her, but she didn't want him to leave. Her dreams had expanded to the point where contraction would kill her. They both knew that. And knew she wanted what he offered, that she dared to dream large dreams now that so much had come about— more than she had ever known could happen back when her day was circumscribed by Mother and friends and Koch's supermarket. She watched his set face as he waited for her answer. Finally she nodded.

"I can see where you would need to know everything." Again she paused, waiting for some lessening of will in him. She needed friends. Needed him. Needed people around her. Something happening again. Mind playing tricks—more tricks—seeing things: this child who couldn't really be there. Ghost? Ghoul? What? What? No one must know. No doubts allowed to creep in to taint her growing power.

He waited. Watched her. Made no move. His sandy eyebrows went up in question but he said nothing, sipping at his coffee while still watching her over the rim of his cup.

"I don't think there is anything in my life you need to worry about," she went on. "David is my first and only lover. We may marry someday. Not now. We don't live together. We do sleep together. He is a dedicated policeman and I'm dedicated to my work. If I can use this gift to alleviate the suffering of parents or a husband or wife, if I can lessen someone's pain, even a little—then I'll do it. The money is incidental. Except that I need to live and as anyone knows living is expensive...."

"Especially if you like good living," he broke in. Laughed.

"I don't consider this apartment or my clothes outrageously expensive." She flushed, angered by his flip tone. "Others live a hell of a lot better than I do. I don't see why I..."

"Hey." He put up his large, blunt hands, warding off attack. "I'm for money and the good life. Just don't lay too much of that 'out to save the world' bullshit on me. Don't ever kid a kidder, honey. I'll promote you and help you make the biggest dollar you can while you're hot. When you cool down, you'll be back on your own. I warn all my clients—the good life ain't forever. Grab it while you can."

"You make me sound like some kind of a charlatan." Her voice was bitter, a frown pulled at the corners of her eyes.

"We're all charlatans. Not that I don't believe in your psychic power, I do. But I know the public. They want new blood constantly. I'll tell ya, it's like feeding Christians to the lions. You gotta keep the bodies fresh. When the lions are done they're done, so enjoy the pageant while you can. No feast lasts forever, you know."

She shuddered. "You make it all sound so...so brutal."

With a single gesture, he brushed it all away, as if nothing mattered, as if he had been stating unimportant trivia which shouldn't bother her.

"That's the way it is. But don't worry. My job is to get you up there to begin with. And I will—with your help and your trust. Now, I'd like to go over what I've been able to accomplish so far. And I'd like to get bio material from you. We..."

The doorbell again. Still troubled, Mattie rose reluctantly.

"Oh, David." Relief at the sight of his ruggedly familiar face swamped her. "I'm so glad you're here."

She hugged him, not seeing the look of displeasure crossing his long face as he caught sight of Bobby Sanderson so comfortably ensconced on the sofa.

He handed her his topcoat. With lowered voice, he asked, "What's he doing here?"—indicating the man in the living room.

"Just planning the publicity," she said hurriedly, rushing on breathlessly to the more important matter she had to discuss. "I saw her last night." She was holding his hands, looking into his eyes, knowing he would be pleased with her. "The blond girl. I saw her—lying on a sofa. She's alive, David. Alive! Don't you think we should call her parents and tell them? They'll feel better at least."

He thought for a minute, hands holding her shoulders, stooping to kiss her. Still in thought, he said, "Any clue as to where she might be?"

"No." Mattie shook her head. "Just the candles again. And an old flower print sofa. Nothing from the outside."

"Hmmm. I don't know. Maybe better not get their hopes up." He walked into the living room, nodded to Bobby, and sat down.

"Found another body, Mattie?" Bobby asked.

"No, the girl is alive." Her voice betrayed her excitement. "I was just telling David I thought he should let her parents know."

"Good idea." He seemed to be thinking then got up and paced from the front windows back to the sofa. "I'll call the newspapers. Make a good story."

"No." David's voice was hard and authoritarian. He was sitting on the edge of his seat, pulled forward as if to leap at Bobby. "That could jeopardize the girl's life. Make her captor act."

"More likely he won't act if he knows Mattie's on to him," Bobby disagreed. His smile was patronizing. "Be more likely to set her free, I would think."

"Unfortunately what you think isn't what actually

happens. Criminals like to clear the decks. Take no chances on being identified. No, this has got to be kept under wraps." He turned to Mattie. "I'll call the girl's folks, but first it's got to be understood: no publicity."

She nodded, sipping slowly at her breakfast of black coffee.

He got the number from an address book in his suit pocket and went into the bedroom to phone.

"Why didn't you tell me about seeing the girl?" Bobby demanded as soon as David left the room.

Mattie shrugged, hesitated. "I'm used to telling David first, I guess. Didn't think to mention it to you."

"You better get used to mentioning things to me. I've got to know everything that's going on from here in. And another thing, that guy can't give me orders—not if I'm going to do the best job I can. Let's get that straight right now." He half grinned but anger showed.

Mattie didn't know what to say. She didn't want to be caught in the middle, with the two of them trying to run her life. She loved David—but Bobby was offering the world.

"He has always taken care of everything." Her voice had none of the certainty she wanted. It sounded diffident and placating.

"Now I'm here. And I have to be given everything too." His hands massaged each other with what could have been irritation, or perhaps anticipation. He nibbled briefly at his lower lip in what Mattie soon would know as a nervous gesture accompanying excitement—taking in the flesh in small bites and chewing at it.

"You mentioned plans you've made," she coolly changed the subject.

They exchanged a glance in which she signaled he had overstepped the limits of her desire for celebrity, and he signaled back that this was only a minor skirmish.

Chapter Seven

Why was it nagging? This whole thing? Why? Could it be he was jealous of this Sanderson guy and wanted to make trouble? He didn't think that was it. Hoped not. Just a cop's instincts. That old black man hadn't been lying. The concern there had been real. At least real enough to him to make him call a cop. Not a normal event for Mr. Williams, David realized. And that small fact mattered.

His desk was covered with work, reports to write, other cases to go over. The men in Detroit's homicide division never lacked for work, even though things were better now than they had been a few years back.

But something kept him from digging into the waiting paperwork, that little nagging something set off by the old man's phone call. He knew it would bother him until he put it to rest, until he could close every door to doubt by tracking all possibilities and proving them impossible.

The worn swivel chair squeaked beneath him as he leaned back, put his hands behind his head, and let his eyes wander over the view out his fifth floor window, over the city streets.

It wasn't doubt of Mattie. There was no question that she had anything to do with the murders. No doubt. But there could be other links. Somehow they might be connected.

One of the murderers was behind bars. That friend of Esther Shell's husband—the black woman found at the bottom of the steps in that abandoned house. How could he figure in if they were all connected? That one'd confessed to killing Esther because she was cutting out on her husband. Vindicating his friend, he'd called it.

Couldn't be a connection. But still there was something.... something. Every cop knew this vague uneasiness,

144

a sense of a piece missing. But not always to be trusted, this sense. Not always an infallible gauge of how he was doing.

Still, many a hunch solved a crime. It was part of the job to follow up on everything.

He reached for the phone on his desk only to pull his hand away again. Seemed so disloyal to Mattie, checking up behind her back. And checking on what? He didn't even know what questions to ask.

Where to start? Not with her mother—that woman would fall to pieces if she thought he was asking questions of her on official business.

David reached out again for the phone, consulted a directory of Michigan police numbers in his drawer, and dialed.

The Shores police sergeant was friendly, which didn't always happen when he had to call a suburban department. It only took him five minutes to get the name he wanted, the name of the first murdered girl's grandfather. That girl found in a culvert. It took another five to get his number out of a reluctant information operator.

Fred Gibonski.

"Sure you can come on out here, but I don't see how I can help you. Months ago now. These goddamned cops out here done nothin'. Nothin'. Now you want help with some Detroit murder? Nothin' I can do, but you can come on out."

The man's voice was agitated, grew more so as he worked himself into anger and self-pity. David knew he'd hear all about the inefficiency of the police when he got out there.

A small, square, brick house miles inland from the lake, it was almost lost behind untrimmed bushes which covered the house number. The general air of the place was of a failed search for the American dream and a settling for the small and cheap

When David knocked a voice called through the door telling him to come on in.

In one corner of the tiny living room, darkened by the bushes outside the windows, a TV set glared. Across from it, on either end of the sofa, sat a man and a woman.

Both were in their sixties. She was neat. Gray hair cut and curled. Her dress was cotton but pressed, starched. She wore lipstick and rouge. Obviously dressed for company.

He slouched on the sofa in a sleeveless undershirt and no-color pants. Feet in worn slippers. Beside him, on a littered table, was an overflowing ash tray and a much-stained coffee cup. His hair, the fringe left around his balding head, was a fading orange.

He rose, but not all the way, to shake the hand David offered. He waved David to an armchair.

"Sorry," he pointed generally to himself, "but I'm retired. Don't dress for nobody."

His wife made a noise and fluttered a hand at him.

"My wife, Gladys." He indicated the woman with a dismissing wave of his hand. "Don't know how I can help you on Detroit killings when the cops here can't even find the bastard what killed my granddaughter. Seems like you fellows do better to work together on these things 'stead of separate, like you do. Just makes me sick, thinking of that bastard out there, maybe killin' other girls." He paused to shake his head. Gladys dabbed at her eyes with a lace-edged handkerchief. David jumped in to ask his questions before the man really wound himself up. Got so mad he'd throw him out of the house.

"You ever hear of an Alfred Williams? Black man? 'Bout your age?" David asked. The man's tongue stopped as if paralyzed. He met David's eye but didn't say a word, lips still parted to form the next complaint.

"Alfred Williams," David leaned forward, repeating.

Fred Gibonski gulped air for a minute and sat back against the sofa, diminishing in size.

He thought then shook his head. "No, can't say I ever heard of 'im. Course I've met a lot of men in my time. Lot of 'em. No provin' that I never met the man, but right off I'd say no, never knew 'em."

"Odd." David let the single word hang there in the semi-darkness, unexplained. The man and woman gave each other a swift look before returning their eyes to David.

"What do you mean, odd?"

David shrugged. "Just that this Alfred Williams says he knows you, from old days together as union organizers."

The man frowned and then smiled a little. "Really? Well what do you know. Guess I might have met him at some time if he says so. Don't remember all the men I met."

"Alfred Williams is the grandfather of a little boy who was also murdered. He thought it was odd that you both had family members murdered and both worked for the union."

"Well, say now, you know how many men are with one union or another? I'd say almost all around here."

"But he says there was another one, father of Esther Shell. Girl was murdered in Detroit. Says he was in the union at the same time and that all three of you worked together."

"No kidding." Fred reached for a cigarette, put it between his lips then pulled it away, spitting tobacco strands and pulling paper from where it had stuck to his dry lips. He jabbed it back into his mouth, lit it. "Don't remember the names. But what's this got to do with my granddaughter's murder?"

David shrugged. This was the question he dreaded. He had no answer for the man.

"Just looking for any connection, maybe some union connection," David braved it out.

"This Shell girl," Mrs. Gibonski opened her mouth. "She the black girl killed a few months back? The one killed by her husband's friend. What could her murder have to do with the other two? I don't understand."

Another unanswerable.

"We don't know," David fell back into evasiveness. "Just don't want to miss any connection here. Now, Mr. Gibonski, while you were in the union did you ever hear of a guy named Small? I believe it was Donald Small. You ever hear that name?"

The reaction was immediate. The man's face blanched, eyes half-closing as if to keep emotion hidden.

"Small you say?" The words came slowly. "Why you askin' about this one?"

"Just another connection. Did you know him?"

Gibonski shook his head. "Nope. Never heard of him."

David stayed only a few more minutes, certain he would get nothing out of this man. But he was far from

satisfied with the answers. Obviously there was something
he wanted very much to hide. Or maybe, like the other
one—Williams—cops just made him nervous.

He drove back downtown along Jefferson Avenue,
taking his time, thinking.

He just couldn't leave it alone. Not like this. Nothing
to hang together but enough there to form a puzzle. All
his warning buzzers were sounding. These men both hid
something. What? What? And could it effect Mattie.

"That girl's got more to do with 'em than she's tellin'."
The old man's words circled round front and center
again.

Perhaps ask Mrs. Small. Jesus, but he hated to do
that. And for sure it would get back to Mattie. There was
enough getting between them now. This would be another
wedge. She would see it as disloyalty, even bitterness and
jealousy on his part.

No, he would put off seeing Mattie's mother until he
had no place left to go.

That meant Esther Shell's father. He was the next one
to try the names on.

The entrance to Belle Isle was just ahead and, on
impulse, David swung the car that way, crossing the old
balustraded bridge and circling right. At the casino he
parked, walking down to the canal beside the garbage
littered water.

Not many came here now. Not in early spring. But a
good place to walk, to think, to work out problems. He sat
on a bench and watched a popcorn box float past him on
the brown water. A skinny squirrel darted up and back,
approached obliquely to see what offering might be tendered,
then, finding none, ran up a nearby tree to swear.

See the Shell girl's father. Or maybe go talk to the
man who killed her—the husband's friend. And if there
was still nothing after all that he would drop it. He made
the deal with himself but continued sitting, watching the
dirty water.

I don't want to hurt her, he kept telling himself. But a
man can't ignore his conscience.

Chapter Eight

For a week there were no recurrences. She saw nothing of the child, though she watched constantly, never opened a door—to her apartment, to the street—without carefully checking first.

She began to relax, even to laugh at herself, at her inordinate fear of some pathetic kid who'd probably developed a case of hero worship. Who knows? she asked herself one evening, maybe the kid's family moved near here, too. And the kid spotted her one day, recognized her as someone from the old neighborhood, and decided to hang around.

She was alone in the apartment. Getting to be unusual, her being alone. More and more she was surrounding herself with people. David almost always there. And Bobby—planning, planning, always planning. She thought of him and laughed. He worked hard. Never lied to her. Never flattered—damn him. All right out in the open. Strange man.

She was still trying to find the blond girl. In her hands, twisted around her fingers was a gold necklace with tiny gold lock and key. It belonged to the kidnapped girl, delivered to Mattie by a devastated father. She was going to try again. Hoped to receive some clue as to where she was being kept. Something that would help locate her before she was murdered.

The chair, placed before the window so she could concentrate on a single star in the night sky, was comfortable, relaxing. Slowly, muscle by muscle, limb by limb, she told her body to relax, felt the tautness melt, even felt the skin of her forehead soften and clear away frown lines, felt her lungs expand and contract and slow, was aware—almost simultaneously—of every muscle, every pumping vein, every artery of her body—slowing, relaxing, controlling....

Counting backwards from sixty, telling herself silently between numbers that she was going deeper and deeper into a trance, she felt the familiar darkness begin to encompass her. Languidly her eyes closed as she welcomed the deepening chasm in her awareness, slid unafraid into the state she sought.

But something irritated, scratched at her waning consciousness, tore into the warm cocoon wrapping itself around her. It nagged, snapped her mind awake.

A sound. Coming from somewhere in the apartment. Somewhere...

She shook herself. Sat forward in the chair. Alert and listening now. Nerves surfacing like antennae.

A gentle, quiet knocking...

But from where?

She listened.

The front door, of course.

Irritated, she pushed back the chair and hurried across the living room.

Her hand went out to grasp the knob releasing the lock when she froze.

The timid knock came again. Then came the sound of breathing, as if someone out of breath rested against the door panel.

Waiting for another knock, mesmerized by the deep even breaths just a half-inch away, Mattie almost missed the added sound, the tiny-voiced whisper. It repeated. This time she heard it clearly.

"Martha." Whatever was outside the door was calling her by name in a childish, fluted tremor. "Martha. Let me in." The voice was pathetic. It pleaded.

As if frozen, Mattie stood motionless on her side of the door, hands braced against the wood, horror crawling over her skin as the voice continued to call her name, begged her to open the door between them.

Unable to stand any more, Mattie screamed at the thing: "Go away, for God's sake. Leave me alone!" at the top of her lungs. She held her breath, listened. For a while there was silence. Nothing moved beyond the door.

Then, with suddenness, the door moved, shook as if being struck with a hammer.

"You let me in! You let me in! You let me in...."

Mattie ran, turned and ran as fast as she could; had to be away from it; escape.

She slammed the bedroom door behind her, frantically pushed a bureau across her to hold it closed, then crawled into bed, covering her ears with her hands, then with the pillows. Anything to shut out that hideous voice still calling insistently: "MARTHA! LET ME IN!"

"How about the Southfield Hadassah?" Bobby was hunched over a legal pad making notes and lists. "Break your talk in before you get to Miami. Be a good audience."

"And you help me with the talk?" She was pacing in front of the window, nervously looking out at the sailboats maneuvering around long, cigar-shaped ore carriers headed up toward the Soo locks. She checked her watch and looked expectantly toward the door. It didn't take Bobby long to pick up on her nervousness.

"Boyfriend trouble again? Hope it's not me."

She shook her head.

Bobby shrugged. "Good. Too much ahead of us for petty business. Hey, you sure are fidgety. What the hell's up anyway?"

Mattie shrugged and walked over to collapse into a chair.

"Bad night." She mumbled something more.

"You look like hell."

"Don't I know it." She gave him a look that emphasized the circles beneath her wide eyes.

"Want to talk about it? Or is it personal?"

"No. No." She reached quickly for her coffee cup on the table between them, drank some of the cold liquid, and set the cup back. "Maybe I should tell you... at least a part of it. Really business, I guess. That girl. The one I've been trying to find. I think I found her last night. A dream. I had a dream after...well..."

She put both hands up to support her head, weariness and pain draining the little strength she had left.

He sat forward, to the edge of his chair, and leaned toward her.

"Yeah? Where? Is she alive? Hey, this will make a great story."

"I don't know if she's alive. I saw the house—one of those old brick houses, you know, built close together, high porch all across the front. And there was a main street and a huge golden star. A street sign said Gratiot—clearly, very clearly—and then the gold star and an alley and the house, with a purple door...."

"And?"

"And nothing."

"Didn't you see the girl?"

She let her head fall back against the chair, eyes closed. "No. And I'm afraid, Bobby."

"Afraid? Of what?" Impatience crossed his face.

"When I see the outside, the person is dead. Every time so far."

"But you don't know that."

"I feel it."

"So, what have you done? Called the police?"

She nodded. "I called David's office. He wasn't in yet. They're trying to locate him. He'll be right over when he hears."

"But why wait?" Bobby stood up, rocking on the balls of his feet. "Let's go looking. Save time. We'll call him when we find the place."

"I...I can't." Her eyes were wide open. "I've always gone with David."

"Listen." He was shrugging on his suit jacket. "If we go I can call the newspapers as soon as we find the house. Get the story in with the news that she's found. Maybe a picture of you this time—on the scene. Come on."

"But...no...what if she's dead? It'll be like taking advantage. I..."

"Look." He towered above her, bent slightly forward at the waist, almost menacing her. "You're either in this game or out of it. You want to be known everywhere for your divining, or you don't. Tell me which it is 'cause I'm getting tired of this reluctant virgin bit. Hey, no..." his hands went up as he saw she was upset with him, "I mean it. We either jump in right now and do it right or I'm walking out. My time's too valuable for this shit."

Anger activating her, she moved up to face him but wilted as he stood resolute. She had come too far already—

in expectations, dreams, in desire—ever to slip backward. She didn't dare chance it. Her angry expression melted, replaced by a sheepish smile and a toss of her head.

"Come on," she said.

"Nothing yet?" he asked as both pair of eyes swept from one side of Gratiot to the other.

She shook her head.

Old abandoned warehouses—one after another. Boarded buildings. Occupied buildings with doorways protected by heavy metal grates. Pawn shops. A few seedy discos. Nothing familiar. Nothing leaping in memory from that miasma of dream. No golden star.

She was weighted down with fear that the girl would be dead. "Why couldn't I have seen the outside of the place before?" she finally said aloud. "Why can't I save them? I don't understand a God who gives a gift like this. It's sick. Sick."

Bobby looked over at her, but said nothing. He let her calm down. After a while he changed the subject.

"There," she interrupted him, pointing at a large golden star stuck on scaffolding on the roof of one of the antique buildings. She sucked in her breath.

Gold Star Bakery, the sign beneath the star said.

"Down here?" he asked, indicating the side street as he wheeled across traffic and signalled a left.

"Yes," she answered, gulped breath as if she would drown.

He turned, cutting in between cars which honked their outrage.

A sidestreet of old brick houses with wide, roofed porches across the front. An alley...

The purple door.

She pointed, crying out.

He called the number she gave him. Then he called the newspapers.

The police cars—four of them—arrived just as the reporters' and cameramen's van pulled into the curb across from the house with the purple door.

David ran up to her, concern and anger fighting on his face.

"Why this?" He leaned in toward her, indicating the newsmen standing in the street awaiting the police action, one cameraman idly shooting film of a manhole.

Before Mattie could answer, Bobby leaned across.

"My doing. Sorry. Just thought she should get the credit first-hand this time." He was smiling up at David.

"Great." David tore away from the car, running to join the two other detectives approaching the house, guns drawn.

Four of the uniformed men were on the front porch knocking. One kicked in the purple door and they rushed inside. The detectives had gone around back. It was suddenly very quiet in the street.

Mattie could feel the pressure of her heartbeat at her temples. Strangely at one with the car, with the scene through the window, and with the silence, she sat motionless as if frozen in place.

When Bobby opened his door the unexpected movement startled her. She brought her hands up to her breast as if to hold her heart from leaping through.

"I'm going to go talk to the reporters. Let 'em know you're here."

"Not now," she breathed, reaching to hold him back.

"Yes, now." He ignored her, getting out and slamming the door, creating a thunderclap in that uncanny stillness.

She watched as if she were home watching television. Bobby advanced, shook hands, turned and pointed. Notebooks came out, men spoke. Finally one cameraman advanced toward the car only to be stopped by movement from the house. Two cops galloped down the front steps to their cars. The newsmen converged.

Soon more police were coming out, cameras were whirring and clicking, reporters talked over each other.

Bobby was somewhere in the middle of all of them. Mattie stayed in the car watching.

From the center of the maelstrom, David walked out, toward her.

She didn't really need to ask. His face told everything.

He opened the car door, slid in under the wheel, and looked at her. His face seemed to be alive with twitches and tics. His teeth were clenched so hard his jaw appeared frozen.

Before she could say anything to him, he broke, hands slapping the wheel to cover his despair.

"I can't stand anymore of it." His voice was taut, cruel. "I just can't take it. Not another one dead. I knew it. I knew it when we went in there. I just knew it." He hunched over the wheel, fighting for control.

She didn't dare touch him. Pity would only hurt him right now. He needed time to overcome the pain.

So involved was she with his sorrow she had no time to take cognizance of her own. But it was there. Waiting.

"You've got to try harder next time," he was saying. "Try to find them before this happens. See the murderer beforehand. Something more than what we have been doing."

The attack not only surprised her, but threw her into confusion; she didn't know which emotion to deal with first: pity, sorrow, anger.

David was looking toward her, his face still flushed, eyes focused in an accusatory stare.

"And I don't think you should be going off on any tours. Not when your work here is so important. You've got to put more effort into early divining. Or even into seeing the murderer. That's your gift. Not public speaking." He shook his head, turned to where a group of detectives were gathered in front of the house. "I'd better go back." He made a move to get out. "You go on home. Wait for me there."

"I can't," she choked out. "Bobby is talking to the newspapers. I'll have to wait."

His head snapped toward her. "They'll want pictures of you. He'll exploit this girl's death just to get your name spread around."

"I did find her, David." Her voice was controlled, very low. She smiled ever so slightly.

"For what purpose? For this?" He swept a hand up to indicate the milling people in the street. "Or because you've been given an extraordinary power to use to help people?"

"I don't have a label for it. I just know it works. And the more who know about me, the more I can help."

"You sound just like him." He lifted his chin, indicating Bobby, who was approaching with reporters in tow.

"Maybe because what he says is true. Just maybe he has my best interests in mind more than you do," she snapped back at him. "At least he doesn't blame me when the body is found. As if I had some part in the death. Or could have done something about it."

They looked directly into each other's eyes, a great deal of anger playing between them.

"I didn't mean to sound as if I blamed you." He tried to take her hand. She pulled away. "I was just upset. You know I didn't mean..."

"Losing your faith, David? Didn't take long did it?"

"No," he denied, shaking his head. "Nothing like that. It's just..."

"Just?" She waited. He said nothing more, only looked at her.

Bobby was at the car. The reporters began questioning her as David opened the door. Then he was gone and photographers surrounded her.

Chapter Nine

"David? No. I haven't seen him today. Is this Martha? Well, hello. Such a long time since you came to dinner. And now David says maybe you two will get married, eh? That's nice. But you should come to visit more. Families should stay close, don't you think? Oh—I saw by the six o'clock news that you helped find another dead body. Tsk, tsk— such a shame. So young." David's mother's voice droned on and on, painfully loud through the phone.

"Just tell him I called," Mattie finally said, hanging up.

She walked over to her desk, intent on forgetting about him, intending to take care of some bills, make a list of clothes she would need for her first big tour trip to Florida—but he wouldn't stay out of her mind.

She needed him. Badly. If only he would get over his reservations about her psychic ability, about Bobby, and move in here.

I would be safe then, she told herself, and paced a narrow path across her living room.

Nothing could get at me if he were here. If only...

She was glad to be going down to Florida for a while. Do her good, she knew, to get away, needed the rest. Nerves. Bad nerves. Eyes playing tricks. Ears playing tricks—whispering, always whispering in corners...

The apartment no longer pleased her as it once had.

I'll find a new place when I get back, she promised herself as she paced, nervously rubbing her hands together. She had even considered moving back with Harriet. It was what Uncle John wanted. And she wouldn't be alone then....

If only David weren't changing so.

She loved him. But he wanted to make her doubt. He'd been so sincere about his reverence for her gift before, as if he'd actually believed he was the keeper of the flame and if he ceased to watch over her the divination would stop, her visions darken. Now, since Bobby, his doubts were growing until he frightened her.

Why was he treating her as if she were a guilty party when she used her power?

And what of Bobby's cynicism? His emphasis on money? His slick machinations—could that destroy the gift too?

The doorbell interrupted her thoughts. She stopped pacing to hold very still without breathing, waiting, fearing that voice.

Finally she crossed to the door and with words catching asked, "Who is it?"

She wanted it to be David, was surprised at her own disappointment when Bobby answered.

"Hi." He strode right in. "Knew you'd be up to catch the eleven o'clock news. How'd you like the six o'clock? See channel seven? Really gave it the air time, didn't they? You can't buy that kind of time, you know? Not for any money. Better than pure gold. And still better—the wire services picked it up. Story in all across the country."

He plunked himself on the sofa, arms spread out across the back. "Told you I'd make you famous, baby."

"Or infamous." She closed the door, first checking the hall out of habit.

"No more of that stuff now." Bobby's voice was harsh. When she looked around toward him, she could see his face set in lines of paternal displeasure, his chin stuck out, beard bristling. "We've got a job to do."

She knew she should protest, but she was too tired to care. With a dismissive shrug, she joined him on the sofa.

"Wanted to discuss a few more ideas with you. Figured I might as well get right on 'em."

When the phone rang, he clucked his tongue in displeasure as she got up to answer.

"Mattie?" David. "Mother said you called."

"Of course I called." She was immediately angered at the distance in his voice. "Why aren't you here? You knew I would be expecting you. I need you here with me. Please, David, I really need you."

"Just too tired to go over it all again tonight." His voice did sound weary. "You know where I stand. Seems to me the next move is up to you."

"You mean give up any plans to spread word of my power? Give in to you completely? Is that it?"

"Now, Mattie," his voice hesitated. "Don't put it that way. You know how much I love you. We have something very special. I just can't stand to have us destroyed, that's all. What kind of man..."

"Mattie," Bobby called from the bar where he was noisily mixing a drink. "I don't have much time and I'd like to get these things worked out tonight."

There was a pause at the other end of the line as David heard the voice and the words. Mattie knew instinctively that Bobby's presence here, now, somehow made things much worse. There was a fleeting thought at the back of her mind that Bobby knew this would happen when he dropped in. But there were too many words and emotions to be juggled to give this much more than a second's thought.

"That guy's there, isn't he?" David's voice was ice-hard.

"Yes, but only..."

"You just can't see what he's doing to you, can you? Wringing gold out of a miracle like some cursed Judas and you're playing right along. You better wake up, Mattie. Before it's too late for all of us."

The phone went dead. She put down the receiver and turned to confront Bobby, smugly sipping a Scotch and leaning back against the bar. The phone rang again.

Hoping it was David and they could now talk this whole mess out, she grabbed up the receiver.

"Martha? Eh... Mattie? It's me, Patsy. How ya doing?" The diffident voice seemed to strain through the phone, reaching out to touch Mattie in some intimate, encircling way.

"Oh—Patsy." She rolled her eyes at Bobby. "I..."

"Caught you on the news tonight and in the papers. God—that's really something, ain't it?"

"Look, Patsy, I'm really kind of busy..."

"Sure," the voice faded, dropped slightly. "I figured you would be. It was just that I read where you're going on tour and I wondered if you'd made up your mind about that job as secretary yet."

"Look, Patsy," Mattie's irritation and impatience wouldn't be suppressed any longer. "I never promised you that job. And I've been telling you all along that you just don't have the right qualifications...."

"But I've been going to night school," the voice rose on a note of hope again. "It was a surprise. I been studying shorthand."

"Patsy," Mattie sighed in desperation. "I need someone with a lot more skills than just shorthand."

"Well like what?"

"Like I just don't care to discuss it now. I'm busy and I'm just not about to hire a secretary on the spur of the moment." All patience gone, Mattie tapped her foot, caring little what she said. She just wanted to get rid of her.

There was a pause on the other end of the line. Mattie hoped Patsy had hung up, but her voice came again.

"Tolly's gone." The words were little more than a choked whisper. "He's gone, Mattie. Said he wanted to try in New York. He's gone. For good. I asked if I could write him, but he said he was no good at letter writing, but if he ever got back to Detroit he'd look me up. Just like that. As if we didn't have nothing between us. Just like that."

Mattie sensed the pain in Patsy's voice. She bit her lip and closed her eyes tightly. She had so much pain of her own to handle, why should she be saddled with this now too? But yet, she couldn't just turn her back on a friend....

"Maybe he'll be back, Patsy. Don't be sad," she tried to put genuine concern in her voice.

"You know what that means? Back to those guys from the bar. And the way things were before Tolly. Nothing." She gulped and sniffed. "Do you think I could come down and see you, Mattie? I really need a friend right now."

"Oh," Mattie hesitated, disconcerted by this additional demand on her. "Well... I'd like to see you, Patsy, really, but my PR man is here and we're working on future plans and..."

"Gee—sorry. Why didn't you tell me before?" The voice was flustered. Unlike Patsy. "I'm sorry I interrupted. No, of course I won't bother you. But let's get together real soon. We were always so close. Remember how I used to tease the old ladies and how you..."

"I'm really busy, Patsy," she cut in. "I'd like to talk but... you understand."

"Sure. That's O.K."

"But we must make it very soon. That's a promise," Mattie said brightly, already bending toward the phone cradle.

"Sure." The voice on the other end was drifting away as if that mind, too, was already elsewhere. "Soon."

As Mattie hung up, she looked over to Bobby, who winked broadly and put up two fingers in a V for victory.

"Now you're learnin'," he complimented Mattie. "Now you're learnin'."

Chapter Ten

"Martha, let me in."

The voice whined against the door. The words were tentacles worming their way through cracks to slide into her head, torture her mind.

"Go away," Mattie whispered from her chair. Her hands gripped the arms, nails digging into the fabric. She stared toward the door, watched it move inward as it received another kick.

"No! I won't go away." The child's voice strengthened. She began to laugh. "I can get in anyway, if you let me or not. Yes, I can. I can do anything I want. And you can't stop me."

"Go away." Now it was Mattie whose voice failed her. "Who are you? What do you want? Why do you keep bothering me?"

"Martha!" The child's voice was hurt, disappointed. "Don't you know me?"

"No. No, I don't. Go away you awful little girl. Just leave me alone."

Laughter peeled against the door, then away, down the hallway, and silence.

As soon as she could control her trembling fingers, Mattie picked up the phone and dialed.

"Lilith?" Mattie grasped the phone with both hands, hugged it to her. "This is Mattie Small. Remember? Tolly Pritchard's friend?"

"Yes. Surely. I remember you." The voice sing-songed the words back at her over the wire. "You are the diviner, the one who locates the dead."

Mattie hesitated. "Could...could I come see you today?" Her voice quavered. "Something is happening. I don't know what to do."

"But of course. Come right away," the Jamaican voice lulled. "I will try to help you."

The shop was exactly as it had been, with Lilith, large, solid, waiting in the middle, hands on ample hips, face worried as she took note of a thinner, harried-looking Mattie.

"Something is after you that's for sure," she greeted Mattie. "Something bad. Very, very bad."

She made a motion toward the floor with one plump hand and sank to a sitting position, patting the floor for Mattie to join her.

"Something else is happening. What is it?"

"There's a child, Lilith. I don't even know if this child is real but it's after me, after me more and more."

"Shhh…" she calmed Mattie who was growing hysterical. "What kind of child is it?"

"A little girl. About four or five." Mattie gulped air and attempted to control herself. "You're gonna think I'm crazy but I used to see her going to school when I lived with my mother. Now I've moved miles from there and the child turned up, waiting on the corner for me."

Lilith shrugged. "Coincidence? Probably nothing more."

"No, listen," Mattie begged her attention. "The girl is in my building now. She rings my doorbell, knocks on the door, demands to be let in."

"Have you called the police? Your doorman?"

"I…I don't think anyone but me can see her." Mattie sucked in air as the words came out. It was the first time she'd admitted this fear, even to herself.

Lilith said nothing, merely raising her eyebrows in surprise, and carefully studying Mattie's face.

"She's so bold now. She pounds on my door. But no one else seems to hear. Not one neighbor has complained. And it gets so loud." Mattie's heart was skipping beats, she put a hand to her chest to quiet it. "At first she was so shy. Now she's awful. It's gotten so bad that I'm…I'm afraid of her. If I open that door as she asks, I just know something terrible will happen."

"Hmmm." Lilith considered the problem then shut her eyes and remained silent. When she opened them she stared directly at Mattie. Lifting her hands she moved them over and around Mattie's head without touching her. She ran them down Mattie's arms the same way, ran them in front of her, again and again. She then returned her hands to her lap, watching Mattie closely as she waited.

"I remember now. Your tarot cards gave me trouble. Some blockage, as if the cards told too many futures." Her voice was husky, deepened by the concern shining in her eyes. "There is still something here I do not understand. Something beyond my skill to discover. But I will try to help you. Wait. I want to read something to you. Something that is important."

She rose to her feet gracefully, her robe swinging rhythmically. She went to one of the book shelves and returned with a large book cradled against her chest. She began to thumb through it, dark eyes squinting as she searched.

"Ah, here. Maybe this is a clue to your problem. The author is discussing how psychic powers are not always the exclusive province of deserving people. Evil ones may possess them too. And they may direct their evil powers with what this book calls a beam of psychic malevolence."

She looked meaningfully at Mattie and closed the book.

"Your child could be this beam directed at you by someone who wants to hurt you."

"But who? There's no one. I can't think of anyone at all who could hate me like that. And I don't know anyone with the kind of power you're talking about..."

"Then we must act without knowing. Someone has turned this power loose on you. Many times the form of a child is taken. But it is not the child which threatens, it is the one whose power manifests that child." She rose again, going to a side table where she rummaged through her possessions, returning with one of the black candles. One formed as a woman.

"Since this thing takes the form of a girl-child, I think it is a woman who is after you. To combat her you must take these—" she held up two small bottles of oil, one tinted blue, the other red. "Tonight you will anoint the candle with these oils and light it. You must then meditate on the child. You must wish her gone. See her gone. In your mind—visualize. Send her away!"

Lilith's voice deepened again, took on a dramatic emphasis that she punctuated with a flinging motion of her arms.

"Will . . . will that end it? Will the child leave me alone then?" Mattie, wide-eyed, curls unkempt, leaned toward Lilith as if to draw strength.

"That will end it, my dear." Lilith's eyes lighted briefly on her before turning away. "Unless it is something else."

"Something else? What?"

"Something I cannot help you with." She turned away, made a move to get up, but Mattie held on to her arm, forcing her to stay, face her again.

"What do I do if it doesn't work?" Terror was written in every line, every darkening circle of Mattie's face. "I'm so afraid of it . . . her. Who else can help me?"

A look of sympathy crossed Lilith's plush features. But all she did was shrug. "Only God. Only God can help you if my power is too weak."

"But what will happen? What will happen to me?"

Lilith didn't answer. She got to her feet and with surprising coolness bid Mattie good-bye.

Chapter Eleven

The Atlantic Ocean was a deeper blue than she had ever imagined it could be. From the plane she looked down on mile after mile of open water and a hot sun splashing off the clean white hotels along Miami's oceanfront.

Never having been anywhere before, Mattie was like a child in her excitement, peering out the window, holding on to Bobby's arm with the death-grip she had applied at Metro Airport in Detroit and had not loosened yet.

"It's gorgeous!" She looked away long enough to beam at him. "I just can't believe anybody down there will ever have heard of me or want to listen to me speak."

"Don't worry," he said. "I've seen to that. There've been stories in the papers about you all week, flyers around college campus, plenty of notices, radio spots. Don't worry, there may not be a brass band at the airport, but I guarantee there'll be requests for interviews, radio shows. You'll do fine."

"You sure?" She turned her large eyes on him, afraid now that she was not good enough, poised enough, to handle this kind of thing. Movie stars and hotshot celebrities gave interviews for a living, not supermarket cashiers. Could she handle it?

"Sure, baby. You had that Hadassah in the palm of your hand, didn't you? They ate it right up. I tell you, you've got a natural feel for giving people what they want. Those women wanted gory details—you gave 'em blood and guts. They wanted to be moved with stories of children found and you gave it to 'em."

Tossing her head with a short, scoffing laugh, Mattie said, "You wrote the damned thing."

"Yeah, but it was in the delivery. All in the delivery." He settled back for the landing, a wide grin across his face.

Miami and Miami Beach were like a stage-set for a Disney movie. So spotlessly clean and polished and unreal. After Detroit, Collins Avenue could have been that golden street the European immigrants always sought. But...gold leotards and tennis shoes! Wedgies with rhinestone heels! A male in pink suit, maroon silk shirt open to his belt buckle, which itself was a joy to behold— mother-of-pearl spelling: FLORIDA.

She poked Bobby, who was intent on transporting the luggage from the care of the limo driver to the care of a bellman. He looked at the people she pointed to and laughed.

"That's nothing. Transplanted New Yorkers in drag."

Minutes after she was settled in her hotel room, the phone rang. Mattie hoped it would be David, but it was a reporter requesting an interview. Bobby told him to come on up.

Three more times while the reporter was there the phone rang. Each time Mattie expected it would be David and only half heard the reporter's questions as she tried to listen to Bobby's responses.

Gulping scotch and soda to slake her thirst, after a time she found she was beginning to unwind, to ignore the phone and the hope she had riding on each call. It was as if the muscles all along her body suddenly relaxed. She lay back in the chair and let Bobby order another bottle and more ice and soda, taking an even larger, deep amber drink.

She dared to close her eyes a moment, balancing the glass in her lap. Her mind roamed. It wasn't a trance. No—more freeing than those pinpointing, nose-to-earth searches. A phantasmagoria of busy colors shaping spear-like flashes behind her eyes. Good to see nothing. A twenty-first century stage curtain of intersecting lasers. NO SHOW TODAY. Hooray! Mind freed from hunting images imposed by the *in extremis* fears of the dying. Good to have mind freed. Child gone.

It *was* gone. Hadn't been seen, or heard, since that day she went to Lilith's shop and came home to burn the candle, feeling silly and superstitious. Still she had burned it. Gladly. Even praying over it as the wax fell and the flame deformed the image. With eyes squeezed shut, determined to rid herself of this thing, this child, this succubus, she pictured the little girl and sent her to hell. She visualized the small body burning, writhing in agony just as the fire consumed the twisting wax.

It had worked. For days Mattie would not allow herself to believe her gone, but the child hadn't appeared again. The freedom from fear made Mattie euphoric.

She felt a hand on hers, bringing her thoughts back to the hotel room. She felt the glass being eased out from her fingers and then she felt as if she were floating. Being carried up and away. Up and away. Up and...a... way....

So good. Mindless. She let go of all thought and let the alcohol have her....

*   *   *

Bobby stirred and moved slightly beside her on the bed. A sick feeling in the bottom of her stomach made her fear to think beyond a need to visit the bathroom.

Clothes still all on, she noted with relief. Rumpled, but still there.

And he was dressed. Right down to his Gucci loafers.

All right. Everything all right. She moved, jostling Bobby who rolled toward her, one of his arms moving and falling directly across her breasts.

"Jesus," she swore under her breath. Who wanted him waking in this position? Embarrassing for both of them. But how to move. To get out from under this pinioning arm without disturbing him.

She edged over, getting one foot on the floor. With that leg pushed against the bed she had some leverage, but as she attempted to slide out from under his grip, the arm moved, the hand slid directly over her right breast, resting over the crown.

Suddenly the hand closed tightly, even painfully on her breast, and the man beside her gave a deep chuckle.

"Tryin' to get away, eh?" He rolled up on his side to look gleefully down into her startled face. He had been awake all along, playing a game. Making a fool of her.

She looked up into his eyes, crinkled with malicious laughter. A deep, instinctive fear moved through her. A fear screaming warnings about this laugh, this look, and her vulnerability.

Again she attempted to roll out from under his grasp. He squeezed tighter and laughed until she could not catch her breath.

"Since I'm gonna make a star of you, what say I make you first?" His breath was thick and slid fuzzily off her cheek.

"Let me go." Her teeth were clenched, were ready to snap if necessary. "Or you'll be making a star out of somebody else pretty quick."

He released her, laughing as he rolled away. "Ooooh, threats. You need me. And you do want to make it big, don't ya, Mattie? Want it bad. I'll bet you can see your name in headlines already."

From the bathroom doorway she turned, saying, "I don't want it quite as bad as you seem to think. There is a line, Bobby. Don't cross it again or I'll drop this whole goddamned business right now and go back to David. All your help sure hasn't made me any happier. So what good is it?" She was controlled and thoughtful. "And you watch who the hell you pull your tricks on. You hear? You're an employee, you bastard you. Just a lousy employee."

He laughed again, uncaring, arms up, hands tucked under his head.

It was unbearable. Unthinkable that he would mock her, laugh as he was doing. She must be crazy, she thought. Completely crazy. Why was she here anyway? Why was she allowing him to treat her like this. He had to be stopped. Shut up....

The nearest thing to hand was a green vinyl Gideon's Bible. She grabbed it up and heaved it at him, striking him a hollow thump on the rib cage.

As she turned to hunt the next, more damaging thing to throw, he leaped from the bed and grabbed her, turning her toward him and pinioning her arms to her side. The laugh was gone, replaced with an angry scowl, lips parted and pulled back with the exertion of holding her as she kicked and bit at him.

He forced her backward until the edge of the bed hit the back of her knees and she fell with him on top of her. They lay there glaring at each other.

As her anger subsided and her body relaxed, his tautened, pressing tightly against the hump of her.

"Nothing like a good workout before a good fuck," he whispered warmly down into her face.

"Unless this is a rape, all you're getting is the workout." She pushed at him and he rolled quickly away from her.

They stood up, staring at each other. Finally she walked into the bathroom, shutting the door behind her.

When she came out, he was on the phone. He left soon after without another word between them.

She should have said more, she told herself when he had gone. Fired him. Told him off.

But he was right. She did want what he offered. The specter of Patsy's life and Koch's supermarket were too frightening. Any hope of avoiding those dark shadows of imminent possibility was worth holding on to. At any cost.

Any cost at all.

Chapter Twelve

"Morning, Sergeant," the portly duty officer greeted David and stood to escort him down the long, green hallway.

"Lieutenant," David corrected then smiled in embarrassment and shrugged, waiting to follow the man.

"Promotion, eh? Congratulations. Been breakin' a lot of big cases lately, I hear. Good for you." The man moved with a side-to-side roll down to a metal door. He knocked. They stood waiting, David wanting to get this over, never having learned to take trips here, to the Wayne County Jail, for granted. Always ill at ease, no matter that he might be here two, three times a week. It was the gray stone walls, metal bars at the windows. He had only to walk in, hear the first lock click behind him, and he started to sweat as if he were trapped.

The door opened. David walked in and took a seat at the long, metal table, grained to imitate wood. Chairs of cheap, green vinyl. Tile floor—white and black—scarred, marred by dark lines made by synthetic heels—nervous feet scuffing back and forth, back and forth.

Depressing place. David settled himself, hands clasped before him on the cold table.

"Be bringing him directly," the officer in charge informed him. David nodded as answer. The man returned to his chair, picking up the *Police Magazine* he was reading.

Quiet in here. A wall clock ticked. That noise would drive him crazy, he knew. Especially if he had years to go. Drive him crazy.

All time seemed to hang heavy right now.

Mattie was gone, down in Florida, and the city was strangely empty without her there to call, without her voice on the phone, needing him.

Funny how that worked. Missing her one minute,

mad and jealous the next. Down there with *him*. The two of them. And she such an innocent. Like the sacrificial lamb—Mattie, and that Sanderson guy. He knew what that one was. No illusions. A user. He would use Mattie every way he could until there was nothing left to use. And she was falling for it.

With the jealousy came anger and a certain freedom from the pain of missing her. It also brought objectivity about her and the gift. And about the investigation he was carrying on without her knowledge. He'd been feeling guilty, going on with it behind her back. Now that she was gone his conscience eased a little, enough anyway to let him ask for this visit with Gary Jones, the man who murdered Esther Shell.

The trial was just over. Guilty beyond question. That much was settled anyway.

Another door was opened. They brought the young black man into the room, indicated that he should sit across from David.

Thin, with delicate features: high-ridged nose, finely outlined lips, soft, almost feminine eyes with long lashes—Gary Jones didn't fit any preconceived idea of a murderer. There was a look to most murderers, a cockiness, coarseness that David had come to expect. None of that was evident here. Looked like a nice kid. Just a nice ordinary kid.

David introduced himself. Shook hands. The man's head dipped down; he kept it that way and waited.

Twenty-four years old, David knew. The bowed head showed hair bravely corn-rowed, black welts of knotted hair down wide beige rows.

Whipped. Beaten. Subdued. Not literally, but the system did that. No fight left. Trial could have flattened him. Or memories of murder.

"I wanted to talk to you about Esther Shell," David started, only to have the man make a show of disgust and turn away without looking up.

"Now wait—I'm not on the case or anything." David reached an arm across the table and held the man's fragile shoulder, reassuring him. "And anyway, the trial's over now."

The man mumbled something and David had to ask him to repeat it.

He glanced up, eyes filled with mistrust and anger.

"I said yeah, and I lost. Means prison. Hard time, man. Hard time."

"What did you expect? You killed the girl."

The eyes burned. "Sez you."

"And the evidence. And the jury." David let the word come out forcefully. Only way to deal with convicts, from a position of power. All they respected.

Gary Jones waited.

"I want to talk to you about Esther Shell because the name keeps coming up in other murder cases."

There was an immediate reaction. "You can't pin no more murders on me."

"Hold on," David quieted him. "That's not what I'm here for. I came to see you because some things have come up in these other cases that I don't understand. Now, don't get me wrong, there's nothing new that will get you off the hook on this one: there's just, well, a connection between Esther's father, Johnny Flash Gordon, and two other men he used to work with. All of 'em had children or grandchildren murdered. I'm just checking it out so I don't miss anything."

Jones thought a while, eyes avoiding David's. Finally he said, "My lawyer's going to appeal. I don't want to queer that by..."

"Off the record. I'm not assigned to your case. Just trying to fit everything together. See—no tape recorders, no stenographers. Nothing you say to me will go any further."

"Sure. The damned room's probably bugged."

"For what? Wouldn't be admissible evidence in court, and anyway Gary, you've already been tried and found guilty."

He sat in silence, thinking again before muttering. "What do you want to know?"

"You've got no previous record. I checked. Nothing against you. But you went down for murdering your buddy's wife. Why not leave the revenge to him? How come?"

"If only I knew the answer to that." He squirmed and shot David a sharp look before saying more. "Couldn't help it. Not my choice."

"Not your choice—to kill her? Hell, man, they all say that."

"Now look here, I'm tellin' the truth. You wanna listen? I tried tellin' those cops who picked me up. I tried tellin' my lawyer. And I tried tellin' that jury, but nobody wants to hear what happened. Nobody cares 'cause they think I'm lying. But I'm not, man. Not lying at all. If you want to hear about it then you gotta hear it all and let me tell it or—nothin'—I'm givin' you nothin'."

David stared back, skeptical, but nodded that he would listen.

"I saw her—Esther—with this Freddy guy, a big mother from the west side. But—shit, that was nothin' new. She was always messin' around on Davis. That's my friend, Davis Shell. He knew it. He catch her times and beat the livin' shit out of her, but she goes right back. Well, I see her standin' outside of this bar. That Freddy guy goes on in so I pull up and tell her to get in. Esther never was too hard to get along with. She just kinda laughed and gets in the car."

He stopped, assessed David's face, then went on.

"This is where it starts. Where I can tell you what happened but I can't say why. I never...never meant to hurt her. We was never like that. I always figured what was between her and Davis was their business. Not that I wanted to see her messin' up, but she knew she didn't have nothin' to be afraid of from me." He paused again and drew in air, as if each sentence was coming harder.

"Except this time. It was as soon as she got in my car. I never felt anything like that before in my life. Like something took me over, my mind, my body, my hands, and I was somebody else."

David started to say something but Jones raised a hand. "Let me tell it," he insisted and kept on. "I'll swear to you I didn't even have a beer that night. Never do drugs. A little weed back in high school but I stay away from that stuff now. Got a job. Well—had a job. Even takin' night classes in law enforcement. Gonna be a cop if I could." He stopped to let the irony of his ambition sit between them. "Anyway, as soon as Esther got in that car I felt hatred for her like I never had for no other human being. From that minute there was no way I wasn't gonna kill her."

"Tryin' for irresistible urge, huh?" David drew a breath and looked from the man's face, contorted from the effort of telling the story, eyes glistening with tears.

Gary was shaking his head. "I can't even put it into words, the way it was. I felt this pure hatred, like that was all there was in the world and nothin' could stop it. Pure hatred and I guess you could say pure evil."

The man shivered, waves of feelings shaking his small body. "Shit," he swore violently. "I wouldn't ever want to think that was me. Too awful. Too goddamned awful."

David nodded, silenced by the obvious pain the man was suffering.

"I'll tell you somethin' though." The face lightened a little. "Davis, her husband, my friend? He comes here to see me. Believes me too. He knows I wouldn'ta hurt Esther if that somethin' didn't come on me. See? Even Davis believes me."

Something wrong with the guy. Some disconnection in the brain probably. Terrible thing, but what did it really have to do with Mattie? David asked himself after the guard took Gary Jones back to his cell.

Nothing to do with Mattie. The guy killed Esther Shell, even admitted it. But not the others. So there were other murderers. Others perhaps suffering from similar disconnections in the brain that made killers of them. But that had nothing to do with the woman who found the bodies of their victims through her psychic power. Nothing.

He was relieved. Saddened for the man sitting in jail who thought himself innocent, but relieved anyway. He would stop now. Had done all anyone could expect of him. And Mattie was in the clear.

Chapter Thirteen

The cavernous lecture hall was a huge half-barrel in Toulouse-Lautrec blues and reds. Exposed metal beams formed an exoskeleton which the vivid colors were designed to mask but didn't.

The sound system, like all institutional sound systems, was bad. Mattie could hear her voice crackling through speakers imbedded in elbows of metal around the room.

Surprisingly—at least it surprised Mattie—the hall was full to S.R.O. Required attendance, she told herself. But the quality of the questions after her talk showed a familiarity with her and with her work.

Bobby had done his job. Done it well.

A tall thin boy with pimples stood to ask, "You call this a gift but in some ways it's a curse too, isn't it?" His voice cracked on the question.

Mattie was tempted to ignore him, go on to someone else. She dreaded this question, hated to think of her divining in terms of a curse. It had been so good for her, brought so much change into her life. And yet—perhaps.

"It could be a curse too, I suppose." She gripped the podium with both hands, still thinking. "But only if it is perverted. If I respect the gift, I'm sure it will bless me."

Not to dwell on this aspect of her gift, Mattie looked quickly away from the youth who still stood, expecting her to expand on her answer. She searched among the waving hands for a nice, innocuous face, a person who would ask one of the usual questions: How long have you known you were a psychic? How can a person develop these powers? —any one of the ten or twelve which she had ready answers for.

Earnest young faces, rows of them, all looking up toward her, waiting to be enlightened.

Her eyes searched the front rows. One blond girl was smirking—probably thought up some smart-ass question. To the side...by the bright blue wall...

Mattie sucked in her breath and held it, as if she could thus freeze the scene before her, stop it, erase it, and not let it become real.

The strawberry raincoat. A tiny, pensive face looking up with all the others.

Her heart began a rush of beating that made her feel faint. She put her hand out to clutch the podium, support herself so she wouldn't fall.

She was back. Had followed her to Florida. Not destroyed at all. Even more powerful. Their eyes met and Mattie felt herself being drained, losing control.

Had to get off the stage, get away.

"Excuse me, I'm...not feeling well," she leaned against the podium and mumbled into the microphone before stumbling off the stage and into Bobby's arms, polite applause following her.

"Get me out of here." She clutched at Bobby.

"Sure. Sure. Sick, eh? Too bad. But you did a good job. They got their money's worth." He put an arm around her and directed her toward the door. "You get back to the hotel, rest a little. You'll be O.K. Too much all at once. Too many people. We've got a late dinner with some locals but you'll be O.K. by then. Lay down awhile."

At the hotel he left her alone to rest. She had an hour to herself. But rest wasn't what she needed. To think, think clearly, incisively, comprehend what was happening to her—that's what she needed. She rubbed at her temples to ease the beginning ache, and longed for David, just to have him close, to have him protect her from this...this madness.

Lilith! She might be able to help. Maybe she had burned the candle at the wrong time, wrong place. Maybe there was some other ceremony that could rid her of the child.

In her bag. Lilith's number.

The woman answered her phone on the second ring.

"Lilith, this is Mattie Small." She fought to keep her voice steady. "I'm down in Miami and the child is here. She's come back. What can I do now?"

The line was silent. Finally Lilith drew a deep, uncomfortable breath. "I cannot help you anymore. That child is something I do not understand. Maybe black magic. I don't mess with black magic."

"Lilith, please." Mattie felt panic growing inside. She couldn't be left alone with this...this thing. She needed help. "Please help me. Am I losing my mind, is that what you're saying?"

"No." The word was slow in coming. Not reassuring. "But I do not know what it is. It might be evil. Could turn on me if I try to help you anymore. I know. I've seen things not to be explained. I would help you, yet..."

"Listen. Listen. Please." Mattie's voice was agonized. "It follows me. What is it? What can I do?"

"I am sorry, I don't know. Except, perhaps, well...no, I cannot say." Lilith's voice hesitated, she seemed eager to get off the phone.

"If you know something, Lilith, for God's sake tell me." Anger was seeping up through the panic.

"I know nothing. I can only make a guess. Maybe... maybe you have control of this child. Maybe it waits for you to direct it. Or maybe, it directs you."

Before Mattie could say more the line went dead.

A crushing headache borne of nerves and pressure was robbing her of desire to do any more than stay in her darkened hotel room. Only sleep could cure her, make her fit for another day of interviews, help her understand what was happening to her. But Bobby had a late dinner planned with some local celebrities to insure pictures would be taken and delivered to the newspapers. He came for her at seven. There was no getting back to her room for hours. By then her eyes were deeply ringed with circles and the pain and exhaustion left her unable to sleep until after two seconals and hours of tossing. And then the dream rushed forward.

Walls were gray. Cinder block. Machines—huge. Floor to ceiling. Set in long rows with men pulling and hauling and straining over levers that conveyed parts of things along narrow moving belts.

Even in that uncanny silence of dream, where reality

has no true relation to vision, these machines were terribly real, these men firmly related in motion and space to their huge automated servants: teams of men and machines in motion.

Factory walls. Factory dirt. Oil. Grease. Grime. Factory synchronous motion.

She was a fixed eye staring in. A convex lens recording as a man in dark blue shirt and pants walked past and out of her field of vision.

Slightly round and stooped, the figure was familiar.

And then the eye shifted. She was in a room lined with bins of metal things, set in rows and running up the walls. The blue outfitted man stooped over one of the bins. Reaching in, he pulled out metal parts, compared and discarded them—oblivious to her intruding eye.

She was not ready for what happened next.

With sudden, startling motion, the man jerked stiffly erect. In his back, dead center, like a painted bull's-eye, a round hole appeared—red and blue.

The man's head turned slowly, coming around toward her with the exaggerated movement of a marionette. The wide-opened eyes, slackened jaw, the look of fear and shock disrupted the face, but Mattie knew it at once. It should have been scowling, demanding to know if she was taking good care of her mother: Uncle John.

Mattie woke exhilarated, gasping for breath as if she had run a great distance. Wonderful! Wonderful!

No. No. Horrible! Horrible! She fought for control of her mind. It was as if she were the killer, standing behind him, firing shots at his back. Same view a murderer would have. But she had seen no one but Uncle John. No one.

Just a dream. Just a dream.

She sat up and turned on the light beside the bed. Two-thirty, the clock said.

Could she take the chance that this was only a dream? It had the vividness of her visions. Or could this be a prophecy?

She knew she would have to call home. Warn Harriet to warn Uncle John. Maybe someone at the plant with a grudge. He must be warned.

The phone rang a long time before Harriet's apprehensive voice answered.

"Mother, it's Mattie."

"What's wrong?"

"Nothing. Well—yes—something. I just had a terrible dream. Is Uncle John all right?"

Harriet sucked in her breath loudly. "John? Why yes, far as I know. What was the dream about?"

"Oh—well—just bad. Do you think you could call there and call me back. Just so I don't have to worry. Tell 'em I had a dream he got hurt at work and I want him to be careful—of anyone who might hurt him."

Her mother's voice timidly asked, "Was it a dream or one of those visions, Mattie?"

"I don't know. Just a dream, I think. Call, Ma, and call me back so's I don't worry. All right?"

"What'll I tell 'em?"

"Just what I told you."

"It's going to scare them to death." Harriet was reluctant, her voice thick and growing testy.

"Please, Ma. It's important."

"Well—O.K. I'll call you right back."

Mattie put the phone down slowly, not really wanting to sever connection with the woman and with ordinary life.

It should have been a matter of ten minutes at most. After twenty minutes, Mattie was too nervous to lie still. She got up and opened the drapes, but the starry dark only intensified her isolation. She paced from bed to TV set to window and back. No call.

Should she call again? What could be the matter? They wouldn't carry on one of their extended conversations at this time of night. Maybe Mother couldn't reach Aunt Jenny. But where could she be...?

Certainly not called to the auto plant where he worked. No. She didn't see murders. Hadn't ever. That had been a dream, not one of her psychic visions. A dream...

She lay back down. Nervously she reached for the phone, but pulled the hand back. If Mother called and got a busy signal, she might not try again tonight.

Time dragged on interminably. There was no way to clear her mind and think of other things: the radio show tomorrow; an interview in the afternoon on a local TV show; a meeting with the parents of that boy who disappeared....

That child, haunting her. Always just before she found a body. *It directs me!* No...no...mustn't think...

Certainly she could not use the time for a trance. There was no concentration possible until she heard, knew it had only been a dream.

The phone didn't ring until four. She was on it in the middle of the first ring.

"Mother? Where have you been? Why..."

"Mattie? It's me. David. Your mother called, asked me to call you." The familiar voice went straight to some center where it struck chords of longing and guilt. They had hardly been speaking when she left.

"David." The word was tense with conflicting emotion. "Tell me. What is it?"

"She asked me to call you," he repeated. It was evident he was stalling for time. Delaying. "Er—she went over to your Aunt Jenny's."

"But why? I only asked her to call there. You see, I had this terrible dream...."

"Yes. She told me about it."

"But why did she call you? It's the middle of the night, for goodness sake."

"Oh, that's all right. I'm on a case, so I was here at headquarters."

"David, will you tell me what's going on before I scream?"

"Well—it seems your mother called your Aunt Jenny. Got her out of bed. Your uncle wasn't at home. He started on the night shift a week ago. Your aunt called the plant, and, well—it seems there was some trouble there."

"Oh no." Mattie covered her mouth with a hand. She could feel the pressure of blood pounding in her head. "Not what I saw, was it? Not that!"

"I'm afraid it was. A man your uncle had an argument with the day before over a seat in the lunchroom. Guy brought a gun in tonight. Told police he only meant to scare him. Yeah—scared him all right."

"And I saw the whole thing." Her voice was choked. Even she couldn't believe what was happening to her now.

Not this—to have witnessed his murder—her own family. Too much to bear. She sobbed into the phone, slumping backward on to the bed and dragging the phone from the nightstand so it bumped to the floor.

"Mattie! Mattie! Are you all right?" The voice was faint, almost spectral.

She moved the receiver up to her ear. "Oh, David, this is just horrible. I can't endure it. I won't be able to stand it if I'm going to have to watch the murders too. I won't be able to. I'll lose my mind. Poor Uncle John. Oh, poor Uncle John. And—and poor Aunt Jenny."

"Your mother and her friends have gone to be with her. But it's you I'm worried about. Are you O.K.?"

She clutched the phone as if at any moment he would be cut off from her again.

"I'll be home on the first plane I can get. Tell Mother, all right? And tell Aunt Jenny how sorry I am." Her face was wet with tears. As soon as she hung up, having assured David she would call and let him know her arrival time, she called Bobby, waking him.

"Please, Bobby, come to my room. Something's— something awful has happened."

Chapter Fourteen

The room was filled with rows of chairs on which old people dressed in black perched unhappily. Some leaned their arms on the chair in front of them, talking in low tones, ever alert for the entrance of a new family member and fresh grief. Two sparse bouquets of multi-colored glads guarded the coffin set importantly on a catafalque at the front of the room. On the lower half of the polished box there sprawled a large, expensive spray of roses and lilies.

Uncle John was prettily painted with pale pink lips and a slight hint of cheap rouge. His coarse-pored face, smoothed and at rest, showed a boyishness the hard knowledge of his eyes had always masked. All signs of violence were hidden by the undertaker's art, except that his hands weren't clasped on his chest clutching a rosary against whatever future there might be. The shattered hands had been buried in the closed bottom half of the box, giving Uncle John a stiff, military bearing.

Mattie looked down at the face of the man she had known well. She could not block out the last time she saw him. Nor the violence that swept him away.

Uncle John was at peace at last. She knelt down on the padded kneeler set before the coffin but she couldn't pray, not so conspicuously, with the whispering behind her, telling excitedly of her visions, her deathwatch at her uncle's murder. The voices grew louder.

A hand was on her arm. She looked up into David's concerned face and stumbled to her feet, reaching to take his hand.

"I . . . I'm sorry I didn't come home at once. There were appointments scheduled, Bobby and I . . ." she stammered out, her eyes searching for signs of censure, but she saw only compassion and kindness there. He looked heavier, more solid, a compact man rather than the thinner, younger man she carried in her head.

"Everyone understands," he soothed. Her eyes filled with tears. Of course they understood. Getting ahead took precedence. They understood, these simple people. Understood ambition that burned out all other thoughts. Not only understood but made allowance for human failings—expecting little for themselves while allowing space for her, one of the anointed ones with a ticket up.

"They do, don't they?" She looked steadily into his face as if he might disappear.

"Was it true? You saw him murdered?" a distant cousin probed, a thrill in her voice.

"When did all this start?" the husband wanted to know. Others gathered around. She couldn't get away. Couldn't find David again. She was forced to relive the scene over and over until after a while it was only a play, its reality diminished, and she could deliver it with the panache they expected.

That evening, Mattie returned after dinner to field more questions from curious relatives and comfort her mother and aunt as best she could. She was relieved to see David come through the arch and hurry over to her. A newspaper was tucked under his arm.

He greeted Mattie somewhat abruptly, and when they had a moment alone he took the newspaper, opened it, folded it to display a story on the front page, and put it into Mattie's hands.

The headline read: Psychic Sees Uncle Die in Vision.

She didn't need to read the story to know what it said. Bobby. This had to be his doing. But that was his job, to promote her. He had to take advantage of every opportunity that presented itself. Didn't he?

David motioned toward the lobby with his head. She followed. They moved on outside. He took her arm and led toward his car, opened the door for her to get in, then went around to the other side.

"You read that?" He pointed toward the paper as he settled behind the wheel.

"No. I didn't know anything about it."

"Your friend do that?" His voice was hard.

"I suppose so."

"And you don't mind that he capitalizes on a family tragedy this way. That everybody's going to think this was your doing?"

"Why are you so mad?" she broke in on him.

"I just hate to see you exploited like this," he said. "When are you going to wake up to what's happening? See what compromises you're making? For what? Some cheap glamor? This?" He slapped the newspaper again.

"My aunt will love it." Her voice was even, knowing.

"That's ugly." He turned away from her.

"But true."

"Maybe she doesn't know any better. You do. You've got to know it's wrong to profit off the dead bodies of your family."

"Oh come now, why so dramatic? It was all right to profit from dead bodies as long as it benefited you."

His head remained turned away from her, fingers drumming against the steering wheel.

After a time, he said, "That's the third or fourth time you've said that to me." His voice dropped. "I guess it's how you feel, that I exploited you, so why not this Sanderson guy? And why not exploit your family? That way of looking at things justifies anything. And it all comes back to me."

"Look, I'd better go back in." She reached for the door handle. He stopped her.

"I love you, you know. Still want us to get married." His voice had the earnestness of a young boy. "But there's so much coming between us."

"Bobby Sanderson for one, right?" Mattie held her head high, away from him. She was fighting exhaustion and tears. "So what's the next step? I get rid of Bobby or we're through?"

"I'd hate to think it."

"So would I." She held back emotion, feeling only empty.

"Maybe now that you're home we can work this out." Silence.

"I just am not sure I know what it is we have to work out," she said after thinking for a while. "I can't give up my work. Not now."

"I know that. But I won't compete with Sanderson."

"I see."

There was little left to say. They went in together and all left soon afterward, David driving the women back to the flat on Mt. Eliot. From there Mattie took a cab to her apartment, over Harriet's objections. She hadn't wanted David to drive her. No more time alone to talk and beat each other to death. She was tired. Disturbed. She could use a little kindness, a little thoughtfulness. But no more recriminations.

She promised the women to pick them up in the morning—early—for the funeral.

Unpacking still to do. On returning from Florida she had stopped by here only long enough to drop off her luggage. Guilt over her late return made her rush to the funeral home. Now it all had to be done. Clothes sorted, clean from dirty, dresses hung up in the closet. Tedious work.

She emptied one case and was swinging another one on to the bed when a movement from the other side of the open bedroom door caught her eyes. Just a blurred motion, something flitted out of sight, beyond the doorway.

"Who's there?" Mattie stood very still, eyes cocked toward the door, waiting to catch whoever it was.

There was no answer but there was sound as if someone brushed the wall, tapping fingers playing over the plaster.

Mattie held her breath, listened, then called out again, voice less controlled, "Who's there?"

A half-suppressed giggle bubbled into the bedroom, striking Mattie's ears as if the sound screeched through bare electric wires.

"No," she whispered, shrinking back away from the sound. "No."

A flash moved across the open space where Mattie stared, just an instant's view of a childish face, of a strawberry-splashed raincoat. A second high, fluted giggle. Then quiet. Impersonal quiet as the apartment and all things in it held their breath, waited along with Mattie.

The ringing of the doorbell cut across the quivering silence as if ripping its way through the rooms. Mattie remained motionless, unable to comprehend the sound, unwilling to focus her mind enough to center on the chilling fact that the child was in there with her now, inside the apartment. No more worry about keeping her out. She had gained entry somehow.

Mattie's first conscious emotion was fear followed quickly by anger. This couldn't be happening. It wasn't logical, couldn't be real. If it were, then the child was in here, hiding someplace, could be caught.

The bell rang again.

Mattie forced herself to move toward the bedroom door. She stood and examined the living room. Empty. She crossed to the door. Opened it to Bobby, who stood grinning at her, newspaper in hand.

Not allowing him a word, Mattie turned back into the apartment.

"Remember that child I told you about?" She nervously

searched from one corner of the room to another. "She was just in here. Someone must've let her in while I was gone. Help me find her, Bobby. I've had enough of whatever this silly game is."

"In here?" He was confused, stopped just inside the door then closed it behind him. "Sure, we'll work together. But it just doesn't seem possible she's..."

"She is all right. I saw her. And this time I'm gonna get the little bitch and make her leave me alone once and for all."

She moved slowly across the room, checking every possible hiding place while Bobby followed, his face more bemused than concerned.

They went through the bathroom, kitchen, pantry, hall, every closet, the bedroom—and found no one, nothing.

Bobby patted her shoulder, consoling her. "Just the strain of the last few days. Eyes playin' tricks. I wouldn't worry about it. Get this funeral behind you, grab a little rest, and you'll be good as..."

"Shut up," Mattie ordered, eyes burning at him. "I don't need your bedside crap. That kid was here. I saw her. Heard her. Someone's doing this deliberately and I'm gonna find out who and why. With your help or without it."

"Sure, sure," he claimed. "Do whatever I can to help, you know that. Whatever I can."

She gave him a look that spoke eloquently of what she thought of his sincerity and sat down in the corner of the sofa, curling up into a ball, holding herself tightly, arms around knees.

After mixing himself a drink, Bobby picked up the paper he'd brought and dropped it beside her.

"You see that?" he asked.

She said nothing.

"Guess you saw it already."

"Had my nose rubbed in it would be more appropriate."

"It's a great story. A good attention-getter. Who didn't like it?"

"David."

"Why?"

"He thinks it was insensitive."

"Did your aunt complain?"

"No."

"There you see. Your friend's nose gets out of joint about everything."

She'd gotten up, walked into her bedroom where she proceeded to put the remainder of her clothes away. Bobby followed, moved a pile of her underthings aside and sat on the bed. "Sometimes I wonder about that guy. He's so damned prissy. If he wasn't a cop I swear I'd think he was queer. I mean—still living at home with mother, after all. Jesus. Isn't he ever gonna grow up?"

"That's not fair, Bobby. It's traditional in Italian families for the unmarried child to take care of his mother. And believe me, I'm living testimony that he's not gay."

"Good in the hay, huh? Never would've thought it." He smiled up at her.

She laughed, more relaxed now, and finished tucking clothes into drawers and closets, coming finally to sit next to him on the bed. Her shoulders hunched forward, showing her fatigue.

"What's wrong?" Bobby slipped an arm around her.

"Oh, I don't know. So much, I guess."

"Want to tell me or would you rather I just leave."

She looked at him and smiled, tiredness outlining her large eyes. "It's that child. And my uncle's death. All of it. And, of course, me and David. I guess he's jealous of you. Delivered almost an ultimatum: you go or we're through."

For once Bobby didn't have a snappy comeback. He fell into deep thought, then looked into her eyes, saw the tears there and, putting an arm around her again, drew her close, kissing her lightly on the forehead.

"Tough. Real tough for you." She rested her head against his shoulder. It felt good there. Simple. Uncomplicated.

With an index finger Bobby lifted her chin so she looked up at him. He smiled again and bent to kiss her with pressure and length that left her without breath.

He seemed so different from the usual flamboyant Bobby, as if he intuitively knew what she needed from him.

He kissed her again. She could feel the quickening begin in her: lips aching to touch his, tongue searching another, body straining toward him—back arching, breasts pushing forward—desiring touch. She wanted to forget everything beyond Bobby's kiss, Bobby's touch, and his soft voice murmuring against her hair. One night—simply to lose herself as she felt at the moment, without problems of conscience, religion, any of the many dictums against sexual pleasure. She was tired of all of it. All the fighting...

She lay back as he pushed slightly. He came with her, slipping his hand into the gap in her robe. She sighed as he held her breast carefully, cupping it tenderly, then running a finger up over the nipple until it stiffened.

Mattie offered no help, no hindrance. She let him move her, responded as her body told her to without artifice or design.

Later they made love again and lay naked afterward.

"I guess tragedy makes me horny," she giggled. "My fiance all but dumps me, my whole family is mourning, and here I flop into bed with you."

Propped against the headboard, Bobby lighted a cigarette. He only shrugged.

"I thought it would help." He blew a smoke ring out and reached down beside the bed for an ashtray.

Tone so detached, it stopped Mattie midway in her thoughts. Did he mean it to sound the way it did?

"All part of the job?" She watched him from the corner of her eye, saw a smile curve across his lips.

"Why not?"

"You bastard!" She reached around for a pillow, grabbed it, swung it at him, hitting him and sending the ash tray bouncing across the carpet.

"Hey!" he shouted, arms up to protect himself. "Cut it out."

She raised the pillow again, laughing this time, about to strike the cowering figure, when she caught sight of the doorway and the small figure outlined there.

Mattie drew in a breath and dropped the pillow, hands scrambling for the sheet to cover her nakedness.

The narrow face was set in a look of intense curiosity. The eyes went from Mattie to Bobby and back to Mattie, making Mattie cringe with fear.

In a moment the solemn face began to move as the thin lips curved upward, first into a familiar smile and then the mouth opened into loud, dirty laughter.

Mattie covered her ears, burrowing downward into the bed as if for protection. Her hands reached out to Bobby for help, but he was still busily protecting himself from the pillow, oblivious to the obscene laughter filling every corner of Mattie's mind.

Chapter Fifteen

"I told ya there would be more," the voice said. David recognized it immediately. The impact of the words was intense, as if expectation had built a pyramid of fear that crashed around him now as the man spoke.

"If you woulda listened to me you woulda known who'd be next. Only be one of two men. Those were the last. But, Jeez, she got him directly. Wish she woulda done me that way. 'Stead of my grandson."

Alfred Williams. The black man whose grandson had been found in that garage.

"Mr. Williams, why don't you tell me why it could only have been one of two and also just what in hell you're gettin' at."

"Jesus Christ! I didn't know this John Fletcher was her uncle! He didn't really have nothin' to do with it. But he got involved." The man's voice stopped, then, as if gathering new force, he started again.

"I called Old Flash Gordon. And I called Fred Gibonski. Tole those ole boys it was time we tole the truth about your girlfriend and those murders. She already got one chile from each of our families. What next? And now her uncle." He paused but David didn't interrupt. The man was talking as if under compulsion. From experience David knew to let him go on.

"But those two don't see it that way. They're scared. I figure I'm too old now. Don't matter. Just want this killin' stopped." He paused and waited for a response this time.

"Scared of what, Mr. Williams?"

"That's what I want to tell ya. Meet me at the Pussy Cat again. I gotta get this over with."

Lester, behind the bar, waved a greeting and pointed a chubby finger toward the back where Alfred Williams, looking sunken and old, sat at the same table between the juke box and the men's toilet.

"You want anything?" he asked out of ritual, impatient to get on with it.

David shook his head and sat down, waiting then while Alfred Williams drank down his beer and motioned to Lester for another.

"I'm kind of in a..." David began.

"Yeah, yeah, I know. In a hurry. But I'm putting my whole life on the line here. Those other two guys think I'm crazy. The fourth guy—the only one she hasn't touched yet—is too big. Won't even take my calls. So I'm on my own here."

"So?"

"What I'm gonna tell you happened years ago. Maybe twenty-five or more. Me and these other three guys were working for the union, trying to get these little shops organized. Well, sometimes things got rough. Nothin' was easy then. Shop-owners pay guys to keep us out. Sometimes they'd even pay a guy to run for office in the union, or maybe get to be shop steward and then force a vote to get us out. Those were early days, rough days. Me and these other three were called organizers. But we was troubleshooters. Lots of trouble. Once in a while some shooting. As often as not be one of us get it. But once—this one time—something got all screwed up. One of these guys who was double-crossin' us, being paid to undermine the movement, got killed. Shot. We was only supposed to rough the guy up but, man, things got outta hand. Somebody—wasn't me—pulled a gun and shot him."

"What's that got to do with anything?" David frowned, afraid he was wasting time again.

"That guy was Donald Small, your girlfriend's daddy."

David drew in a breath. Held it. The connection. It was happening, all tying together whether he wanted to see it or not.

"That's impossible," he said. "Mattie told me her father was killed in an accident. Car wreck. He wasn't shot."

"That was all taken care of. He was shot all right. And his kid was there when it happened."

"There! What the hell are you sayin'? She'd know if she saw her father shot. That's not the kind of thing she'd just for..."

"You wanna hear me out?"

David stopped talking, nodded.

"We was in this alley by his house. Hey, I'll never forget that chile's face. She just stood there lookin' up while we talked about killin' her too. No. No. We wouldn't a done it. We weren't really killers. The other just happened...."

"Just happened." David's disgust leaked up and surfaced.

"I know. I know." The man's head went down. When he continued his voice was subdued.

"After that we went right to a phone and called the guy who sent us out on the job. We didn't know what to do. Meant big trouble and a setback for the union. Leastwise, that's what this guy was worried about. He made a few phone calls and got back to us. We was to go back there if we could, get the body, and make it look like an accident."

"Well, to old Fred, accident meant car. So we went back there, back to that alley and—Jeez, I hate to even think about it." He stopped again, wiping at his grizzled face with his hands. "That li'l chile was sleepin' with her head against her daddy and he was dead. Rain comin' down. Right on the ground, asleep near her daddy. That 'most killed me." The man shook his head.

"This uncle of hers, John Fletcher, he met us there and took the little girl home while we got her daddy outta there, into his car and ran that into a lamppost. No problem about that. Somebody paid off, I guess. No more trouble...till now."

"You mean his wife, his daughter, even Mattie's Uncle John never said a word? Why would they hush it up? And what about Mattie? You mean she knows?"

"Don't think she really knows. John Fletcher was on our side. He took care of everything. Tole the wife a story and got the union guy to offer her money. A lifetime pension if she shut up against nothin' if she caused trouble. Scared, alone, with that chile to raise, she took money. That's it." He spread his hands then wrapped them around the fresh beer and drank it down.

"But Mattie must know about this." David couldn't leave it alone.

Williams shrugged. "Well, ya know now. The uncle took care of everything, that's all I know. Bet he got himself a nice piece of change out of it too."

David sat back, shook his head, and tried to think.

"O.K. now. All three—four—of you were in on this killing. Even five, with the uncle. But where does Mattie fit in? She's not doing the killing. Christ sakes, she was in Miami when her uncle was shot. And you're not even sure she remembers what happened that day."

"Aw, she must know. She's gotta be doin' them, or got someone doin' 'em for her. You don't think all of these murders are a coincidence, do ya?"

"I talked to Gary Jones, the guy who strangled Esther Shell. He admitted killing her but he has no connection with the others. And this last one, Mattie's Uncle John, happened while Jones was in jail. You trying to tell me she's got a gang working for her? It won't wash. None of it."

"She find the bodies, don't she? All nice and neat. You really believe in her visions? Shit, man, you the dumbest cop I ever did meet."

It was more than confusion that ripped at him. It was alternating belief and disbelief, alternating horror when he thought of the child and anger when he thought she was hiding all this from him.

He didn't know where to turn, where to start. He was oddly stymied, as if his years of experience as a cop never happened, as if his mind refused to confront an unsolvable problem.

He'd left the dim bar with nothing settled. The man demanded to know what David would do but, having no idea, he couldn't answer.

What was there to do? What was procedure? Investigate? But investigate what? A twenty-five year old killing that was made to look like an accident? A wife and daughter who hushed up a man's death in exchange for some security? Where should he start?

Only two places open to him. Mattie or her mother. Both impossible. He couldn't. Ruin everything between them. And for what? She hadn't murdered those people. Couldn't possibly have had anything to do with those deaths. But why this strange connection? Why? Why?

His mind didn't want to accept the question. An ineffable fear settled over him. Fear of a loss greater than he could tolerate. He closed his mind down. Refused to be drawn further into the nightmare. He spoke to no one about what he knew.

Chapter Sixteen

Patsy decided she didn't want to die in the dark. Alone was bad enough. But not in the dark. In slippers, she padded the rooms of the house, turning on every lamp, switching every wall switch, until the house glowed with light and she felt less alone and less afraid.

She went into her pink and white bedroom, opened packages laying about on the floor, then lifted bundles out, taking them back to the bathroom where she held them up in front of the mirror.

"See?" she said and the image smiled, eyes staring into hers. "New sheets and pillow cases. Cost over fifty dollars. But I charged 'em. Won't the bed look nice?" The image nodded.

She lowered the eyelet-trimmed sheets and pillowcases. They were slick, cold to the touch. Pretty. Unspotted. Unmended. She bowed her head away from her image and thought of Marilyn Monroe.

On silk sheets, the article said. She died between silk sheets dressed in a satin nightgown, phone within reach.

Classy way to go. Real class.

She faced her image again. White, white hair, like Marilyn. Nothing else. Jaw too square, bony. Mouth too big. Eyes like marbles, round, hard. Eyebrows two pencil lines drawn down the middle of nude, shaved skin.

"And you should see what else I got. Wait here. I've gotta show you this."

She came back and held up a purple, satiny nightgown, patting the straps to her shoulders over her blouse, admiring the wide ecru lace bands decorating the front, dipping beneath the bodice to firm up the breasts that would fill it.

"Pretty, huh?" She smiled at herself then looked away, feeling suddenly that no matter what she bought it would all look sleazy when they—whoever they were: firemen, policemen, neighbors?—broke in to find her. Don't think about it, she warned herself, don't think.

What to do first now? This was the appointed time, and she liked order. Kept the little house inherited from her mother in perfect shape.

Check that first.

Nothing out of place. Clean towels in the bathroom. No dishes on the kitchen sink.

In the bedroom she stripped the bed and put on the new sheets, billowing them, smoothing them in place, snapping the corners under the mattress. No blanket.

She stripped off all her clothes, hanging the blouse and slacks in the closet, rolling down her knee-high nylons, removing them, and sticking them in a drawer.

"Damn!" There were rings around her calves where the elastic of the knee-highs had dug in. But that would be gone by the time she was found, she decided, and slipped the new gown over her head.

She ran her hands over the smooth material. Felt rich, slinky.

Next: hair and make-up. Jesus! It was like gettin' ready for a date—a terrific date—biggest of her life!

She smiled quickly and moved back to the bathroom, where she began to wash her face briskly with a cloth, removing all residue of make-up.

She brushed the white-blond hair out and fluffed it, like doll's hair, into a rigid pageboy. She gave it a blast of hair spray to hold it then gave it another so the pillow wouldn't muss it.

Next she made-up her face, drew new black lines for eyebrows. Etched liner around the eyes. Drew a lipstick brush around her lips and filled in from the tube of orange.

She stepped back. Looked at herself and smiled again.

The smile faded as the eyes looked deeply: woman to image. She sighed and opened the medicine cabinet, removing three bottles from three different drug stores and bearing three different doctor's names.

All three recommended sleeping pills for the patient who couldn't sleep nights, suffered nervousness.

She had plenty of pills.

Lifting the glass of water and clutching the three bottles of pills, Patsy went back to the bedroom and set the glass and vials down on the nightstand.

A note, she wondered. To who? Who would really care? Mattie? Just make her feel guilty. And she wasn't. Not really. Some people were lucky. Dreams came true for them....

She lay down and pulled the cool sheet up over her, arranging the folds precisely, loving the luxury of the new white cotton. She fluffed the pillows and tried lying back to see how her hair would stay. Just one place it pushed forward. She patted it back in place.

Opening the bottles, she dumped the first of the pills on to the sheet beside her, then, one by one, she swallowed them.

Too slow a process, she decided, and opened the other bottles to pop handfuls into her mouth until they were all gone.

She wiped the ring the glass had made on the bedstand then set the glass down.

Again she arranged her nightgown, her pillows, her hair, and the sheet covering her, snuggling down into the softness and newness of things she'd never been able to buy before.

It had been a long day at Koch's supermarket. So many old ladies. Mrs. Koch bitchin' cause she took too long on her break. Rain. Cold. Empty house...phone never rang...

Tomorrow would be different....

Chapter Seventeen

The phone rang constantly the entire week following her uncle's funeral. Mattie was interviewed by both Detroit dailies and featured on the local morning TV show, "Good Morning, Detroit," hosted by an affable man who obviously didn't believe a word she said. Radio shows featured phone conversations with her. People in restaurants recognized her and stared.

Mattie kept herself busy. Too busy to think. And she kept the apartment filled with people. With so many always there the child wouldn't dare appear again.

David called. He came daily but there was no time to talk. She would see him come in, stand on the fringes of the group, and watch her, his long face expressionless. And then he would be gone without a word. It was not until she would think of him, look up, search the many faces, that she knew he had already left. No good-bye. Just gone.

Things were moving fast now. The volume of mail increased drastically.

A wire service story ran all across the country and brought pleas for help to find missing relatives from as far away as Alaska. A secretary was a must now. Bobby promised he would find one and reported, with a wink, that he was enjoying the labor. Mattie only hoped Patsy wouldn't be hurt too badly when she learned of the hiring. But there was little time to think about Patsy's hurt feelings either. So much happening. Days so full...

She devoted mornings and late evenings to her trances. Afternoons and evenings were spent with new friends flocking around, eager to be in touch with this mystical power she had, charmed by her celebrity. The liquor bill, just for the weeks since the funeral, was five hundred dollars, but she had no time for the minor details of life. Bobby took care of all that. He was even screening the clients now, making the first run-through of the letters each day, deciding which were possibles and passing only these on to Mattie. The rejects were sent a form letter explaining that Miss Small had too many cases at present and regretted she could not accept another at this time.

Bobby was really strutting. He looked great when he walked in that afternoon in his pale Bill Blass suit. Meticulous. Smile wide in a tanned face. She could see the news was big. But he was going to savor teasing her with it. She watched as he threaded his way through people in all sorts of stylish undress, stopping to kiss women who offered up purple lips, to shake hands and laugh with casually dressed men.

She was in the middle of an avid claque, young women who flocked around to ooh and aah over her stories, to question her methods in hopes of reaching the extended place where present, past, and future merged. They stood oh-mouthed and saucer-eyed and dispersed when Mattie waved them away so she could find out Bobby's news.

"Just got confirmation from Gil Tabok's producer," he launched into it as soon as she had a moment alone with him. "You're in—this September. Only thing left to discuss is length of time and what you'll talk about."

"Gil Tabok's show? New York? God, Bobby, that's the top. Are you sure? They really want me?"

Excitement linked them. Eyes glowing, they hugged each other. Bobby let out a whoop the others couldn't help but notice. They crowded around as Bobby broke the news. Champagne appeared and the party went into full swing.

Later, alone in a corner of her bedroom with Bobby, she held on to him and made him tell her again to prove she had not been dreaming.

"Gil Tabok's show? September?"

He laughed at her.

"I've made it, haven't I, Bobby? I mean really made it. Right to the top. That girl who worked in the supermarket is dead, isn't she? No more Martha Small. God, Bobby, I can't believe this has all happened to me. It's so...so unreal. And I have you to thank, Bobby. You've done everything you promised. And more."

He didn't bother looking humble. Instead he nodded, agreeing with her and more than willing to accept congratulations.

"Now we'll have to keep you up there. That's harder than getting there. But I can do it. If I have your full cooperation." He sobered, looked into his glass and then at her. All traces of laughter gone.

"Of course I'll cooperate. Haven't I been doing just that?"

"Not completely. You're always pulling away from the job we've got to do. It's time for you to decide once and for all which way you want to go."

"I thought I've made that very clear from the beginning." She frowned and sank to her dressing table chair, where she picked up a lipstick brush and worked on the line of her lips.

"Not always."

"And?"

"And I think it's time to dump David." He watched her work at repairing her careful make-up, not missing a single delicate stroke with her brushes and pencils. She remained silent for a time, thinking.

"He's barely in my life now," she finally said guardedly, blending shades of gray and brown shadow into her eyelids with quick, professional strokes.

"Oh, he's there all right. Like some kind of ghost haunting you. The guy's here every day. Hangs around watching as if he'll jump up at any time and accuse you of all sorts of sins."

"With good reason, probably." She put down the brush and looked at herself—full face.

She wanted all of this. But she loved David too.

"Shit!" Bobby said. "What reason does he have to judge you? Didn't he get a promotion out of your work? Wouldn't he like to keep you in a nice neat box all to himself? And he calls that sharing your talent with the world."

Slowly she turned in her chair to face Bobby, who was red-faced with anger.

"That's enough, Bobby. Stop right now. You hear?"

He flinched, overcoming his anger, but not prepared for
her tone of voice. His face made the adjustment from
anger to annoyance.

"I mean it, Bobby. My problems with David are my
own business and I'll settle them without ultimatums from
you. You're doing a good job for me, but it's only what you
promised when I hired you. And don't forget—I pay your
salary."

"Oh, so it's back to employee, huh? I thought we'd
gotten beyond that. The job I'm doin'—you know I'm
breakin' my ass for you. That's not something you can buy,
that kind of job. You know that, don't you? That what I'm
doin' can't really be bought?" There was hurt in his voice
but his eyes remained appraising, as if he was still in the
process of adjusting to her about-face.

"It can be bought," she said, eyes level. "Because I am
buying it."

The door opened, interrupting. A full-blown, middle-
aged woman with dry blond hair and enormous glasses
stuck her head around the corner, searching them out.

"There you are." She hesitated, catching the expressions on their faces. "Oh—sorry—I just...your mother
and aunt and some other ladies are here."

"Hell!" Mattie shook her head, anger veering in another direction now. "What do they want at this time of
day for God's sake? I've got work to do."

The four women had not moved from just inside the
front door. They eyed the slit skirts and forties hair styles
on the women collected in Mattie's living room. And in
return the women raised plucked eyebrows at the dowdy
old ladies.

"What's this?" one cool young woman asked another.
"A cleaning ladies' convention?" They snickered. Bella
Schwartz drew herself up to full bosom and frowned
ominously in the young woman's direction.

"Mother." Mattie approached, obviously put out with
them. "I was just about to clear the place and start my
evening sessions."

Harriet winced at her daughter's high, false tone.

"Hi, Aunt Jenny." Mattie had taken both her hands to
offer consolation. "How are you doing?"

"Fine. Fine." Jenny sniffed and took a bunched handkerchief from her pocket to wipe at her runny eyes. "Just so much trouble. So much trouble."

"Oh, you're no trouble to anyone." Mattie smiled brightly at her, misunderstanding.

"No. Not me—I mean..."

Harriet interrupted. "Let's go into your bedroom, Martha. We've got some bad news."

Bobby excused himself when the women entered the room where he was sitting on the bed, waiting to resume this quarrel.

"I'll be back later," he said and left.

"Now what is this about?" Mattie demanded, standing and forcing the women to stand too.

"It's about Patsy," Harriet started, only to be interrupted by Mattie.

"No Ma, if that's why you came, forget it. I feel just as sorry for her as you do but I can't hire her. She has no training. And—after all—could she fit in here?"

Juliet reached out and placed a hand timidly on Mattie's arm. "She's dead, Martha. She died last night."

The information didn't sink in easily. The words floated for a time on the surface of her consciousness and meant nothing. Mattie searched the old faces ringing her as if meaning might be written across them. But the faces were blank, only recording, watching her reaction.

"Dead?" she questioned angrily. "How can Patsy be dead?"

"She took pills. That's all we know. She took too many pills and killed herself. Mrs. Koch went there when she didn't show up for work. Found her like that. Dead."

"Suicide," Juliet whispered the word.

"Suicide!" She couldn't believe them. Wouldn't. Patsy had to be alive someplace. She couldn't be dead...yet.

There was no way to stop what was coming. No way to turn quickly enough to keep them from seeing. She heard her own voice take on joyful sounds and then she laughed aloud, and laughed again as the bubble inside her burst and spit out merriment.

"My God!" Bella stepped back away from her. Mattie put out a hand to reassure her but drew it back as she doubled over with laughter.

"Is it a nervous breakdown?" Juliet asked, pulling away in fear.

"What's the matter with you?" Aunt Jenny demanded, angry at the inappropriate response.

"There, there," Harriet soothed and pushed her backward toward the bed, where she got her to sit down.

Mattie let herself be manipulated and coddled until she was in control again and could cover her face with her hands.

"Hysteria," Bella pronounced and they all looked pityingly at Mattie.

The women wanted to stay but Mattie couldn't let them. She wanted to be alone, she said, thanking them for clearing the apartment of the others and for calling David. He would be enough.

She asked for him. To have him hold her, feel sorry for her, tell her Patsy's death wasn't her fault. She wanted him to tell her everything was all right. They were still going to get married. That nothing was complicated. No ghostly child haunted her, no tangled lives tugged like horsemen at her legs and wrists, threatening to pull in all directions.

But when the bell rang it was Bobby. He heard. Sympathized. And wouldn't leave.

When David arrived his greeting was warm and loving, until he spotted Bobby standing by the window.

"Your mother said you were alone. Needed me." He looked from Bobby to Mattie, who was sunk in a chair, eyes staring straight ahead.

"I do, David. It's so impossible to believe she would do something like this to me." She put out a hand to him. He took it and knelt next to her chair, touching her hair, her cheek. "It couldn't have been because I wouldn't give her a job. She understood about that. It must have been over Tolly—he left her, you know? Without a word. And she really loved him."

David looked away from her. "Probably for a lot of reasons. Some we'll never know."

"But you don't think it was because of me, do you? She understood I couldn't employ everyone. Nobody can. That wasn't it, was it?" Her large eyes searched his.

He shrugged, moving away from her.

Bobby came over to the place beside her chair which David had vacated. He settled casually between them, sitting on the arm of the chair and resting his forearm over the back, behind Mattie. She didn't notice. David looked from one to the other of them, noting the easy intimacy.

"A girl like that could have a thousand different reasons to commit suicide. Nothing going for her. A life of the same ahead. No wonder."

David didn't answer.

"Nobody's fault but her mother's—for having her in the first place."

"She was Mattie's friend." David's voice hardened. The look on his face was meant to silence the other man.

"That was before. Mattie outgrew her when she left the supermarket and got famous. Sure she feels sorry, but really, that girl was stale news. You know yourself, people outgrow people, move on. Too bad, but that's life."

"That how you feel?" David ignored Bobby, speaking directly to Mattie.

Thinking, she roused herself to answer. "I feel terrible. I really do. And I don't want to be guilty of her death. Just 'cause I was luckier."

She leaned her head back, closed her eyes. David made a move toward her but Bobby hunched forward, taking her in his arms and murmuring low, comforting words against her head.

David stood where he was a moment, watching them. A knowing look crossed his face. He stepped past the chair where they sat together and went quickly to the door.

Turning to look back at the two of them, he opened the door and left the apartment.

It was half an hour before Mattie realized he was gone.

Part Three

Chapter One

He parked the car at the curb and sat looking toward the gray shingled building. The downstairs, a shop, had fly-specked windows displaying shelves of plaster molds: dogs and cats; even a Nefertiti, Queen of the Nile, looked out on the empty street. Garish finished pieces stood among the others to demonstrate what could be done with the stark, white molds.

His mother would love to own one of those gilded cherubs for her living room, David smiled to himself. Before Mattie, he'd never thought to question rococo gilding and fringe and plastic wraps on everything.

He looked to the upper flat, at windows from which light had fallen on them that first night, when Mattie had been afraid her mother would see them.

When Mattie had been afraid...

It seemed impossible now that there had ever been such a time, a time when she shyly touched his hand, when everything was new to her, as if she'd just been born... was innocent.

For weeks he'd done his best to ignore what his

conscience screamed. This was no time for confrontation with Mattie. Their relationship was too fragile, too tenuous to stand the strain of his doubt. But he couldn't ignore it any more. Patsy's death somehow acted as the final nudge. Another fortuitous death. He knew Patsy had bothered Mattie, made her feel guilty and ashamed for turning on her. Now that pressure of guilt was gone. Saved by death . . . again.

Too neat. Life wasn't like that. Not life as he knew it from the Detroit streets. Deaths had reasons and explainable causes.

David had the feeling that Harriet was looking out the window, apprehensively waiting for him. He'd called, told her he wanted to talk to her today.

It was as good a time as any, with Mattie in California, called out there by some movie star whose daughter was missing.

David took a deep breath and got out of the car.

They were all there. Middle of the afternoon. Bella, Juliet, and Harriet.

"Well, well, David. Come on in. You know Bella Schwartz and Juliet Swiderski. Good to see you." Harriet opened the door wide, inviting him to join the coffee klatch at the kitchen table.

"This about a wedding?" Bella asked slyly, getting a nudge from Juliet.

Bewildered, he stammered that no, that wasn't what he'd come about and maybe he'd better see Mrs. Small alone.

"Alone! Me? Whatever for? My friends know everything there is to know about me, David. Nothing to hide." She plumped herself down on the empty chair after setting a cup of coffee in front of him and pushing the sugar bowl and milk carton his way.

"It's about your husband." He watched her face express the emotions in her mind. Surprise. Shock. Wariness. Fear.

"My husband! Donald? Whatever could you want to know about him?"

The three women exchanged alarmed glances and sat up stiffly.

"This is hard to go into," David hesitated, aware of

the step he was taking. "But I've been told a story about Donald Small's death that conflicted with the story Mattie told me."

"What did you hear?" Bella asked, eyes boring toward him.

"Mattie once told me her Dad was killed in an auto accident, coming back from a fishing trip, I believe. But a few weeks ago a man, for reasons I'd rather not go into right now, came to me and said he was there when Donald Small was shot, killed in some union hassle."

"Why there's no truth to..." Juliet began to sputter, moving her body in agitation, upsetting her mug so that coffee spread across the stained oilcloth. All three women went into action, leaping for a dish cloth, sopping up the mess, and pouring Juliet another cup. "No truth at all," Juliet finished her defense when they were seated again.

"Wait." Harriet stopped her, turning to David, face set in lines of worry. "Why is this important, David? Why now? Does it have anything to do with Mattie's gift?"

He nodded, "Maybe."

"Something strange there, isn't that true? I don't mean her psychic powers, but about the bodies she found at first...and about her Uncle John's death. Maybe Patsy's too."

Harriet met his eyes and he saw in them the same confusion he'd been suffering.

"I knew it," Harriet breathed and slouched back in her chair, face pale and sick.

"Best not to jump to conclusions, Harriet," Bella warned. "Best not to dig up the past either. You did what you had to, for Martha's sake. Can't undo what's been done."

"Yes, Harriet," Juliet jumped in again. "Just leave it alone. No good'll come of bringing it all up now."

"No good'll come of going on, ignoring that all those first dead people were connected in some way to people in the same union as Donald. You know John warned me that something stranger than anybody thought was going on with Mattie's visions. He told me about these men being union organizers and, as far as he could remember, that they were the men who killed Donald."

"Then your husband was murdered just as I was

told." David heaved a sigh, relieved and troubled at the same time. But at least that much was out in the open.

"Don't blame Harriet," Juliet leapt to her friend's defense. "There was nothing else she could do but go along. Her brother-in-law came in here, I remember the evening well. I'd just come by for a visit—we didn't see each other so much then, what with families and all. The way he explained it there'd been some trouble, a bunch of union organizers met Donald out on the street on his way to the store with Mattie. Seems Donald was some kind of double-crosser, selling out to the employer of the shop where he worked. The men accused him and they all got into a scuffle and somehow Donald was shot and killed."

"That's what they said about him but I still don't believe it." Harriet had tears gathering in her eyes.

"But why didn't you call the police?" David was incredulous.

"John, my brother-in-law, said that would only cause the union trouble and solve nothing. He swore it was an accident."

"And offered money?"

Here Harriet squirmed uncomfortably. She turned to Bella, who came to the rescue.

"He offered a lifetime pension from the union. Enough money to take care of both her and Mattie, for as long as they needed it," she said. "Course it don't amount to much with today's inflation, but how could she have turned it down? There was no insurance. Harriet's got no job training. All she knew was stayin' home, takin' care of Donald and Mattie. She was so scared. Scared to death. What she did was leave the decision up to her brother-in-law and he decided she should take the money and shut up."

"But—Mattie! This man said she was there when her father was killed."

Harriet's face was wet with tears now. All she could do was nod.

"Then she knows about all of this? And has kept it quiet too?"

Harriet shook her head vehemently, denying but unable to speak.

Juliet squirmed, said, "We all made her forget." She

toyed with her coffee cup, glancing at David, then away.

"Made her forget. How?"

"John Fletcher's idea," Bella took over again. "Over and over we told her how her Daddy died in a car wreck. At first she'd try to talk about what happened in that alley, but we all corrected her, repeated the car wreck story until she accepted it as truth and forgot what really happened."

"And you thought you could wipe something like that out of her mind? Just like that?"

"We did." Bella was defensive. "We got her to believe our story all right."

"And people began to die...." David looked from one old, worried face to the other.

"Is there a connection, David?" Harriet wiped at her eyes with a tissue Juliet provided.

"Connection?" His voice was distracted, far away from them. "Connection?...I don't know."

"I've felt it too," Harriet admitted. "So scared to even think it. But maybe this is our fault some way."

"I can't really see how," he admitted. "Except I can't get the thought out of my mind. That little girl sees her father get killed and years later the men responsible and their families begin to die. Connections are impossible. Anything I can come up with is too fantastic to be true. But still..." He shook his head, overwhelmed with the problem.

"But still?" Harriet watched him, waiting. He only shrugged, looking away from her blotched and suffering face.

"You gonna tell Mattie now?" Bella demanded.

David shrugged. "I've got to think first, but—yes—I think I have to. Only way to end all this once and for all. Unless you want to do it?" He looked toward Harriet, who put her head down.

"I can't," she said, voice muffled. "I'm too afraid of what we've done to her. I can't. You do it, David. You do it."

Chapter Two

The air in the apartment felt used, disturbed, as if someone had been moving there just moments before she walked in. As if they had stopped suddenly on hearing her key in the lock.

Uneasy, Mattie set her small case down in the living room and ran her eyes over what she could see of the apartment. Everything just as she had left it. Perfect order. She frowned, feeling a chill move down her arms and across her shoulders. She tried to shrug off the feeling. Made herself move as if nothing were wrong.

"Air conditioning set too low," she muttered, walking to the side wall where she adjusted the thermostat. The humming undertone that had greeted her stopped. Waves of silence seemed to roll toward her from the other, unseen rooms. Again she attempted to shrug off the uneasiness, picked up her traveling case, and walked toward the bedroom, stopping to flick on the radio.

The throb of a rock beat eased the quiet.

The doorbell rang, startling her. Doorman with her luggage. She pointed toward the bedroom and dug a few dollars from her bag to tip him.

She closed the door behind the man and kicked off her shoes. Back in the bedroom she opened the first of her striped Gucci cases, dreading still another unpacking.

Los Angeles had been too much—of everything. People. Color. Cars. Ideas. And too draining. Followers everywhere. Almost cultists. They hung on her every word with slack-jawed adoration. She was California's saviour of the month, a concept to run from. And she had. Completed the job, found that movie star's kid, and left.

Wearily she gathered up an armful of dresses and carried them to the closet, sliding the wide door open and

210

walking in. At a sound that seemed to come from behind her, she stepped back into the room. On edge, wary, she searched the room. There was nothing out of place. No one there. She decided it was the air conditioning shutting off and went back to her job.

As she transferred dresses, one hanger to another, she wondered again at her lack of emotion, at the growing empty space inside that refused to fill in.

It could be because of David, she thought, guilt enveloping her.

She had betrayed him. Slept with Bobby.

But David wasn't her husband! He had no claim on her.

HELL!

The dress in her hands caught and snagged on the hanger. Disgusted, she threw it to the floor.

Irrationally angry, she picked up a hairbrush and sat down at her dressing table to run the brush quickly through her shorter than ever curls.

Tired of carrying all this guilt and pain, she told herself. And what the hell did she owe him anyway? They weren't married. But that didn't stop him from laying the guilt on her. Unfair! Unfair!

She brushed at the curls, watching the bouyancy, the life of them. She avoided her darkly circled eyes.

She put the brush down. Headache again...should see a doctor.

Her fingers rubbed at her temples as she attempted to forestall the ever growing, crushing pain that would close in soon. Purposefully, to be busy and not have to think, she got up, intent on unpacking.

The quiet around the edges of the music still made her nervous. Nothing seemed to reach the corners of the rooms today. Too many dead areas where people should be.

Phone calls. Make a few phone calls, she told herself, but moved instead to lie down on the bed.

Only comfort...only real comfort...

She awoke because of a single sound in the apartment. Coming to so suddenly, she couldn't be certain what the sound had been, from where it had come, or if it had been real or a part of a dream. Opting for the last explanation, Mattie pulled herself from the bed to the bathroom where she let cold water run over her hands and then ran her hands over her face, waking herself, letting cool fingers massage her temples where pain still lingered.

Looking into the mirror, checking the ravages of the trip—skin, hair—she caught a slight movement reflected behind her, the swiftest of movements across the open bathroom doorway.

Not quite certain of what she had seen, she stood very still. Made no sound. Her eyes remained fixed on that spot in the mirror. Her hands clutched the edges of the white enameled bowl.

The sound of a small laugh made Mattie's body turn to ice. There was no other warning. She was there, mirrored in the doorway. Watching. The old raincoat—yellowed. Strawberries—faded. The same peaked face. The eyes...

Mattie let out the breath she held, afraid, as she did, that the noise would bring the child at her. She inhaled and held it, watching, mouth open, as the child tilted her head first to one side then the other in imitation of cuteness.

Large blue eyes met her in the glass. There was no timidity in that small narrow face. The girl was only curious.

They stood very still, watching each other. Mattie knew excruciating fear. The child stared boldly.

They stood with eyes locked, no noise, not even of breath catching, falling, rising. When the child moved one foot forward it shocked Mattie, as if something agreed between them was being violated.

With a knowing air, the little girl smiled, showing a space where a tooth was missing.

Mattie's stomach tightened. She could feel vomit rise in her throat.

The face was grotesque. The face of a child but with knowledge written there no child should know.

Mattie kept her eyes trained on the glass where both images were captured, willing herself to hold the girl there. She couldn't turn to face her, didn't dare to, yet felt so exposed, her back vulnerable to attack. Eyes were beginning to burn. She couldn't blink. Couldn't risk breaking the spell locking them in place.

But the child could risk it. She took another teasing step forward.

A low scream escaped Mattie.

As if spurred by excitement, the little girl took another step across the white tiles of the bathroom yet no sound came from the plastic raincoat or from her small brown shoes.

Blood pounded in Mattie's ears. Except for that, Mattie could hear nothing. Hearing was gone, turned inward, tuned to her bodily processes so enflamed by fear.

"No," she moaned and moved to put out a hand to stop the child. Her eyes watered from the strain of keeping them riveted on the mirror. She didn't dare blink. The menace, the gloating on the girl's face told her this was no friendly visit.

The small figure blurred, began to swim in place. Mattie feared fainting. She would have to face what was coming. Gradually she took in a deep breath and backed from the bowl to flatten herself against the wall, fingers pressed tightly to the icy tiles.

They faced each other directly.

With a mocking look of surprise the child put a tiny hand up to her mouth and took one slow step closer.

Mattie was panting. Her mind was whirling. She tried to gain control of it, to reason. This was only a child. What could she do to a grown woman? Had to get hold of herself. Stop being afraid. Confront her. Throw her out.

Had to find strength to get angry, to get this thing—this deranged thing—out of the apartment.

But her body wouldn't move. As if she were losing control, her legs were slipping out from under her. She felt herself begin to slide down the wall like a rag doll.

Fear. Fear was doing it. Couldn't feel her legs. No control. Hands going dead too. Unable to move arms.

Mattie gulped air. Opened her mouth to order the child to leave, to scream at her, but choked on words that wouldn't form. Throat useless. Arms, legs, hearing—all gone.

*The child was stealing her! Bit by bit, she was stealing her,
devouring her like some hungry animal!*

She felt herself slide unhindered to the floor, could
see her arms and legs at impossible angles.

Eyes and mind still there. Must fight to keep them.

The girl gave another giggle and folded her arms
across her chest, watching Mattie even more closely. "Too
bad for you," she said.

Mattie saw the mouth move. Strained to hear. Couldn't.
When the words blasted in her brain from the inside,
echoing with terrible precision, Mattie knew the child
would win, and she settled, with surprise, to watch the
end.

There was a blow Mattie was only dimly aware of. It
picked her limp body up and slammed it down on the
floor. There was no pain but it tipped her head and her
view of the girl tilted to one side.

Fear seemed to be gone now. She was not afraid,
just...interested in what was happening...and sorrowful.

The child was growing in size. Without moving another step she was leaving the floor. As she rose her small
body expanded until it blotted out the doorway behind
her, blotted out the room, the light, until she filled all
space and hung, huge, above Mattie. The coat, the face,
the eyes meshed and hovered ethereally, a part of the air,
expanding and diminishing with the breaths Mattie dragged
in and out.

God! God! Please help me!

Mattie's mind formed the words but they went nowhere.

The yellowed plastic was a curtain pressing toward
her face. Strawberries were huge bloody splotches. It
touched her skin, enveloped her, cut off what breath she
had left.

She choked. Air all gone. Light blocked. It pressed
...pressed...until her brain prepared to burst.

She raised the body from the floor and shook it, like
an old fur piece, to get the kinks out.

Hand out in front. Nice.

Other hand—hmmmmm.

Skin had blue marks where the body had hit the floor

with too much force. The marks hurt but she ignored this. Knew they would go away. Couldn't be helped anyway. It took that last burst of power to get control.

First to a sitting position. Hands traveling over the silk textured skirt then down the sleek, nylon-clad legs. So smooth, fully-rounded to her touch.

Standing now, unsteady, she looked into the mirror and ran a finger across the lips. Then she traced the line of the nose, the arch of an eyebrow. She pulled at a curl, let it bounce back and giggled with happiness at the strange feel against her head.

Standing on tiptoe she pulled the blouse down taut and turned from side to side. Breasts! She ran a hand over the swell of them, caressing the gentle curve. She smiled. Was happy.

"Mine," she whispered toward the mirror, voice quivering. "Mine."

Doing a little dance in place, she clapped her hands then found she had to clutch the washbowl to steady herself.

After a time she regarded the mirror and made a gesture of dismissal.

You can come on back, Martha. But only when I say. Ya hear? Me. When I say. I won. I just won the whole game.

She gave the mirror another check and patted primly at the hair before going back to the bedroom to choose the outfit they would wear that evening.

Chapter Three

Something terrible was wrong with her....

When David walked in Mattie ached to have him take her in his arms and make the world go away. She needed a safe place, just for a while, her own magic circle where she could hide until the fears and dreads assailing her would stop.

He had called, just as she knew he would. "I have to see you," he had said in a voice which meant more trouble.

If only she could forestall David's naked truth. She needed time. Peace. *Something was Wrong....*

She ran her arms up around his neck and pulled him down to kiss her but he backed away, gently removing her arms from where they held him.

"This has got to be said, Mattie. And I don't have much time. We've got a kidnapping on our hands. Union president, Ralph Molino. Could be a murder. I've only got an hour or so but there are things we've got to talk about."

She felt the tension in his arms and back. Tension that couldn't let up, she knew, until he did what he considered his duty. No escaping David's duty.

She gave him a bright smile, leaning away to look up at him. "So serious?"

He nodded.

She sighed and turned to walk over to the bar where she poured drinks for both of them. She really had been through enough already for one day, she thought, as she added more gin than tonic to her glass. Waking as she did, hours blank as if the clock had spun itself around when her back was turned; and dressed in that outfit, one she would never have chosen...she couldn't account for any of it. And since then—strange impulses, like being directed from inside by someone laughing at her.

Horrible. Incomprehensible. Must be a result of the headaches. Going insane. Brain tumor. Had to be some reason for a void in memory, for this evil worm within her brain chewing pieces of her life.

She was scared, and growing more frightened. Now he brought additional trouble.

"Couldn't we just be close tonight? No suspicions. No problems. Just tonight?" She handed him his drink which he set aside and ignored.

"It's about this psychic power you have." He went on, taking her hand and moving her to the couch. She sat and put her hands on the coarse fabric of the sofa as if for something to hang on to.

"What about my power? You're not going to start the same thing all over again, are you, David? I . . . I couldn't take it."

He was shaking his head, face solemn, even worn-looking, as if whatever he had to say had been working inside him.

"A man called me, a man named Alfred Williams." He stopped, watching her closely as if waiting for a response. She made none. He seemed to be studying her. She looked away. "Said he knew of a connection between those first bodies you found."

"A connection! Now come on, David, you know I had nothing to do . . ." her voice trailed off in fatigue.

"A union connection." Again he was watching her, waiting.

"Union? I don't understand." Her voice was quieter, less sure of itself. A new twinge of fear moved in her, quickening, as if her body were tensing for a blow.

David looked away. "This Williams guy is the grandfather of that little boy you found in that garage, the first one you helped me with. He was a union organizer about twenty-five years ago. He says two men he worked with at that time were Fred Gibonski, whose granddaughter was murdered in St. Clair Shores—you know, the first one you saw—and a John Gordon, whose daughter was Esther Shell—you remember . . ."

She nodded quickly, yes, she remembered.

"Coincidence," she said, round eyes huge and frightened.

"There's more. It has to do with your father."

"My father? With his accident?"

He nodded. "Only it seems . . . well . . . it seems he wasn't killed in an accident."

"There! There now! That proves the man's crazy. My father died in a car accident, coming home from Harsen's Island." She flounced away from him, face set.

He was shaking his head. "I had a talk with your mother, Mattie. She admitted it."

"Admitted what?" The twinge of fear was expanding into anger. She turned on him.

"That your father was shot in a scuffle with some union guys."

"You're a liar," she exploded, reaching out and pushing at him, slamming her hands against his chest, taking him off guard, knocking him sidewise.

He righted himself and grabbed on to her hands, holding her by both wrists as she screamed at him. Without a word he held her until she quieted, his eyes searching her face, going over every feature.

"Tantrums won't change anything." His voice was very low and in control. It cut through the anger she felt and finally quieted her.

"None of this is true, David. Believe me," she begged.

He just looked at her.

"Then what...I don't understand. I've always been told...."

"Money. Your Uncle John arranged a union pension in exchange for your mother's silence."

"Money. To cover up my father's death? And these men, these three you named, they killed him?"

"Four. There were four."

"Uncle John in on it too?"

"He wasn't the fourth, but he made the arrangements afterward."

"And he's dead too." She closed her eyes, face sick. "My God, David, what is it? What could be causing this? I didn't even know."

He let her hands go, pulled her toward him and held her. When he spoke his voice was shaking.

"You were there, Mattie. When they killed him. You were there with him. Even after he died. You were there."

Her eyes flew open. She sat away, looking deeply into his face.

"I'd remember something like that, David."

"They wouldn't let you. Every time you tried to talk about it they told you this other story until you believed it and forgot what happened."

"They? Who is they? You mean my mother?"

He nodded. "And Bella, Juliet, your aunt and uncle."

She had no words. There was nothing that could be said. Her mind raced and rejected thoughts.

"I don't believe it, David. I don't care what any of them say. I just don't believe it. That's not something you could make a person forget. And my father killed by

union organizers? Impossible, he was a real union man.
Why, we have scrapbooks...."

"But it's true. And we have to think what it means."

"What can it mean? I know I'm not killing anyone.
For God's sakes, why would I kill children? And my own
uncle? You know I had nothing to do with the murders.
You know that so what can you be thinking?"

"I don't know," he shook his head. "I don't know. But
I think you'd better stop. Stop all this chasing after rainbows.
I think you'd better get rid of Sanderson. Stop taking
money and..."

Her mind was in a turmoil but the refrain here was
familiar: Sanderson. Could it be? She closed her eyes to
shut out David. She took a deep breath and concentrated
on control, feeling confusion rolling in her brain.

"Is that what this is all about?" she asked, lips drawn
tight. "About Bobby? Did you make up these terrible lies
because you're jealous of him? Is that it?" She pulled away,
was staring coldly at him. She waited.

David shivered, reached for her, but she pulled away.

"They're not lies, Mattie," he said the words firmly
and tried again to hold her. She shrugged him off.

"I don't know what to believe." She got up to walk
over to the large window and stare down at the city. "I
don't even know you anymore. Could you say such things
just to get even? Just to get rid of Bobby...?"

"But it is the truth."

"So what!" she turned and screamed at him. "What
does all that change? I don't remember anything about
being there when my Daddy died. Not a thing and I don't
believe it. This is all coincidence. Coincidence. Or because
these men were evil I picked up on them first. I don't
know...there's some explanation. But don't expect me to
stop. This is a blessing from God and I'm using it to
help...."

"Is it a blessing?" he stopped her. They both stood,
facing each other, challenging one another to speak the
whole truth.

She turned away first. Stood looking out the window.
She rubbed vigorously at her forehead. He waited. She
was silent a long time. When she moved again it was to
rush over and throw her arms around him, laying her

head against his chest. They stood like that for what seemed a long time. Finally she said, "Let's not fight anymore." She was begging in a small, coaxing voice. "We mustn't fight. Just show me that you love me."

The voice wheedled in a way that was totally unlike Mattie. Suspicious, David pushed her to arm's length and examined the downturned face. Her eyes flashed up over him. They were filled with tears but beneath the tears there was a beam of mischief. She glanced down again, hiding them. With a movement, she wiggled her hips, pushing against the hands holding her away from him, indicating she wanted to be close, move against him.

She lifted her mouth upward, but her lips were different, puffy. They made kissing motions. From beneath half-closed lids the blue eyes stared keenly.

This wasn't Mattie. There was no mistaking it. She was someone else, a caricature of Mattie, a diseased creature. He was repulsed.

Bewildered, he held her away though she struggled to get close to him, to twine her arms around his neck.

"Don'cha want me?" Her voice weaseled into his mind. It was seductive, sex offered in every syllable. But it was also frightening. He shuddered again, backed away from her.

"What's going on, Mattie?" he demanded. "What's happening to you? This isn't..."

"Hmmmm," she only murmured softly, smiled, and worked her way in close, her mouth finding his, tongue darting at him, hands moving over him.

She was pushing backward toward her bedroom, hands, mouth, body exciting him. Soon his mind had no power left to question as he returned her kisses and followed where she led.

Chapter Four

Bobby came in brandishing the next morning's newspaper, smiling so that his tanned face, with the thick sandy brows and beard, was unusually open and alive.

"You read this? Big union man kidnapped. No one knows where he is. Alive or dead. Can you just picture the explosion if you found him? Fantastic! Right?" He moved the paper in front of her eyes.

"You mean free? Gratis? Help the police? Something like that?" She was suffering from a headache caused by a night of related dreams, all with the underlying theme of loss: Patsy, David, Uncle John...and she was tired of pain, had enough of it.

"Hell no. I mean big bucks. Union bucks. I'm going over there this morning. Sell that vice-president on you, on hiring you. The publicity, especially coming right on the heels of that Hollywood thing, will be fantastic. Super. Really super." Ebullience carried him away. He poured himself a cup of coffee and sat down opposite her at the tiny kitchen table.

"You know," he went on, "I've promoted some second-rate country singers, a couple of hopeful starlets, and even one half-assed comic, but this is my biggest coup—what I've done for you. And it keeps getting bigger. Hell, who knows where it will all end. If I pull this off—keep your fingers crossed, baby—you'll be known around the world. How's that for keepin' my word to you? Make you a name, I told you, around the world—and, by Christ, I'm doin' it."

"I think I've had a little to do with it myself." She was weary of his inflated ego, weary of him.

"Hell, you'd still be traipsing along behind that cop if it weren't for me," he scoffed and held his cup out for more.

She got up to get the coffee pot, coming back to fill both cups. With a sudden laugh, she set the pot back on the stove.

"You know something, Bobby?" She was shaking her head. "I was just thinking. My mother's doing the same thing I am right now: heating the coffee, pouring it for friends..."

"What the hell is that supposed to mean?" He was immediately on the defensive.

"Oh, nothing." Her smile weakened. "It's different, I guess. You're not Bella and Juliet. I'm not my mother. This isn't a god-awful flat on Mt. Eliot. But it just seemed for a minute like no matter how I fight I can't ever really escape. Maybe thirty-three was too late to break away, you think?"

He pushed his chair abruptly back from the table, arrogance piqued by her self-absorption.

"What in hell you want to bring me down for? I come in with great plans and all you can worry about is if you're like your mother. Hey, let's get with it here." His fist hit the table, cups sent wobbling.

Ignoring Bobby, not even hearing him, Mattie looked up at the noise. "I've been thinking about what you said once, Bobby, about moving to New York. Getting farther away from here. Maybe that's a good idea."

"Not now," he disagreed, tasted the coffee, then sopped up the mess in his saucer with a paper napkin. "This union thing is centered here, in Detroit. You're not going anywhere until this is over." He paused, speculatively eyeing her. "Anyway, you can't run from what's bothering you, you know. What you want is to have no past, and life doesn't work that way."

"Tell me about it," she scoffed, giving him a look that said what she thought of his insight. "It's more than that, Bobby. Things are happening to me. I...I don't think I'm feeling well and..."

"Hey." He got up from the table and came over to put an arm around her shoulders. He bent forward and nuzzled her neck. "Need another dose of Sanderson healing?"

Deep in thought, she leaned against him, cheek against

his chest, then, realizing who he was and what he had said, she pushed him away. "No more gigolo love, thanks," she laughed.

He let her go immediately and, shrugging, went back to his coffee while she calmed herself.

"David's found a connection," she said finally, voice strained. "He's found a connection between those first bodies I saw and my father's death. He think's I'm responsible somehow."

"He say that?" He stared across at her, met her look.

She nodded, then amended, "Well, not exactly, but that was the implication."

"Bastard!" Bobby spit out the word. "Just his jealousy. He know you and I made it together?"

She nodded again. "I think so."

"There. There's your reason for what he's doing to you. Trying to make you unsure of yourself, making you doubt your sanity even. Don't listen, babe. Ignore him. Why you let him go on hanging around is beyond me anyway."

"I love him."

"Shit! Like you'd love a good dose of the clap. If that's love I'm glad I never caught the fever."

"But some of the things he told me make sense. He's not dreaming up what happened."

"So? You know you had nothing to do with the murders, right? You know you find dead bodies through these visions, or trances, or whatever you call 'em, right? Then what do you care what connections he makes? Let him make 'em till he drives himself nuts for all I care. As long as you're in the clear there's nothing for us to worry about, right?"

She nodded again.

"And quit worrying about your past." He finished the coffee, pulled a notebook from an inner pocket, consulted it, and stood. "If I told you my past you'd mess your drawers. My old man ran me off when I was thirteen. Told me I cost too much to feed and to hit the road. Old bastard. I hope he's dead now. Well, I've got to get over to the union. Gonna bring you back a plum, baby. You be here working?"

"I think I'll go home," she answered after a while. "I think I'll go see my mother. Call me there if you want to. I need to know some things."

With a short, bitter laugh Bobby said, "Mattie, you don't even know where home is. You're just like me—a goddamned orphan."

"I hope not," she whispered, watching his face, a forlorn look crossing hers.

"Go home," he said, softening. "You'll see."

Chapter Five

"Martha! Martha! Martha!" Juliet was the first to see her as she let herself in the door. "Look who's here, Harriet. Martha." She clapped her hands in excitement.

Harriet rose and hurriedly pulled off her apron as she did only when the insurance man came to call.

"No, Ma. Sit. Sit. I'm not company." She waved her back to the kitchen table where the three were having another of their endless cups of coffee.

"Here. Sit with us, Martha." Harriet motioned to a chair and looked deep into Mattie's face as if to read the signals there and find out if today was the end of her world.

Mattie saw, sensed her mother's concern, and dreaded having to pull the curtain aside after all these years. But it had been, and still was, a curtain between them—Daddy's murder.

"Hot, eh?" Bella took a deep swig at her cup then, red-faced, puffed out her cheeks and gave a tremendous blow as if to cool them all. "Never slept at all last night. Toss. Turn. Toss. Turn. Too damned hot. Bet that place of yours is cool, eh?"

Distracted, Mattie nodded.

"Yes. Cool." She turned to her mother, who looked so different suddenly. Grayer than she remembered. Skin faded. A pale contrast with her burnt-hennaed curls. Mattie hadn't seen her since before the California trip, and the change was striking.

"How's everything been, Ma?" Mattie couldn't take her eyes off her mother's face; she suddenly recognized with a sense of shock how familiar the face looked now that it was marred with age and trouble. Her own face. Mattie's.

If she allowed herself to think too much about it, Mattie knew it might drive her crazy. Like being haunted by her own ghost. Or facing a fate she fought desperately to avoid.

"'Bout the same." Harriet was shrugging off the question. "You want coffee?"

"No. Too hot. Terrible for September."

"Best thing for you when it's hot," Juliet put in. "Drink something hot. Cools you off."

"Makes me sweat," Bella disagreed.

"That's 'cause you gulp it. You should sip it."

"Baloney! Cold stuff. That's what cools you off. Stands to reason."

"My doctor said hot liquid," Juliet frowned in Bella's direction. "Heat up the inside and the outside feels cool by comparison. That's the scientific explanation."

"That the same doctor told you you were pregnant when you had that gallstone that time?"

"Yes. I've always had Dr. Tyscka. Wouldn't let anybody else touch me. And he didn't say I was pregnant, just said that could be one of the things it was and we wouldn't know until the tests came back."

"Can't you just see if you'd gone into labor and—plop— this little gallstone'd rolled out on the table?" That sent Bella bellowing with laughter as Juliet fumbled for one of her tissues and Harriet frowned at the pair of them.

"I want to talk to you, Ma." Mattie ignored the other women and spoke confidentially to Harriet.

Harriet's eyes flew open. For a moment she couldn't catch her breath, a hand moving up to tap her chest as if begging for help.

Mattie half rose to help her but she whispered, "No, no, sit. I'm all right. Just my age. And the heat. Don't sleep well these..."

"Ma," Mattie insisted on her attention. "We've got to talk about...about my father. I know, about his death. David told me. Now I need you to tell me. I need to hear it from you and I'd like you to tell me without these two here."

"Oh, Mattie..." Harriet started to cry, hanging her head forward limply from her shoulders as if she had no strength to keep it aloft.

Afterwards, Mattie reached out to touch her mother's faded and freckled hands, clasping each other before her on the table. "Don't you see what you did to me? The memory's still in here. Locked up tight. I don't know if that's what triggered the visions or not, but I know it shouldn't have been bottled up all these years. The wall between me and the rest of the world got too high. It's always there, always there because the rest of my world lied to me. And now other things are happening...the child...she..." It was gone, what she wanted to say. Gone. She shook her head but the memory was erased. Strange. She knew there had been something she wanted to say....

"I'm so sorry...." Harriet dared to look at Mattie. "So sorry. I never wanted to hurt you, you know that. Thought it was for the best..."

Mattie took a deep breath. Sweat broke out on her forehead. She tried again to think what she had wanted to say but came up with nothing. "I know, Ma. I know," she finally said.

Further recriminations would have been cruel. No need for cruelty. But what? She felt so...so unsatisfied.

"Been a while, hasn't it? Since you been here." Bella broke into the silence after a while, trying for her normal voice. "Since your Uncle John's funeral."

Mattie nodded and realized by entering into the fantasy of "all's well" she was relinquishing her right to punish them, to walk out and be free forever. She looked at each of the three old women. Only Bella's eyes met hers. She nodded, agreeing with Bella's question.

"How's Aunt Jenny? She doin' all right?"

It was Harriet who nodded, gingerly drying her eyes. "Kids are good to her. But you know Jenny, she's still playin' it up for all it's worth. Cried enough tears to fill Lake Michigan." Harriet shook her head. "Always did enjoy trouble, her own as well as anybody else's." The other two nervously clucked with Harriet over her sister-in-law's perversity and watched Mattie's face.

"How's it feel to be home?" Bella asked Mattie. "We read about you out in Hollywood. You meet many movie stars?"

It was, question by question, tiny step by tiny step, back to business as usual. Mattie didn't believe them. Five minutes for a lifetime of treachery. And now they were slipping away, back to the old world, and she was letting them. She even realized she wanted it as much as they. This new texture to their long-term relationship was too prickly to be sustained. It felt wrong, uncomfortable. Nothing was worth this cliff-hanging suspense between them. With relief she turned to Juliet and smiled as the woman went off into raptures over Mattie's career and good fortune.

Their questions were endless. She excused herself when she could take no more. She went down the hall to the bathroom, followed by Bella's jocular, "You remember where it is, don't ya?"

The dull white tile, the pink shower curtain with a poodle printed on its crackled surface reminded her of that Sunday evening David and she made love and the women had come back from Toronto to find them together. Not quite a year but so long ago.

She let the water run to cover her stay there, then opened the bathroom door and went the few steps farther down the hall to her old room.

Jesus—like a shrine.

Just as it had always been, since she was a child. Slant ceiling. Stuffy with heat. Flowered paper. Flawed lampshade. Long dirty string hanging from a center light. Exactly as she left it. She could walk back in tomorrow and shrug her old life on as easily as shrugging on the cardigan sweater laying over the ladderback chair. Frightful thought.

She threw herself on the bed, wadding the comforter and pillow beneath it in her hands, burying her head in the nest of cloth, stifling the scream growing from some untapped place inside her.

Dear God, he *is* dead. Dead.

Tears ran. She held up one hand to examine it as if through a cloud. It had the feel of his hand clasp, felt alive with the electricity of his grip. Just yesterday...

Blue...blue pants: rough; smell of wet wool...

Rain, Ma said. Raining. Begged him to go out...my fault...all my fault.

Head hurting. Terrible pain closing in.

Not my fault. They're all liars. Want me to be blamed, feel guilty, absolve them.

Shit! She flounced around to lie on her back, the faint odor of disturbed dust rising from the bed.

They knew all right. They knew. And she would fix 'em for what they did. Fix 'em....

Mattie opened her eyes wide, shocked as she listened to the words coming from her own mouth, mean, vindictive words she didn't recall formulating in her brain. But there they were.

She put her feet to the floor, took a deep breath, made a decision, then got up and crossed the room, pulling aside the figured curtain covering the closet opening, pushing aside the clothes left hanging, searching the floor, hunting for the pile of scrapbooks she had left in one corner. She separated and moved the clothes down the wooden rod, working her way toward the right.

Her hand hit the slick surface and pulled to move it out of her way, pulled toward her. She was looking down, hunting for the scrapbooks, didn't see the raincoat until her face was only inches from it.

Plastic yellowed and brittle. Strawberries faded. Strawberries. Red splotches...

Mattie inhaled suddenly, covered her scream with a taut hand.

The strawberry raincoat...but how had she forgotten? It had always hung here. Always...but...

Then the child must be a trick of her own mind. A phantasm made up from buried memory. But why? Why? And what had just happened to her that she couldn't remember, couldn't quite grasp, something to do with that awful child? Something...no, no, it wouldn't come.

She grasped her head in both hands and held it still until the wild thoughts quieted.

Too much for one human being to take: divination, a child who didn't exist, fame, buried memories...too much, that was why the black periods...strain beyond endurance.

She forced herself to relax, to take a deep breath.

All could be explained. She needed to rest, to think without pressure from anyone. She needed peace.

Chapter Six

"They won't go for it," Bobby was saying over the phone. "Say they don't want to make a three ring circus outta this thing. But, hell, I just don't think they want to find the guy."

"That's too bad." She had trouble working up a sense of disappointment. Her mind was tugged in too many directions.

"Don't worry. I've got other irons in the fire. Your Bobby doesn't lay down on the job."

"What else is there? Who else would pay?"

"Never mind. This time I'm not talking until I peddle the idea. Should have an answer by tonight. Or, at the latest, tomorrow. Don't worry if you don't hear from me. I won't call until this is worked out one way or the other."

She hung up, conscious only that she had hardly heard what he said, too preoccupied.

Getting up to answer the phone, she had glanced at the clock. *One-thirty!* She was stunned. Four hours gone. She had sat down for only a minute at nine-thirty that morning. It should be ten, at the most, ten-thirty. But four hours were just erased from her life. And it was happening repeatedly.

That morning she had taken three aspirins but they'd worn off now. Head hurting again. Pain seemed to outline hours of every day, at least the hours she was conscious of, hours that weren't totally missing—gone—as if they were being sucked back into some black hole.

Yesterday evening she had found herself walking down a street she didn't know, couldn't remember how she got there or why she was there. Just walking. All time before that moment was lost.

She curved her fingers around the phone, held it tightly. She had been trying to recall the past, dredge up memories buried under years of lies, but they wouldn't come. Maybe that was why the blank hours? Her mind's way of protecting itself. But then why would she be outside, walking where she'd never been before? Why blanks in her memory that had nothing to do with the past? And why these strange feelings, tugs at emotions, hatreds she wasn't aware of, words and voices in her head?

And trying so hard to remember the day Daddy died...

She was still holding the phone when it rang again.

David. Voice weary.

"You sound so tired," she told him.

"I am. This case is breaking me instead of the other way around. But I've got some time. Till tomorrow. Noon. Can I come over?"

"Sure," she agreed. "But, David, I can't take much more. Not while I'm—well—I'm so unsure about everything. Come on over but let's be the way we used to be. Just for today."

"Can't. That's why I'm coming. We have to talk."

"I understand," she hurried to say, placating him. "I know. But just today—no pressures. No recriminations. I...I...please?"

"This is too important, Mattie. Something's come up and we've got to face it, all of it. And I...I have a suggestion. An idea that might help."

"I went home, David." Her voice held pain. "I asked my mother and got the truth. So I believe you now. Still, I don't see how it affects my work."

"Did you remember? I mean, after you talked to your mother, did anything come back?"

"Nothing. Nothing at all. Except...except something about...eh...what was it now? There was something I wanted to tell you but it's gone, wiped out. Christ, David, this is happening all the time. What's wrong with me?"

"I'm coming over, Mattie. We'll talk then."

She hung up but vowed there would be no more pain today. She needed a break from fear.

They might have been two polite strangers sitting across from each other in her cool living room, drinks in hand, pleasant smiles, consciously animated faces. Two strangers who had not a clue how to proceed.

She greeted him with a kiss that seemed to embarrass more than excite him. He laughed self-consciously as she helped him out of his jacket and ran her hands over his back. With a shiver, he pulled away, waving a hand slightly as if to hold her off.

It annoyed her, that gesture of dismissal. It angered her that it seemed of no importance that she wanted him now—first—before—and the hell with drinks, lunch, and talk.

She sat and sipped and stewed.

"You saw your mother?" He drank half of his Scotch down in a few gulps then lowered the glass to look intently at her. "But nothing came back, eh?"

"Not really." She shrugged, looked away from the probing eyes. "I've tried but I seem to have a big black box in my head, and it's locked. No way to get inside."

Both lost in thought, they sat without speaking for a few minutes until David asked, "You still seeing that child who was hanging around here? You still see her?"

"Who?"

"That child. Remember?"

She tried to think. "Oh, the day I got back from California. She was here, I think, in the apartment. Seems I saw her...then she just disappeared. I haven't seen her since."

"Hmmm." He sat quietly for a moment. "You ever wonder about that little girl? I mean, did her appearance here, right in your apartment, shock you?"

"Of course. Little monster had no business hanging around like that." Her anger showed. "Guess she got scared off, though. Gone now."

"Strange, don't you think?" He was watching her face. "I mean, her getting right in here."

"What do you mean strange? Nervy, that's for sure."

"Are you certain she was real, Mattie? She couldn't have been another manifestation of your psychic power, could she?"

At first she was startled, then puzzled.

"Why...why do you ask?" She tried to think, but the thoughts she reached for were blocked, stayed just out of reach. "Seems like there was something...something wrong. Yesterday, at my mother's. Something I wanted to tell you. Now it's gone."

He looked worried, watching her fumbling with her mind. He reached over and took her hand.

"Listen, forget it for now. I've learned some new information you should know. It's about Ralph Molino." He stopped, cleared his throat. In his mind he was going over the phone call he'd gotten just the other day from Alfred Williams—the drunken call in which Williams gloated over his foreknowledge of Molino's kidnapping and let drop a few more pieces of this horrifying puzzle. David wondered how much he should tell Mattie. Her eyes were on him. "You know, Mattie, this union thing. Seems Molino's the one who shot your Dad. Now he's missing too."

She felt as if the room were closing in. No, it was more than that, her brain screamed. She didn't want to know any more, put a hand out to stop him. But he was determined.

"Another one of my victims?" Her voice was bitter. She waited.

"I never said..."

"Yes you have. Over and over. In different ways. You think I'm involved somehow."

"Mattie, I..."

"I might as well tell you, Bobby's trying to get someone to pay me to enter the case, to try to find him." The words came out even. Her eyes never left his face.

"Terrible idea."

"According to you Bobby's never had a good one."

"This isn't about him, Mattie. Believe me it isn't."

"That's hard for me to do, believe you."

"Look." He moved closer to her, held on to her hand. "I've been thinking. Why don't we try hypnosis again. Age regression. You should be an easy subject. Try to take you back to that day when you were five. Bring the child out."

"Child? Child? What child? What do you mean?" She was panicked.

"You. When you were five." He spoke calmly. "That's what age regression does, takes you back to your childhood."

"Oh...yes, but Tolly..."

"Doesn't matter. I called Lilith. Said she could do it. Take you back to that day, see if the memory surfaces."

She pulled away from him, gathering her robe closed across her breasts. She didn't like this. Not at all. For a time she was silent, thinking. Then she asked, "Why can't we leave it alone, David? Why do I have to go back and relive something that horrible? Maybe it's a blessing I can't remember. Can you imagine what it must have been like? To see my Daddy shot?"

"I've thought about that. But we've got to try. This can't go on with us not even knowing why it's happening or if there really is a connection. We can't just let it hang there like this."

"*You* can't! I can gladly ignore the whole damn thing." She turned from him when she heard her voice rising with frustration.

"This is murder, Mattie. We have to know."

"That's because you're a cop. I swear I think that badge is engraved on your soul. I don't want to know what I'm not supposed to know. I only want my life to go on just as it is. I'm not going to help destroy it because of your guilt."

"But, Mattie...", his voice softened, "just the hypnosis. Let's try it and see."

She hesitated, her eyes large. Slowly she admitted, "But I...I'm afraid."

"Don't be. I'll be there. And we do have to know. We have to."

"All right. But if nothing comes of it I want you to drop all of this. Drop all this digging into my past." She stood, pulled her hand from his.

He shook his head miserably. "You know I can't promise. I . . . I just can't."

"Bastard," she muttered after he was gone.

Liked that word.

Good one.

Big, round word.

BASTARD.

The silk robe swished around her as she walked. She flounced it back and forth and listened to the murmur of cloth on cloth. Nice.

Now, what to do all afternoon?

Only one thing appealed. Scrapbooks.

Look at 'em again. All those men Daddy knew.

All those men . . .

She bent over, laughing at some secret, then brought the heavy books to the sofa, where she settled down to browse through her own garden of delights.

Page after yellowed page. Articles browning, curling from dried paste. Brittle.

No matter. All there. Faces she'd looked at a thousand times . . . no, a million times.

She turned a dusty page.

"*Enjoying the outing Sunday are Mr. and Mrs. Fred Gibonski and their granddaughter.*"

"*Winners of the three-legged race were Johnny "Flash" Gordon, and daughter Esther.*"

"*Prettiest baby contest winner, Billy Williams, beams at his grandfather, Alfred Williams.*"

On picture after picture she rubbed a chubby finger over the faces. Some were completely rubbed away.

And the most recent scrapbook: pictures of the new president, Ralph Molino. A large man, rumpled suits . . . faceless, empty space where features should have been.

After a time she closed the book and leaned her head back against the sofa, concentrating deeply. One hand made a tentative movement upward, then it formed itself purposefully and came up to fit the thumb neatly into her mouth.

Could concentrate now. Could really think about those men who hurt Daddy.

Chapter Seven

When the phone rang it cut into her sleep like a deep and painful wound. She didn't want to be awake. No. Let her alone. Let her sleep. But it insisted. She pushed the scrapbooks away, got up. David? No, he was gone. The phone rang again.

Bobby.

"Wake up there," he shouted at her. "Papa's brought home the bacon." Jubilance rushed his words. He gave a whoop.

"It's all arranged. 'The Tabok Show' thought the idea was great. Two appearances instead of one. Maybe more."

"Wait. Who...what are you talking about?" She tried to clear her head so it would absorb the information.

"What I tried to sell the union. Tabok's producer loved it. They're going to hire you to find that union guy. Great gimmick, eh? You go on first and tell your story. They explain they've hired you. Work up the publicity. You know the scam. Then you go back when you find him."

"When! Whatever happened to 'if'?"

"Forget 'if.' Your hit rate's getting close to ninety percent. That's good enough to take to the bank." He was annoyed.

"When do I have to be there?"

"Tomorrow night. They want it fast. Beat the cops before they come up with something. Never know. That's the only thing could queer the deal. So—anyway—I've got reservations for tomorrow morning. Nine-thirty plane. Pick you up about eight. We can have breakfast at Metro—

O.K. Oh—yes—I want you to wear that gray crepe dress. Doesn't hurt to give 'em a little T and A while you're showin' 'em what you can do. Keeps their attention."

The phone rang again as soon as she hung up. This time it was David.

"Hi. Sorry I had to leave things hanging like that. But I wanted to get this session set up right away and ... and I had to get back," he finished lamely. "Listen, I've arranged with Lilith for tonight, if that's all right?"

"Oh—I don't think so, David. I've got to be in New York tomorrow. Bobby got 'The Tabok Show' to hire me in the Molino kidnapping so I really have to pack and ..."

"You're going through with it?" he broke in. "Even when we don't know so many things about what's going on?"

"I have to. We've signed."

"All the more reason to get this over with tonight then." His voice was brusque. "Maybe still change everything."

"Change what? How could it?" She was annoyed. "I have a contract."

"And you want all of that anyway," he added.

She paused. "Of course I do."

"Fine. Do what you like afterward. But do this tonight. Give Lilith a chance. You agreed?"

"David." She paused then breathed deeply before going on. "All right. Bring her here. Eight o'clock. But don't expect anything to change my mind."

Chapter Eight

"Sure, I'm Mattie. And don't call me Martha cause that's a dumb name."

The tone was high and childish, answering Lilith's question in a small voice coming from the lipsticked mouth. The face was as it had been, deftly made-up, but changed.

There was a pouting softness around the lips. Her wide eyes went from one to the other: David to Lilith, and then to scan the room.

"What is this?" The child looked gravely around her and then back to Lilith and David. "You're Lilith, aren't you?" Her bright eyes landed on the big woman with curiosity. A touch of wariness moved over the features. "What do you want?"

"Just to talk to you, m'dear. Just to talk. Don't be frightened by us. We don't often bite little girls, ya know." The laughter in Lilith's voice soothed the child. She leaned back slowly, eyes moving from one to the other of the people before her. She was on guard, not ready to trust either.

"And can you tell me how old a girl you are, Martha?"

The child bit at her lips, angrily looked away and back. She folded her arms across her chest, took a deep breath, but didn't answer. She was obviously angry.

"Mattie, dear?" Lilith prodded. "Can you tell us your age or is it you don' know how old you are?"

Reluctantly Mattie spread one hand open, five fingers stuck up stiffly.

"Five. Ummm—I see. Yes. That is a very nice age to be, I'm sure. And do you go to school, Mattie?"

The child nodded then looked toward David. She gave him a slow, knowing smile, narrowing her eyes.

A shudder passed over David's body. Reflexively, he pulled away, as if to hide behind Lilith.

Lilith's voice was a tranquilizing monotone. The soft, high notes of her sing-song Jamaican accent were as hypnotic as repeated drum beats.

It had taken her only moments to hypnotize Mattie. The slow, backward regression to the age of five had taken longer. It was a calibrated descent through the years of Mattie's life, formulated by Lilith so as not to move her too quickly, shock her system in any way.

"Now, m'dear, I am going to test your memory, see how well you recall special days. It is your birthday. Your fifth birthday. Do you remember your fifth birthday, m'dear?"

David sat very still, fearing even his breathing might be a distraction.

She nodded. "I remember."

"Good. Very, very good, little girl. Now tell me about this celebration of your birth. Who was there? Do you remember?"

"Let's see." The brows came together. "Mr. and Mrs. Schwartz, Uncle John and Aunt Jenny, and my cousins. And Mrs. Swiderski, and Mommy and Daddy. That's all, I think. I had a real big cake. With a picture on it."

"That's good. Very good. So your Daddy was there too?"

She nodded. "You wanna know what presents I got? 'Cause I can tell you."

"No, Mattie. I want to know about your Daddy."

The room was still. David held his breath, waiting. The little girl turned away again but then faced Lilith and appeared to give in.

"Daddy? You sure you wanna talk 'bout him?"

"Yes, Mattie. Tell me about your Daddy. What does the man look like? Where is he now?"

Her eyes went down to her hands. She mumbled. "He looks fine." She shifted about in the chair uncomfortably then brought one leg up, tucking it under her.

"Now, little girl, what do you mean when you say fine? How does the man look?"

"I love Daddy very much." She settled her face into stubborn lines.

"Oh, we know that, Mattie. Of course you love him very much, but..."

"I got a raincoat and hat and umbrella for my birthday, from my Aunt Jenny. They all got strawberries on 'em. All match, too. All three. I like 'em a lot." As she spoke her expression passed from the excitement of telling about her prize to something else. Sadness. "But those men stepped on my umbrella. And my hat fell off and I forgot to pick it up. But somebody did. I found it home. And Ma never said anything about the umbrella. I guess she forgot. She musta forgot or she'd yell at me for losin' it. But it wasn't my fault. Those men..."

"Would your Daddy yell at you too? About the umbrella?"

"He can't. They did something to 'im. He can't say anything because those men hurt him."

"Did your Daddy ever come back after those men hurt him?"

She shook her head no.

"Can you remember that day? Can you tell me what happened that day? When you went for a walk with your Daddy?"

She nodded then sat thinking for a few minutes, the fingers of one hand picking at her lower lip as she concentrated.

"Me and Daddy went for a walk. To the store. He held on to the umbrella because I'm not big enough and he'd get wet if I carried it. We were going to the store, to get Ma some stuff. These men, four of 'em, came up and started yellin' at my Daddy, and pushin' him. They were ugly men. They pushed Daddy down and there was a big noise and they came running back. They stopped by me but then they all left and I went to get Daddy but he was just layin' there with garbage and everything on him and he wouldn't get up."

"What did you do?" Lilith prodded.

She thought deeply, the thumb of her right hand pressing against her lips, fingers curved around it. "I just sat down."

"Right in the alley?"

She nodded. "I couldn't leave Daddy and he wouldn't wake up."

"Did you ever see your Daddy after that?"

The head slowly indicated no. "I shouldn'ta fell asleep. They took him away when I was asleep. Those men came back. I know it. And Uncle John too. But I was sleepy. I didn't see everything."

"Later, after you were home again, what reason did your mother give for your father's never coming back?"

The child frowned and slipped the thumb tentatively between her lips.

"You mean when she said Daddy got killed in an accident?"

"Yes. What did she say about that?"

"She lied. They all lied to me. That dumb Martha believed 'em but not me. I pretended but it wasn't true. My Daddy got hurt by those men but Ma lied. You're not supposed to lie either. But Mrs. Schwartz and Mrs. Swiderski an' Uncle John an' Aunt Jenny all told the same lie. That other Martha believed it 'cause she never knew any better but not me." Here she pointed roundly to herself, tapping her chest with a rigid finger.

"That other Martha?" Lilith inquired. "Which other Martha?"

"You know. The one who growed up. Her. She believed 'em even though I tried to tell her different. She never did nothin' about it neither." She shook her head as if to impress these grownups with the uselessness of some people.

"Never did nothing about what, Mattie?"

"About what those men did to Daddy. Never did nothin'."

"But what could she do? The girl didn't even know the truth, don't you remember?"

"But I kept tellin' her. She just wouldn't listen."

"Do you know anything about these visions of dead bodies and murders that Martha has?" Lilith nonchalantly slipped in the question.

The child was surprised. She pushed back against the chair and looked menacingly at her. She said nothing for a while. Lilith and David waited, watching. Finally she nodded.

"You know about them?" Lilith prodded.

"I said yes, didn't I?" She was angry with her. "I know Martha has 'em but they won't hurt her."

"Do you know what causes them?"

The child looked away from Lilith's face then looked directly at David. He sat back, away from her.

"You're David. I know you." The look she gave him was so lewd David's face burned with shame, though he didn't know why he should feel that way.

"You better not hurt Mattie." Her face, Mattie's face, hardened as she spoke, eyes narrowing, lips firm. The face became grotesque with its make-up covering a child's features. Suddenly the child seemed old to him. Evil. "You just leave her alone or you'll be sorry. You just wait and see."

Unable to control himself, David made a move toward her, angry. Lilith restrained him, holding him back with her strong hands. "Let me," she coaxed. "You will drive her away."

"Why did you threaten David?" Lilith kept her voice calm.

The girl looked away again. Refused to answer.

"Ask her about the child Mattie's been seeing," David whispered to Lilith, who nodded.

"Now, Mattie, tell me, do you know about this little girl who the other Mattie has been seeing everywhere? Can you tell me anything about this experience?"

Mattie pursed her lips and shook her head. "That was a real big surprise. I mean that she could see me like that." She leaned earnestly toward Lilith. "Boy oh boy, what a shock it was the first time she waved. I thought I was gonna fall right down. That was fun, her bein' able to see me like that. But it kinda scared me too 'cause it was like she was gettin' stronger and I was gettin' weaker and she's not the one who knows how to do things like me. Something's always been wrong with her. I don't know what it is, but if I don't tell her what to do she just kinda does nothing."

She stopped only for breath, hurried on.

"When she was growin' up I thought I would too—grow up. But I never did. Stayed just the same. It was like gettin' lost in here. This body grew, had things happen to it, but I was kinda swallowed up, no real place of my own." She shuddered. "But then I had power she didn't have. I knew how to do things, could take care of things, not let people hurt us." She stopped suddenly, yawned. "I'm too tired to talk anymore. Can't we stop?"

Lilith hesitated then nodded that yes, that was enough and told her to lean back, close her eyes, sleep.

Curled sideways in the chair, the girl gave them one last baleful look before tucking her thumb into her mouth and closing her eyes.

"Well!" David sank back and looked expectantly at Lilith, who shrugged her shoulders.

"Poor child." Lilith's face expressed her sympathy. "Poor little girl, to see her father be murdered so. No wonder this poor innocent thing suffers."

David listened, let his eyes move over the sleeping

woman, then looked back at Lilith speculatively. "Must've been terrible, I'll admit. But what I wonder is just how innocent she is. What was this power she spoke of anyway? And what has she been doing with it? Didn't it strike you odd that she talked as if she were separate from Mattie, as if she were a different person?"

"Well...yes, that is not usual but..."

"There's something wrong here, Lilith. Something we haven't found out yet."

"You mean...something evil?" She raised her brows, watched him.

"Think about it. This five-year-old acts like a person separate from Mattie. Do you know some rationale that would fit here? If you do, please tell me."

"How, now, my friend. There are always reasons. Some not as possible as others, but always there are reasons for strange things to happen."

"Please. I'm serious, Lilith. Let me know what you think."

"Well." She settled herself comfortably in the chair, turned away from Mattie. Her voice stayed low. "I do not know for certain, David, what this can be. Perhaps what psychiatrists call a split personality."

"But she talked about the body growing and she didn't. That doesn't sound like a personality fragment to me. That sounds like a separate person. Or am I wrong? I tell you, my mind just can't handle all of this."

"Calm. Calm yourself. Perhaps it is not a mental illness then. I don't know." She raised her shoulders then dropped them. "We are all many selves, you know. The child in all of us remains a child all our life, influences many things we do. Some never really grow beyond that child. Most—wouldn't you say?—never grow beyond teen years even though the body ages. But these selves, child, teen, adult, they grow together, form a single being. Not like this." She motioned toward Mattie.

"You think she should see a psychiatrist?" he asked. "But what about this psychic ability? Is that what the kid means by her 'power'? And how does it tie in with this two person business?"

Lilith drew a deep breath, thought a moment, then answered carefully, "There are other possibilities..."

"Such as?"

"Possession, for one." David was shaking his head. "Now don't scoff. That it happens is fact, a proven fact recognized by all the churches of the world. To believe in God and goodness one must also believe in Satan and evil. Yes, evil. But, don' worry, I do not believe this is an imp of Satan residing in your friend's body. If it were I would have known it immediately. They make themselves known. And, dear friend, we would need a priest here to protect us." She paused, assessing his reaction and ability to listen to more.

"No, this is possession of a very different kind. Your friend chooses to be possessed, possessed by a part of herself that split off at age five and took a different, abnormal direction. Either guilt over her father's death or fear of being killed herself stopped the growth at this age. Or—and this is what I believe—this part of her stopped growing through hatred so intense she could think of nothing, ever, but those men who hurt her father. You've seen her here tonight. A little girl who never grew. My heart cries for this child, David. I weep for a little girl, no more than a baby, who sees her father murdered before her eyes, is then lied to, confused, not allowed to let out these feelings. But—and I don't mean to offend when I say this—I have the feeling, one I noticed from the first time she came to my shop, that your friend, or the child who is also your friend, has deliberately and tragically chosen to be evil in order to get revenge."

"Evil! But you said it wasn't some imp or..."

"But evil nonetheless. Just as the worst tendencies within us cannot be blamed on the devil but rather on our own baser instincts, hers—Mattie's—have been given form as a self within a self. For twenty-nine years she has practiced evil, indulged hatred. She is quite the expert now, wouldn't you say?"

He frowned toward her, speechless for the moment. Then a movement from Martha startled them both.

Lilith whispered hurriedly, "She will come out of it naturally, through sleep. Be careful."

"How can I help her?" His face was gray, beard shadowing his cheeks. "Does a real Mattie even exist?"

Lilith shrugged and picked at a ragged nail. "I don't

think there can be a real Mattie. She was partly the old Martha and partly the child. But perhaps you can help the old Martha. In fact, if you don't, the deaths will continue. You must help her be rid of the evil, but when the evil dies so will the psychic power and so will the child. You must tell her all of this. Tell her what has grown independently—as a cancerous growth would—within her, and then help her to grow strong enough to recapture her mind. She is the only one capable of stopping this."

Mattie moved again. Lilith lowered her voice to a whisper.

"She will be herself when she wakes up. Give her time to rest before you tell her what we now know."

He nodded then smiled as Mattie sat up and stretched. But the face was not what he expected. It still smirked, still smiled crookedly. She leaned toward Lilith and David and, dropping the smile, bared her teeth, hissing, "You just try to get rid of me. We'll see whose power is stronger. You just try and hurt me."

Shocked, the two sat frozen as she laughed at them then sat back into the chair to glare malevolently, until her eyes closed and she slept.

When she next awoke she was confused, apologetic, and nervously complained of having another terrible headache.

David decided not to tell her what he knew. Not yet. First he had to believe it himself.

Chapter Nine

The monkey squatted, stared into space, and urinated on the floor beside Mattie's foot.

"Chico! Shame on you." The girl clucked at the grinning monkey and gave a tug at his leash.

Bobby, leaning forward, hands clasped nervously between his knees, eyed her with disgust. "Well? Aren't you gonna clean it up?" He pointed to the puddle trailing across the speckled tiles, running in a rivulet with the dip of the floor toward Mattie's shoe. "You want my client to slide out of here on a pool of monkey piss?"

The woman pulled the monkey to her, gave Bobby a look that told what she thought of animal-haters, and came over to dab at the puddle with a handful of tissues.

Mattie only half watched the exchange. Her nerves were screaming, her stomach a live squirrel rolling and scrambling inside, blood pounding through her temples. This sitting and waiting was making all her hysterical symptoms even worse.

In the green room with her, waiting to go on the "Tabok Show," were the young woman with the weak-kidneyed monkey and a distinguished gentleman who silently clutched the book he was touting and stared up at the bank of monitors broadcasting the show in progress. A sad old comedian paced, head hanging forward, hands behind his back, cigarette clinging to a dry lip.

Mattie sympathized with the monkey and wondered if she had time to make one more trip to the bathroom. What if her stomach should rumble on camera? What if she should pass gas? Or even throw up on Gil Tabok?

"Hey, catch that promo?" Bobby was nudging her, pointing at the monitors. "You'll come after the monkey."

Someone called her name and led her to a spot behind a curtain to wait. She was sure she would faint before those curtains parted. But within seconds she heard that famous lilting voice announce:

"Let's give her a warm welcome folks—Mattie Small!"

Her head went up. She pasted on a smile, assumed a confident air, and marched out, greeting Gil Tabok, who kissed her warmly and sat her beside him on a love seat.

Applause she had been oblivious to until now cut into her consciousness as she turned toward this well-known face, his mouth poised, waiting for quiet so he could ask her a question.

"Funny," he said. "You don't look psychic."

A wave of laughter greeted that. She simply went on smiling at him. "Not going to zap me are you?" He gave her a boyish grin, putting her at ease.

She shook her head at the small, ultra-neat man.

"Sorry. Left my zapper at home." Mattie kept a cool smile which set her apart from this nonsense. He winked, reassuring her it was going fine.

"But seriously, Mattie." Tabok switched to business as if a circuit in his head clicked from laughter to main idea. "I understand from our producer, Ted Cicero," here he doffed an imaginary cap toward the patient man standing just off camera, "that he has hired you to find Ralph Molino, the missing union president, through your power of divination." He paused. She nodded.

"How do you go about doing a thing like that?" His look was serious, truly interested. She felt less a spectacle, more a professional. She relaxed, trusted this little man not to betray her, and began explaining the process, how and when she first noticed she had this gift, and then related some of the cases she had solved. She agreed that it was kind of spooky, but gave him her spiel about doing good for people; ending a parent's doubts, saving the police necessary time in an investigation, ending the ordeals of so many.

"And then many times I find the missing person alive." She went on to tell of finding that movie star's daughter.

"Do you think that could happen in this case?" he asked.

"I have no idea. I'm not even sure I'll see anything at all. It might come to nothing," she warned.

"But you will try, right? I mean, you will try to find Ralph Molino and report back to us whatever you see—or divine." He turned to face the camera directly, his face deadly serious. "Because this show is taped, we will give the police any information Mattie Small receives as soon as we get it. By the time we're on, the police might already have found their man." He grinned, shook his head slightly. "We're only doing this in the interest of helping the police solve the case, and at the same time provide a real life test of psychic phenomena, so a lot is on the line here. Right?" He turned to Mattie for confirmation. She nodded. He continued. "We're not giving any guarantees that this will work because, as you can see, Miss Small can't give any either. This is just the network's way of doing what we can to help solve a baffling mystery."

He paused, cut to a commercial.

"That'll be on the front page of every newspaper in the country by tomorrow morning," he winked at her. "Should be good publicity for all of us. Puts a lot of pressure on you, though. Wish you luck." He grinned that boyish grin again and the cameras were back on, with the sad comedian, now wreathed in smiles, joining them.

She didn't have to say another word. Afterward, happily, she hurried from the studio to the St. Moritz, where she was staying.

Bobby left her to go make a few phone calls, see if the story was going out on the wires, to do a little of what he called "movin' and shakin'."

In her room she lay across the velvet bedspread. Pain was gathering across the top and back of her head, knots of it, gearing up to unleash a barrage that would devastate her.

Maybe it was more than anxiety over the Tabok appearance. She couldn't get David out of her mind. Something to do with her own fear that he was right, that something was wrong with her, something terrible. That revelation didn't come as any surprise anyway. She knew she wasn't normal, knew something was horribly wrong. She'd known it since the beginning. Since first experiencing that disgusting, demented joy at finding a dead body. That euphoric happiness. Like a ghoul. A vampire. Some filthy bloodsucker. How was it no one had noticed? Not any of them. How many times she had been forced to hide the smile, the laughter ready to crack through and betray her. What was it, she wondered? Insanity?

All it could be. The visions, dreams, the child, divination, now blackouts...all of it symptoms of a sick mind. David was right to worry.

Then why go on? she asked herself.

But why shouldn't I go as far and as fast as I can—until it's all over? If I'm going insane anyway...

David said he'd talked to her as a five-year-old. He talked to the child and she knew all about her Daddy's death. Recalled being there when he was murdered. She remembered and Mattie didn't.

Christ. She massaged her temples, trying to alleviate the pain. Like a parasite, some thing living in me. Alive. An evil worm in my brain. Knowing itself. Knowing me. Knowing even more about me than I know. Another personality? God! What now? Psychiatrist? Mental institution? No! No!

He had asked her again to stop. To forget the Tabok Show, stay out of the limelight, just until they had this whole divining business figured out.

"No," she'd told him. "I'm committed. And I need the money. It's too late for that, David. Much too late."

A shudder passed over her. She got up and went to the mirror, looking intently at herself as if to see within, to the place where this child lurked.

"What are you doing to me?" she whispered to the reflection, "Why? Who are you?"

The pain closed down as if an iron cap were being drawn across her head. She moaned and felt her way back to the bed. She couldn't fight it.

Too much lately. That was it. All happening so fast. Pressure too great to stand. Or maybe it went deeper than that. If her head didn't threaten so she would examine her feelings, sort out the contradictory messages she had been getting, and attempt a plan for herself. Such a thing must be possible, she knew. To plan and work within that plan.

To plan. Hold on...to who she was. Think! Think!

Fear. Always fear. It followed joy. Something so awful about the progression of joy and fear and elation and horror: warring emotions. Of two different people? God— please, no. No.

A moan escaped her. Something so unholy about it from the beginning. Something even—God help her—evil.

She rubbed gently at her temples and began to use the techniques of self-hypnosis to relax herself. Concentration was difficult. Her mind craved activity.

This was the only out given her, wasn't it? she thought desperately. Without the gift she'd still be drab Martha Small, cashier at Koch's supermarket.

But to always have to war with ghosts. Everywhere— ghosts. Of herself as a child. Ghosts of herself as an adult. Daddy. Patsy. Uncle John.

Ghosts.

Haunted.

God help me.

The bell was ringing inside her head. She rolled over to snap the alarm off, but the bell went on. Her head was throbbing. Sleep had not helped.

The bell rang on and on...

She sat up, looking at the clock she had tried to silence. One-thirty! It must have rung itself out hours ago. She had missed the show. Damn.

Her brain finally accepted the fact that the phone was ringing.

"Mattie Small?" a quiet, refined male voice asked.

"Ummm?"

"I can't say who I am, but I'm calling with a business deal for you." The voice was low and sensual in her ear.

"Business deal?"

"Yes. I caught the 'Tabok Show' because I'd been told you were being hired to mentally locate Ralph Molino's body. I'm ready to offer you three times whatever the show is paying you to back off and stay out of this messy business."

"Body? How do you know he is...?"

"There'll be no more questions. If you agree, I'll send you $1500 right now, by messenger, and another $1500 when we hear you've withdrawn."

"What? That's crazy. Of course I won't withdraw. I'd look like an idiot."

"I see you don't quite grasp my meaning." The voice became stern and paternal. "Nor do you seem to realize how very serious this whole affair is, and what trouble you might be heading for."

"I...I don't understand." Her mind cleared instantly.

"I think you understand perfectly."

"Is this a threat?"

"Very definitely. And I wouldn't take it lightly. You had better accept my offer. It won't be extended twice."

"And if I don't?" Anger was rising in her.

"I think I made myself clear, Miss Small."

"Not clear enough. You're saying that either I accept the money, withdraw my help, and look like a fool and a liar coast to coast, or you'll do something to stop me?"

"Not me!" Distaste lubricated the man's voice. "There are others..."

"Others who will hurt me?"

"You. Or someone close to you."

"Go to hell, you bastard." She slammed the phone down so hard it leaped from the hook and had to be replaced, with more clatter.

She picked it up immediately and dialed Bobby's room. At first he couldn't comprehend what she was telling him.

"Threatened you? Just some nut...no, eh?" There was a pause as he thought. "Let me get this to the papers. Damn—almost two o'clock. Missed the morning editions but we'll catch the afternoon, which will be better anyway—a follow-up story. Yeah, better anyway. Sit tight. Don't open your door. I'm calling the cops about getting you some guards, but don't open your door until you know it's me. I'll take it from here."

"He offered three thousand dollars for me to drop it," she said, suddenly scared.

"Cheap bastards. Screw 'em. We're gonna end up making millions out of this."

"He said they could hurt someone I love. Could that be my mother, or David? There's no one else..."

"How about me?" His voice was insinuating.

"Not a chance."

Chapter Ten

The light was yellow, flared into a trumpet's horn of gold from which a halo expanded and encircled visual space set within a black void.

At first the light blinded her, content as she was within darkness. Then it comforted, as a warm place in cold would, as a safe place away from the dangerous. She felt it

slip over her skin like liquid sun, until her body was a part
of the light and she a part of the corona, until she slipped
downward into the bell of the horn, toward the radiating
center.

And now her mind joined the center as a bee extracting
nectar enters the flower, and the light narrowed. And
paled.

And she slowed...

Until her mind was located in a room. With no
awareness of the breathless body transporting it, the mind
—with single eye—searched.

A grinding sound filled the room. A motor straining.

"I can't do this," a deep voice said. "It's making me
sick."

"Just shut up and get it over with," another, deeper
voice growled.

Someone else said, "Christ, the goddamned drain's
closed up again. All we need's to have a goddamned
plumber in here. Get a stick, will you?" There was a
mumble of voices. A few coherent phrases as they struggled with something, but no faces with the voices.

Her eye focused. She could make out the room: bare,
cement block, cement floor, long, gleaming stainless steel
counters and tables, and on one of the tables, piled like
slaughterhouse waste, a tangle of bleeding arms, legs,
hands, feet. And a head—a grisly, waxen effigy—it stood
just a little apart, severed low on the neck so that it sat
almost upright as if on its own pedestal. The eyes were
closed. The skin drooped, was yellowish. The facial expression was of one asleep.

It was a face she knew. Or a death mask of a face she
knew, had seen in the newspapers many times, had collected in her scrapbooks: Ralph Molino.

She wanted to turn away from the sight, but her mind
had no eye to close. She watched.

An arm was grasped by rubber-gloved hands and
disentangled from the mass. Upright, too stiff to be bent,
the arm was lifted whole, pointing upward. The gloved
fingers dug into the fatty flesh near the elbow.

The arm was fixed into a large machine and then
came the grinding sound again as the motor strained on
the difficult job. The hands pushed hard on the arm,

feeding it into the hopper, slowly shortening the length of it.

"Shove it harder. There...uh...push it down. The only way. You gotta keep feeding it into the hopper or the goddamn thing clogs and stops. Chop the next one in half. Do half at a time like the legs. Easier," a man's voice said.

"Christ! I'm really gettin' sick I tell ya. I'm gonna heave," another male voice answered.

"Go on. Get the hell outta here. We'll do it."

"I'll be right back. Just let me get some air."

There was the sound of feet adhering slightly and tearing away from the cement as a pair of sneakers might. Then a heavy door sucked open and closed.

"Crummy bastard," the deeper voice muttered.

"Don't blame him. This is the shittiest goddamned mess I ever got into." A pause. "How come we get stuck with this? We didn't have nothin' to do with killin' him. Those guys weren't even supposed to, what I hear." His voice rose at the end to reach over the grinding sound.

"Who you gonna trust to make hamburger outta this guy? Huh? The heat's gonna be on forever. Feds'll never give up on it. We make 'em look bad. Who you gonna trust with pressure like that on, eh? Bad enough there's the three of us."

Half an arm was being chewed by the machine.

The pile was diminishing. Only red gore left. And the head.

A hand reached out, grabbed it by the hair.

"Ummm—won't fit."

"Get a cleaver. Over there. Behind you. One of the big ones. Yeah. See? Now right down the middle."

A crack of steel into bone and then into wood. She had to watch as eye separated from eye and the two halves of the face fell away from each other. One half was lifted. Then the grinding sound again...

She was on a street, looking up at a sign. A sign she knew. A street she knew. In Hamtramck, the small Polish city within a city.

"Hiram's Meat Packing" the rectangular red and white sign said.

She knew where Ralph Molino was—at least for the moment.

As the light faded and the scene began to contract, hurrying away from her as she had earlier rushed toward it, jubilation hit her.

Jubilation. Joy. She was ecstatic.

She knew! Only she—and the murderers.

She delayed opening her eyes, keeping her eyelids as still as possible, maintaining the deep breathing accompanying a trance, savoring as long as possible the excitement of knowing she had reached the pinnacle of her powers.

Washing through her in waves of joy was the pleasure of seeing that man dead, dismembered and piled like garbage waiting to be ground into dog food. Fitting. Fitting. Laughter bubbled but she subdued it.

Wonderful!

The pinnacle!

She'd done what no other person on earth could. Her name would be known from one end of the world to the other. The babble of other tongues shot through her brain. Now there were no limits to her world, no inaccessible corners shut to her. To her, who had known only limits, the world was infinite. Without limit. No one could stop her. Not with the power she possessed. More power than any of them suspected: over who shall live and who shall die.

The pinnacle. Let them all tremble. Let any one of them dare cross her....

At that moment the phone rang. She heard Bobby say "Damn" as he got up to answer it. Since when had Bobby been in her room? she wondered vaguely.

"It's your mother, Mattie." Bobby was poised at her arm. "I told her you were busy but she won't take no."

Mattie raised a hand to silence him as she took the phone, bent her head a minute, closed her eyes, then came up slowly looking bewildered and frightened.

"Mattie? Mattie? That you?" Harriet shouted into the phone. "It's just awful. Terrible," she moaned into Mattie's ear. "Juliet. It's Juliet. Oh, my God, to think it would all lead to this. She's gone. Just gone. Disappeared."

Mattie caught her breath and tried to shake off the strange sense she had of listening from a distance, of not really being involved. "Juliet? You mean...gone? She's gone? But where? I mean...where?"

"We don't know. Even called her son but he hasn't talked to her since her birthday. Four months ago. Oooh, Martha...Mattie. The police think they meant to get me and got her instead. It's horrible, Mattie. Just horrible."

"Hello? Hello? Mattie? It's me, Bella." She must have taken the phone from the hysterical Harriet. "It's true. Juliet's gone. Don't know where. Just gone. We looked everywhere. They think she's been kidnapped."

"Mattie?" Harriet, calmed, in charge again. "We don't know what to do unless you can find her before they—oh, my God!—before they hurt her. You know how timid she is. They're gonna scare her to death. Come home, Mattie. Come home and help. Please."

"I will, Mother," she whispered into the phone. "I will."

Chapter Eleven

"I have to talk to the child again." David was kneeling in front of her, holding her hands as she sat on the edge of her bed, her old bed in her old room in the Mt. Eliot Street flat.

"Not now." Mattie tried to get away from him. "I can't take any more. Anyway, there's no reason for that. I know about my father's death. Why dredge all of that up again? Juliet's what's important now. Finding her before they kill her."

His narrow face was drawn, gray beneath a couple days' growth of beard. She had never seen him look so worn. His eyes, when she trusted herself to look into them, were wild, fanatical.

"But there's more you don't know. About the power that child has. About what she really is." He stopped then began again, overcome with anxiety. "I think she knows about these murders, including Molino's. She may even know where Juliet is. Please, Mattie. Let Lilith hypnotize you."

"But that child is just a part of me. You talk as if she's a separate human being. That's crazy."

"This whole thing is. But, believe me, I'm very serious. It's got to be stopped. Got to be finished once and for all. It starts with that little girl. It's got to end there. When Lilith talked to her she claimed she was the powerful one, directs all you do. You've got to be aware, Mattie, in order to fight her, stop her, win."

She was looking at him in disbelief.

"One more time," he begged. "I know what questions to ask her now. I'll know everything and how to fight her."

"Fight her? You're talking about me, David. *Me!* I don't understand." She frowned, pulled slightly away as if in defense of herself.

"One more time," he begged. "I should know everything then. It's...well...she seems to have developed powers—psychic abilities—that she used to destroy people. It started with hatred for the men who killed your father. Then it moved to your Uncle John. Even...well...others."

Her disbelief and anger were immediate. "Are you trying to say I killed all those people? That's crazy. Why do you want to do this to me, David? Why would you want to hurt me like this?"

Pain crossed his face as he watched the changing emotions in her eyes.

"I don't want to hurt you." He held on to her hands. She tried to push him away. "Let's get it all into the open. Right out where we can deal with it. I'll tape the session. You won't have to believe me, you can listen to it yourself. But let's get this over with, Mattie. I can't stand much more."

She considered for a moment. "One more time, that's all? Then you'll drop all of this nonsense, you promise?"

He nodded.

She was still, thinking. After a time she asked, "What did she say about me? What could she know about me? I thought all that would happen was I would regress to when I was five and talk about what I knew up to then. How could I, at five, even know about myself years later? That can't be, can it?"

She searched his face for answers. He fumbled for words.

"I . . . I don't want to hurt you, Mattie. I love you. You know that."

"But? What else is there, David? Tell me."

He swallowed hard, stalling, seeming to need time to think. Finally he said, "She claims she's the child you saw. Claims she was shocked when you first waved, had no idea you could see her although I guess she's been watching you for years. She's . . . she's a whole person, Mattie. While you grew she turned inward, learned how to tap psychic powers. Used them to kill . . ."

"Kill! My God—you mean it *has* been me? All along? I am the killer?" She pulled away from him, eyes huge.

"No. No. It's her. The little girl. She's like some evil thing, broken off and growing crooked, growing in the dark. And now she is stronger, wants to take over completely . . ."

When she could speak it was with a voice diminished by shock. "Is that why I lose hours? Why I'm not aware of so much? My God, I've read about things like this but . . . never . . ."

He nodded. "We'll have to fight her. I'll help."

"But how?" One tear crept slowly down her face. "And what do I win? Something in me has been killing. I'll be the one to go to prison."

"We won't let that happen. It's not you. It's her."

"And who will believe that? A jury? A judge?" Her shoulders shook briefly as a tremor passed through her body.

"Look." Claiming control of himself, David tried now to calm Mattie. "Let me talk to her again. Let's find out the whole truth."

"And the truth will set ye free." She was empty, defeated.

"Let's find out the whole truth and take it one step at a time."

She nodded. "Now. Right now. We'll do it and be finished with this. I feel so weak. So drained. I can't take much more horror either."

"Now you're five years old. Five years old. Five years old." Lilith's controlled voice droned on and on in the quiet of the twilight room as she took the relaxed woman back over the years to her childhood.

"Yes. Five. I'm five. And my Daddy's dead and you want to know about Mattie's visions. Right?" The face once again had softened to childish outlines, lips puffed and pouty, eyes wide, clear. But she was looking beyond Lilith to David. The look in the eyes wasn't childish. It was angry. Vengeful. "I'm talking to you, David."

"Yes. I hear you." Both Lilith and David were startled. David moved in closer, into the circle of soft light falling over the chair where Mattie sat, one foot tucked under her, back straight and alert.

"I'm gettin' tireda all this," the girl complained, frowning. "What do you want to know?"

"Are you responsible for the visions?"

"Course." She looked away, disgusted. "Course I am. Who'd you think? Her? Ha! Ha!"

"Are you responsible for the deaths too?" David asked and held his breath.

"Ha! Wouldn't you like to know. And what if I was? So what? Those men hurt my Daddy in the worst way. They should be hurt too." The look she gave David was defiant.

"Then you did kill all those people?"

"All what people?"

"All the bodies—the people Mattie saw, you killed them?" His voice was slow, reluctant to know.

"Not alla them." She narrowed her eyes. Watched him closely.

"But some?"

She nodded reluctantly. "Some."

"Which ones?"

"The ones that had something to do with killin my Daddy. Them. But not Patsy." She shook her head. "Not her. She did that alone. Not me."

Lilith and David both drew in a breath at the same time.

"But three of the men are still alive?" David said, unbelieving.

"I know that." She looked directly at David and compressed her lips. "But I made 'em suffer even worse. Ma always said to me when I hurt myself—'Ooh, I wish it was me. It hurts me more when you're hurt.' So I hurt those men more. I got the thing they loved most of all in the whole world. With Mr. Gibonski it was his granddaughter. Mr. Williams too—his grandson, Billy. With Mr. Gordon it was his daughter, Esther. That'll make 'em suffer for years."

"But you killed children, and a young woman." David's voice filled with the horror he felt. He pulled back, away from her. Her eyes stayed on him, boring toward him. Reading him. Playing with him. He knew she had decided to make him hear it all.

A smirk worked across her face.

"That's too bad," she finally answered. "They shouldn't've killed Daddy. And they wanted to kill me too."

David swallowed the fear he was feeling and opened his mouth to ask another question, stopping when he saw the child's eyes narrow and a wide smile curve up the lipsticked mouth.

"You enjoy it, don't you?" David whispered, swallowing fast as bile rose into his throat. "You enjoy killing."

The smile got wider, became cute and playful as she nodded. "Yes. They shouldn'ta hurt Daddy. And people shouldn't bother me and Martha, make us unhappy. Course, 'fore long that won't matter. Be just me. Mostly me now."

"That means you killed three—no, four people?"

"More than that." She waggled her head back and forth in time to some internal music.

"Who else?"

"Let me see." The innocent eyes rolled up as she thought. A finger rested on her bottom lip, pressing, making a pale indentation where the lipstick came off. The child took the finger away, noticed the lipstick on it, and rubbed it on her pale blue skirt. "There was Uncle John," she said. "Mr. Molino. And one more—but not yet I don't think. Soon. But not yet." She looked directly at David.

"Five! My God! Five people? But how? How, Martha? You couldn't do them yourself."

"I wouldn't do that. I don't have to."

"Then..."

She shrugged, stopped to yawn, turned back to them with a conspiratorial smile playing across her face. "I know how to do it. Practiced a long time. Before I could only hurt people, when I was in school. While Martha cried about somebody in school being mean, I'd think about them, picture something awful happenin' to 'em. After a time it just began to happen. Just the way I pictured. Steve Craig was mean. Called me stupid. I kept picturing the train behind where I lived running over him. Just gettin' even for me. And one day it did. He lost a leg and I wasn't sorry one bit. And Sally Florek too. She was terrible. Made up rhymes about me. I remember this one: Little Orphan Annie...Oh, well...anyway I kept seeing her get hit by this car, a blue car. And she did. Hurt bad. Out of school all one semester. And I wouldn't sign the get-well card Miss Spencer passed around our classroom 'cause I didn't want her to get well."

She stopped, waiting for a reaction; then, receiving none, she frowned and went on. "It's easy now. 'Member what you told her, Lilith? That people could send out evil that could kill? Boy, I wanted to laugh when I heard. I can do that. I really can. You just think about a person, picture 'em until you find this kinda energy goin' out of you and you keep sayin': Kill! Kill! Kill! Like that. And you cover 'em with bad thoughts. Cover 'em with bad until that's all there is around them: evil. Death. Death. Death..."

She put a hand to her mouth and giggled behind it, hunching down as she enjoyed her joke.

"Evil aura? Is that it?" Lilith watched her, fascinated.

She nodded. "Any evil any where around comes to 'em then. And any evil person. Any evil within a person. And they can't get away either cause they're marked. They're a victim for all the evil anywhere around 'em. I remember once, in church with Daddy, the priest talked about the evil surrounding everybody. I remembered that. It works good."

"And then Mattie finds these bodies?" Lilith asked.

The little girl nodded, looking smug.

"But how? How does she know where to find these people?"

"That's easy." The child waved her hand in imitation of an adult gesture. "I concentrate on the person. Think about 'em. Then Mattie goes to sleep and it's like zeroing in. Anybody can leave their body if they want to, go anywhere too. You can't do anything there, can't move things or touch people, but you're there, just like you got up and went. Mattie don't like it now, seein' all those dead people, but she knows that's all she's got, the only thing keeps her out of that supermarket." She shrugged, mugging at David. "I do 'em. She sees 'em. They're gettin' bad now. The dreams. Boy, this last one ... WOW! But soon it'll just be me. Won't have to worry 'bout her. And when I take over—*all of you just better watch out!*"

David watched her mobile features as she bragged. He felt sickened. "God help us," he whispered beneath his breath.

"You wanna know why I told you about everything?" she asked, leaning the upper part of her body toward him, going on without waiting for a response. "'Cause I want you to know what I can do to you if you tattle on me."

"Kill me? That it?"

"Well." She became coy. "I'm not sayin' any more, but you just leave us alone. Or else maybe something even worse than happened to that last man will happen to you."

"Last man? You mean Ralph Molino? You know what happened to him? Is he dead?"

"Ooh boy, is he!" She fell sideways in the chair, laughing.

David choked, got control of his voice again with difficulty. He asked, "Where Martha? Where is Molino?"

She shrugged, sat up straight, and primly pulled her skirt down.

"Ask her. She knows. I already gave her the visions."

"Why didn't she tell me?" The voice echoed around him as if the space they occupied was a huge hollow vault.

"Awww—something about protecting that Juliet—Mrs. Swiderski. She's afraid they'll kill her if she tells. But that's O.K. anyway. She's supposed to be next. For what she did to us. Tellin' all those lies. Her and that fat Bella. And Aunt Jenny, her too." She glared.

Lilith hurriedly came forward to give David time to control himself.

"But what of those others Mattie found? What of them?"

"That was to get her famous and rich. When it worked, after the first two, I thought it would be good to make her famous. She's always so sad, 'cause of what people did to her. It wasn't fair. So I did that—let her find other people. I could help with that. No harder than finding the ones I wanted dead." She smiled quickly, almost shyly at David. He remained speechless.

"And how did you know so much about those men, the ones who killed your father? How did you pick your targets?" Lilith went on.

"We kept scrapbooks. Lotsa pictures. They were all there. I recognized them right away. Every one of 'em. At union picnics they could bring their families. Always had a special child they were huggin' for the camera. That's the one I got." She emphasized her words with a beat of her fist on the chair arm.

"That makes you a murderer," Lilith accused.

"I don't care. They killed my daddy."

"But Mattie will be blamed."

The child shrugged and gave a sly glance toward David.

"Won't have to worry about her soon. Soon be just me. She'll go away for good. But that's O.K. 'cause she don't know how to live anyway. Always moaning about something. Don't know how to have fun. Not like we do, eh, David?" She gave him a lewd wink. His face burned.

She lowered her voice. "I like bein' in bed with you, David. You know what I like best about..." She was going on, tormenting him.

"*Shut up!*" he shouted and put his hands over his ears.

Lilith's eyes widened. Fear spread over her face as she saw he was breaking and the child was feeding on the weakness.

"STOP! Right now!" Lilith ordered. Rising from her chair, she stood over the girl.

"Stop it yourself, fat bitch." The child dismissed her, but huddled down, pouting.

Fighting for control, David drew deep breaths and willed his anger to subside. His face was burning. She had gotten to him. He had to regain ground. Fight her.

"Now don't tell on me." She was leaning forward, shaking a finger at him. "Don't you dare tell. Or I'll kill you too. Or maybe your mother—the old witch."

He felt the last ounce of strength drain from his body as terror struck him.

"You'll kill no more." Lilith, hands on hips, drew up to majestic height. Her words were a pronouncement.

David shook his head and watched the large woman approach the child, who cowered away from her. Somehow, suddenly, he sensed unfairness here. The child so small. The woman huge, grotesque, ugly.

The little girl and the hovering woman faced each other. Their eyes met, held, spit hatred. Then the child's face changed as if it went slightly askew: the eyes were unfocused, the jaw a little slack. She might have shifted to some other thought.

David watched as Lilith stood very still. A look of disbelief crossed her face. Then the look turned to one of horror as she spun around to face David, searching his face as if hunting for signs of . . .

Of what? David wondered, noting with disgust the sweat covering the fat woman's face; the shine and dark wrinkles of her double-chinned neck.

She was awful, even gave off a stench he hadn't noticed before but now found repugnant. She was a large excrescence violating the room with her presence, dirtying both him and the little girl she menaced. The smell of her was in his mouth and nostrils. He could feel the slimy fat on his hands as if she exuded grease into the air, as if her very existence soiled him.

He watched the sweat pour faster down the pudgy cheeks, leaving lines, like snail paths, behind. Her eyes fixed on his and he shuddered, repulsed. How had he depended on this thing, this quivering mass of flesh.

She was hardly human. He stood. Had to do something to it. Stop it somehow. Ugly thing.

It put a pink-palmed hand up to stop him, backed

away, and tripped, sprawling heavily backward on to the bed.

David heard the little girl's laugh and almost joined her, would have if the sight of this flowered pile of garbage floundering like a stranded jellyfish didn't agitate him, didn't drive him to rid himself of the sight of it.

If she didn't need killing so badly...

Awkwardly the woman rolled off the bed and stood on the other side. Her mouth moved. She seemed to be calling his name but his ears refused the word. His head filled with other sounds as if things in flight jammed his brain.

The muscles in his arms ached. Looking down, he saw his hands had curled, fingers bending into claws.

How he wanted those claws on the neck of that thing stupidly staring at him.

He reached out to grab the robe it wore but it pulled away, snatched the material from his hands, and ran toward the door.

Sounds of howling within and without his head startled him, threw him off the track of his quarry just long enough for it to reach the door and pull it open.

It was going to escape him. He lunged forward and threw himself at the door, striking the wood panels and knocking it closed.

The thing looked at him with terror in its eyes but he felt no mercy. He reached out for its throat, got a firm grip, and squeezed until his body shook with the effort it cost him.

"What's all the noise in...DAVID! WHAT'S GOING ON? STOP THAT!"

The door had opened and Bella was tugging at his hands. He looked at her, not understanding, then looked at the woman he was choking. Instantly his hands flew from her neck. His mind cleared. He was aware of her gasps, her weak cries. The woman helped Lilith out of the room.

He stood absolutely still as the truth of what he had become and who ruled his mind swamped him.

The girl was smiling, satisfaction written on the painted face. With an air of nonchalance she reached up and rubbed at her nose.

"You did that to me," he choked and made a move toward her. "I could kill you."

The smile remained in place. No fear showed. She only narrowed her eyes and looked at him.

Chapter Twelve

October sun crept up the sloping walls of her bedroom as she lay staring blankly toward arches of water stains on the ceiling. In a little while she would get up and pull the dirty string, lighting the bare bulb overhead. She would try to use it as a catalyst to trance state. It had not worked so far. Maybe this time.

Out in the kitchen she could hear the mournful voices of Harriet and Bella, like two useless parts of a trio, talking to the guarding policeman, pouring cup after cup of coffee into the men, filling him with old complaints and all the fears their tired bodies quivered with as they waited to hear of Juliet's fate, waited for Mattie to find her.

But she couldn't do it. Couldn't seem to go into a trance. It was as though the secret she kept, of Ralph Molino's whereabouts, filled her to capacity and until she emptied there was no room for more knowledge. Or, more likely, she thought, the horror of what waited was too much to bear.

Perhaps she should have told Bobby she knew what happened and where Ralph Molino was. But he would use it, sacrifice even Juliet for this one. And she was certain that wasn't the thing to do—break the story. Maybe her knowledge—and silence—were the only weapons she had to fight them with, the only way to get Juliet back. She couldn't bring herself to tell. So fearful again. Indecisive.

Certainly couldn't tell David. He would do what he had to, she knew. Do his duty. There was no other way for him. And anyway, he blamed her for the murders. Said she was responsible...

She shut her eyes tightly and reached for the cool cloth she'd put on the bedside chair, pressing it to her head, across her aching eyes.

Pain again. Always pain. As if the child David said possessed her were contained within her skull—pushing, pushing—like some abnormal fetus trying to be born.

David had talked to the child a second time. Said she'd threatened him, threatened Lilith. Attacked them...

Unbelievable, of course. But there had been the mess in her room. Her books, pictures, clothes, shoes all scattered everywhere as if someone had thrown a tantrum. Still... unbelievable.

Her eyes traveled up toward the bare lightbulb. She could feel something click in her mind, as if a switch were turned to "off." There would be no tunnel. No white light. No knowledge.

"Goddamn this thing to hell." She turned her face into the pillow and cried. Why not now? When she might possibly save Juliet who only got caught up in this thing because she, Mattie, had wanted that pinnacle so badly. A straw in a maelstrom. Poor timid soul. And the very thing that got her into this—the gift—would no longer work to get her out.

Self-hypnosis was impossible. She had no power of concentration. Body rigid, mind alert and painfully aware of her shame—she was still barren.

Creaks of the old springs sliced into the pain when she got up from the bed and shuffled out to the kitchen where she joined them for coffee. Neither Harriet nor Bella would look straight at her. No one uttered a word of blame. They didn't have to.

Juliet was paying the price Mattie's freedom cost.

"Should've got a call from 'em by now," the mournful policeman muttered. "Usual in these cases, you know. They took her for a reason. Surprised they haven't called with the demands."

"If only the newspapers hadn't printed the story," Harriet lamented. "I don't think they should've done that. Usually kidnappers warn you not to go to the police or anything. Ooh, I hope they don't hurt her." Tears welled again.

"That Bobby tell the papers?" Bella asked, looking sideways at Mattie who nodded. "Shouldn't have. Shouldn't have. You should've told him not to, Mattie."

"They know by now they got the wrong person," the cop shook his head. "Not good. Not good at all."

"I think Bobby felt they'd let her go when they found out she wasn't my mother," Mattie defended him. And, indirectly, herself.

"More likely they'd just do away with her." The cop's insensitive words set the two women to sobbing into hankies.

Mattie grabbed the aspirin bottle from the cupboard. At the sink she ran a glass of water and swallowed three pills. "I'm going back to bed," she muttered. The two women paid no attention but rocked back and forth, giving small sounds of grief.

Mattie lay in darkness concentrating on the throbbing in her head and the low voices coming from the kitchen. After a while the voices faded into a buzz inside her head and she slept.

It was the golden light. At last.
Then white...
Instantaneously she was hurtling forward and then the light opened up and:
There were cases marked catsup and carrots and green beans piled to varying heights in rows along one wall. A single, bare window high on a wall let in the artificial light of a streetlamp. A washtub stood along another wall and beside it, between it and the adjacent wall, was an old wooden kitchen chair. Hunched forward, permanented hair standing on end, face gaunt and hideous with fear, Juliet sat on the chair, her plump body tucked into itself as if to make her disappear, her legs stretched out at an awkward angle—tied to the front chair legs, arms secured behind her.

In front of Juliet was a shaded, overhead lamp that swung just above a little table.

As the lamp slowly swung, it shone first on one figure, then another. Mattie's mind registered the two men. Both dark figures only. Indistinguishable. Shadows.

Juliet whimpered.

"Shut up, bitch," one of the figures growled.

There were cards on the table. Hands came out to play, narrow hands, large knuckles, almost deformed. Hands on the other side of the table felt for an ash tray, tapped off a large ash from a cigarette, and reached for cards dealt out.

"Come on. I paid to see you," one urged. The voice was crude, slurred words together. It held arrogance.

"Sure. Sure. Just that the dumb bitch bugs me. All that goddamn whimperin'. More trouble than she's worth. Wrong one, Christ!" This one was silent for a while, studying his cards, then laying them on the table and pulling a small pile of coins toward him. "What do you think they'll want us to do with her?"

The first figure shrugged. "Who the hell knows? Maybe she's still good for a trade. Just relax. They'll let us know."

Small noises continued to come from Juliet. Her head was down and tears wet the front of her dress.

The sound became muffled first, then the light faded.

"David, it's Mattie. I'm home. At Mother's. Please come right over. Now. I just had a dream—I saw Juliet. Yes. Please come."

Harriet and Bella, wrapped in chenille robes (Bella was staying with them until this whole mess was finished), stooped toward the phone as she spoke.

"He's coming?" Bella asked.

Mattie nodded. "As soon as he can."

"She's alive. I'm so relieved," Harriet said. "Maybe now David can find her before it's too late. How did she look? Was she frightened?"

"She looked all right," Mattie hedged, not wanting to burden them as she was with the horror of Juliet's imprisonment.

His eyes were sunken, the depths emphasized by dark smudges. A haunted look kept them moving back and forth, never lighting on anyone for long. He hadn't slept. And he was thinner. Mattie hurriedly prayed his mother didn't blame her for the way he looked. It was the job.

This Molino case. He even looked older. She tried to remember him as he had been that day he walked into Koch's asking for her. So different. Her mind must be playing tricks. He can't have aged this badly in less than a year.

"I saw her." She clutched at his arm, pulling herself close to him, looking directly up into his face. "I saw her, David. It's some kind of warehouse. There were cases of things. Like catsup and beans and things. Stuff a grocery store would stock. Does that help? Does it?"

A muscle in his left cheek went into spasms causing the eye to twitch. He put a hand up as if to hide it and edged away from her, loosening her grip on his arm.

"Don't know, Mattie. Let's sit a minute. Figure it out. Just tell me all of it. Anything at all." He took a seat in the Morris chair, brought out his notebook, and waited.

She repeated the dream. Then repeated it again. And again.

Finally he gave up and read his notes, shaking his head, rubbing wearily at his eyes.

After a while he said, "Not much here to go on. Is this all you can tell me?"

She nodded.

"Nothing else?"

She thought a minute and shook her head.

There was a moment of suspended movement between them as if both held their breath. He broke it by asking, "And nothing on Molino?"

His eyes slid to her face and away. Then back again, questioning. She looked down at her hands.

"No. Nothing."

"Mattie." His voice demanded her attention. "Have you seen Molino? Don't lie to me."

She looked at him. Their eyes held a moment before she turned away. "Why would I lie?"

"I don't know. I hope not so Bobby can get you back on that 'Tabok Show.' Just to grandstand."

"My God! David! What do you think I am? I already told him to cancel that, tell them anything. They know about this kidnapping, they'll understand."

"Understand? That bunch? You're kidding yourself.

If you broke the Molino thing on their show it would be just that much better with a kidnapped woman involved. Don't underestimate Bobby Sanderson either. Ten to one he has no intention of canceling that show."

"You're being cynical." She turned away. He reached out and put his hand on her chin, forcing her to face him. He smiled. She couldn't help but smile back. She reached out to run her finger tenderly over his cheek.

He began to say something but choked on his words.

"What is it, David?" She bent close to him, arms trying to encircle his body. "David. Stop. Please. I can't stand it..."

His hand closed on her arm and held her tight beside him until the grip began to hurt and she pulled away.

When he leaned back, head against the crocheted antimacassar, his eyes were closed. He kept them closed as he said, "The child said she showed you what happened to Molino. I know you know."

There was stunned silence.

"She lied to you," Mattie got up and began walking away from him. "She lied to you. I haven't seen anything but Juliet. And don't you think you should get busy looking for her? There's not a lot of time, is there?"

He came after her, pulled her back to face him and roughly kissed her. "I loved you so much," he choked out. His eyes bore down into hers.

"Not now, David. Please." She pushed at him, not wanting complications added to an already overly complicated time.

"I don't know what to do, Mattie. I don't know..." The voice was broken, pained to the point of hysteria. "I love you but I can't..."

"Please!" She pushed him away firmly. "We've got to get Juliet back. As soon as possible. We've got to. And, David, I'm through with divining. No more dreams—ever. No more visions—nothing. I won't be able to stand it. It's destroying me just as you said it would. I've got to stop. Got to stop—for good."

His shrug said it mattered little now.

"Too late for that," he mumbled, heading for the kitchen. "I'm afraid it's too late."

*   *   *

Later, after David left to go back downtown, Harriet and Bella found Mattie crying in her room. They got her into bed but she would not sleep, demanding all the lights be left on. When they tried to leave her she screamed for them to stay, so all three spent the night together—sitting up, staring into space, Bella and Harriet on chairs, Mattie in bed, her back pressed against the old headboard, eyes red-rimmed, never closing for more than half-seconds at a time for fear of horrible sleep overtaking her.

From time to time during the night Harriet and Bella heard her whisper, "I can stop it. I can."

That was all that was said throughout the long night.

"I can stop it. I can."

Chapter Thirteen

The strain of the night and day were telling on her. She felt the pain in her head expanding. Her eyes burned and teared. She yawned repeatedly but still couldn't sleep. Wouldn't sleep. The trances were a thing she could control, snap herself from in time. But not the dreams. She would be forced to watch Juliet suffering again if she let herself sleep. She would have to watch as that poor, frightened woman went out of her mind with fear. Too terrible. It *was* a curse—this goddamned gift—a horrible curse over which she had no control. It was consuming her and all she came in contact with. And the suffering because of it! My God! The suffering!

"Please help me stay awake," she begged of Bella and Harriet, two sorrowful figures hunched in chairs beside her bed. "Please don't let me sleep."

"But maybe you could find her this time," Bella suggested. "If you could see a street sign or a place that could be identified…"

"No!" she cried, reaching for Bella's plump hands. "No. I can't. Not again. Don't let me sleep. You hear? Don't let me sleep."

Again the light was a blinding white. But, as if to hasten unnecessary preliminaries, she sped quietly through it back to that room.

It was exactly as it had been except a single figure sat at the table this time. Juliet remained tied, her housedress pulled up over the sprawled legs, arms tied behind her. Her head was up, face tight from dried tears, mouth working.

"Please, sir," her urgent voice cracked over the words, so weak. "I do have to go to the lady's. Could you let me loose long enough to visit the bathroom, please?"

"I said I can't." The coarse-voiced one turned his head toward her, but only momentarily, as if she didn't actually exist. "Not when I'm here alone. Can't take a chance on you pullin' something."

"I'm an old lady," she tried wheedling in a terrible simpering voice. "What could I do to you? Really, sir, I am in pain. I really need to..."

"Hey, bitch, shut up!" he shouted and pretended to get up, as if he were coming for her. "Pee your pants. Who's gonna care? You're not gonna be here long from what I heard."

"You mean I can go home soon?" The happiness in her words was heartbreaking.

He only laughed. There was silence for a while.

"I really have to visit the lady's, sir. I'm sorry, but the pain..." she began again.

"Listen old lady. One more word and I'll kick the piss outta you. I said pee your pants and leave me alone."

Silence again until the sound of liquid trickling on to the floor could be heard throughout the basement.

The man began to laugh.

Juliet's eyes were closed, tears running from beneath the lids and covering her flaming face.

Mattie was screaming with the horror of it. It took hours for Harriet to calm her. Even then she would not rest but sat stiffly upright, staring about her, nervous and wide-eyed as if she feared sleep could surprise her from any corner.

Chapter Fourteen

"I don't know any more than I did," she whispered to David, who sat beside her on the sofa. "It was all the same. Nothing new. Same profile of a man. Only one though. David, I can't stand to have to watch her like this."

He was bending over a notebook, jotting down a few notes. "And what about Molino?"

He wasn't looking at her. That made it easier to lie.

"No," she said. "Nothing yet."

The thought that they might kill Juliet if she told what she knew still haunted her. If only they would contact her, make some demand, she could promise silence in return for Juliet's freedom. But then how could they be sure she would keep her word? She wasn't dealing with honorable men, after all. Why should they believe her?

Perhaps they would hold Juliet until all trace of the man was gone, and then release her when it would be too late for her to hurt them. But would they release her then? She could identify the two who held her. At least from their voices.

Why couldn't she get something definite on where she was being held? Why did the full visions come only after the person was dead?

It was evening when Bobby called from New York.

"Anything yet on this union guy?" he asked directly.

"God, Bobby, it's been terrible here," she said. "I keep seeing Juliet but no clue as to where she is. This is horrible."

"Too bad, Mattie. Sorry to hear it." The tone was unemotional, even bored. "But on this Molino business—nothing yet, eh? Can't you get yourself off of Juliet and on to our man? Tabok and his producer are getting impatient. I'm catching lots of heat here to get moving. The newspapers are full of nothing else. We've got to strike now."

"I can't get my mind off Juliet. She's suffering because of me. And if she dies it'll be my fault. I've got to try to save her."

"Find Molino and they'll probably let her go. Or the feds'll find her."

"Before they kill her? Impossible. And why would they let her go? She's seen them."

"Then break the news that you're watching them. That you've seen them. Lie a little. Say you can identify them. What good would it do them to kill her then?"

Skeptical, she considered a moment. "I hadn't thought of that. Maybe you're right, Bobby. Instead of telling them what's happened to Molino, I'll tell the newspapers I can see 'em. Maybe David would go along..."

"Hey, whoa there. Go back a little," he interrupted. "You said *what happened* to Molino. You know something you're not telling?" His voice was harsh. "'Cause you better be leveling with me, you hear? I've brought you this far, better not turn on me now."

She hesitated, uncertainty hauling her this way and that. It was too much responsibility to bear alone. She did know what happened to Ralph Molino and where he was—or what was left of him. Would that knowledge hurt or help Juliet?

Mind not working. Unclear. Hurt or help?

"I did see him, Bobby," she admitted, voice intense, thick with the ring of fear. "At least I saw what was left of him. But I won't tell you where. Not yet. I've got to think. Give me just a day to work out what's best. I wouldn't want to live if they murder Juliet because of me. Patsy—Uncle John—now Juliet. I couldn't tolerate more guilt. Please, Bobby, please—tell Tabok, but explain why I can't come on the show until Juliet's safe."

"You're gonna have to if she's not freed soon. Maybe your only hope."

"That's no hope."

They hung up, agreeing he was to call again in the morning.

David dropped by later but he had nothing new on Juliet. Nothing but fatigue to offer. The distance between them was as wide as the day before.

He noticed her dark, shadowed eyes, stark against her pale face. She looked to be on the verge of madness. The carefully done hair was matted and dirty. No trace of make-up remained on her face. Harriet, worried, said Mattie was throwing up everything she ate, which wasn't much to begin with. She was thin. Her silk blouse and wraparound skirt looked big, like hand-me-downs from some wealthy relative.

"I wish I could end this for you." Emotion and fear checked his voice.

"I wish you could too." She looked dismally beyond him, large eyes taking in what appeared to be hidden space. "I wish someone could end this."

"You've seen nothing else? I mean nothing that would help find her?"

She shook her head.

"And nothing on Molino? That would help. Maybe through finding him we'd find her."

"It's not the same place. She would be dead before you got to her." Her voice was flat and tired.

"What do you mean it's not the same place?" Instantly he caught her. "You do know something, don't you?" He coaxed, coming closer. "You know where Molino is." They sat at the kitchen table. He leaned even closer. "You better tell me, Mattie. Don't try to use this as some publicity stunt. Lives are at stake here."

"Publicity?" She began to laugh. "You really think I would take a chance on Juliet's life for publicity?" She was too exhausted to do more than make a half-hearted show of scorn.

"No." He softened toward her, remembering the child. Nothing was Mattie's fault. She needed the help of a doctor, a psychiatrist, as soon as this was over. "I know you've had your reasons. To protect Juliet. But you've got to trust me. To tell me where he is. It's the only hope we

have of finding Juliet. They'll never let her go. She could
identify 'em. You know they'll never let her go."

She was rubbing at her temples, wincing with the pain
she was trying to stop.

Her eyes were closed, face pinched, unhappy. "So
many greeds and pressures and lusts...I...I can't help
you yet, David," she whispered. "I've got to think."

"When?" His hands tightened on her arm, grasped
her, demanded she recognize his dominance over her.
"Don't tell Sanderson. I've got to have a couple of hours
head start. Will you give me that much?"

"Yes," she answered. "Yes."

Chapter Fifteen

The news out of New York broke on NBC's "Today Show"
the next morning. Jane Pauley interviewed Bobby Sanderson
who told about the threats after Mattie's appearance on
"The Tabok Show" and about the subsequent kidnapping.
He then, with very little prodding from the smirking Ms.
Pauley, launched into the sensational disclosure that Mattie
had gone into a trance and traced the union leader, Ralph
Molino. Knew where he was.

Smiling as he made gestures meant to indicate this
was big news, he declared he could say no more but that
the information as to Molino's whereabouts was in the
hands of "The Tabok Show's" producers and a few other
people. "To protect Ms. Small, of course," he added.

To Mattie's horror, as she sat alone watching, he went
on to promise her appearance on "The Tabok Show" in a
day or two to make full disclosure.

As the faces of both self-satisfied people faded from
the screen to be replaced with another face selling dog
food, the phone, in the hall, began to ring.

The policeman on guard answered it. She heard his low, muttered responses and heard him hang up.

"Lieutenant Bernabei," he came through the low arch to tell her. "Says he's coming over."

She was alone in the living room when he got there. He was cold, walked in and settled into a chair without speaking. With slow, deliberate movements, he pulled first a notebook and then a pen from his inner pocket. Only then did he look over at her and speak.

"Now you'll tell me everything." He lifted the pen, raised an eyebrow at her, and waited.

"You saw that show this morning." It wasn't a question.

"Mother always watches the 'Today Show.' She called me as soon as she saw who was on."

"Mother. Of course," she said, sighed.

"She's not an issue any more." He was stiff, unyielding. "All I want from you is information or I'm arresting you for obstruction of justice or any other damn thing I can think of."

"I didn't tell Bobby anything, you know." She said it wearily, hugging the old chenille robe tightly around her shivering body. "All he knows is that I had a dream and saw the man. But I do know what happened to him and where he is. Or was. I couldn't tell because I'm afraid for Juliet. Don't you see? If the police go hunting for him they'll just kill her."

He was silent, assimilating the new information, seeming confused by another reversal of fact. Finally, after long thought, he looked at her and asked, "Why'd you let him give that story out? Just as likely they'll kill her now, you know. Didn't he think of that?"

"Bobby doesn't seem capable of two thoughts at once."

He was quiet again. Then, "You'd better tell me all of it. Let me handle it from here on," he frowned. "I can keep it quiet and we might still trace Juliet."

"I don't know . . ."

"I don't think you've got a choice. You'd better tell me."

"Well—maybe, if we worked together. I'll even attempt self-hypnosis—try to find her. Maybe this time—a clue—something."

She told him of the grisly scene she had witnessed. Of the Hiram's Meat Packing sign and of its location. She told him of the three voices she had heard and lastly of that terrible head.

"Jesus," he whispered. "We figured it was something like that. Mixed in cement. Buried in garbage. Something. This is even worse. I wonder what they did with him? I mean...with what was left."

She couldn't answer him or even think about it.

"We'll have to get over there. You know that." He got up to leave. "You keep trying to find her."

She nodded.

He stopped, cleared his throat as he tucked the notebook away. "I'll do my best to find her before they do anything. But what Sanderson's done makes it doubtful. I want you to understand that and not get your hopes up. And Mattie—how's it been? I mean about the blank hours. With that little girl..."

She lifted her shoulders and dropped them. "Nothing. Here at home I seem to be...well...normal, I guess you'd call it. More like I used to be."

"Good." He seemed relieved. "That's good news."

"Anybody wanna play gin rummy?" Bella riffled a deck of cards, shuffled them, and looked at the other three expectantly. Harriet was cooking. Mattie shook her head. But their police guard said he figured he would like to play and sat down at the table.

"Don't see how you can play cards," Harriet scolded as she lowered the flame beneath a pan of boiling potatoes. "Can't think of anything but poor Juliet."

"Me either," Bella reared back defensively. "But, damn it, just sitting here day after day is getting boring."

"Just think how it is for Juliet." Harriet's look and words were censorious and meant to find their mark.

"I don't think of anything else. But does playing a game of rummy with Officer Witkowski hurt anything?"

Harriet sniffed and pushed a meatloaf into the oven.

"Well, if it's so awful, I guess we better not." Bella's injured tone was aimed at Harriet while the words were directed toward the policeman. "Not if she's going to act like she cares more for my friend than me just because I want to help pass the time a little."

"I didn't say anything like that."

"That's what you meant and you know..."

Mattie left the room. Everyone's nerves were tender. Too many days of waiting. Flat too small. A kind of boredom no one wanted to admit to was settling in on them, as though shock and horror and worry had had their innings and now a desire for normalcy was creeping back. As if human beings could only sustain a tragic sense for just so long.

She curled up on the sofa after snapping on the television. As the picture came in and cleared she could see words crawling along the bottom of the picture, beneath the faces of two soap opera actors.

"...found today. Details sketchy. News at 5:30."

Immediately the phone rang. The policeman answered it and did the talking.

Mattie let her mind be absorbed with the soap opera, not noticing that the policeman came into the living room.

"Eh...Miss...eh...Small." He leaned over toward her. "I just got the news that they found that union guy's body. They're sending a detective over here to stay awhile because they figure if anything's going to happen it will be right away. But you're not to worry. They don't really expect trouble here. Too late. Looks like the one in trouble is your mother's friend—that Juliet Swiderski. Looks bad."

Sitting up, she stared at him, not understanding.

"Who called you?"

"Detective Bernabei. Seems like he found the guy. Or what was left of him. Beat out the FBI and everybody. Gonna be a big promotion for him out of this, you can bet. Good news for our department. Those federals sometimes make us look bad. They come in like they know everything and..."

"And he gave the information to the newspapers?" she asked, feeling a cold sense of foreboding creeping over her.

"I suppose so. He said it will be on TV soon." He looked toward the set.

"Did he say anything about me?"

He shook his head. "No, nothing as I remember. Just said to give you the news. And said you should pray."

"What about Juliet? Didn't he say anything about her?"

The man shrugged his shoulders. "Nope. Guess he figured this'll flush out those guys."

"And maybe not." She sat very still beneath the Bleeding Heart of Jesus and tried to make herself go numb so as not to think the thoughts going through her brain or feel the emotions those thoughts triggered.

Another death...and another...another...another... without end...

Chapter Sixteen

The three women sat before the television set as though mesmerized, watching as the blurred figures interviewed and were interviewed. Scenes, retracing the finding, unfolded: packages of frozen meat which proved to be human. The grisly tale was told at length by the same newswoman who had interviewed Mattie all those months before. David was the hero of the story.

"And where did you get your information?" the newswoman asked. "How did you find Ralph Molino?"

"I'm afraid my sources are confidential. You understand." He was looking very official, very serious.

"Is that confidential source the psychic you've worked with before, Mattie Small?"

David frowned. "I assure you we found him through only good police work and a great deal of cooperation between all departments."

"You tell him, Mattie?" Bella leaned over, touching her knee to get her attention.

She nodded.

"Guess he wants to protect you."

She nodded again.

"And what of the kidnapped woman, Juliet Swiderski? Do you think she will be released unharmed?" the woman asked him.

"We're working on that right now." He stopped, cleared his throat. "Expecting a break any minute."

Harriet's rosary beads clicked faster. Mattie sat forward on the sofa and whispered toward David, "But they'll kill her! My God, he knows they will. Tell them I've seen 'em." She leaned toward the screen and whispered at him. "Scare 'em, David. Say something. It's the only hope we've got."

Later that evening when the telephone rang Mattie knew who would be on the other end, knew not through an intuitive sense but more through a sense of inevitability, as though there was only one move left in this game being played with her life. With a touch of black mischief she picked up the receiver and said:

"Hello, Bobby."

"*You bitch!*" he greeted, his voice a growl between clenched teeth. "You gave it to that fuckin' boyfriend of yours. I know he didn't break it alone. So don't lie to me. It's all over the TV here."

"I won't lie to you." She was too tired for this, brain only half functioning, no longer caring about any of them, about herself, even about Juliet. It was as if all this had happened a long time ago, to a different person. Almost meaningless. Her voice carried her detachment.

"You blew it," he roared. "Forget Tabok. He doesn't want to see you. No fee either. And after all my god-damned work. Well, baby, I made you and I'm gonna break you. I'm callin' a press conference now to tell 'em what a phony you are. I'll fix you good. Nobody plays games with Bobby Sanderson. I'll make your name shit in . . ."

"Thanks, Bobby," she said and, smiling, hung up on him.

"Who was that, Mattie?" Harriet asked as Mattie reentered the living room and lay, zombie-like, on the sofa full length, staring up at the dark painting on the wall.

"Jesus Christ," Mattie whispered, too tired to say more.

"It wasn't about Juliet, was it?" Harriet panicked at her daughter's reaction. But Mattie shook her head.

"You tired, Mattie?" Bella leaned toward her then motioned to Harriet with her head that they'd better leave her alone.

"You want an afghan over you?" Harriet worried just above her.

"Afghan?" Mattie repeated, looking toward neither of the women.

"How about a pillow?" Bella suggested, half-whispering as she would in a sick room.

"Pillow?" she repeated the word, then suddenly she became agitated, reaching out for her mother. "No, no pillow. Don't let me sleep. *For God's sake don't let me sleep now.*"

"But you're exhausted, Mattie. Just look at you. Now put your head back down and rest your eyes a minute. Go on now."

"But . . . Ma."

"Go on now. Me and Bella'll be right out in the kitchen. You want my beads?" She held out the rosary to Mattie who turned away.

"Well." Harriet was a little put out. "Don't forget Jesus is right above you there. He'll look out for you."

Mattie's chest heaved, whether in laughter or a shudder Harriet couldn't tell and decided not to ask. "Enough's enough," she told herself, pitying her worn daughter.

She knew that quality of light and hated it. It was the white of the skin of dead things; the white of a certain snail; albino white; sky white; rabid-froth white. Melting into it, she wanted to drown there rather than be transported to what she knew must be beyond. But she moved, mind accelerating, rushing forward at incalculable speed until the room was whole and suffused with the clarity of a spotlight.

"That was George." A voice said to a thin figure leaning against a wall just out of the light. The figure was smoking in jerking nervous movements.

"Yeah?"

"Says to take care of it—now."

"Jesus. Poor old lady."

There was only a single moan from Juliet, but her eyes were wild, hurtling back and forth in her head.

The thin man reached inside the shirt he wore and moved toward her, his back to Mattie. Juliet's eyes moved faster, face working, fear driving reason away. The man reached her and put the gun to her head, pulling the trigger; Juliet's head slumped forward.

In a whirl, Mattie next saw a street of stores. A bowling alley was at the corner. Pin-Down Lanes, a sign in the shape of a bowling pin read. And next to that: George's Mini-Market. Then a shabby shoe repair shop. And more beyond...and more...and more...

It was over.

She knew Juliet was dead.

Her screaming brought the police guard, Bella, and Harriet.

When the screaming turned into laughter they called a doctor.

When all the patient could say was "I've been cursed. I've been cursed," the doctor sank a needle into her arm.

Part Four

Chapter One

Fairy lights twinkled on the Christmas tree and reflected back into the room from the wide windows. Otherwise the apartment was dark. Dark and silent. Tremendous relief after months at home with Harriet and Bella trembling around and over her as if she would fly apart at any misplaced word, as if she were a woman of glass and might shatter if they didn't maintain twenty-four hour guard.

Good to be back in her own place. She ran a hand appreciatively over the fabric of her chair. The charm bracelet on her arm jangled, lonely notes reverberating in the dark quiet like music over a lake.

After a time her arms and legs felt cramped. She got up to look out the windows, down on the Christmas lights of Detroit and Windsor winking through layered air and bare trees. It was a gigantic toy city spreading out below, a decorative village beneath the Christmas pine David had set up to cheer her homecoming.

She couldn't have come back here right away. First there were weeks in Ford Hospital being healed mentally and physically. There was Juliet's funeral. She still couldn't stand to be told how few came, how few cared, or to think how little Juliet's life had meant. And there were the scathing news stories. The phone here must have rung for weeks. Not too many knew to reach her at her mother's.

But that had all quieted and still the letters came, begging letters, asking her to help. People still believed. That helped, knowing people had faith in her. Helped and...well...validated her work. Not that she dared mention her work to David. He grew livid at the thought.

Still...money was growing short. Another three, four months and she might have to give up this place. And then what?

Her face reflected back at her in the shine of Christmas lights. Raising her chin, she ran a finger over her bottom lip then licked at the finger and ran it around her mouth until her lips glistened. She fluffed out her curls, loving the gentle touch of her own hand combing through her hair. The sensation made her shiver. Sensual and tingling, the feel of hair being mussed.

Thinner. She ran a hand down her body. Still tired at times. Easily exhausted. The doctor agreed she had been through a great deal in the last year. No wonder she broke down, they all said. What was amazing was that she had stood the pressure that long.

She checked her watch. Couldn't make out the small dial in that light, so walked to the kitchen where she briefly snapped on the bright, overhead fixture so she could see the wall clock.

Nine o'clock. David was late. It was to be a quiet Christmas Eve alone, just the two of them. But first—his mother. She insisted he go with her to an aunt's house for the yearly festivities. Must have taken longer than he thought. She frowned, wondering if his mother was deliberately keeping him away. Be like her.

Ten minutes later, before she had time to get angry, he was there.

"Are you staying?" she asked, voice husky with emotion.

He held her close to him and whispered "Yes" into her hair, then held her away, smiled, and said, "First I want you to open your present. Never really shopped for a woman before. Always got my mother a toaster or a steam iron."

"You better not've bought me anything like that." He led her to the tree where they both knelt to the floor. She pulled her pale silk robe around her, arranging the folds as he set the package in front of her.

She smiled and accepted his gift. He was looking better than he had throughout their ordeal. Not completely well, but better. Dark circles remained as though he slept fitfully, but he'd gained weight, lost that haunted look.

"Open it," he urged.

It was a Florentine jewelry box of inlaid wood. In the box were two rings: a diamond solitaire and a single plain gold band.

"David," she breathed, holding the rings up to the tree lights where the diamond picked up rainbows. "Oh, David."

"I hope the timing is right." He watched her face for a look of acceptance or rejection.

He waited for her response.

It came slowly after her first excitement died.

"We haven't talked about marriage in months," she frowned, setting the rings gently back into the grooves of the jewel box. "I...I don't know. It's too soon. Don't you think?" Her eyes went over his face. "I mean...too soon to think about any commitments."

A deep breath. "I just wanted you to know that I still felt the same. Want us to be together..."

"But not like this." She pulled her legs around and got up from the floor, walking over to curl up on the sofa.

"Like what?" he demanded of her, trying to keep anger out of his voice.

"Not as a...a failure. Like you're pitying me." The word was said with revulsion. She couldn't look at him. He sat near her.

"You're not a failure. What in hell are you talking about? I want a wife, Mattie, not a business partner."

"That's not enough." The answer was swift. She stopped and met his look dead on, pushed away the hand he put out toward her.

"But..." he started to protest. She stopped him.

"David. Look, I'm still getting letters. Requests for help. Bobby hurt me, but not as much as we thought. People still believe. I can start again. I..."

"NO!" He was up and grabbing on to her, yelling directly into her face as she watched him in astonishment.

"David! I know it was bad, what happened. But I didn't really have anything to do with those murders. I could never believe I could. So why shouldn't I go on using the gift as long as I'm careful and, of course, don't get involved with any more public relations men?" Her laugh was bitter.

"You did have something to do with the murders. And you can't start again or more people will die because of you." He took hold of her arms and held her fast though she squirmed to get away from him. "Look. The child told us how she murders, how she spreads evil over her victims, marks them as a target. She told me and Lilith and she warned me not to stop you or I'd be next."

She leaned stiffly away, straining to be let go. "That's insane! *You* should have been in that hospital, not me."

"Believe me, I'm not crazy," he pleaded with her to understand, holding her. "I can prove it. Call Lilith. She heard it all too. I know you think you're cured because the child didn't show up at the hospital. But, I tell you Mattie, I'm still scared. Those people did die. And that child wanted them dead. I think she was real. At least for a time. And maybe could come back. Get out through these dreams again. She says she learns, gets stronger. Don't start it. The next one she gets could be me, or your Aunt Jenny, Bella—who knows?—even your mother, or mine. And anyone else who gets in her way."

Mattie's eyes were wide with horror. She clutched at the neck of her robe where he had pulled it open by holding her tight.

"You want to stop me just as you always have. Just like the others. I don't believe your lies." Her words were deliberate, clipped. She was in control, while he was almost frenzied. "I'm going on with my work, David. I don't have a choice."

He drew in this breath and held it as he searched her face. "I'll have to stop you." His words came out steady.

"Try," she spit up at him.

"Mattie...I..." he faltered first. "I don't want to hurt you...."

Her head was down. The first change he noticed was in the feel of her arms. The narrow limbs seemed stouter, thicker, but without womanly grace. Before any difference really registered, she kicked him hard, her pointed slipper catching the bony part of his shin where it would hurt most. His hands flew to his leg, letting go of her. When he looked up the face was scowling down at him, careful make-up somehow askew as the lips pouted crookedly and the narrow cheeks plumped.

"O.K." the angered little girl's voice said. "That's all for you. I warned you before and now look what you did." Her hands were on her hips. She stood with legs apart, feet splayed out. All semblance of a woman's body appeared absorbed into the thick trunk of the child, breasts sunken, waist lost. The robe hung open across her chest in hideous caricature of seductiveness.

He straightened to face her, fear shutting off words. To hurt her meant hurting Mattie. And wasn't she, after all, only a five-year-old? Or was she a thirty-four-year-old with the black and white conscience of a five-year-old? He didn't know. Couldn't think. Scared. The face before him was a hideous mask of evil, made worse by the twisted features of a child.

He put his hand up to signal a truce, a period of calm, to hold her at bay, but she would have none of it. *"You go on home."* The child screamed, stood straight, wobbled slightly on the high-heeled slippers, then pointed toward the door. "And don't you ever come back here again. You can't hurt us like this. That's all over. You go on. Hear me? Go on." She took a step forward. The menace implied made him shrink away from her.

Vaguely he heard a whimper, knew it was his own voice. He threw his hands up to protect himself and tasted vomit in his mouth as he half-crawled away from her.

"I'll stop you," he threatened though his body shook. "I'll get you declared insane. You'll be locked up. It can't go on." The words poured out as he backed toward the door, bumped it, and felt for the knob. She stood with hands on hips, glowering. Then she started to snicker, the painted lips quivering with merriment. She threw her head back and laughed at him.

He got through the door. The sound grew around him, followed him out into the hall and stayed in his head as he made his way down in the elevator.

Chapter Two

"Merry Chris..." the doorman started to greet David as he ran out of the building and headed for the parking lot.

The man narrowed his eyes, staring after him. He stood within the glass doors and watched, finally giving a shrug. No use standing around outside. They won't be coming back until the early hours of the morning. Out celebrating, all the tenants were. Christmas Eve and all. No need standing out in the wind. Getting colder. More snow expected.

He watched David again, not certain why, until he was out of sight.

"Lousy bastard," the man muttered. "Knew he wouldn't let loose of a buck. Not even for Christmas. And him in and out every day, seeing that psychic on the twentieth."

"Lousy bastard," he decided again and made no effort to contain his scorn.

David didn't even hear the man's greeting. Too wrapped in emotion, with desolation and fear at war in his head.

She was lost to him. No chance for them now. That child was in control. Had to be stopped. But hurting the child, hurting "it," meant hurting Mattie.

No choice left. He'd call Pontiac State Hospital. Get ahold of a psychiatrist he knew there, tell him what happened, and see about having her committed. Probably Harriet would have to sign the papers. But once she knows...

He was sure she expected the child to return, had

already accepted the inevitability of the child's ascendance, her power over the weakened Mattie. She'd seemed to know. And to be prepared for Mattie's confinement—or death.

The end for Mattie meant the end for him. But it had to be done. Had to stop her. This was the only chance for any of them—other than killing her and killing himself.

Have her committed. Put away for good. Keep that child drugged. Under control.

Maybe she'd get help there. Maybe the child would give up, disappear again.

He found his blue car, unlocked it, and pulled from the lot, heading for the expressway and home.

The street was lit up green and gold for Christmas. He wanted to cry and at the same time felt too empty of everything for tears. It was almost as though Mattie had died, back a few months ago, and tonight had been a visit with a ghost. He could accept what had happened, if he had to. Believe that Mattie wasn't really there anymore. But had she ever really been there? Or was it possible the child played grown-up all along? Probably never know. Too much to comprehend, all of it, this condensation of evil and hatred trapped in a child's body, growing as the body grew as if it were a physical appendage: an arm, fingernails...evil.

He turned the car on to the approach to the expressway and noticed the lights of the car behind him weave slightly to the right then back in lane.

Oh-oh, David warned himself. A Christmas office party drunk heading out to the suburbs. He'd keep an eye on him until he got past.

But the car entered the expressway directly behind him and stayed there, though the roadway was nearly clear with long stretches between cars.

When the car did pull out to switch lanes David slowed a little, to make sure he got past him. The green Camaro pulled back too, drawing alongside of him and staying there.

David steered carefully, very aware of the car that was pacing him. After a few minutes he looked over at the driver.

In the shadows of the car, David could see the man

turn to look at him. An overhead streetlight caught the eyes. They flinched as they met David's, flinched then narrowed. At that moment the man jerked his wheel to the right, driving his car directly into David's Chevette. There was the thump and screech of metal on metal as David's car pulled to the left and he heard a tire blow.

The wheel almost tore out of his hands. His car smacked back into the green Camaro next to him before he could slow it and pull over on the shoulder.

When he had the car off the road he stopped, noticing that the Camaro had also pulled from the road and was parked behind him.

Taking a couple of deep breaths, fighting for control before he faced the damned drunk, he gripped the wheel in both hands. He heard the car door slam, steeled himself, then opened his door and moved to get out, to confront the drunk.

But the man was beside him before he could get completely out of the car and on his feet. A fist slammed into his shoulder, knocking him backward. His head hit the doorjamb, his legs sprawled out on the cement.

"What the hell!" David put up an arm to protect himself as the man drew back his fist again. "Hey! You ran into me, fella," David yelled at him and tried to scramble back up on his feet before the guy could strike again.

"You damned liar." The fellow held his fist. He was trembling. Didn't look drunk. Business suit. Late thirties. "You pulled right into me. What're you on? Sniffing coke or something? It's your kind..."

David slipped a hand into his jacket, pulling out his wallet as he held the other hand up to ward off more blows.

"Police," he said, flipping the badge at him.

"All the worse, you crummy...you crummy...you should know better. And it won't stop me turning you in either."

"Listen fella..." David eased himself into a standing position. He could grab his gun now if he had to. The man must be crazy.

An old, brown Oldsmobile slowed as it passed them, then pulled over just ahead, stopping. The doors opened and three men in their early twenties got out and sauntered toward David and the threatening man.

David's head was turned toward the three approaching men to tell them everything was under control and they could just keep going when the man hit him again, this time in the head, slamming his jaw against the door and opening a gash along his chin.

"You..." David drove a fist into the man's stomach, doubling him over, then brought a knee up, hearing the sound of bone on bone as he cracked the guy's jaw.

The three gave a whoop and started running.

"Whoo, they're really going at it," David heard one cry out with satisfaction as they approached.

Two stopped and leaned on the hood of David's car. They watched, then idly began rocking the car. The other, older one, came around to where the man in the suit lay on the pavement holding his jaw. David was slumped on the front seat, a bloody handkerchief pressed to his face.

"Police officer," David managed to say to the grinning face sticking in the door, almost at a level with his own.

"Shit man, don't give me that. You got a badge?"

He nodded, feeling around for it then remembering it had been in his hand when he was hit. "Must have dropped on the street." He tried for authority in his voice even though his jaw was hurting like hell.

"Says he's a cop," the man leaned back to yell the news to his two friends.

"Hey, officer, you got a blow-out. You know that?" one in front, stringy blond hair sticking from a dirty woolen cap, called. He was standing near the left front of the car. The other one, standing on the right, bent down then slowly stood, closing a knife in his hand and giggling before saying, "You got a blow-out here too."

David felt the other side of the car going down and knew what the man had done.

"Let's take a look at those back tires." The two agreed and moved down the side of the car.

David slowly moved his hand, to slide it into his coat, get his gun, but the one standing directly in front of him put a hand on his, stopping him. The man then pressed something in his hand and a long blade shot out, a blade he stuck under David's chin, pricking the skin.

"You don't want to do that." The man leaned in again, smirked in David's face.

David moved back and just to the side of the knife as he reached up and grabbed the hand that held it, throwing his weight against the body leaning over him and driving it back against the car door. The man's head hit the top of the car and then bounced against the window. Stunned, he slid to the ground as David leapt over him, kicking him as he went, stumbling, righting himself, then turning to run around the car and up the embankment, where he slipped on the light cover of snow.

He heard them shout behind him but didn't stop, not even to pull his gun. Too many of 'em. They could get him. He ran, his feet sliding, scrambling to reach the top of the embankment. He climbed the metal fence.

He raced across the deserted street toward a row of darkened houses. Public housing. Must be the one just before the Warren exit, he thought quickly, trying to figure where he was.

At the third house he ran up the narrow walk, heart racing, blood pumping. They hadn't followed. He could hear them still down at his car, yelling and whooping, probably tearing the car apart, robbing that other guy. They knew he was on foot, that he could wait.

Had to get to a phone.

Houses all dark.

Still he'd have to call from one of them. No badge to identify himself. He patted his pockets again. No. Gone. He leaned against the rickety porch rail and let his chest heave as he struggled to calm himself.

A phone. He'd have to try doors. Knock. Get somebody up. Bad neighborhood for that. And those guys back there might already be looking for him.

He moved back up the street and hurried across winter-killed lawns down the block, choosing a path they'd be unlikely to follow.

The dark was intense. More than once he stumbled over the broken sidewalk as he made his way to the first corner, stopping there again, holding his breath, listening for voices following him.

Nothing.

In the next block, second house, a Christmas tree lighted the front windows. People still up. Cars parked in front. A party.

He made his way up the front steps to the door and knocked.

The voices inside stopped. Then he could feel the boards of the porch shake as someone walked toward the door. A lace curtain at the window was twitched aside then dropped. The door opened the width of its chain.

"Whacha want?" a woman's voice asked, suspicion thick in the words. The sound of Christmas carols on a radio was loud behind her.

"Police officer." David leaned heavily against the house, resting on one taut arm. "Had trouble on the expressway. Can I use your phone, please, ma'am?"

"You got I.D.?"

He shook his head and was made aware again of the open wound on his chin. "Lost it in the scuffle."

"Then get the hell off my porch." He could see her eyes gleaming over the chain, eyes that seemed to want to kill him. "You ain't gone right now and I'm gettin' a gun. Charlie!" She was yelling back over her shoulder to someone in the house. "You get your gun and git over here."

David knew this was no empty threat. The woman would kill him if she could. Those eyes were eyes he'd seen before. The eyes of the man who had deliberately run his car into him. The eyes of the man with the knife. Eyes filled with hatred and loathing.

He backed away, down the front steps. His face hurting, his mind reeling.

Was the whole world crazy?

It was like being caught in some insane time warp. Everywhere he turned people attacked him...wanted to kill him.

TO KILL HIM...

AND HE KNEW WHY...

He backed away and began running again, running down the street. Running without stopping, fast at first, then slower, slower, until he was sobbing and dragging himself along.

A main street. He crossed. Mack, the sign said. He knew where he was. He also knew where he had to go and what he had to do.

It was the child. She was spreading her web of evil over him, tightening it so there would be no escape. No matter who he turned to. Tonight he was the victim. No friend, no stranger would be able to help him. She had marked him as if he wore the scarlet letter. Marked him to die.

Chapter Three

Late. But that was good. People off the streets. He couldn't trust anyone to help him, they'd kill him, everyone—even his friends. Kill him and live afterward with the horror of not knowing why.

Trust nobody.

Empty lots around him. On Rivard, heading south. He crossed Eliot, passed an old, empty church. More open lots. He kept going. Knew he was somewhere behind the Eastern Market with its daytime crush of farmers' stands and crowds of shoppers. Deserted and dead at night.

Lucky he knew the city so well. Just get out to the Fisher Freeway, get around that somehow and he'd find his way back to her apartment house. Had to get there. Had to...

The temperature was dropping. He pulled his coat tighter around him and hunched forward, making his way down one dark block after another. Soon it was snowing again, dry white powder gathering in swirls on the pavement, then large flakes sticking to his coat, to the sidewalk, making his urgent march that much more difficult.

Warehouses. Everything empty. No cars. He stuck to the west side of the street, away from the buildings, until he saw movement on the sidewalk ahead. He stopped, waited, narrowing his eyes against the snow and the dark.

A figure was draped across the sidewalk. David moved into the street, keeping the figure in sight at all times. An arm waved. David heard muttering sounds and allowed himself to breathe.

An old drunk. God, but he was relieved. Still he continued over to the warehouse side of the street, hoping to hug the buildings in case of other surprises.

Behind him the drunk shouted something and David heard a bottle hit the pavement and shatter, bits of glass striking the back of his pant legs. He didn't turn. Just kept forging his way ahead. His one thought, expanding in his brain: get to Mattie and kill her!

He began to run again, fighting darkness, wind, and snow.

No way of knowing how far yet. He knew generally, but it was different on foot. Space seemed to expand. Minutes by car could be an hour on foot.

Toward the river. He had to make his way south, staying off main thoroughfares but always moving in the direction of Mattie.

Christ, but his jaw hurt. He put a finger up to touch it and felt the hard ridge of dried blood. Still sticky. Seemed to be oozing some but the hell with it. No longer mattered.

His life was finished. After he killed Mattie no one would believe him about what she really was. About the concentrated evil formed into a being. No one would believe. End of his career. End of his life. Prison probably. No worse than what he would have to live with. Kill her. Kill her as soon as she opens the door. Take out his gun and kill her. Mattie. He loved Mattie. But the child would be there now. Poor child. God, what they put her through! But God, what she'd become.

He shook his head. Can't feel pity. No more than he could for a starving animal attacking a human being. It was still all a matter of survival. Hers or his—and all the others she would murder.

Had to get down to Lafayette. Feet ice-cold. Shoes not meant for walking in snow. Hands stiff and shoved into his pockets. He moved his feet along, cursing under his breath.

Just one street over from the market section now. Fisher Freeway in front of him. But sheer concrete cliffs faced him on either side of the freeway. No way to cross here.

He turned down the street to his left, slowing now as his throat and lungs burned with the cold.

Russell Street. And an overpass. Only way. So open here. If anyone was searching for him he'd be exposed. No choice.

On the other side of the overpass the east side of Russell was lined with poultry and fruit markets. The west side was the red brick wall of Stroh's Brewery.

Gratiot Avenue. Again he was in the open. But few cars were out. The snow-haloed streetlights shone on a desolate scene of blowing snow and a single car parked just down the block.

As he crossed, dragging himself as hard and as fast as possible, he noticed the lights on that single car come on. It pulled from the curb, sliding in the wet snow at first, then moving slowly forward. He couldn't be certain through the snow, but he thought it was an old, brown car.

He reached the other side of Gratiot and ran, slipping, almost falling down between the warehouses. There was an alley, the first one he came to. He rushed blindly down it, feeling the building now and then for direction, falling over garbage cans and tripping on tin cans being blown in circles on the alley pavement.

He stumbled, slammed his shoulder into the building, and fell.

Out on the street he could hear voices and the sound of a car motor. He lay still, using the garbage cans as a shield, not breathing. After a few minutes the car pulled away. Still he waited, not daring to take a chance on going back out there yet in case they waited for him.

Something rustled in papers nearby. He prayed it was the wind, but the rustling kept on when the wind died. It came closer, grew louder. There was no choice left to him. He'd have to get out of there.

He put a hand down to brace himself, to push himself up, but his shoulder couldn't stand the pressure, it hurt too badly. He lost his balance and fell heavily again, dragging one of the garbage cans down with him. One hand went out behind to break the fall. As he slumped back to a sitting position he felt sharp pain in his hand, the hand out behind him.

He screamed and tried to pull the hand away, realizing then that something held it fast, that teeth were sunk into his flesh.

With all the force he could muster he picked the hand up, heavily weighted with a scrambling rat that held on. He slammed it against the building again and again until the teeth were jarred loose and the animal fell to the ground away from him.

He struggled to his feet and ran toward the mouth of the alley, heedless of the brown Oldsmobile and the men searching for him. He continued to run until his lungs were seared to scalding by the cold breath he gulped and the pain throughout his body screamed at him to stop, stop, stop....

His mind moved beyond fear now. He was a man with a single idea. Kill. Stop the torture. Kill.

The street curved into another with a brick wall stopping him from going on in the direction he must follow. The wall curved around, kept going. He moved one way, then another, searching until he found one of the passageways he knew had been placed in the wall.

He was on Antietam Street now. Had to go south. To his right. Streets so chopped up here. Curved every which way. Stopped dead at apartment houses, rows of townhouses.

He hurried on. Not far now.

Back on Rivard.

Walking in the middle of the street, away from the bushes and trees lining the curb.

Lafayette. Just ahead.

Terraced landscaping.

Across the parking lot.

Cold forgotten. Pain forgotten. One thought.

The door...

"Just a minute there," the doorman, lounging in the lobby, shouted after him. "No one goes up unannounced. Hey you—WAIT!"

David made his way across the lobby, concentrating only on dragging his body a little farther, a little farther, a little farther...

"Get the guard," the doorman was calling to someone behind him.

An elevator stood open. He pulled himself in and punched her floor number, allowing himself to lean his head against the panel and close his eyes for a minute.

He only needed a little strength now. Just enough to do what he had to do.

The elevator stopped, door opened. With exaggerated care David moved his body again, stepping out into the hall.

Her door was three down from the bank of elevators.

He slipped his hand into his coat and pulled the thirty-eight from its holster. He snapped the safety back and then let his fingers tighten around the gun's handle.

Hold it steady. Steady. That was all he would let his mind think as he pushed her bell and waited.

She must have been in bed. It seemed a long time before he heard someone approaching.

"Who is it?" Her timid voice called behind the door, stopping his heart. He shook his head and firmed his resolve.

Fast, he told himself. Fast. As soon as the door opens. Fast. Over with...

"David," he managed to answer.

There was a hesitation. No sound. And then he heard the chain sliding across and the lock snap back.

He brought the gun up though tears were already clouding his eyes. The door began to open....

"Hey! You there! Drop that thing!" a voice from the bank of elevators yelled toward him.

He turned slowly, reluctant to be disturbed. A man in uniform was standing there. An older man. Gun in his hand. Hatred in his eyes.

The gun went off.

"Christ, lady, I didn't mean to kill him." The guard stood over David's body, slumped sideways into Mattie's doorway, dead eyes staring opaquely. "I didn't mean to shoot to kill. So close. I could've just hurt him. Why'd I shoot like that? Why?" The middle-aged man's face was sick with shock as he looked from the bleeding body to the woman standing in the doorway.

She was staring down at the man slumped at her feet. She seemed so cool, as if this had nothing to do with her. As the guard watched, horrified, her lips curved up in satisfaction, parted, and a smile moved across the sloppily lipsticked mouth.

The guard shuddered at the sight of her, lowered his gun, and backed away. "I never meant to kill the guy," he murmured. "Never meant to kill the poor bastard."

"I know," she nodded in appreciation. "I know."

ABOUT THE AUTHOR

ELIZABETH KANE BUZZELLI has been a journalist and a teacher. She has written several books on local history and spent ten years researching the life and work of Emily Dickinson, about whom she has published numerous articles. The mother of five children, she lives in southern Michigan during the winter and northern Michigan during the summer—back in the woods with two Siamese cats, a yellow Labrador named Andy and an always pregnant raccoon. She is presently at work on a new book.

*Not since NURSE has there been
a book as powerful and revealing as*

THE
NURSE'S
STORY

by Carol Gino

"Carol Gino has written a wonderfully moving book.
She tells THE NURSE'S STORY with just the right
blend of emotion, compassion and wisdom."
—Harold S. Kushner, author of
WHEN BAD THINGS HAPPEN TO GOOD PEOPLE

Based on the author's sixteen years as a nurse, this is a book
that will forever change your assumptions about the medical
profession. Here is the first truly candid portrait of the role of
a nurse—the wrenching emotional conflicts, the bittersweet
victories, the life-and-death struggles that take place virtually
every day. THE NURSE'S STORY is a story of courage and
strength, tragedy and triumph—a remarkable testament to the
power of the human spirit.

Read THE NURSE'S STORY, on sale October 1, 1983,
wherever Bantam paperbacks are sold.

Hair-raising happenings that guarantee nightmares!

You'll be fascinated by unearthly events, intrigued by stories of weird and bizarre occurrences, startled by terrifying tales that border fact and fiction, truth and fantasy. Look for these titles or use the handy coupon below. Go beyond time and space into the strange mysteries of all times!

☐	20920	THE CHILDREN by Charles Robertson	$3.50
☐	23740	GIFT OF EVIL by Elizabeth Kane Buzzelli	$2.95
☐	23518	THE DISCIPLE by Laird Koenig	$2.95
☐	22687	THE TRUE BRIDE by Thomas Altman	$2.95
☐	24010	KISS DADDY GOODBYE by Thomas Altman	$3.50
☐	23356	HOUSES OF HORROR by Richard Winer	$2.95
☐	22616	THE DEMON SYNDROME	$2.95
		by Nancy Osborne Ishmael	
☐	22748	MOMMA'S LITTLE GIRL by George McNeil	$2.95
☐	22634	THE AMITYVILLE HORROR by Jay Anson	$3.50
☐	24008	MORE HAUNTED HOUSES	$2.95
		by Winer & Ishmael	
☐	23755	HAUNTED HOURES by Winer & Osborn	$2.95
☐	23670	WHAT ABOUT THE BABY by Clare McNally	$2.95
☐	23834	GHOST HOUSE by Clare McNally	$2.95
☐	23065	GHOST HOUSE REVENGE by Clare McNally	$2.95
☐	22520	GHOST LIGHT by Clare McNally	$2.95
☐	20701	THE EXORCIST by William Blatty	$3.50
☐	22740	HALLOWEEN by Curtis Richards	$2.95
☐	20535	50 GREAT GHOST STORIES	$2.95
		by John Canning, ed.	
☐	20799	50 GREAT HORROR STORIES	$2.95
		by John Canning, ed.	

Prices and availability subject to change without notice.

Buy them at your local bookstore or use this handy coupon:

Bantam Books, Inc., Dept. EDA, 414 East Golf Road, Des Plaines, Ill. 60016

Please send me the books I have checked above. I am enclosing $_____
(please add $1.25 to cover postage and handling). Send check or money order
—no cash or C.O.D.'s please.

Mr/Mrs/Miss_____

Address_____

City_____ State/Zip_____

EDA—11/83

Please allow four to six weeks for delivery. This offer expires 5/84.

DON'T MISS
THESE CURRENT
Bantam Bestsellers

RELAX!
SIT DOWN
and Catch Up On Your Reading!

☐	05034	**BALE FIRE** by Ken Goddard (Hardcover)	$14.95
☐	23678	**WOLFSBANE** by Craig Thomas	$3.95
☐	23420	**THE CIRCLE** by Steve Shagan	$3.95
☐	23567	**SAVE THE TIGER** by Steve Shagan	$3.25
☐	23483	**THE CROOKED ROAD** by Morris West	$2.95
☐	22913	**HARLEQUIN** by Morris West	$3.50
☐	20694	**DAUGHTER OF SILENCE** by Morris West	$2.95
☐	22746	**RED DRAGON** by Thomas Harris	$3.95
☐	23838	**SEA LEOPARD** by Craig Thomas	$3.95
☐	20353	**MURDER AT THE RED OCTOBER** by Anthony Olcott	$2.95
☐	20662	**CLOWNS OF GOD** by Morris West	$3.95
☐	20688	**TOWER OF BABEL** by Morris West	$3.50
☐	22812	**THE BOURNE IDENTITY** by Robert Ludlum	$3.95
☐	20879	**THE CHANCELLOR MANUSCRIPT** by Robert Ludlum	$3.95
☐	20720	**THE MATARESE CIRCLE** by Robert Ludlum	$3.95
☐	23149	**SMILEY'S PEOPLE** by John Le Carre	$3.95
☐	23159	**THE DEVIL'S ALTERNATIVE** by Frederick Forsyth	$3.95
☐	13801	**THE FORMULA** by Steve Shagan	$2.75
☐	22787	**STORM WARNING** by Jack Higgins	$3.50
☐	23781	**SNOW FALCON** by Craig Thomas	$3.95
☐	22709	**FIREFOX** by Craig Thomas	$3.50

Prices and availability subject to change without notice.

Buy them at your local bookstore or use this handy coupon for ordering:

Bantam Books, Inc., Dept. FBB, 414 East Golf Road, Des Plaines, Ill. 60016

Please send me the books I have checked above. I am enclosing $_____
(please add $1.25 to cover postage and handling). Send check or money order
—no cash or C.O.D.'s please.

Mr/Mrs/Miss_____

Address _____

City_____ State/Zip_____

FBB—10/83

Please allow four to six weeks for delivery. This offer expires 4/84.